P9-DOF-671

TRANSIT

ANNA SEGHERS (née Netty Reiling; 1900–1983) was born in
Mainz, Germany, into an upper-middle-class Jewish family. She
was a sickly and introverted child by her own account, but
became an intellectually curious student, eventually earning a
doctorate in art history at the University of Heidelberg in 1924;
her first story, written under the name Antje Seghers, was
published in the same year. In 1925 she married a Hungarian
immigrant economist and began her writing career in earnest.
By 1929 Seghers had joined the Communist Party, given birth
to her first child, and received the Kleist Prize for her first
novel, *The Revolt of the Fishermen*. Having settled in France in
1933, Seghers was forced to flee again after the 1940 Nazi
invasion. With the aid of Varian Fry, Seghers, her husband, and
two children sailed from Marseille to Mexico on a ship that
included among its passengers Victor Serge, André Breton, and
Claude Lévi-Strauss. After the war she moved to East Berlin,
where she became an emblematic figure of East German letters,
actively championing the work of younger writers from her
position as president of the Writers Union and publishing at a
steady pace. Among Seghers's internationally regarded works
are *The Seventh Cross* (1939; adapted for film in 1944 by MGM),
one of the only World War II–era depictions of Nazi concentration camps; the novella *Excursion of the Dead Girls* (1945);
The Dead Stay Young (1949); and the story collection *Benito's
Blue* (1973).

MARGOT BETTAUER DEMBO has translated works by
Judith Hermann, Robert Gernhardt, Joachim Fest, Ödön von
Horváth, Feridun Zaimoglu, and Hermann Kant, among

others. She was awarded the Goethe-Institut/Berlin Translator's Prize in 1994 and the Helen and Kurt Wolff Translator's Prize in 2003. Dembo also worked as a translator for two feature documentary films, *The Restless Conscience*, which was nominated for an Academy Award, and *The Burning Wall*.

PETER CONRAD was born in Australia, and since 1973 has taught English literature at Christ Church, Oxford. He has published nineteen books on a variety of subjects; among the best known are *Modern Times, Modern Places*; *A Song of Love and Death*; *The Everyman History of English Literature*; and studies of Alfred Hitchcock and Orson Welles. His most recent book is *Creation: Artists, Gods and Origins*. He has contributed features and reviews to many magazines and newspapers, including *The New York Times*, *The New Yorker*, *The Observer*, the *New Statesman*, *The Guardian*, and *The Monthly*.

HEINRICH BÖLL (1917–1985) was one of Germany's foremost post–World War II writers. He wrote short stories, essays, plays, and novels, the most famous of which are *Billiards at Half-Past Nine*, *The Clown*, *Group Portrait with Lady*, and *The Lost Honor of Katharina Blum*. Böll was awarded the Georg Büchner Prize in 1967 and the Nobel Prize in Literature in 1972.

TRANSIT

ANNA SEGHERS

Translated from the German by
MARGOT BETTAUER DEMBO

Introduction by
PETER CONRAD

Afterword by
HEINRICH BÖLL

NEW YORK REVIEW BOOKS

New York

THIS IS A NEW YORK REVIEW BOOK
PUBLISHED BY THE NEW YORK REVIEW OF BOOKS
435 Hudson Street, New York, NY 10014
www.nyrb.com

The translation of this work was supported by a grant from the Goethe-Institut,
which is funded by the German Ministry of Foreign Affairs.

Library of Congress Cataloging-in-Publication Data
Seghers, Anna, 1900–1983.
 [Transit. English]
 Transit / by Anna Seghers ; introduction by Peter Conrad ; translated by
Margot Bettauer Dembo ; afterword by Heinrich Böll.
     pages cm. — (New York Review Books Classics)
 ISBN 978-1-59017-625-2 (alk. paper)
 1. World War, 1939–1945—Refugees—Fiction. 2. Marseille (France)—Fiction.
I. Dembo, Margot Bettauer, translator. II. Title.
 PT2635.A27T713 2013
 833'.912—dc23

                    2012044953

ISBN 978-1-59017-625-2
Available as an electronic book; ISBN 978-1-59017-640-5

Printed in the United States of America on acid-free paper.
10 9 8 7 6 5 4

INTRODUCTION

THE STORY told by *Transit*—about refugees attempting to escape from Europe as Hitler's armies advanced—is one that Anna Seghers had lived. As a Communist, she had been arrested by the Gestapo when Hitler seized power in 1933. After her release, she migrated to Paris, and after the Germans invaded northern France she fled to Marseille—the city "where Europe ends" as the narrator of *Transit* dolefully notes. Along with Lisbon in neutral Portugal, Marseille was one of the few ports that offered an exit from a continent that was closing down. Here Seghers joined the crowd of harried strays she describes in her novel, scuttling from one consulate to the next in an attempt to assemble the visas and permits required for their onward journey. Not for the last time, modern life had turned into the enactment of a Kafka novel: Seghers and countless others were like Kafka's Joseph K trying to get his credentials as a land surveyor recognized by the officials in the impenetrable castle.

While Seghers fretted in one or another of those Marseille waiting rooms, her friend Walter Benjamin, who also abandoned Paris when the Nazis marched in, killed himself in a town on the border between France and Spain. Benjamin was hoping for a visa that would allow him to cross the Pyrenees and travel on to Lisbon, from where he hoped to sail to the United States. Threatened with deportation to France, he took morphine pills. Seghers was luckier. In March 1941 she managed to obtain the necessary permits, and secured passage on a ship bound for what was still, for terrorized Europeans, the New World. She began to write *Transit* soon after her arrival in Mexico, where she settled. It was first published in English and Spanish translations in 1944; it did not appear in German until 1948, three years after Seghers returned to her native land. True to the left-wing faith of her youth, she lived in East Berlin until her death in 1983.

Sailing to Mexico, Seghers told friends that she felt "as though I had been dead for a year." This was not quite the same as asserting that she now felt alive: she placed herself in the transitional state of Marie, the heroine of her novel, who may or may not have died when a ship like the one on which Seghers was traveling hits a mine and who is now, thanks to the narrator's wishful imagination, "ripped from the Underworld by sacrifices and fervent prayers." Although Seghers adopted the persona of a narrator who plots unscrupulously to get onto one of those ships, *Transit* takes a sadder, longer view of her own experience. It observes events from what might be the vantage point of the gods, looking down—or in Seghers's case looking back since, when she wrote it, she was already "over there," enjoying the resurrection her characters dream of—on the spectacle of human folly, the delusion of human hope, and the alternation of anxiety and ennui that consumes our days.

The perspective places individual fates at a distance. The characters who crowd the Marseille waterfront gaze out toward a vanishing point on the horizon that is obscured by mist; Seghers seems to be quizzically peering in the opposite direction, across the ocean that divides the continent she identified with renewal from the old one which was in terminal decline. The chronology to which the story refers is not that of the newspapers: it deals in epochs, where disasters cyclically recur and nothing new ever happens. Biblical catastrophes are the stuff of daily life, and the last days always seem to be arriving. The concentration camp inmates resolve to break free "before the Last Judgment"; in Marseille a travel bureau looks like "the administrative offices for the Last Judgment." A ship leaving for Brazil reminds the narrator of Noah's Ark—an inevitable analogy, further elaborated in Erich Maria Remarque's very similar novel *The Night in Lisbon*, where the refugees clustered on the quays in the Portuguese capital see every boat as an ark, with America as the

Ararat where it will, with luck, come to rest. Completing the allegory, Remarque fills in details of the Old Testament deluge, sent to exterminate errant mankind: it was happening again on dry land as Hitler's armies trampled Europe. The myth, as Seghers retells it in *Transit*, omits the olive branch: the characters spend much of the novel scrambling to qualify for berths on a ship that we already know, if we remember the opening sentence of the book, will sink.

Seghers captures the atmosphere of Marseille with gritty exactitude: the cheerless winter sun, the trees rigid with cold, the hydrants opened in the morning to clean the streets that merely sluice dirt downhill. But her contemporary snapshots record only the surface. This city is a time tunnel, through which the wind has always been blowing, with clouds of dust and crowds of people swirling before it. The same gossip has been exchanged around the harbor—which opens onto a sea that was once considered to be the uterine center of the earth—since the time of the Romans, Greeks, or Phoenicians, while the same food has been consumed for all those centuries. Who'd have thought that pizza, a local speciality, was so antique, so venerable, not after all the invention of Dr. Oetker or Papa John? The narrator loves the cave-like pizzerias of Marseille, where the wet dough has been flattened with a bent wrist since time immemorial. (He also makes this overfamiliar dish look new, thanks to a fillip of metaphorical magic: he reminds us of the surprise we all experience when eating it for the first time. How come something that looks like "an open-face fruit pie" tastes so peppery? Shouldn't the olives that stud it be cherries and raisins?)

Transit frequently removes us from the present in this way and lets us drop, as if through a hole in the floor, into a remote past. An American consul, an agent of what would soon become a new global empire, slips back through a couple of millennia and suddenly resembles "a Roman official ... listening to the emissaries of foreign tribes with their dark and to him ridiculous demands from gods unknown to him." Such temporal recessions induce an abysmal dizziness. Europe simply has too much history: individuals inherit ancestral problems, which have always been and will remain insoluble. On his way south through France, the narrator jokingly calls the bureaucrats who stamp passports "dogcatchers," and wonders why they bother, since this human flood is just the latest case of a churning of runaway multitudes that has been going on forever: "It was like trying to register every Vandal, Goth, Hun, and Langobard during the 'Barbarian Invasion.'" And if the uniformed men who stamp the papers are dogcatchers, then the narrator and his kind are just dogs—ownerless strays and mongrels, a "wretched refuse" that will never be embraced by the welcoming Statue of Liberty in another harbor across the ocean.

Jean Cocteau, on a brief visit to New York in 1949, sat up all night on the plane composing a sermon addressed to the liberators and (he hoped) saviors of self-destructive Europe. "Americans," he said, "the dignity of humanity is at stake." So it is in *Transit*, except that the dignity of our species may already have been forfeited—brutishly denied by the Nazis, sabotaged as well by the treachery and selfishness that are rife among the refugees. The novel's blunt but richly allusive title suggests that these are people in transition, and not only between countries: they commute up and down on what theologians once saw as the great chain of being, some aspiring to the status of spirits, others behaving and even coming to look like beasts. Binnet's mistress has "the head of a wild, black bird," while another woman who has been compulsively crying is left with the puffy red face of a goblin. A suspicious landlady, perhaps "working in disguise for some secret authority as an exorcist," has teeth that grow longer overnight, an inflatable bosom, and a body that probably ends in a fishtail.

We are in the realm of Greek myth, liable to encounter ogres or deities. The gatekeeper at the Mexican consulate in Paris is a glowering Cyclops with one empty eye socket, and in Marseille the narrator finds that the hotel room next to his is occupied by Diana, the goddess of the hunt, who is accompanied by two howling Great Danes. Or rather—as the myth is turned upside down, with human and animal changing places—she accompanies the dogs, since their exit from France has already been arranged by their American owners, and the woman, whose crooked shoulders and garish dress hardly suit the chaste deity, is only guaranteed passage out because she is their guardian.

The narrator's French girlfriend Nadine comments at one point, "You foreigners are all so strange." She means that they are aliens, not members of a common human family—existentially different like the *étranger* in the novel of that title by Albert Camus, which was published in 1942. For good or ill, the metaphors in *Transit* alienate or estrange us from the people to whom they're attached. Does this make the fishy landlady or the weepy goblin dangerous, inimical, subhuman, like the ethnic groups the Nazis wished to exterminate, or are our own definitions at fault? Might we be in the presence of the divine, not the demonic? As H. G. Wells suggests in his descriptions of Martians in *The War of the Worlds*, it's merely our anthropomorphic conceit that makes us think that creatures who don't look like us must be monsters; Picasso's portraits also treat the human face as something provisional, able to be rearranged at will. There's a creepy moment in *Transit* when the narrator stumbles upon a party of drunken Foreign Legionnaires in "outlandish Arabic headgear." One of them is a dwarf, and another—who doesn't think Hitler is such a bad fellow—is so disfigured that he looks "as if neither his mouth nor his nose were in the right place, as if they were flattened over his face." The dead writer Weidel—whose identity the narrator adopts—leaves behind him a manuscript that is, like *Transit*, a modern fairy tale, set in "a forest for adults." Boys turn into bears, girls into lilies; the transformations are uncanny, but Weidel's fictional magic works like a spell, a talisman. These, the narrator feels, are "stories that would have protected me from evil." In fact they teach him how to practice a kind of evil, a sinister enchantment that puts a physiological curse on other people.

Marseille is supposed to be the point of departure for heaven, that fanciful next world "over there," the place where the old Spanish man believes he will "regain his youth or find a sort of eternal life." In fact, the people in the crowd jostling outside one of the consulates are scrambling to board "the last ferry across the Dark River

Styx." They are debarred because they are still vestigially alive and haven't yet suffered enough; the fate worse than death is to be sent back to that bleakly sunlit reality above ground.

Everything and everyone in *Transit* is transitory. The narrator begins by shrugging that all acquaintances are "fleeting," like people accidentally met on trains and in waiting rooms, and he adds that mental impressions also go "right through you, quickly, fleetingly." Even thoughts are fugitives—and from whom or what are they, like those who think them, fleeing? From death, which is moving ever closer with its swastika banner (or with the skull emblems that were the insignia of the SS). The narrator fancies that "Death was also fleeing" and can only wonder "who was at his heels?" In this perpetually moribund Europe, always dying and always being reborn to sicken and die all over again, no finality—not even that supplied by an unhappy ending—can be hoped for.

Hence the narrator's grim admiration for two beggars he sees sleeping at a construction site: they may be the wisest characters in this populous book, because they are so inertly resigned. The tramps in Beckett's *Waiting for Godot*—written in 1948–49, not long after the publication of *Transit*—share the vexatious vital itch of Seghers's refugees. Stalled and impotent, they still feel compelled to pass the time with their games and whimsies. The tramps in *Transit* are beyond that, unconcerned about the passage of time and indifferent to history, and they are therefore at peace. Louse-ridden, scurfy-skinned, they are "unaffected by what was happening in their country—feeling as little shame as trees do, molding and decaying. . . . They had as little thought of leaving their homeland as trees might." These homeless men are rooted; they are fixtures, while everyone else is passing through, wind-blown.

Transit is about society and politics, but it is also, more intriguingly, about literature, its deceptions and its bad faith. Can it, in circumstances like those Seghers describes, save lives? And if not, what good is it? The narrator is an inadvertent writer, or perhaps—because he plagiarizes an entire life—a fraudulent one. He does have a knack for it: even before he becomes a posthumous continuation of

Weidel, he admits that "I'd always enjoyed unraveling tangled yarn, just as I had always enjoyed messing up neat skeins of yarn." He is describing the process of weaving and interweaving that produces textiles as well as literary texts; writers, who are both orderly and anarchic, create messes for characters and readers in order to have the pleasure of disentangling them. The narrator's imposture is his apprenticeship as a novelist. To create a character is to inhabit the identity of someone other than oneself; the man in *Transit*—unencumbered by a name of his own—enjoys a double or even treble existence, passing himself off with forged documents as a refugee called Seidler, although the authorities take him to be Weidel. But he has a sense of morality that many writers lack, and knows that what he's doing is an ethical crime.

To make matters worse, the book Seghers has him write, the one that we are reading, belongs to a genre he dislikes, for his own worldweary reasons: it's a thriller, and as he says at the start, immediately after his digression on pizza, he is sick and tired of "suspenseful tales about people surviving mortal danger." The mere business of writing reminds him of the meaningless "paper jungle" in which he is trapped—a thicket of documents, none of them worth the paper they are written on, despite the officious stamps and letterheads. He even has an aversion to reading, especially novels, which are "invented stories about a life that wasn't real"; he wants another life for himself, "but not on paper." He despises the pompous Strobel, who thinks he deserves an American visa because he has written "countless articles against Hitler." Does Strobel really fancy that there's some moral equivalency between his rhetorical posturing and the courage of the narrator's one-legged friend Heinz, "beaten half to death by the Nazis in 1935" and then sent to a concentration camp?

This uneasy literary conscience prompts the confession the narrator makes near the end, when he tells an American official, in a spasm of self-contempt, "the full truth." Is life and its agony merely the raw material for art? "It seems to me," he says, remembering his time in captivity with other writers, "that we lived through these most terrible stretches in our lives just so we could write about them:

the camps, the war, escape, and flight." It might be Seghers's re-proach to herself. Perhaps she felt guilty about her survival, or was unable to forgive herself for having chosen art not action.

This could be why her narrator, previously so sly and cynical, un-dergoes a last-minute conversion and opts for political engagement. To me, it's not entirely convincing. Explaining himself, the narrator seems to be making a prepared speech, rather than allowing us to be privy to his thoughts. When he describes his sudden determination to resist the Nazis and says that "Even if they were to shoot me, they'd never be able to eradicate me," he sounds oddly like Hum-phrey Bogart's Rick, who in 1942 in *Casablanca* makes the same un-characteristically noble choice by giving up his place on the plane to Lisbon. Hollywood certainly took an interest in Seghers: her second novel, *The Seventh Cross*, about a manhunt for seven prisoners who escape from a concentration camp, was filmed in 1944, with Spencer Tracy in the leading role. (The adaptation of course overlooked the fact that in the book Tracy's character was a doctrinaire Commu-nist.) It's revealing that in *Transit* Seghers tries literally to ground the decision of her narrator by giving him his own version of the Nazi cult of blood and soil. What he vows to defend is the hills and mountains of Provence and he emphasizes above all the crops that grow from that earth, "its peaches and its grapes." Napoleon said that an army fights on its stomach. Was Seghers implying that only the thought of food and wine could persuade a Frenchman to take up arms?

The narrator's sentimentalized change of heart is forgivable enough: Seghers needed to go on hoping, and could hardly risk damaging the morale of those who were standing up to Hitler. The end of the war, however, did not do away with the misery of displace-ment and deracination. Today, the characters Seghers describes are everywhere. People-smugglers cram them into airless trucks and drive them between continents. They wade across the Rio Grande, or crowd into leaky boats to travel from Cuba to Florida or from Indonesia to Australia or from North Africa to Italy. For a while they slipped out of a camp for asylum-seekers near Calais and made nightly treks on foot through the Channel Tunnel to reach England. They even sometimes stow away in the undercarriages of jets flying from Pakistan to Europe: recently one of them, ejected when the incoming plane lowered its landing gear, plummeted out of the sky onto a suburban street in London.

Those of us who travel for pleasure, rather than to save our lives, have our own reasons for sympathizing with *Transit*. We live in a world where people are in constant circulation, where borders have supposedly become porous and distances are abbreviated by jet engines and by electronic communications—yet never has travel been more like travail, bedeviled by bureaucratic obstacles and by the apparatus of security and surveillance that subjects our every movement to scrutiny. In 1969 Brigid Brophy published a fantastical novel called *In Transit*, an unwitting comic sequel to Seghers's book. The protagonist is a transsexual who is in transit at the airport in Dublin, which he or she calls "a free-range womb" where "you too can be duty free." In the heady spirit of the 1960s, Brophy sings the praises of mobility and elasticity, predicting that in the future it will be as easy to flip genders as to flit between countries. It is her novel, not Seghers's much older one, that now seems wistfully out-of-date.

The narrator of *Transit* refers to an earth that has become "uncomfortable," and later notices the instability of "this trembling earth." Our discomfort is now more intense, as we begin to sense that the earth is not merely tremulous but convulsed, furiously protesting against our depredations. The human race now plays the role of Hitler's army, overrunning and ravaging an entire planet, not just a single continent. And where else can we hope to go? There are no safe havens left, no "fabled cities of other continents" where we can start life all over again or rescind the iniquities of history. It is sobering and alarming to rediscover this book: what Seghers saw as an emergency has now become what we call normality.

—PETER CONRAD

TRANSIT

I

I

THEY'RE saying that the *Montreal* went down between Dakar and Martinique. That she ran into a mine. The shipping company isn't releasing any information. It may just be a rumor. But when you compare it to the fate of other ships and their cargoes of refugees which were hounded over all the oceans and never allowed to dock, which were left to burn on the high seas rather than being permitted to drop anchor merely because their passengers' documents had expired a couple of days before, then what happened to the *Montreal* seems like a natural death for a ship in wartime. That is, if it isn't all just a rumor. And provided the ship, in the meantime, hasn't been captured or ordered back to Dakar. In that case the passengers would now be sweltering in a camp at the edge of the Sahara. Or maybe they're already happily on the other side of the ocean. Probably you find all of this pretty unimportant? You're bored?—I am too. May I invite you to join me at my table? Unfortunately I don't have enough money for a regular supper. But how about a glass of rosé and a slice of pizza? Come, sit with me. Would you like to watch them bake the pizza on the open fire? Then sit next to me. Or would you prefer the view of the Old Harbor? Then you'd better sit across from me. You can see the sun go down behind Fort St. Nicolas. That certainly won't be boring.

Pizza is really a remarkable baked item. It's round and colorful like an open-face fruit pie. But bite into it and you get a mouthful of pepper. Looking at the thing more closely, you realize that those aren't cherries and raisins on top, but peppers and olives. You get used to it. But unfortunately they now require bread coupons for pizza, too.

I'd really like to know whether the *Montreal* went down or not. What will all those people do over there, if they've made it? Start a new life? Take up new professions? Pester committees? Clear the forest primeval? If, that is, there really is a genuine wilderness over there, a wilderness that can rejuvenate everyone and everything. If so, I might almost regret not having gone along.—Because, you know, I actually had the opportunity to go. I had a paid-for ticket, I had a visa, I had a transit permit. But then at the last moment I decided to stay.

There was a couple on the *Montreal* I knew casually. You know yourself what these fleeting acquaintances you make in train stations, consulate waiting rooms, or the visa department of the prefecture are like. The superficial rustle of a few words, like paper money hastily exchanged. Except that sometimes you're struck by a single exclamation, a word, who knows, a face. It goes right through you, quickly, fleetingly. You look up, you listen, and already you're involved in something. I'd like to tell someone the whole story from beginning to end. If only I weren't afraid it was boring. Aren't you thoroughly fed up with such thrilling stories? Aren't you sick of all these suspenseful tales about people surviving mortal danger by a hair, about breathtaking escapes? Me, I'm sick and tired of them. If something still thrills me today, then maybe it's an old worker's yarn about how many feet of wire he's drawn in the course of his long life and what tools he used, or the glow of the lamplight by which a few children are doing their homework.

Be careful with that rosé! It tastes just the way it looks, like raspberry syrup, but can make you incredibly tipsy. It's easier then to put up with everything. Easier to talk. But when the time comes to get up, your knees will be wobbly. And depression, a perpetual state of depression will take hold of you—till the next glass of rosé. All you'll want is to be allowed to just sit there, never again to get involved in anything.

In the past I often got embroiled in things I'm ashamed of today. Just a little ashamed—after all, they're over and done with. On the other hand, I'd be dreadfully ashamed if I were boring someone. Still, I'd like to tell the whole story, just for once, from the beginning.

II

Toward the end of that winter I was put into a French work camp near Rouen. The uniform I had to wear was the ugliest of any worn by World War armies—a French *prestataire*'s uniform. At night, because we were foreigners—half prisoners, half soldiers—we slept behind barbed wire; during the day we performed "labor service," unloading British munitions ships. We were subjected to horrible air raids. The German planes flew so low, their shadows touched us. Back then I understood what was meant by the phrase, "In the shadow of death." Once I was unloading a ship, working alongside a young guy they called Little Franz. His face was as close to mine as yours is now. It was a sunny day. We heard a hiss in the air. Franz looked up. And then it came plunging down. Its shadow turned his face black. Whoosh, it crashed down next to us. But then, you probably know as much about these things as I do.

Eventually this came to an end too. The Germans were approaching. What had we endured all the horrors and suffering for? The end of the world was at hand—tomorrow, tonight, any moment. Because that's what we all thought the arrival of the Germans would mean. Bedlam broke out in our camp. Some of the men wept, others prayed, several tried to commit suicide, some succeeded. A few of us resolved to clear out before the Last Judgment. But the commandant had set up machine guns in front of the camp gate. In vain, we explained to him that if we stayed, the Germans would shoot all of us—their own countrymen who'd escaped from Germany. But he could only follow the orders he'd been given, and was awaiting further orders instructing him what to do with the camp itself. His superior had long since left; our little town had been evacuated; the farmers from the neighboring villages had all fled. Were the Germans still two days away, or a mere two hours? And yet our commandant wasn't the worst guy on Earth, you had to give him his due. This wasn't a real war for him, not so far; he didn't understand the extent of the evil, the magnitude of the betrayal. We finally came to a kind of unspoken agreement with the man. One machine gun would remain at the gate, because no countermanding order had arrived. But presumably if we climbed over the wall, he wouldn't aim at us too deliberately.

So we climbed the wall, a few dozen of us, in the darkness of night. One of our group, Heinz, had lost his right leg in Spain. After the Civil War was over he sat around in southern prison camps for a long time. The devil only knows how and through what bureaucratic mistake a guy like him, who really was useless for a labor camp, should have been transported north to our camp. And so Heinz had to be lifted over the wall. After that we took turns carrying him as we ran like crazy through the night to stay ahead of the Germans.

Each of us had his own particularly persuasive reason for not falling into German hands. I, for one, had escaped from a German concentration camp in 1937 and had swum across the Rhine at night. For half a year afterward I'd been pretty proud of myself. Then other things happened to the world and to me. On my second escape, this time from the French camp, I remembered that first escape from the German camp. Little Franz and I were jogging along together. Like most people in those days we had the simplistic goal of getting across the Loire. We avoided the main road, walking instead across the fields. Passing through deserted villages where the unmilked cows were bellowing, we would search for something to sink our teeth into, but everything had been consumed, from the berries on the gooseberry bushes to the grain in the barns. We wanted something to drink, but the water lines had been cut. We no longer heard any shooting. The village idiot, the only one who'd stayed behind, couldn't give us any information. That's when we started feeling uneasy. The lack of human life was more oppressive than the bombing on the docks had been. Finally we came to the road leading to Paris. We certainly weren't the last to reach it. A silent stream of refugees was still pouring south from the northern villages. Hay wagons, piled high as farmhouses with furniture and poultry cages, with children and ancient grandparents, goats and calves. Trucks carrying a convent of nuns, a little girl pulling her mother in a cart, cars with pretty women wearing the furs they had salvaged, the cars pulled by cows because there were no gas stations anymore; and women carrying their dying children, even dead ones.

It was then that I wondered for the first time what these people were fleeing from. Was it from the Germans? That seemed pretty futile since the German troops were after all motorized. Was it from death? That would doubtless catch up with them along the way. But such thoughts came to me only then at that moment, when I saw these most wretched and pitiable refugees.

Franz jumped onto one vehicle, and I found a spot on a different truck. On the outskirts of a village, my truck was hit by another truck, and I had to continue on foot from there. I never saw Franz again.

Once more I struck out across the fields. I came to a large, out-of-the-way farmhouse that was still occupied. I asked for food and drink and to my great surprise the farmer's wife set out a plate of soup, wine, and bread for me on a garden table. She told me that after a long family argument, they had just decided to leave. Everything was already packed; they had only to load their truck.

While I ate and drank, planes were buzzing by pretty low. But I was too tired to look up from my plate. I also heard some brief bursts of machine-gun fire quite nearby. I couldn't figure out where it was coming from and was too exhausted to think much about it. I just kept thinking that I'd be able to hop onto their truck when the time came. They started the engine. The woman was running nervously back and forth between the truck and the house. You could see how sorry she was to leave her beautiful home. Like others in such circumstances, she was hurriedly gathering up all sorts of useless stuff. Then she rushed over to my table, took away my plate and said, "*Fini!*"

Suddenly I realized she was staring, her mouth wide open, at something on the other side of the garden fence; I turned around and saw, no I heard—actually I don't know whether I saw or heard them first or both at the same time—motorcyclists. The sound of the truck engine must have drowned out the noise of their motorcycles approaching on the road. Two of them stopped on the other side of the fence; each had two people in the sidecar, and they were wearing gray-green uniforms. One said in German, so loud that I could hear it: "Goddam it, now the new drive belt is torn too!"

The Germans were here already! They'd caught up with me. I don't know how I had imagined the arrival of the Germans: With thunder and earthquakes? But at first nothing at all happened besides two more motorcycles pulling up on the other side of the garden fence. Still, the effect was just as powerful, maybe even more so. I sat there paralyzed, my shirt instantly soaking wet. Now I felt what I hadn't felt during my escape from the first camp, not even while I was unloading the ships under the low-flying planes. For the first time in my life I was scared to death.

Please be patient with me. I'll get to the point soon. You understand, don't you? There comes a time when you have to tell someone the whole story, everything, just the way it happened. Today I can't figure out how I could have been so afraid, and of what. Afraid of being discovered? Of being stood up against a wall and shot? On the docks I could have disappeared just as easily. Of being sent back to Germany? Of being slowly tortured to death? It could have happened to me while I was swimming across the Rhine. What's more I'd always liked living on the edge, always felt at home with the smell of danger. As soon as I started thinking about what it was that I was so incredibly frightened of, I became less afraid.

I did what was both the most sensible and the most foolish thing I could do: I remained sitting there. I had intended to drill two holes into my belt, and that's what I now did. The farmer came into the garden with a blank look on his face and said to his wife: "Now we might as well stay."

"Of course," his wife said with relief, "but you'd better go to the barn. I'll deal with them; they won't eat me."

"Me neither," her husband said. "I'm not a soldier; I'll show them my club foot."

In the meantime an entire convoy of motorcycles had driven up on the grassy plot on the other side of the fence. They didn't even enter the garden. After three minutes they drove on. For the first time in four years I had heard German commands again. Oh, how they grated! It wouldn't have taken much more for me to jump up and stand at attention. Later I heard that this very same motorcycle column had cut off the refugee escape route along which I had come. And that all this discipline, all these commands, all these orders had produced the most terrible disorder—bloodshed, mothers scream- ing, the dissolution of our world order. And yet thrumming like an undertone in these commands was something terribly obvious, in- sidiously honest: Don't complain that your world is about to perish. You haven't defended it, and you've allowed it to be destroyed! So don't give us any crap now! Just make it quick; let us take charge!

Suddenly I felt quite calm. I thought, I'm sitting here, and the Germans are moving past me and occupying France. But France has often been occupied—and the occupiers all had to withdraw again. France has often been sold down the river, and you, too, my gray- green fellows, have often been sold down the river. My fear vanished completely; the whole dreadful swastika episode was a nightmare haunting me; I saw the mightiest armies of the world marching up to the other side of my garden fence and withdraw; I saw the cocki- est of empires collapse and the young and the bold take heart; I saw the masters of the world rise up and come crashing down. I alone had immeasurably long to live.

In any event, my dream of getting across the Loire was now at an end. I decided to go to Paris. I knew a couple of decent people there, that is, provided they were still decent.

III

I walked to Paris; it took me five days. German motorized columns drove along beside me. The rubber of their tires was superb; the young soldiers were the elite—strong and handsome; they had occupied a country without a fight; they were cheerful. Some farmers were already working the fields on the side of the road—they had sown their crops on free land. In one village bells were ringing for a dead child who had bled to death on the road. A farm wagon had broken down at one of the crossroads. Perhaps it belonged to the dead child's family. German soldiers ran over to the wagon and fixed the wheels; the farmers thanked them for their kindness. A young fellow my age was sitting on a rock; he was wearing a coat over the remnants of a uniform. He was crying. As I walked by I patted him on the back, saying, "It will all pass."

He said, "We would have held the place, but those pigs gave us only enough bullets to last an hour. We were betrayed."

"We haven't heard the last of this," I told him.

I kept walking. Early one Sunday morning I walked into Paris. A swastika flag was actually flying before the Hotel de Ville. And they were actually playing the *Hohenfriedberg March* in front of Notre Dame. I couldn't believe it. I walked diagonally across Paris. And everywhere there were fleets of German cars and swastikas. I felt quite hollow, as if emptied of all emotion.

All this trouble, all this misfortune that had befallen another people had been caused by *my* people. For it was obvious that they talked like me and whistled the same tunes. As I was walking to Clichy where my old friends the Binnets lived, I wondered whether the Binnets would be sensible enough to understand that, even though I was one of these people, I was still myself. I wondered whether they would take me in without identity papers.

They did, and they were sensible. In the past this sensibleness of theirs even used to bother me! Before the war, for six months, I'd been Yvonne Binnet's boyfriend. She was only seventeen. And I, fool that I was, had fled from my homeland to escape the mess, the evil fog of dense emotions. I was secretly annoyed at the Binnet family's clear-headed common sense. I thought all the family members were just too reasonable in their view of life. For instance, from their sensible point of view, people went on strike so that next week they could buy a better cut of meat. The Binnets even thought that if you earned three more francs a day, then your family would not only feel less hungry but also stronger and happier. And Yvonne's good sense made her believe that love existed for our pleasure, hers and mine. But I knew deep down in my bones—of course I didn't tell her this—that love sometimes goes along with suffering, that there's also death, separation, and hardship, and that happiness can overtake you for no reason at all, as can the sadness into which it often imperceptibly turns.

But now the Binnet family's clearheaded common sense proved to be a blessing. They were glad to see me and took me in. They didn't think I was a Nazi just because I was a German. The old Binnets were at home, as well as the youngest son who wasn't yet in the army and the second son who had shed his uniform in the nick of time when he saw how things stood. But their daughter Annette's husband was a prisoner of the Germans. She now lived at her parents' house with her child. My Yvonne, they told me with embarrassment, had been evacuated to the South, where she had married her cousin a week ago. That didn't bother me at all. At that moment I wasn't the least bit in the mood for love.

Since their factory was shut down, the Binnet men stayed at home. As for me, all I had was time. So we had nothing better to do from morning till night than talk about what was going on. We all agreed on how much the invasion of Germany suited the rulers here. The elder Binnet seemed to understand quite a few things as well or better than any Sorbonne professor. The only thing we disagreed on was Russia. Half of the Binnets claimed that Russia was thinking only of itself and had left us in the lurch. The other half claimed that the French and German rulers had agreed that their armies should be launched at the Russians first instead being used in the West, and it was this that had thwarted Russia. Trying to make peace among us, old man Binnet said that the truth would come to light, that one day the files would all be opened, by which time he'd be long dead.

Please forgive this digression. We're getting close to the main point. Annette, the Binnets' older daughter, had been assigned some work at home. I had nothing better to do, so I helped her pick up and deliver her laundry bundles. We took the Métro to the Latin Quarter. Got off at the Odéon stop. While Annette went to her shop on Boulevard Saint Germain, I waited on a bench near the Odéon station exit.

Once Annette took a long time. But what did it matter to me? The sun was shining down on my bench; I watched the people going up and down the Métro stairs; two women were hawking *Paris Soir*, shouting in an ancient mutual hatred for each other that increased whenever one of them took in two sous more than the other. For to be honest, although the two women stood next to each other, only the one was making any sales, while the other's pile never got any lighter. The bad saleswoman suddenly turned to the lucky one and cursed her wildly. In a flash she flung her entire rotten life at the head of the other woman, interrupting herself only to cry out, *Paris Soir*!

Two German soldiers came over and laughed. That really annoyed me, as much as it would have if the drunken newspaper seller were my French foster mother. Some women porters sitting next to me were talking about a young woman who had cried all night after being detained by the police because she was walking with a German soldier while her own husband was a prisoner of war. The trucks of refugees kept rolling down the Boulevard Saint Germain without interruption. Between them darted the small swastika-emblazoned cars of German officers. Some of the plane tree leaves were already falling on us, for that year everything was drying up early. But I kept thinking about how heavily time weighed on me because I had so much of it. It really is hard to experience war as a stranger among a strange people. Just then, Paul came walking along the avenue.

Paul Strobel had been in the camp with me. Once while we were unloading a ship, someone had stepped on his hand. For three days they thought his hand was done for. He had cried back then. Actually I could understand that. He prayed when we heard the Germans were already surrounding the camp. Believe me, I could understand that too. Now he was far removed from such situations. He was coming from the direction of the Rue de l'Ancienne Comédie. An old buddy from the camp! And in the middle of Swastika-Paris! I called to him, "Paul!"

He was startled, but then he recognized me. He looked amazingly cheerful and was well dressed. We sat down in front of a little café on the Carrefour de l'Odéon. I was glad to see him again. But he seemed pretty distracted. Up to that point, I had never had anything to do with writers. My parents saw to it that I was trained as a mechanic. In the camp everyone knew Paul Strobel was a writer. We were assigned to unload on the same dock. The German planes were heading straight for us. While I was at that camp, Paul was a sort of buddy of mine, a somewhat funny, slightly crazy camp pal, but always a pal. Since our escape I hadn't experienced anything new, and for me the old stuff hadn't yet blown over. I was still half in escape mode, half in hiding. But I could tell he had finished with that chapter of his life; something new seemed to have happened to him that gave him strength. All the things I was still deeply caught up in were just a memory for him.

He said, "Next week I'm going to the unoccupied zone. My family lives in Cassis near Marseille. I have a danger visa for the United States."

I asked him what that was.

"A special emergency visa for especially endangered people," he said.

"Are you in special danger?" I just meant to ask whether he was perhaps endangered in a more unusual way than the rest of us in this now dangerous part of the world.

He looked at me in surprise, a little annoyed. Then he said in a whisper, "I wrote a book and countless articles against Hitler. If they find me here—Why are you smiling?"

I wasn't smiling at all, I was in no mood to smile; I thought of Heinz who had been beaten half to death by the Nazis in 1935, who was then put in a German concentration camp, escaping to Paris, only to end up in Spain with the International Brigade where he then lost a leg, and who, one-legged, was then dragged through all of France's concentration camps, ending up in ours. Where was he now? I also thought of flocks of birds being able to fly away. The whole earth was uncomfortable, and still I quite liked this kind of life; I didn't envy Paul for that thing he had—what was it called?

"My danger visa's been confirmed by the American Consulate at the Place de la Concorde. My sister's best friend is engaged to a silk merchant from Lyon. He brought me my mail. He's driving back there in his car and will take me with him. He just needs to get a general permit saying how many people he's taking. That way I can circumvent the German safe conduct."

I looked at his right hand, the one that had been stepped on back then. The thumb was a little shriveled. Paul hid his thumb. "How did you get to Paris?" I asked.

"By a miracle," he said. "Three of us escaped together, Hermann Achselroth, Ernst Sperber, and I. You know Achselroth, don't you? His plays?"

I didn't know any of his plays, but I did remember Achselroth. An exceptionally good-looking fellow, who would have looked better in an officer's uniform than the dirty *prestataire* rags he wore like a *Landsknecht*.

He was famous, Paul assured me. The three of them had gotten as far as L. and were pretty much exhausted. Then they came to a crossroads, a real parting of the ways, Paul said, smiling—I liked him very much then, and I was glad to be sitting there with him, both of us still alive. Anyway, he said, it was a real crossroads, with a deserted inn. They'd been sitting on the steps of the inn when a French military car drove up, stuffed with military supplies. The three of them watched as the driver began dumping everything out. Suddenly Achselroth went over to the fellow and exchanged a few words with him. The rest of us weren't paying much attention. Then Achselroth climbed into the driver's seat of the car and roared off, without even waving good-bye. The French driver took the other branch of the crossroad and started walking toward the nearest village.

"How much do you think he gave him?" I asked. "Five thousand? Six?"

"You're crazy! Six thousand! For a car! And an army car at that!

And don't forget, the driver's honor had to be paid for, too! On top of the price of the car. Desertion while on duty, that's treason! He must have paid the man at least sixteen thousand! We, of course, had no idea that Achselroth had that much money in his pockets. I tell you, he didn't even turn once to look at us. How awful it all was. What a mean, rotten thing to do!"

"But it wasn't all mean. Not all of it was awful. Do you still remember Heinz, the one-legged guy? They helped him get over the wall back then. And they didn't leave him behind, I'm sure they had to carry him. Anyway, they schlepped him all the way into the unoccupied territory."

"Did they get away?"

"I don't know."

"But that guy Achselroth, he made it. He's already on some ship, on his way to Cuba!"

"To Cuba? Achselroth? Why?"

"How can you still ask why? He just took the first visa and the first ship he could."

"If he had split his money with you two, Paul, then he couldn't have bought himself a car." The story as a whole amused me because of its utter consistency.

"What are your plans?" Paul asked. "What are you going to do now?"

I had to admit that I hadn't made any plans; that the future was hazy for me. He asked whether I belonged to any party. I said no. Back then, I told him, I'd ended up in a German concentration camp without belonging to any party, because even without belonging to a party I wouldn't put up with some of their dirty tricks. I escaped from that first concentration camp, the German one, because if I was going to kick the bucket I didn't want to do it behind barbed wire. I was also going to tell Paul how I'd swum across the Rhine, at night in the fog; but it occurred to me that by now there'd been lots of people who'd swum across lots of rivers. And so I didn't tell him my story so as not to bore him.

Annette must have given up on me and gone back home by

herself long ago. I had thought Paul wanted to spend the evening with me. He was silent now, looking at me in a way that puzzled me. Finally, in a changed tone of voice, he said, "Listen, you could do me a huge favor. Would you?"

I wondered what he wanted me to do. Of course I was willing.

"In the letter my sister's friend sent me—she's the friend I mentioned before, the one who's engaged to the silk merchant who wants to take me along in his car—in that letter she enclosed a second letter addressed to a man I know well. The man's wife had asked her, as a favor, to see that the letter was delivered to him in Paris. Actually, in her letter she said that the man's wife had been desperate, had pleaded with her.

"The husband had stayed in Paris; he couldn't get out in time; he's still here. You've surely heard of the writer Weidel, haven't you?"— I'd never heard of him. Paul quickly assured me that this wouldn't affect the favor he was asking of me.

He suddenly seemed uneasy. Maybe he'd been uneasy the whole time and I just hadn't noticed. I was curious to find out what all this was leading up to. Mr. Weidel, he continued, lived quite nearby, on the Rue de Vaugirard. In a small hotel between the Rue de Rennes and Boulevard Raspail. Paul himself had already gone there earlier today. But when he asked whether Mr. Weidel was in, they gave him a strange look. The woman who owned the hotel had refused to take the letter. Yet, she had given only an evasive answer when he asked whether the gentleman had moved elsewhere. Would I be willing to go to the hotel again with the letter and ask for the man's address so that the letter could be delivered to him? Would I be willing to do that?

I had to laugh and said, "Of course, if that's all there is to it!"

"Maybe he's been picked up by the Gestapo?"

"I'll find out," I said.

Paul amused me. On the dock, while we were unloading the ships, I hadn't noticed if he was any more afraid than the rest of us. We were all afraid, and he was too. In our shared fear he hadn't said anything more stupid than the rest of us. Like the rest of us he had

slaved away, because when you're afraid it's better to be doing something, and better yet to be doing a lot, than to wait for death, shivering and trembling like baby chicks waiting for a hawk to swoop
down on them. And this keeping busy in the face of death has nothing to do with bravery. Don't you agree? Even though it's sometimes
mistaken for bravery and rewarded as such. But at that moment Paul
was certainly more afraid than I was. He didn't like this Paris, three
quarters of it deserted; he hated the swastika flag, and saw a spy in
every man who followed him. At one time Paul probably did have
some success as a writer; he had wanted to be incredibly successful
and he couldn't bear to think that he was now just a poor devil like
me. So in his mind he twisted it around, feeling terribly persecuted.
He firmly believed that the Gestapo had nothing better to do than
to wait for him in front of Weidel's hotel.

So I took the letter. Paul again assured me that Weidel had really
been a great writer. It was his way of making my errand less unpleasant, which was unnecessary in my case. Weidel could have been a tie
salesman, for all I cared. I'd always enjoyed unraveling tangled yarn,
just as I had always enjoyed messing up neat skeins of yarn. Paul
asked me to meet him the next day at the Café Capoulade.

The hotel on Rue de Vaugirard was a tall, narrow building, an
average Paris hotel. The owner was quite pretty. She had a fresh, soft
face and pitch-black hair. She was wearing a white silk blouse. I asked
without thinking whether she had a room available. She smiled even
as her eyes looked me coldly up and down. "As many as you want."

"But first, there's something else," I said. "You have a guest here,
Mr. Weidel, is he in by chance?"

Her face, her attitude, changed in a way you only see among the
French. The most courteous composure can suddenly turn to furi-
ous anger when they lose control. She said, quite hoarse with fury,
"For the second time today someone's asked me about this person.
The gentleman has moved, how often do I have to explain that?"

I said, "You're explaining it to me for the first time. Would you be
so kind as to tell me where the gentlemen is staying now."

"How should I know?" the woman said. It began to dawn on me

that she was afraid, but why? "I don't know where he's staying now. I really can't tell you anything else."

So the Gestapo's picked him up after all, I thought. I put my hand on the woman's arm. She didn't pull it away, but looked at me with a mixture of scorn and unease.

"I don't know this man at all," I assured her. "Someone asked me to give him a message. That's all. Something that's important to him. I wouldn't want to keep even a stranger waiting." She looked at me carefully. Then she led me into a small room next to the hotel lobby. Finally she came out with it.

"You can't imagine what a lot of trouble this person has caused me! He came on the 15th towards evening; by that time the Germans were already marching in. I chose to stay; I didn't close my hotel. You don't leave during a war, my father used to say. If you do, they'll mess everything up and steal everything. And why should I be afraid of the Germans? I prefer them to the Reds. They won't lay a hand on my bank account. Anyway, Mr. Weidel arrives and he's trembling. I find it odd that somebody should be trembling with fear of his own countrymen. But I was glad to have a paying guest. I was the only hotel open in the entire quarter. When I gave him the registration forms to fill out, he asked me not to register him with the police. As you must know, Monsieur Langeron, the chief of police, emphatically insists that all foreigners be registered. We have to maintain order, right?"

"I'm not so sure," I replied. "The Nazi soldiers are all foreigners too, unregistered ones."

"Well this Mr. Weidel, in any case, made a fuss about his registration. He hadn't given up his room in Auteuil, he said, and he was still registered there. I didn't like it one bit. Mr. Weidel had stayed at my hotel once before with his wife. A beautiful woman, only she didn't take care of herself and cried often. I assure you, the man made trouble everywhere. All right, so I left him unregistered. Only for that one night, though, I told him. He paid in advance. The following morning the man doesn't come down. In short, I go up and open the door with my master key. I push back the bolt with this contraption I had made. She opened a drawer and showed me the device, a cleverly designed hook. "The man was lying on his bed, still fully dressed, a little glass bottle empty on the night table. If that little bottle was full originally, then he had enough pills in his stomach to kill all the cats in our quarter.

"Luckily I have a good friend at the Saint Sulpice police station. He was able to straighten it out for me. First we registered him for the day before he died. Then we arranged his burial. That man really caused me more trouble than the German invasion."

"In any case, he's dead," I said and got up to leave. The story bored me. I had witnessed too many messy deaths. Then the woman said, "Don't think that my problems are over. This man has actually managed to create trouble for me from beyond the grave."

I sat down again.

"He left a suitcase. What am I supposed to do with it? It was sitting here in my office when the thing happened. I'd forgotten about it. I don't want to stir things up again at the police station."

"Well, throw it in the Seine," I said, "or burn it in your furnace."

"That's impossible," the woman said, "I can't take the chance."

"Well, after all, if you were able to get rid of the body, I'm sure you can deal with the suitcase."

"That's something quite different. The man is dead now. It's in the official records. But the suitcase is a forensic object, it's tangible property, it can be inherited; claimants might turn up."

I was already sick of the whole affair. I said, "I'll be happy to take the suitcase, I don't mind. I know someone who was a friend of the dead man; he can take it to the widow." The hotel owner was quite relieved. But she did ask me to fill out a receipt for her. I wrote a false name on a piece of paper that she dated and receipted. She shook my hand warmly, then I left quickly. I had completely lost the favorable impression I had formed of her earlier. No matter how pretty she had seemed to me initially. I suddenly saw in her long, cunning head only a skull to which little black curls had been attached.

IV

The following morning I went to the Capoulade with the suitcase. I waited in vain for Paul. Had he left in a hurry with the silk merchant? Was it because of the sign on the café door, "No Jews allowed," that he didn't come? But then it occurred to me that he had recited the Paternoster when the Germans arrived. Besides, the sign had already disappeared by the time I left the Capoulade. Maybe one of the customers or the proprietor himself had thought the sign too ridiculous; maybe it had been flimsily tacked up, fallen off, and not been important enough to anyone to be nailed up again.

It was a beautiful day, the little suitcase wasn't heavy. I walked to the Concorde. But even though the sun shone brightly that morning I was overcome by the kind of misery that the French call a "*cafard*." The French lived so well in their beautiful country; everything went so smoothly for them—all the joys of existence—but sometimes even they lose their joy in life and then there is nothing but boredom, a Godless emptiness: a *cafard*. Why should I be spared? My *cafard* had already set in the day before when I no longer thought the hotel owner pretty. Now the *cafard* swallowed me up, body and soul. Sometimes there's a gurgling in a large puddle because inside there's another hole, an even deeper puddle. That's how the *cafard* was gurgling in me. And when I saw the huge swastika flag on the Place de la Concorde, I crept down into the darkness of the Métro.

A *cafard* had also taken hold of the Binnet family. Annette was furious with me because I hadn't waited for her the previous day. Her mother thought it was time that I got some sort of identification papers, and the newspapers were saying there would soon be ration cards for bread. I didn't eat with the family that day because my feelings were hurt. I crawled into the hole under the roof that was my room. I could have brought a girl up with me, but I didn't feel in the mood for that either. They talk about fatal wounds and fatal illnesses; they also speak of fatal boredom. I assure you, my boredom was deadly. That evening, out of sheer boredom, I broke open the lock on the suitcase. It contained little more than paper.

And out of sheer boredom I began to read. I read on and on. I was spellbound, maybe because I'd never before read a book to the end. But no, that couldn't be the reason. Paul was right. I didn't know anything about writing. It wasn't my world. Yet I think the man who'd written this was an expert in his art. I forgot my *cafard*. I forgot my deadly boredom. And if I'd had fatal wounds I would have forgotten them too while I was absorbed in reading. And as I read line after line, I also felt that *this* was my own language, my mother tongue, and it flowed into me like milk into a baby. It didn't rasp and grate like the language that came from the throats of the Nazis, their murderous commands and objectionable insistence on obedience, their disgusting boasts.—*This* was serious, calm, and still.

I felt as if I were alone again with my own family. I came across words my mother had used to soothe me when I was angry and horrible words she had used to admonish me when I had lied or been in a fight. I also stumbled on words I had used myself back then, but had forgotten because I never again felt the emotion I needed to express them. There were new words, too, that I sometimes use now.

The whole thing was a fairly complicated story with some complicated characters. One of whom, I thought, resembled me. The story deals with . . . oh no, I'd better not bore you with that. You've read enough stories in your life. For me, you might say, it was the first. I'd had more than enough experiences, but I'd never *read* anything! This was something new for me. And how avidly I read it! In the story, as I said, there were a lot of crazy characters, really mixed-up people; almost all of them got involved in bad, devious things, even those who tried to resist. I had read entranced like this, no listened, only as a child. I felt the same joy, the same dread. The forest was just as impenetrable. But this was a forest for adults. The wolf was just as bad, but it was a wolf who bewitched grown-up children. And the old fairy-tale magic that turned boys into bears and girls into lilies took hold of me anew in this story, threatening again with grim transformations.

But the people in this story didn't annoy me with their infuriating behavior, as they would have done in real life, stupidly allowing themselves to be taken in, heading toward disastrous fates. I was able to understand their actions because I was at last able to follow them from the very beginning to the point where it all came together as it had to. Already they seemed to me less evil—even the man who resembled me like a pea in a pod—only because the writer had described them. They all became clear and pure, as if they had done their penance, as if they had already passed through a little purgatory, the small fire that was the dead man's brain.

And then suddenly, after some three hundred pages, everything stopped. I never found out how it ended. The Germans had entered Paris. The man had packed up everything, his few belongings, his writing paper, and left me alone looking at the last, almost empty page. Again I was overwhelmed by an immense sadness, by deadly boredom. Why did he commit suicide? He shouldn't have left me alone. He should have finished writing his story. I could have kept reading till dawn. He should have gone on writing, gone on writing innumerable stories that would have protected me from evil. If he could only have met me in time! Instead of that fool Paul who got me into this mess. I would have pleaded with him to go on living. I would have found him a hiding place. I would have brought him food and drink. But now he was dead. Two typewritten lines on the last page. And I was left all alone! As miserable as before!

I frittered away the next day looking for Paul. He had disappeared. I suppose because he was afraid. And yet the dead man had been his *copain*, his buddy, his pal. I thought of the story he had told me about the man who bought the car at the crossroads. Oh well, Paul himself was a pretty good one for leaving you in the lurch! In the evening I crept up to my hole very early so I could return to my story. But I was disappointed this time. I wanted to read it all again. But unfortunately it resisted me. On my first reading I had greedily absorbed everything. Now I had as little desire to read the story again as I would to live through the same adventure twice, the same series of dangers.

So I had nothing more to read; the man wasn't going to rise from the dead for my sake; his story was unfinished, and I was alone and demoralized up in my hole with his suitcase. I rummaged around in it, finding a pair of new silk socks, a couple of handkerchiefs, an envelope with foreign stamps. Apparently the dead man had collected stamps as a hobby. Well, so what. I also found a small elegant case containing nail files, a Spanish language textbook, an empty little perfume bottle; I unscrewed it and sniffed—nothing. The dead man was probably a squirrel, now he was done squirreling. There were also two more letters.

I read them carefully, though not just out of idle curiosity. Please, you must believe me. In the first letter someone informed him that his story promised to be quite good and worthy of standing alongside all the other stories he had written so far in his life. But unfortunately because of the war no one was publishing such stories now. In the second letter a woman, probably his wife, wrote that he should not expect her ever to come back to him; their life together was over.

I put the letters back. As I saw it: Nobody wanted his stories anymore. His wife had run away. He was alone. The whole world was collapsing, and then the Germans came to Paris. That was too much for him. So he put an end to it. I started fiddling with the broken locks trying to fix them so that I could lock the suitcase again. What was I supposed to do with it? A story only three-fourths completed . . . Take it to the Pont de l'Alma and throw it in the Seine? I would as soon have drowned a child! Suddenly I remembered the letter Paul had given me—and let me tell you right now, it led to my undoing. Oddly enough, up to that point I had completely forgotten the letter, as if Providence had sent me the suitcase out of the blue. Perhaps if I read the letter, I thought, it might give me some clue as to what to do with the things.

It contained two enclosures. One was a letter from the Mexican Consulate in Marseille saying that a visa and travel funds were waiting for him there. This was followed by all sorts of additional details—names, numbers, committees—which I skimmed over. The other was a letter from the woman who had left him, written in the same handwriting. Only now, as I was comparing the two, I took note of the handwriting—tight and neat, like a child's; what I really mean is clean, not neat. She urged her husband to come to Marseille. She had to see him, to see him right away. He must not delay a second; he was to join her immediately on receiving this letter, no matter what! It would probably take them a long time to get out of this cursed country. And the visa might expire. Even though the visa had been obtained, and the trip paid for. But there was no ship that would take them straight to their destination. They had to cross other countries to get there. And those countries demanded transit visas, which took a long time and were hard to get. So everything could fall apart if they didn't get together at once! Only the visa was assured. And even that would be valid only for a certain period of time. Everything now depended on the transit visa.

The letter seemed a bit confused to me. What did she suddenly want from this man whom she had left for good? To leave the country with him, even though she hadn't wanted to stay with him at any price? It occurred to me that the dead man by dying had escaped new anguish and fresh complications. And after I reread the letter and the entire mishmash of wanting to see him again, of transit visas, consulates, and transit dates, it seemed to me that his present resting place was a safe and reliable one and would provide him with perfect rest.

In any case, I knew now what to do with the suitcase. I would take it to the Mexican Consulate here in Paris. The consul would send all the documents to his counterpart in Marseille. Because that's where the wife would be inquiring for news. Or at least this is how I imagined it would work.

So, the following day I asked a police officer where to find the Mexican Consulate. At my question, the officer looked at me briefly. This was probably the first time he, a Parisian traffic policeman at the Place de Clichy, had ever been asked for the address of the Mexican Consulate. He searched in a little red book for the address. Then he looked at me again as if to decipher how I was connected with Mexico. I was amused by my own question. There are countries you're familiar with from boyhood on without ever having laid eyes on them. They're exciting countries, God knows why. A picture, a small snaking section of a river in an atlas, the mere sound of the name, a postage stamp. Nothing interested me about Mexico. I didn't know anything about the country and had never read anything about it, probably because even as a boy I didn't liked to read. I'd never heard anything about the country that had stuck in my mind. I knew that it had oil, cacti, and huge straw hats. And whatever else it may have had, interested me as little as it did the dead man.

I dragged the little suitcase from the Place de l'Alma Métro station to the Rue Longuin. It was a pretty neighborhood. Most of the houses were closed down. The quarter was nearly deserted. The rich had all gone south. They had left in time, before getting a whiff of the war now scorching their country. How gentle the hills of Meudon on the other side of the Seine! How blue the air! German trucks were rolling continuously along the riverbank. For the first time since I'd come to Paris I wondered what it was I was actually waiting for here. Lots of dry leaves lay on Avenue Wilson; summer was already over. Yet it was barely August. I had been cheated of summer.

The Mexican Consulate turned out to be a small house, painted a light yellow; it stood at an odd angle in one corner of a beautifully paved courtyard full of plants. There were probably courtyards just like this in Mexico. I rang the bell at the gate. The single high window was closed. A shield with a coat of arms hung above the inner door. I couldn't make heads or tails of it even though it was shiny and new. I did make out an eagle perched on a thicket of cacti. At first I thought this house was also uninhabited. But when I dutifully rang again, a heavyset man appeared on the stairs on the other side of the inner door. He looked me up and down with his single eye— the other eye socket was empty. My first Mexican. I looked at him curiously. He just shrugged in answer to my question. He was only the caretaker, he said; the legation was in Vichy; the consul had not returned; the telegraph was down. Then he withdrew. I imagined all Mexicans were like him, broad, silent, one-eyed—a nation of Cyclopses! One should get to know all the peoples of the world, I thought. Suddenly I felt sorry for the dead man whom I had envied up to then.

In the following week I went to the Mexican Consulate almost every day. The one-eyed man always waved me off from the upstairs window. I probably looked like a crazy man with my little suitcase. Why was I so persistent? Conscientiousness? Boredom? Because the house attracted me? One morning there was a car parked outside the fence. Maybe the consul had arrived? I rang the bell like crazy. My Cyclops appeared on the stairs, but this time he angrily shouted at me to beat it, the bell wasn't there for me to ring. I walked irresolutely to the next street corner.

When I turned around again, I was amazed. The car was still parked outside the consulate, but now the place was teeming with people. And this crowd had appeared behind my back within a few minutes. I don't know what sort of magnetic force had drawn them there, what mysterious, psychic communication. They couldn't possibly all be from the neighborhood. But how had they gotten there? Spaniards of all kinds were probably hidden away in the nooks and crannies of the city, like me in mine, having escaped much the same way I had. But now the swastika had followed them here, too. I asked a few questions and discovered why they were gathering here. There was a rumor, a hope that this faraway nation would take in all Republican Spaniards. There were also ships ready to sail in the harbors of Bordeaux, and they now felt they were all under such powerful protection that not even the Germans could interfere with their departure. An old, emaciated, yellow-skinned Spaniard said bitterly that it was all nonsense. Although there might be visas available because Mexico now had a popular government, unfortunately you couldn't receive a safe conduct from the Germans. In fact, quite the contrary had happened. The Germans were capturing Spaniards here and in Brussels and handing them over to Franco. Then another man, a young one with round black eyes, called out that the ships were not in Bordeaux, but in Marseille. And they were ready to sail. He even knew their names: *Republica*, *Esperanza*, and *Passionaria*.

Just then my Cyclops came down the stairs. I was dumbstruck. He was smiling. It was only with me that he was grouchy as if I were an imposter. He handed each of us a piece of paper while patiently explaining in a soft voice that we must write down our names so that the consul could see us, one at a time. He gave me one of the forms too, but silently and with a warning look. If only I had allowed myself to be intimidated! On my piece of paper I found the time at which I was to appear. On a whim I wrote down the name I had given the dead man's landlady. My own name never entered the picture.

I was given an appointment for the following Monday, but several things happened in Paris that weekend which proved to be significant for me, too. As elsewhere, the Germans had put up posters in Clichy that depicted a German soldier helping French women and looking after children. In Clichy all these posters were torn to shreds overnight. There were a couple of arrests, and after that masses of leaflets against the Nazis started circulating for the first time. Here they call these little leaflets *papillons*, butterflies. The best friend of the Binnet's youngest son had gotten mixed up in this, and the Binnets feared for the safety of their sons. Their cousin Marcel suggested the boys disappear for a while into the unoccupied zone. So Marcel, the Binnets' two sons, and the friend met up to make plans. I was infected by their travel preparations. Suddenly I didn't have the least desire to hide away in Paris anymore. I imagined the unoccupied territory as an overgrown, wild country, a confused jumble in which a person like me could get lost if he chose to. And if, for a while, my life was going to consist of being chased from one place to another, then I wanted at least to be chased to beautiful cities and strange unknown places. They were glad to have me join them.

The morning before our departure I once more carried the little suitcase to the Mexican Consulate. This time, with the piece of paper I'd been given, I was allowed to enter. I found myself in a cool, circular room that matched the strange exterior of the house. They called out the name I had given, repeating it three times before I remembered that it was mine. My Cyclops escorted me only reluctantly and, I felt, mistrustfully.

I didn't know who the rotund man was who received me. Was he the consul himself, the deputy consul, the deputy consul's secretary, or a temporary secretary? I set the suitcase down under the man's nose, while explaining truthfully that it belonged to someone who had committed suicide but who had a Mexican visa and that the contents of the suitcase should be delivered to his wife. I never had the chance to mention the dead man's name. The rotund man interrupted my account, which apparently displeased him.

He said, "Excuse me, sir. But I couldn't help you even in normal times. Much less now that the postal service has been interrupted. You cannot ask us to put the property left by this person into our courier bag, just because my government once provided him with a visa while he was alive. It's out of the question. Please forgive me. But you must agree. I am the Mexican vice consul, I am not a notary public. While he was alive this man may also have received other visas, Uruguayan, Chilean, what do I know. You could, by the same token, turn to my colleagues at these consulates. But you'd get the same answer. Surely you can understand our position."

I had to admit that the vice consul was right. I felt embarrassed. I left. The crowd outside the fence had grown. Countless shining eyes turned toward the gate. For these men and women the consulate wasn't merely a government agency, a visa wasn't just government office trash. In their desolation, which was exceeded only by their faith, they saw this house as the country and the country as this house. An infinitely large house in which lived a welcoming nation. Here set into the yellow wall was the door to the house. And once across the threshold, you were already a guest.

Walking through this crowd for the last time, everything in me that could hope and suffer with other people was awakened, and the part of me that drew a sort of bold pleasure from my own and other people's desolation, and saw suffering as an adventure, dwindled away.

After that I decided to use the suitcase myself since my backpack was torn. I stuffed my few belongings on top of the dead man's papers. Perhaps I would actually get to Marseille one day. We needed German permission to get across the demarcation line. And so we spent a couple of days, still undecided, in the rural towns near the border. They were teeming with German soldiers. Finally at an inn we found a farmer who owned some land on the other side of the border. At dusk he led us across through a tobacco field. We embraced him and rewarded him with gifts. We kissed the first French border guard we met. We were deeply moved and felt liberated. I needn't tell you that it proved to be a delusion.

2

I

YOU KNOW of course what unoccupied France was like in the fall of 1940. The cities' train stations, their shelters, and even the public squares and churches were full of refugees. They came from the north, the occupied territory and the "forbidden zone," from the Départements of Alsace, Lorraine, and the Moselle. And even as I was fleeing to Paris I realized these were merely the remnants of those wretched human masses as so many had died on the road or on the trains. But I hadn't counted on the fact that many would also be born on the way. While I was searching for a place to sleep in the Toulouse train station, I had to climb over a woman lying among suitcases, bundles, and piles of guns, nursing a baby. How the world has aged in this single year! The infant looked old and wrinkled, the nursing mother's hair was gray, and the faces of the baby's two little brothers watching over her shoulder seemed shameless, old, and sad. Old also were the eyes of these two boys from whom nothing had been concealed, neither the mystery of death nor the mystery of birth.

The trains were still packed with soldiers in ragged uniforms openly reviling their superiors, cursing their marching orders, yet following them nevertheless, the devil only knew where to, in order to stand guard in some leftover part of their country, at a concentration camp or a border crossing that would surely have been moved by the next day. Or they might even be loaded onto ships headed for Africa because a commander in some small cove had decided to defy the Germans, but would probably have already been relieved of his command long before these soldiers could get there. For the time being they marched on. Maybe because the senseless marching order was at least something to hold on to, a substitute for some command from on high, a great rallying cry, or for the lost *Marseillaise*. At one point in the journey they handed us the remnants of a man—a head and a torso; instead of arms and legs, empty uniform parts dangling down. We squeezed him in between us and stuck a cigarette between his lips since he had no hands; it burned his lips, he growled and suddenly started crying, "If only I knew what it was all for."

We felt like crying, too. We were scrambling around in a big senseless arc, sometimes spending nights in shelters, then in the open fields, now jumping up on a truck, then on a freight car, unable to find a place to stay anywhere—to say nothing about getting an offer of work—in a large arc always reaching farther south, across the Loire, over the Garonne River to the Rhône. All those old beautiful cities teeming with wild, disheveled people. But the wildness was different from what I had dreamed of. A local rule prevailed in these cities, a sort of medieval municipal code of law. And each city had its own code.

A tireless pack of officials was on the move night and day, like dogcatchers, intent on fishing suspicious people out the crowds as they passed through, so as to put them into city jails from which they'd be dragged off to a concentration camp if they didn't have the money to pay the ransom or to hire a crafty lawyer who would later split the outsize reward for freeing the prisoner with the dogcatcher himself. As a result, everyone, especially the foreigners, guarded their passports and identification papers as if they were their very salvation. I was amazed to see the authorities, in the midst of this chaos, inventing ever more intricate drawn-out procedures for sorting, classifying, registering, and stamping these people over whose emotions they had lost all power. It was like trying to register every Vandal, Goth, Hun, and Langobard during the "Barbarian Invasion."

I evaded the clutches of the dogcatchers quite a few times with help from my clever buddies, for I had no papers, no documents at all. When I escaped from the camp, I'd left all my papers behind in the camp, in the commandant's barracks. I would have assumed that they were burned by now, if experience hadn't taught me that it's much harder to burn paper than metal or stone. Once, sitting at a table in an inn, we were asked for our papers. My four friends had pretty solid French documents—although the older Binnet had not been legally demobilized. This dogcatcher, though, was pretty drunk, and didn't notice Marcel slipping me his papers under the table after they'd already been inspected. Right after that, in the very same room, the same official led off a beautiful girl while her aunts and uncles, Jews who had fled from Belgium, cursed and lamented the fate of this girl they'd taken along in place of their own child. They had great faith but insufficient identification papers. Now she'd probably be hauled off to a women's detention camp in some corner of the Pyrenees. I've never been able to forget her because she was so beautiful and because of the anguished expression on her face as she was being separated from her people.

I asked my friends what would happen if one of them were to declare himself ready to marry the girl on the spot, right then and there. They were all minors, yet they immediately began to argue heatedly over who would get the girl. They almost came to blows but were too exhausted to fight. My friends were ashamed for their country. When you're young and healthy you can recover quickly from a defeat. But betrayal is different—it paralyzes you. The next night we admitted to each other that we were homesick for Paris. We had faced a terrible, cruel enemy there, almost more than one could endure, at least that's what we thought at the time. But there the enemy was visible. Looking back, it almost seemed better than the invisible, almost mysterious evil of the rumors, bribery, and lies we now faced.

Everyone was fleeing and everything was temporary. We had no idea whether this situation would last till tomorrow, another couple of weeks, years, or our entire lives.

We made what we thought was a very sensible decision. We checked a map to see just where we were. It turned out we weren't far from the village where Yvonne, my former girlfriend, the one who had married her cousin, lived. So we set out in that direction and arrived there a week later.

II

Many refugees had already sought shelter in Yvonne's village, quite a few of whom had been sent to help out on her husband's farm. Still, everyday farm life didn't seem to have changed much. Yvonne was pregnant and she was proud of her new house and farm. She seemed a little embarrassed as she introduced me to her husband. When she found out I had no papers, she sent her husband that very night into the village where he also happened to be the acting mayor. She suggested he have a drink at the Grappe d'Or with his friends and the chairman of the United Refugees from the Aigne sur Ange. He came home at midnight with a little piece of yellow paper. It was a refugee certificate that a man had probably given back when he got a different, better set of documents. Seidler was the name of the man whose second-best certificate ended up being a better one for me. He had emigrated from the Saar to Alsace at the time of the Referendum. Yvonne's husband stamped it again. We looked up Seidler's village in a school atlas, and concluded from its location that, fortunately for me, the village along with the registry of its inhabitants had probably been burned to the ground. Yvonne's husband was even able to get me some money. Since now, with my new papers, I was quite the proper refugee, he had the provincial capital of the département dole out some refugee money that I was supposedly entitled to.

I realized that Yvonne had pushed all this through in order to get rid of me as quickly as possible. In the meantime, my traveling companions had written to their scattered families. Marcel tracked down his great-uncle who had a peach farm near the sea. The younger Binnet and his friend planned to stay with his sister. As Yvonne's former sweetheart, I was a somewhat unsuitable guest here and completely superfluous. Yvonne gave some more thought to my situation, and this time came up with a cousin named George, George Binnet. He had been employed at a factory in Nevers before being evacuated along with everyone else in the factory, nobody really knew why, and was now stuck in Marseille. He had written that he was doing quite well there living with a woman from Madagascar who was also working. Marcel figured that once he was at the peach farm, he could arrange for me to follow him there, and until then I could stay in Marseille. Anyway, the Binnet cousin would be a help to me. By now I felt attached to the Binnet family much like a child who has lost his own mother and hangs on to the skirts of another woman who, although she can never be his mother, still shows him some affection and kindness.

I had always wanted to see Marseille, and besides, I felt like going to a big city. As for the rest, it was all the same to me. We said good-bye. Marcel and I traveled part of the way together. I found myself searching among the throngs of soldiers, refugees, and demobilized troops who filled the trains and the roads for a familiar face, some person whom I had known in my old life. How happy I would have been if Franz, with whom I'd escaped from the camp, had turned up. Or even Heinz. Whenever I saw a man on crutches I hoped I'd see his face with the crooked mouth and the light-colored eyes mocking his own fragility. I had lost something, lost it so completely that I didn't quite know what it was, I'd lost it so utterly in all that confusion that gradually I didn't even miss it very much anymore. But one of those faces from the past, I was certain, would at least remind me of what it was.

Marcel left me, and I went on to Marseille by myself. I was and remained alone.

III

On the train they were saying that the crafty guards at the Marseille station had set up checkpoints and wouldn't let any foreigner through. I had only limited faith in Yvonne's refugee certificate, and so I left the train two hours before it was to reach Marseille and boarded a bus. I got off in a village in the hills.

Walking down from the hills, I came to the outer precincts of Marseille. At a bend in the road I saw the sea far below me. A bit later I saw the city itself spread out against the water. It seemed as bare and white as an African city. At last I felt calm. It was the same calm that I experience whenever I like something very much. I almost believed I had reached my goal. In this city, I thought, I could find everything I'd been looking for, that I'd always been looking for. I wonder how many more times this feeling will deceive me on entering a strange city!

I boarded a streetcar and arrived without being challenged. Twenty minutes later I was strolling with my suitcase down the Canebière. Most of the time you're disappointed when you finally see streets you've heard a lot about. But I wasn't disappointed. I walked with the crowds, buffeted by a wind that blew first sunshine, then showers over us in rapid succession. And the lightness brought on by hunger and exhaustion turned into an exalted, grand buoyancy that enabled the wind to blow me faster and faster down the street. When I realized that the blue gleam at the end of the Canebière was the Old Harbor and the Mediterranean, I felt at last, after so much absurdity, madness and misery, the one genuine happiness that is available to everyone at any time: the joy of being alive.

The last few months I'd been wondering where all this was going to end up—the trickles, the streams of people from the camps, the dispersed soldiers, the army mercenaries, the defilers of all races, the deserters from all nations. This, then, was where the detritus was flowing, along this channel, this gutter, the Canebière, and via this gutter into the sea, where there would at last be room for all, and peace.

I had a coffee standing up with the suitcase clamped between my legs. All around me I heard people talking. It was as if the counter where I was drinking stood between two pillars of the Tower of Babel. Nevertheless, there were occasional words I could understand,

and they kept hitting my ears in a certain rhythm as if to impress themselves on my memory: Cuba visa and Martinique, Oran and Portugal, Siam and Casablanca, transit visa and three-mile zone.

At last I reached the Old Port. It was at about the same time as I arrived here today. It was almost deserted because of the war—just as it is today. And like today the ferry was slowly gliding along under the railroad bridge. Today, though, it seems as if I'm seeing it all for the first time. When I arrived that evening the fishing boat masts crisscrossed the large bare walls of the ancient houses—just as they do now. As the sun set that day behind Fort St. Nicolas, I thought, as very young people do, that all the things that had happened to me so far had led me here and that this was a good thing. I asked for directions to the Rue du Chevalier Roux, which is where George Binnet, Yvonne's cousin, lived. The bazaars and the street markets were teeming with people. It was already getting dark in the warren-like streets, and the red and gold colors of the fruit displayed in the market stalls glowed in strong contrast. I detected an aroma I had never smelled before, but I couldn't find the fruit it emanated from. I sat down to rest a while on the edge of a fountain in the Corsican Quarter, the suitcase on my knees. Then I climbed up a stone stairway without having any idea where it would lead me.

Below me lay the sea. The beacon lights along the Corniche and on the islands were still faint in the twilight. How I used to hate the sea when I was working on the docks! It had seemed merciless to me in its inapproachable, inhuman monotony. But now, having come here after such a long and difficult journey across a ruined and defiled land, I couldn't have found greater consolation anywhere than this inhuman emptiness and solitude, trackless and unspoiled.

I went back down to the Corsican Quarter. It had become quieter in the meantime. The market stalls had been cleared away. I found the house on the Rue du Chevalier Roux. I let the bronze, hand-shaped knocker fall on the great, carved door. A black man asked me what I wanted. I told him I was looking for the Binnets.

From the knobs on the banister, the remnants of colored tiles, and the worn stone crests, you could tell that this house had once belonged to a man of means—a merchant, or a sea captain. Now immigrants from Madagascar, a few Corsicans, and the Binnets were living here.

Binnet's mistress opened the apartment door, and I stared at her. She was extraordinarily beautiful, if somewhat strange in appearance. She had the head of a wild, black bird, a sharp nose, glittering eyes, and a delicate neck. Her long hips, long-fingered, loose-jointed hands, even her toes in her espadrilles—everything about her seemed slightly in motion, the way peoples' faces usually are—as if anger, joy, and sadness were like the wind.

In answer to my question she said curtly that George was on night duty at the mill and she herself had just come home from the sugar factory. She turned away from me and yawned. It brought me back down to earth.

On the stairs, as I was leaving, I bumped into a slender, dark boy who was coming up two steps at a time. He turned around, just as I turned to look at him. I wanted to see whether my arrival fever had also invested the boy with some magic, but he just wanted to see if I was a stranger, a surprise intruder. Right after that I heard Binnet's girlfriend, still standing in the open doorway—undecided, as she later confessed to me, about whether she should call me back and ask me to wait—scolding her son for coming home so late. You'll understand later why I'm telling you all this in such detail. Back then I thought my visit had been a mistake, and that the rest of the evening lay empty ahead of me. I had deluded myself into thinking that the city had opened its heart to me, just as I had opened mine to it, that Marseille would take me in on my first night and its people would shelter me. In contrast to my joy on arrival, I now felt a severe disillusionment. I figured that Yvonne probably hadn't written to her cousin about me, that she'd only wanted to get rid of me. I was also mortified to learn that George was working the night shift. It meant that there were still people who were leading normal lives.

IV

I had to find another place to stay the night. The first dozen hotels I tried were full. By now I was exhausted. I sat down at the first table I found in front of a seedy café in a small, quiet square. The city was dark because of the fear of air raids; yet there were feeble lights in many windows. I thought about the many thousands of people who called this city their own and quietly lived their lives as I had once done in mine. I gazed up at the stars and felt, I don't know why, some consolation at the thought that these stars were probably there more for me and people like me than for those who could switch on their own lights.

I ordered a beer. I would have preferred just to sit there by myself. But a little old man sat down at my table. He was wearing a jacket that, on anyone else, would have been in tatters long ago, but which had found an owner who with dignity and care would not let it go to ruin. And the man was much like his jacket. He might long ago have been lying in his grave, but his face was firm and serious. What remained of his hair was neatly parted; his nails were carefully trimmed. With a glance at my little suitcase, he immediately asked me what country I had a visa for. I told him I had no visa and didn't intend to get one; I wanted to stay here.

He cried out, "You can't stay here without a visa!"

I didn't know what he meant. To be polite I asked him what his plans were. He said he had been an orchestra conductor in Prague and was recently offered a position with a well-known orchestra in Caracas. I asked where that was. He said scornfully that it was the capital of Venezuela. I asked whether he had any sons. He said yes and no—his oldest son was missing in Poland, his second son was in England, and the third was still in Prague. He felt he could no longer wait for signs of life from his sons, or it might be too late for him. I thought he meant death, but he was referring to the conductor's position; he had to start the new position in Caracas before the end of the year. He had already had a work contract before and because of the contract, a visa, and because of the visa, a transit visa, but it took so long for the exit visa to be issued that the transit visa expired in the meantime, and after that the visa and after that the contract. Last week he was issued an exit visa, and he was now anxiously waiting for an extension of his contract, which would mean he could then get an extension of his visa. And that would be a prerequisite for his being awarded a new transit visa.

Confused, I asked what he meant by exit visa. He stared at me in delight. I was an ignorant newcomer, he said. But by giving him the opportunity for a long explanation I would be filling up many lonely minutes for him. He said, "It's permission to leave France. Didn't anybody tell you anything, my poor young man?"

"What purpose is there in holding on to people who want nothing more than to leave a country where they would be imprisoned if they stayed?"

He laughed so hard I could hear his jaw creaking. It seemed to me as if his entire skeleton was creaking. He rapped the table with a knuckle. I found him pretty repulsive, and yet I was willing to put up with him. There are moments in the life of even the most prodigal of sons when they go over to the side of the fathers, I mean the fathers of other sons.

He said, "At least you know this much, my son. The Germans are now the real masters here. And since you presumably are a member of that nation, you must know what German "order" means, Nazi order, which they're now all boasting about here. It has nothing to do with World Order, the old one. It is a kind of control. The Germans are not going to miss the chance to thoroughly control and check all people leaving Europe. In the process they might find some troublemaker for whom they've been hunting for decades."

"All right. All right. But after you're checked out, after you have a visa, what significance is the transit visa? Why does it expire? What is it actually? Why aren't people allowed to travel through countries on their way to their new homes in other countries?"

He said, "My son, it's all because each country is afraid that in-

stead of just traveling through, we'll want to stay. A transit visa—
that gives you permission to travel through a country with the
stipulation that you don't plan to stay."

Suddenly he changed his approach. He addressed me in a different, very solemn, tone of voice that fathers use only when they're finally sending their sons out into the world. "Young man," he said,
"you came here with scarcely any baggage, alone and without a destination. You don't even have a visa. You're not the least concerned
that the Marseille Prefect will not let you stay here if you don't have
a visa. Now, let's assume that by some stroke of luck, or by your own
efforts, something happens, though it rarely does, or maybe because
when you least expect it, a friend reaches out a hand from the dark,
that is, from across the ocean, or maybe through Providence itself, or
maybe with the help of a committee, anyway, let's assume you get a
visa. For one brief moment you're happy. But you soon realize that
the problem isn't solved so easily. You have a destination—no big
deal, everybody has that. But you can't just get to that country by
sheer force of will, through the stratosphere. You have to travel on
oceans, through the countries between. You need a transit visa. For
that you need your wits. And time. You have no idea how much time
it takes. For me time is of the essence. But when I look at you, I think
time is even more precious for you. Time is youth itself. But you
must not fly off in too many directions. You must think only of the
transit visa. If I may say so, you have to forget your destination for a
while, for at this moment only the countries in between are what
matter, otherwise you won't be able to leave. What matters now is to
make the consul see that you're serious, that you're not one of those
fellows who want to stay in a place that is only a transit country. And
there are ways to prove this. Any consul will ask for such proof. Let's
assume you're lucky and have a berth on a ship and the trip as such is
a certainty, which is really a miracle when you consider how many
want to leave and how few available ships there are. If you're a Jew,
which you're not, then you might be able to secure a berth on board
a ship with the help of Jewish aid groups. If you're Aryan, then
maybe Christian groups can help. If you're nothing, or godless, or a

Red, then for God's sake, or with the help of your Party, or others like you, you might be able to get a berth. But don't think, my son, that your transit visa will be assured, and even if it were! In the meantime so much time has passed that the main goal, your primary one, has disappeared. Your visa has expired, and as vital as the transit visa is, it isn't worth anything without a visa, and so on and so forth.

"Now, son, imagine that you've managed to do it. Good, let's both dream that you've done it. You have them all—your visa, your transit visa, your exit visa. You're ready to start your journey. You've said good-bye to your loved ones and tossed your life over your shoulder. You're thinking only of your goal, your destination. You finally want to board the ship.—For example: Yesterday, I was talking with a young man your age. He had everything. But then when he was ready to board his ship, the harbor authorities refused to give him the last stamp he needed."

"Why?"

"He had escaped from a camp when the Germans were coming."

The old man said this in the weary tone of voice he had been using before. He seemed to sink into himself. Yet his posture was too erect—it was more that he sagged. "The fellow didn't have a certificate of release from the camp—so it was all for nothing."

I perked up. The last point he'd made in his somber jumble of completely irrelevant admonitions did affect me. I had never before heard of a harbor stamp. That poor young man! Guilty by lack of foresight. I was not going to fail because of that final stamp. I'd been forewarned. But then, I wasn't going to leave. I said, "Luckily, all this doesn't apply to me. I have only one wish, and that is, to stay here for a while in peace."

He cried, "You're making a mistake! For the third time, let me tell you, they'll let you stay here in peace for a certain length of time only if you can prove that you intend to leave. Don't you understand?"

I said, "No."

I got to my feet. I'd had enough of him. He called out after me,

"Your suitcase!" That made me remember something I hadn't thought about for weeks: the letters of the man who'd taken his life on the Rue de Vaugirard when the Germans marched into Paris. I'd become accustomed to thinking of the suitcase as mine. The few things the dead man had left behind took up very little space under my own stuff, and I had completely forgotten them. I could take them to the Mexican consul now. The dead man's wife would surely ask at the consulate for mail. I wondered why something that had so obsessed me in Paris could have evaporated so completely from my mind once I got to Marseille. So that's the stuff the dead man's magic was made of! But maybe it was my own mind that made stuff evaporate so easily.

I resumed my search for a room. I came to a huge, shapeless square, three sides of which were nearly dark, while the fourth was punctuated by lights that made it look like a seacoast. This was the Cours Belsunce. I headed for the lights, getting lost in a network of narrow alleys. I entered the first hotel door I came to, climbed up a steep flight of stairs to the lighted window of the hotel proprietor. I was prepared for, "Everything's taken," but the landlady shoved the registry book toward me. She watched attentively as I copied the name on my refugee certificate. When she asked for my safe conduct pass I hesitated. She laughed and said, "If there's a raid it'll be your bad luck not mine! You'll pay me now for a week in advance. After all, you're here without official permission. You should have applied first at the Prefecture for a permit to come to Marseille. To which country do you want to go?"

I said I had no intention of going anywhere else. I had finally landed here after having escaped from the Germans and being hounded from one city to another. I didn't have a visa, nor did I have a ticket for a ship's passage, and I couldn't walk across the ocean. She'd seemed quite calm, almost listless at first, but now she looked stunned by what I'd said.

"Surely you don't want to stay here?" she cried.

I said, "Why not? You're staying too, after all." She laughed at my wisecrack.

She handed me a key with a metal number tag. The corridor was blocked by dozens of pieces of luggage and I had a hard time pushing my way through to the room I'd been assigned. The baggage belonged to a group of Spaniards, I discovered. Men and women, who were all planning to leave that night, via Casablanca to Cuba, and from there to Mexico.

I felt reassured. So he was right after all, I thought, that boy on Rue Longuin in Paris by the fence of the Mexican Consulate. Ships were leaving. They were in the harbor ready to sail.

As I was falling asleep that night I felt as if I were on board a ship, not because I had heard so much about ships or wanted to be on one, but because I felt dizzy and miserable, overwhelmed by a surging mass of impressions and sensations I was no longer able to understand. In addition, a racket intruded on my consciousness from all sides as if I were sleeping on a slippery wooden plank in the midst of a drunken crew. I heard pieces of luggage roll and bang in the hold of the ship as the seas grew heavy. I heard French curses and Spanish farewells, and finally I heard, from a great distance, but more penetrating than all the rest, a simple little song that I had last heard in my homeland at a time when none of us yet knew who Hitler was, not even the man himself. I told myself that I was only dreaming. And then I actually did fall asleep.

I dreamed I had left the little suitcase somewhere. I was searching for it in the most ridiculous places: back home in the boys' school I attended, at the Binnets' apartment in Marseille, in the farmyard at Yvonne's, and on the Normandy docks. And that's where it was, the little suitcase, upright on a gangplank, planes diving down, I ran over to get it, deathly afraid.

3

I

I WOKE with a start. It was still dark outside and the hotel was quiet. By now the Spaniards might already be sailing on the high seas. Since I couldn't get back to sleep, I decided to write a letter to Yvonne explaining my situation. I told her I needed a safe conduct for Marseille even though I'd already arrived here safely, that I had to arrive all over again, this time with proper papers and all the legal documentation. As soon as I'd written it, I went out to mail it. As I passed the hotel office, the unattractive, unkempt girl who had the night shift stopped me and asked if I'd paid for my room. I said I had.

"Was I leaving?"

"Good lord, no!"

The stars were fading but it was still pitch dark and cold in the streets. I was impatient for the day to dawn; to light up the city, and at the same time, enlighten me about everything I still didn't know. But nothing and nobody woke up any earlier on my account; the cafés were still closed; I had to go back to my hotel.

The way to my room was again blocked by the luggage of the Spaniards who had intended to sail during the night. But the men were not with them; only the women and children had come back from the harbor, and they were now sitting on the suitcases, complaining and cursing. They had arrived at the pier with all their things, ready to leave. Through the pier gate they'd seen the ship lying at anchor. Then the French police arrived and arrested all the men able to bear arms, citing a treaty agreement with the Franco government. The

Spanish women weren't crying now; they were cursing the situation, sometimes softly, while rocking their children, sometimes out loud, arms outspread. Then, abruptly, they decided they would all go to the Mexican Consulate. Since they had Mexican visas, they were under Mexican protection. They would ask for justice there.

Off they marched. They were led by a young woman who had once been quite cheerful, but was now somber. She held the hand of a little cherry-eyed girl wearing a traveling cape. I joined them, taking along the dead man's bundle of papers. Their mention of the Mexican Consulate had reminded me of the bundle. After all, I had plenty of time! I might as well go with them now. Day had dawned meanwhile, the morning almost too bright for my sleep-deprived eyes. We walked up the Canebière. I was the sole man in the flock of Spanish women and children. They were used to me by now.

It seemed to me that I was the only person on that street who didn't want to leave. On the other hand, I didn't feel I absolutely had to stay. No matter how hard it might be to leave, I thought, I could manage to do it. After all, I'd managed to make it this far, and no visible harm had come to me so far except that the miserable state of the world happened to coincide with my youth. I must admit this was depressing. I thought about Paris, where the trees must already be bare. The Parisians were probably freezing in the cold, thanks to the Nazis, who had stolen their coal and bread.

At the ugly big Protestant church we turned onto the Boulevard de la Madeleine. The women stopped talking. Was this the Mexican Consulate? It occupied one floor in an apartment building that differed in no respect from all the other apartment houses on the block. The front door was the same as the other doors with the exception of a shield bearing a coat of arms, almost invisible to a casual passerby but not to us, anxiously searching for it. The shield had become much darker since I'd tried to decipher it in Paris. I could scarcely make out the eagle perched on the thicket of cacti. Looking at it, I felt my heart constrict with a painful yet joyful wanderlust, a kind of hope, but I didn't know for what. Maybe for the world at large, for some unknown blessed country.

The doorman, certainly no cyclops, but a leathery-skinned little man with small, humorless, intelligent eyes, picked me out of the waiting crowd, I don't know why. He asked me to write my name and why I had come on a piece of paper. I wrote: "With regard to the matter of the author Weidel." I don't know why he thought he had to lead me immediately through the waiting crowd and up the stairs to the narrow little waiting room where there were already about a dozen presumably privileged people. Four Spaniards, three lean ones and one fat one, were arguing vehemently and seemed on the verge of drawing their daggers, yet it was probably some common-place matter that provoked this huge expenditure of passion. A ragged, bearded *prestataire* was leaning wearily against a garish poster of two colorfully dressed children wearing huge hats. It was a tourist poster and dated back to the days when sluggish homebodies were enticed to travel by brightly colored pictures of foreign countries. An old man, breathing heavily, was sitting on the only available chair. There were also some men and women who, judging from the nature and condition of their clothes, their hair, and the way they smelled, must have come from a concentration or detention camp. Then a beautiful, well-dressed, golden-haired girl entered the room, and suddenly everyone was talking at the same time; I wasn't even aware what language they were speaking; it was a kind of choral singing: No foreigners were being admitted to Oran anymore. —Spain wasn't allowing people like us to cross its territory.—Portugal wasn't letting anyone enter.—There was supposed to be a ship sailing via Martinique.—From there you could go to Cuba.—You'd still be under French sovereignty.—But at least, you wouldn't be here anymore; you'd be gone from this place.

I waited, half amused, half bored. Then they called my name and, half amused, half bored, I entered the room of the consular official.

A short young man stood before me. He had extraordinarily in-telligent, alert eyes. When he saw me, they flashed with pleasure. Not, to be sure, because he found my visit particularly pleasant. He was by nature inclined to find each visitor coming to his office stimulating—even if there were a thousand. He may have been unique in his profession. Everything that happened in this room made his eyes sparkle: the wiles used by petty black marketeers to skip to the front of the line, or former ministers and government officials who clearly expected preferential treatment. Shrewdly he scrutinized these petitioners, all hoping to go to Mexico, including the businessman from Holland whose Rotterdam warehouses has been burned to the ground but who still had enough money to offer to pay whatever security deposit was required, or the Spanish Civil War veteran who had dragged himself on crutches across the Pyrenees from one camp to another before finally reaching the Boulevard de la Madeleine. The bureaucrat's eyes seemed to penetrate deep into each of the visa applicants. And once he decided a person met the criteria to enter his country, he did everything to close any gaps in the person's file, to make sure he would qualify for a visa.

Coldly, he asked me what I wanted. I was abruptly pulled out of my lethargy. It was his look, his eyes, flashing with wit and perspicacity, which seemed to spark an awareness of my own wit and intelligence in me.

"I came here about the Weidel affair," I said.

"Oh yes," he replied. "That name is in my records."

He called out the name to the fat man, adding his own curious inflection. While the man was rummaging through the files, he turned back to me and said, "Forgive me if I do something else in the meantime."

I tried to interrupt him; I just wanted to put my package on the table and leave. But he waved me off, obviously hating interruptions. They were already calling in the next applicants. Four Spaniards came in together, but they left shrugging, apparently unsuccessful; the short official also shrugged. Then came the golden-haired young woman. She was looking for her beloved who had served with the Ebro Brigades. The official pointed out to her that he didn't have a list of the brigade members, even as his alert eyes were assessing the young woman and the extent of her affection for the missing man.

She was followed by a businessman exuding visa gratitude, the *prestataire* who had been refused a visa by the United States, a workman who was supposed to paint the consulate, and last of all, a young couple, hardly more than children, holding hands. Even though I didn't know what was being arranged, I recognized the ceremony. They were getting visas. All three smiled. They bowed to each other. I envied them their hand-in-hand escape from here. I was the only one left, sitting there on a chair in the Mexican Consulate office.

In the meantime they'd given the Weidel file to the official. He said, "These are the Weidel documents." I had a hazy recollection of a letter I'd read in Paris. I stared at the documents left by the dead man. Here they were, lying on the desk. Visa by visa, document by document, file by file. Arranged in perfect order with what must have been confident expectation.

I suddenly felt a tiny degree of superiority over the official. Had Weidel still been alive, the official would have had the advantage over him; he would have looked right through him, maybe would even have been amused by him. But now, watching the official carefully study the file with a rather excessive degree of attention, I was the one who was amused. A specter among the visa applicants, a shadow who readily relinquished all his rights. I decided that instead of immediately explaining things to him, I would leave him for the moment to his useless activity.

Suddenly the telephone rang—"No!" the official said, and even speaking on the telephone his eyes flashed, "My government's confirmation has not yet come in." Then he turned to me, "That case is very similar to yours."

Surprised, I said, "Excuse me, you must be mistaken. My name is Seidler. I came only—" I wanted to explain everything in detail. But he, averse to long explanations, interrupted me angrily, "Yes, yes, I know." The entire time he was holding the piece of paper with my name and my request clamped between two fingers. "As I just explained on the phone for the tenth time to one of your colleagues, you can only receive a visa once my government confirms that the name Seidler on your passport refers to the same person as the pen name, Weidel. If someone will vouch for your identity, my government can issue a visa."

At this explanation my head began to hum like a wire struck by a gust of wind—my own alarm system, a kind of automatic alert signal that goes off inside my mind even before I realize I'm about to do something that might get me into trouble or even could, no *would* destroy my life.

I said, "Please listen to me! This is an entirely different matter. I already explained all this to your consul in Paris. Here is a pack of documents, of manuscripts, letters—"

He gestured impatiently, annoyed. "You can submit whatever you want," he began, all the time looking me in the eye. His alert, shrewd glance stirred in me a strong feeling of my own alertness, of an irresistible desire to measure myself against an equal intelligence. "Let's not waste time," he continued. "Time, after all, is as valuable for you as it is for me. You must take the proper steps immediately."

I got up, took my pile of papers. He didn't take his eyes off me. I returned his gaze steadfastly. I asked, "So what are the steps I should take now? Please advise me."

He said, "I'll tell you for the last time: Have the same friends who appeared for your visa, vouchsafe to my government that the name on your passport, Seidler, is the same as the pen name Weidel."

I thanked him for his advice. It took some effort to break eye contact with him.

II

Deep in thought, I walked home. That is, I went back to the hotel I'd been staying in since the previous night. For the first time I looked at it carefully in daylight. The street was narrow and lined by tall houses. I liked it. I also liked its name: Rue de la Providence. The hotel was named after the street. Once in my room, I stepped over to the window and looked down. They had just begun flushing the street and the powerful stream of water swilled a veritable flotilla of rubbish along the pavement.

What was I supposed to do now? I'd been very glad to get a room to myself, but now I realized I had to learn all over again how to be alone. What if there was a raid by the police? What use would its four walls be to me then? I felt profoundly that the one thing on earth I was still afraid of was the loss of my freedom. Under no circumstances would I let them lock me up a third time, no way. That old fool last night, the conductor from Caracas, had been right. You had to get away from this place, and if not, then you needed the unambiguous right to stay. But I certainly wasn't one of the chosen; I had no visa, no letter of transit, and on top of that, no residence permit. My head was buzzing with images that I tried to push aside: the darkened coat of arms, the little official's excessively alert, shrewd look. I couldn't bear being by myself anymore. No matter how cool my reception had been last night, I decided to have another go at George Binnet, the only man I knew here. I walked to the Rue du Chevalier Roux. I took hold of the bronze fist, let it drop.

Although I'm about to bore you some more by talking about the Binnet family, I assure you, we're getting close to the heart of the matter. Then you'll see how some ghosts can slip in through any doors.

George Binnet was the only person who didn't ask me where I was going but rather where I'd come from. I told him what I've told you so far. There was only one thing I omitted completely: the Weidel matter. After all, why should Binnet care that some stranger had taken poison when the Germans invaded? George listened attentively to my story. He was of medium height, a strong man with gray eyes, the Northern French kind. He'd ended up in Marseille because of some stupid arrangements made by his factory. They had kept him on, and when the plant was evacuated, he was evacuated, too. Later the business was dissolved, leaving the workers in the lurch. He now had a poorly paid job working the night shift at a mill. When not at his job, he lived a free, cheerful, and relaxed life. He cherished his girlfriend, that marvelous Madagascar creature, and her son, treating the boy gently so as not to hurt his feelings, for the child was very proud.

That evening Binnet's girlfriend invited me to stay for dinner. From the very outset I felt an aching affection for the boy. He would sit at the table silently listening to my stories. I made a special effort on his account. What made his eyes shine so eagerly? They would never get to see anything beyond this world. Why was his skin such a dark gold? The girl he would some day put his arms around would surely be made of different stuff. Why was he following our conversations so avidly—so tense that his lips quivered?

We were telling stories of this year's tumultuous experiences, of betrayal, and confusion.

We all ate from a large bowl of spiced rice. I felt they were putting up with me, and I was grateful. It's things like the security of a few hours, the quite unexpected feeling of safety at a table where people have made room for you—it's things like that which keep you from going under.

That evening at the Binnets I felt that I'd become calmer. After living by yourself for a long time, it's calming to have people ask you about yourself. My anxiety returned only once I was surrounded again by my four walls on the Rue de la Providence.

I had just lain down on my bed when a hellish racket broke out in the room to the right of mine. I went over to ask if they could quiet down and I found a dozen people, split into two groups, playing cards. From their tattered uniforms and outlandish Arabic headgear I gathered they were Foreign Legionnaires. Almost all of them were drunk, or pretending to be, just so they could yell at the top of their lungs. Even though there was no real brawl, there was an undertone of threat in everything they did or said, even if it was only to ask for a glass or call out their cards—as if this was the only way to get what they wanted. I sat down on a suitcase even though no one had invited me to stay. Instead of asking them to tone it down, I began to drink, too. I wasn't alone anymore—that's what mattered. And the men didn't interrupt their rowdy and feverish gambling; they just let me sit there on the suitcase because they understood why I'd come. That is to say, they knew what mattered most.

A small man whose uniform was in somewhat better shape and who was wearing a clean burnoose looked at me with intense, serious eyes. He had a lot of medals glittering on his chest. The stuff they were drinking was pretty strong, and I began to feel hot.

"What are you doing here?" I asked the fellow with all the medals.

"We're on leave from the transit camp Les Milles. We rented this room together for all the guys on leave. It's our room, you understand? It's our room."

"Where are you going?"

"Back to Germany," answered a dwarf who was trying to de-emphasize his small stature by means of an elaborately wrapped headdress. "We're going home next week."

A man sitting astride the open window, smoking with one leg outside, his handsome, insolent head leaning against the window frame, casually told me their story. "A German commission had arrived in Sidi-bel-Abbès. They ordered all German nationals in the Foreign Legion to go home. They'd been granted a general amnesty! All sins were forgiven!"

"Do you like Hitler?" I asked.

"It's all the same to us," one man said. His face was so strangely disfigured that I had to lean forward to see whether it was the haze in front of my eyes that made it look as if neither his mouth nor his nose were in the right place, as if they were flattened over his face. "Hitler's the same as all the others. Just more so."

The man in the window said over his shoulder, "Better to be lined up against the wall back home than buried here with the Foreign Legion."

"They're not lining people up against the wall anymore," the dwarf said. "Back home they're beheading people."

The man in the window grabbed his own head by the ears, "You can use it as a bowling ball."

The man with the distorted face began to sing: *"In der Heimat, in der Heimat...*" The little song coming from his grotesque face with the twisted mouth sounded simple and beautiful. Either I hadn't been dreaming last night or I was dreaming now, too.

The short man with the many medals sat down next to me on the suitcase. "Me, I'm not going home; I'm heading in the opposite direction. Hitler *does* matter to me. And what about you?"

"I'm staying here," I said. "You'll see. In the end I'll be staying after all."

He said, "You're saying that because you're drunk. No one can stay here." He clinked glasses with me in his earnest, levelheaded way.

I would have liked to put my arms around him, but the gleaming, golden impenetrable fog in front of his chest prevented me from doing it. "Why did they hang that medal around your neck?"

"I was brave."

I curled up on the suitcase. I'd spent most of my money just so that I could be alone in a room. Yet now I felt like going to sleep here. But the short man with the serious eyes pulled me to my feet and with practiced moves led me out of the room. He even laid me down on my own bed.

III

The week had almost come to an end. It was early in the morning when someone pounded wildly on my door. The legionnaire with the many medals rushed into my room. "It's a raid!" he said, dragging me through a small door at the end of the corridor and up a narrow flight of stairs to the attic. Then he ran back to my room and got into my bed with his furlough papers. I discovered a second stairway that led from the attic out onto the roof. I squatted down behind one of the small chimneys.

The wind was so strong up there that I had to hold on to the chimney. I could see the entire city, the hills, the Church of Notre Dame de la Garde, the blue square of the Old Harbor with its iron bridge, and a little later, once the fog lifted, the open sea with its islands. Forgetting everything probably happening below—the police searching all the floors of the hotel—I slid down the roof a few more yards. I could see La Joliette with its innumerable piers and moles. But all the piers were empty. No matter how hard I looked I couldn't find one ship. It occurred to me that yesterday the people in the cafés had all been chattering about a ship leaving for Brazil one of these days. A Noah's Ark, I thought! Not enough room to take all of us! Only two of each animal. Way back then that must have been enough. The arrangement seems to have been a wise one. After all, we're back in full numbers.

I heard a slight noise and started. But it was only a cat. It stared at me angrily. We stared at each other, both of us rigid with fear. I hissed, and it leaped to the next roof.

The sound of a car horn came up from the street. Peering over the edge of the roof, I saw a couple of police officers climbing into their car. Another two came through the hotel door, dragging a man into the street; I could tell from the way they were pulling at him that he was handcuffed to them. And as the police car sped off I reflected happily and wickedly on the fact that it wasn't me.

I clambered down to my floor. In the room to the left of mine a group of hotel guests were gathered around the crying and screaming wife of the man who'd been taken away, trying to console her. Her face was puffy and red as a goblin's from crying. In answer to their questions she sobbed, "My husband just came from the Var. We were going to Brazil tomorrow. He came with a safe conduct. He had no residence permit for Marseille. After all, why would he need one since we were leaving tomorrow. And what if we had applied for a resident permit? We would have been crossing the ocean long before we got an answer from them! Now we'll forfeit our tickets, and our visa is going to expire." You could tell from the impassive faces of the legionnaires standing around her, how many screaming, weeping women they had seen lining the roads on their travels. I couldn't understand a word that was said. Nor was it worth my understanding—a thicket of gibberish, dry and impenetrable.

IV

In the days that followed, my life seemed to have calmed down somewhat. Yvonne sent me a safe conduct, and I took the document to the Office for Aliens on the Rue Louvois. This was my second time there, and this time my visit was official. I was registered and my document was stamped. The official asked me why I was here, for what purpose. By now I was more savvy, and I said I had come to Marseille to prepare to leave. He granted me a four weeks' residence permit for the purpose of preparing my departure. It seemed like quite a long time to me. I was almost happy.

I spent my days quietly and pretty much alone in the midst of this multitude of poor devils all longing to leave. In the cafés I drank the bitter ersatz coffee and the sweet Banjuls wine on an empty stomach and listened in fascination to the harbor gossip, which had nothing to do with me. The weather had already turned cold. But I always sat outside, in a corner formed by a window, protected from the Mistral, which could attack you from all sides at once. The bit of blue water down at the end of Canebière marked the rim of our piece of earth, the edge of our world, which, if you wanted to see it that way, extended from the Pacific Ocean, from Vladivostock and from China, all the way here. There are reasons why it's called the "Old World." But here is where it ended.

I saw a short hunchbacked clerk come out of the shipping company office across the way and write the name of a ship and its departure time on the dry little blackboard outside the door. At once a queue of people formed behind the little hunchback, all hoping to sail on that same ship, forever leaving behind this chunk of earth, the life they had lived up to now, and possibly even death.

When the Mistral blew too hard, I would come to this pizzeria and sit at this same table. Back then I was surprised to find out that pizza wasn't sweet but tasted of pepper, olives, or sardines. I was usually light-headed with hunger, weak and tired, and almost always a little drunk, for I had only enough money to buy a slice of pizza and a glass of rosé. Once inside the pizzeria I had only one difficult decision to make. Should I sit in the chair you're sitting in now, facing the harbor, or in the chair I'm in, facing the open fire? Each had its advantages. I could look for hours at the row of white houses on the other side of the Old Harbor behind the masts of the fishing boats under the evening sky. Or I could watch for hours as the cook beat and kneaded his dough, his arms diving into the fire as he fed it with fresh wood.

Then I would go up to the Binnets' apartment; they live just five minutes from here. Binnet's girlfriend usually kept some spiced rice for me or maybe fish soup. Afterward, she'd bring us thimblefuls of genuine coffee. She used to pick the few real coffee beans out of the monthly coffee ration that consisted mostly of a lot of barley. I would carve something for the boy so that he would lean his head against me, watching me. I felt ordinary, everyday life being lived around me, yet at the same time I also sensed that it had become unattainable for me. Binnet meanwhile would be getting dressed for his night shift. We argued about the things one used to argue about back then—whether the German landing in Great Britain would succeed, whether the Pact with Russia would last, whether Vichy would hand Dakar over to the Germans as a base for their fleet.

Around that time I also met a girl. Her name was Nadine. She had once worked in the sugar factory with Binnet's girlfriend, but had moved on because she was beautiful and clever. Now she was a salesperson in millinery at Les Dames department store. She was tall and walked very erect, holding her small blonde head proudly. She was always beautifully dressed in a dark blue coat. I told her at the outset that I was poor. She said that for the time being it didn't matter; she had fallen in love with me and after all, this wasn't a marriage till death would us part. I picked her up every evening at seven. How much I liked her beautiful, vividly painted lips back then, the strong smell of the fresh yellowish-pink powder that lay like butterfly-wing dust on her face and ears, the real, not painted, shadows of extreme tiredness under her light-colored, clear, hard eyes! I gladly starved myself during the day so that I could take her to the Regence in the evening. It was her favorite café, where the coffee unfortunately cost two francs. Then, each time, there'd be a little argument over whether we'd go to her room or to mine. The legionnaires always clicked their tongues as I passed them with Nadine. I had grown in stature in their eyes because of this girlfriend. We'd hardly gone to bed when they'd start their ugly singing, either to celebrate us or to make us angry or both at once. Nadine asked me who the poor devils were and what they were singing. How could I have explained to her something that I couldn't understand myself, what it was that drew me to this group and away from the lovely girl I was holding in my arms.

Binnet and I enjoyed our women—one was as light as the other was dark. As for the women, they were jealous and couldn't stand each other.

V

In the meantime the month allowed me by my residence permit had come to an end. By now I already felt part of the community. I had a room of my own, a friend, and a lover. But the official at the Office for Aliens on the Rue Louvois had a different view of things. He said, "You must leave tomorrow. We only allow foreigners to stay here in Marseille if they can bring us proof that they intend to leave. You have no visa, in fact not even the prospect of getting one. There is no reason for us to extend your residence permit."

At that I began to tremble. Maybe I was trembling because in my innermost self I knew the official was right. I wasn't part of the community at all. The roof over my head on the Rue de la Providence was questionable. My friendship with George Binnet was untested, my affection for the boy, a fragile connection that did not commit either of us to anything; and as far as Nadine was concerned, wasn't I already beginning to tire of her? So that was the punishment for my lack of commitment during this brief stay here—I had to leave. I'd been given a probationary month, a trial period, and I'd made poor use of it.

The official looked up just then and saw that I had turned pale. He said, "If you absolutely have to stay longer, then you must immediately bring us written confirmation from a consulate that you are waiting here for your departure documents."

I walked back to the Place d'Alma. It was bitterly cold. It was a southern cold that had nothing to do with the time of day; for sometimes the Mistral can turn the midday sun to ice. It attacked me from all sides, probing for my weakest spot.

So now I needed proof of my intended departure so that they would let me stay. I walked down the Rue St. Ferréol. I debated whether I should sit down in the café opposite the Prefecture, but I didn't belong there. It's the café frequented by those who are ready to leave but still have some business to finish at the exit-visa department or at the American Consulate. Besides, tonight might be my good-bye party with Nadine, and I needed every sou for that. By then I was already on the Canebière. For some reason, I didn't go down to the Old Harbor, walking instead in the opposite direction up toward the Protestant church. Maybe that was how I got the idea of turning into the Boulevard de la Madeleine. Or did I go in that direction because it was really where I wanted to go?

A crowd had gathered outside the gloomy building that housed the Mexican Consulate. The coat of arms over the door was almost completely worn away, the eagle unrecognizable. The porter picked me out of the crowd at once with his dry, intelligent eyes as if by a secret sign of extreme and urgent need on my forehead put there by some superior authority at one of the world's consulates.

"No, I'm sorry," said the short official with the flashing eyes, "I'm sincerely sorry. We still haven't received confirmation from our government that you are the same individual as Mr. Weidel. It has nothing to do with any personal doubt or lack of trust on my part. Unfortunately, I can't do anything for you yet."

I said, "I came only—" His eyes challenged mine. I wanted more than ever to be cleverer than he, more cunning, to get my own way, no matter what.

I said, "But I only came to—"

He interrupted me, "Please be sensible. I can't do anything for you until I have my government's notification. I need—"

"Please, let me finish," I said softly; I felt that my gaze was a trace more firm, a trace more urgent than his. "The sole reason for my coming here today is to request written confirmation that there has been a delay in my identification so that I can get an extension of my residence permit."

He thought about this for a moment. Then he said, "That I can certainly give you. Please forgive me."

I walked back to Rue Louvois with my confirmation. They gave me a month's extension. My heart was pounding. How was I going to use this month? I ought to be wiser about it this time around.

Yet I didn't have a clue as to how I could change my life. I could at least act differently toward Nadine—the realization came to me quite unexpectedly. If I'd been forced to leave at that point, I'm sure I would have remembered her as a great passion. But now, at the end of that week, I was suddenly revolted by the smell of her powder, by the fact that even in my arms she never made a single spontaneous gesture, I detested the one-sided smile with which she rolled up her beautiful hair at night. I wanted to find some pretext to skip an evening with her, but I didn't quite know what to do next; I didn't want to hurt her feelings, after all she'd always been good to me. Then she herself came to my aid.

"Don't be angry with me, love," she said, "but from now on I have to work on Sundays and do overtime because of the Christmas season." We knew that we were lying to each other and also that such lies were a lot better, less hurtful that the truth would have been.

VI

By now the last of my money was used up. That still didn't worry me.

When I was very hungry I went to the Binnets. If I was just a little bit hungry I smoked. After not having eaten lunch I would sit down outside the cheapest café I could find. The ersatz coffee there was terribly bitter and the saccharine dreadfully sweet, but back then I was content: I was free; my room had been paid ahead for the month; I was still alive—a threefold stroke of good luck that few people shared with me.

I watched them streaming into Marseille with their tattered banners representing all nations and faiths, the advance guard of refugees. They had fled across all of Europe, but now, confronting the glimpses of blue water sparkling innocently between the houses, they were at their wits' end. For the names of ships written in chalk didn't mean that there really were ships but only a faint hope that there might be some—the names were constantly being wiped off because some strait was mined or a new coastal port had been fired on. Death was moving ever closer with his swastika banner as yet unscathed. But to me it seemed—perhaps because I had met him once before and overtaken him—that Death was also fleeing. But who was at his heels? It seemed all I needed was some time to wait it out, and I would be able to survive him, too.

I was startled by a touch on my shoulder; it was the conductor of the Caracas Spa Orchestra. In the daytime he wore dark sunglasses that made his death's-head eye sockets seem bottomless. "You're still here," he said.

"You too," I replied.

"They gave me my exit visa yesterday. Half a week too late."

"Too late?"

"Because my visa expired at the beginning of the week. The consul will extend it only if the orchestra renews my contract."

"And they won't do that now?"

He said, quite taken aback, "Why shouldn't they? Of course they will. The committees sent me a telegram. If I can just get it done in a month. Otherwise my exit visa will have expired again. You'll experience all that for yourself."

"Me? Why should I?"

He laughed and walked on. His pace was that of an old man, and I thought he would never make it across the Canebière, not to mention other countries and other seas. I dozed in the sun. How long would the café proprietor let me sit there with my one little coffee? Why did I feel so exhausted? I'm still young, after all. Maybe those people boarding the ships are right. I was sure I'd be able to cope with those demon consuls. Then I got a jolt.

Paul was leaving the Café Mont Vertoux across the way. He looked good, wearing new clothes. I dashed across the Canebière and dragged him back to my table. Although he'd never really been my friend, we'd been in the camp together; and he'd also been with me in Paris when the Germans were in control. At that moment I almost kissed him. But he just looked at me—impersonal, detached. And he was in a hurry. "The Committee shuts at twelve," he said. "What is it now? What do you want?"

What is it now? I thought. I realized that he had no idea that this was the first time we'd seen each other since those days in Paris, probably because he met so many people again for the first time every day. "How are you doing, Paul?"

That brought him to life and set him talking. "Terrible! I'm in the most terrible predicament." He sat down at my table, realizing he'd found someone he could tell everything to all over again. "When I first got here, I applied for a residence permit. I wanted to do it all very correctly. I wanted to be absolutely proper and legal. I handed my application in at the Office for Aliens. And because an official advised me to, I personally handed in a second application to the Prefect. You couldn't do more than that, I thought. And I got replies to both my applications. But what replies they were! The Office for Aliens issued me a new ID card—here, take a look—it says: 'Enforced Stay in Marseille.' The Prefecture summoned me and on my old card they'd stamped: 'Must return to his Département of Origin.'"

I couldn't help laughing.

Paul was almost in tears; he said, "Go on, laugh. But I've got to leave the country. Even though I'm on the endangered list, they won't issue me an exit visa. Because at the Prefecture they said I've been expelled from the city."

"Then go back to your last département and arrive here all over again!"

"But I can't do that," he complained, "on the ID card that I need for traveling it says: 'Enforced Stay in Marseille.' Oh, stop laughing! Fortunately I have some friends and they're straightening things out for me, highly respected people they are. After all, I have a Danger Visa."

Those last words were my cue. I remembered the two of us sitting together in Paris on the Carrefour de l'Odéon. That seemed ages ago. I had been going around with the dead man's documents and using his name. It might just as well have been some other name that might have turned out to be useful for my purpose. For the first time I thought again with respect and sadness of the dead man.

"Why didn't you come back that time to the Capoulade, Paul? That was a terrible situation with your friend, you know, with Weidel."

"Yes," Paul said, "it's a sad world."

"It is pretty sad. And yet this man has a visa, a good visa waiting for him at the Mexican Consulate."

"Really? That's odd. Doesn't he have a visa for the States? After all, the kind of people who go to Mexico ..."

"You know, Paul, I think you were right; I don't understand anything about art. But I think your friend Weidel, he knew quite a lot about it."

Paul looked at me strangely. "You've expressed that quite well. He *did* once know something about it. But his last works are—what should I call them—a bit lacking in color."

"I don't know anything about it, Paul. It's only that I read something by this Weidel, the last thing he wrote. I don't know anything about these things, but I liked it."

"What's it called?"

"I don't know."

Paul said, "I doubt very much that a man like Weidel would ever be able to write in Mexico."

I was so surprised to hear him say this that I didn't reply. It seemed there was no reason for me to be ashamed that our reunion should turn out somewhat lame. Paul didn't even know that Weidel was dead. Maybe it was because of all the wartime upheaval that he didn't know. Or should he have known? He ought to have been making inquiries, investigating, and not given up. After all the dead man was one of his own kind. I now had a better understanding of why this man Weidel had gotten fed up with it all. They'd probably left him to his own devices long before that.

Paul said, "The main thing is that he has a visa."

We were silent then and in the silence my mind whirled. I said, "The visa won't work. It's made out to his pen name."

"That happens often. So Weidel isn't his real name? I didn't know that."

"There are a lot of things you don't know, Paul."

I looked him in the eye. And I thought, You're really stupid, Paul. That's what's wrong with you. It's that simple. It's your hidden weakness. Amazing that I didn't see it sooner! You make an intelligent impression because you talk as if you're clever. But I can see the stupidity in your brown eyes.

"What's his real name?" Paul asked.

I thought, You didn't care whether your friend was alive or dead. But this name nonsense has really sparked your curiosity.

I said, "His name is Seidler."

"Very odd that someone would call himself Weidel if his name is Seidler," Paul said. "I'll arrange for my Committee to take on this case, since I'm in a position of trust there."

"If you could manage to do that, Paul, since you have so much power, so much influence over so many people . . . "

"I do have some degree of influence in certain circles. Have Weidel come by to see us."

I figured Paul had installed himself somewhere, entrenched himself behind a desk. Before that I'd always met him in pretty hopeless situations. In Paris. In Normandy. He's stupid, that's for sure. But precisely because of that he's consistent. He uses the meager bit of power he has, the modest amount of common sense he's endowed with to attach himself to someone or something, and this always helps him out. In Paris, if I remember correctly, it was a silk merchant, the husband of his best friend.

I said, "It's not so easy for Weidel to go out among people. He's shy, you know. Why don't you, who can do everything and are so clever, why don't you arrange things for him. It just takes one telegram..."

"I'll ask my Committee. Even though I must say that I don't give a damn about his shyness, as you call it. I think it's an affectation. You seem to have become his coolie in the meantime."

"What have I become?"

"His coolie. We know all about that aspect of Weidel. He always manages to find someone to act as his coolie—until the time comes when he breaks up with each in turn; it always ends in an unholy row. He knows how to cast a spell on people—but only for a limited time. Even his own wife."

"What kind of woman is she actually, Paul?"

He thought a while. "I don't care for her. She's—"

For no reason whatsoever I felt a slight uneasiness. I quickly interrupted him, "All right then, so you'll do whatever you can for poor Weidel. After all, you have some influence among a certain group of people. By the way, could you lend me a few francs?"

"My dear fellow, just stand in line for a couple of hours at some committee."

"Which committee?"

"Good heavens! There are the Quakers, or the Jews of Marseille, HICEM, Hayas, the Catholics, the Salvation Army, or the Freemasons." He walked off rapidly. In an instant he had vanished down the Canebière.

VII

When I arrived at my hotel, the proprietress stopped me. Up to now I had only seen the upper third of her, those parts of her that were visible behind the window at the top of the staircase, from which point she could follow the comings and goings of her lodgers with impartial attentiveness. She was prattling on, telling me how lucky I was because the police had come back and taken away the woman from the room next to mine.

"Why?" I asked.

"Because, since her husband was arrested, she was now living in the city without a man's protection. And all women discovered living here in Marseille without their own husbands or without adequate identification papers are to be interned in the new women's camp, the Bompard."

Obviously her lodger's fate didn't matter at all to her. She was putting aside every franc she collected from her precariously situated guests so that she could start a grocery store as soon as possible. Maybe she was even in cahoots with one of the police officers, the one who led the raids, dividing the reward for each person arrested with him. After all she knew everything about us. So she was living quite the enterprising life in her quiet lair. And all the crying and despair of the lodgers arrested during the raids were transformed into peas, soap, and macaroni in her mind.

During the next few days I tried to follow Paul's advice. But my attempts at the various committees failed miserably. At first I told everyone that I was expecting to get work on a farm, I needed only a little bit of money to tide me over till then. They all shrugged. They gave me nothing, and I didn't even have enough change to buy cigarettes. After that I decided to disregard my parents' deeply ingrained advice, namely, that a man must hold his ground and give up only when there is no other way out. So now I told them all that I intended to give up, to leave. This they all understood. I'm convinced that had I asked for money to buy a hoe so that I could try my luck in a beet field somewhere on this old planet, they wouldn't have given me five francs to buy it. They rewarded only those who were ready to leave, those who were willing to give up everything. So from then on I presented myself as eager to leave, and I got enough money to last me while I was waiting for a ship. I paid for my room; I bought cigarettes for myself and books for Binnet's boy.

My second month in Marseille wasn't quite over but it was well under way. Marcel had written me in the meantime that he was on pretty good terms with his uncle and I could probably come to work on the farm in the spring. If I cited this at the Office for Aliens as a reason for my waiting around, I would certainly be imprisoned or sent back, the devil knows where to. Refugees, it seems, have to go on fleeing; they can't suddenly raise peaches. What I needed to extend my residence permit for the second time was proof that I was waiting here for a visa. So for better or worse, I had to go back again to the Mexican Consulate. At the time I didn't think there could be anything bad about getting this proof; I wasn't taking anything away from anyone else. And it would give me a chance to catch my breath. Innumerable things could happen in the meantime that might change my life. Maybe I'd be able to go to work at Marcel's uncle's farm sooner. The important thing was to retain my freedom. That's what I thought; that's what we'd all been thinking for years. At worst it would be a stamp on a piece of paper. It couldn't hurt the dead man. But once I had it, I could get a safe and useful extension of my residence permit. I was certain that I could really grow some roots once I had a genuine extension of my residence permit. I might even lose my desire to leave.

My heart was pounding as I walked up the Boulevard de la Madeleine. At first, I thought I'd made a mistake about the house number. The coat of arms was gone! The gate locked!

In the blustery wind, a crowd had gathered in the street; people looked perplexed, irresolute. As I approached I heard them bemoan the sad news: the consulate was closed because it was moving elsewhere. No visas were being issued. We can't leave. The last ship might be sailing this week. The Germans might arrive tomorrow.

The bearded *prestataire* joined the group. He said, "Calm down, people. The Germans may come, but you can rest assured there's no ship leaving now. With visas or without. Go home, all of you."

But the people continued to wait there as if the locked gate would take pity on them. The wind, even as it buffeted and pummeled them, seemed also to hold them there together in a vortex of fear.

They looked pale and frayed as if the expected ship were the last ferry across the Dark River Styx; and yet they were barred even from taking this ferry because there was still some life in them and they were destined for extraordinary suffering.

Eventually they dispersed. A tall, elderly man with gleaming white hair remained behind. "I've had enough," he said gloomily. "Do you think I should go to the new consulate when it opens? My children all died in the civil war. My wife died while we were crossing the Pyrenees. I've survived it all. I don't know why, but nothing seems to touch me. Do you think it makes much sense for me, with my white hair and broken heart, to keep on fighting with these stupid consuls here in Marseille?"

"The short consul isn't stupid," I answered him. "I'm sure he'll treat you respectfully."

"My problem is getting a transit visa," the old man said. "Even if they give me a visa here, I have to stand in line elsewhere for the transit visa. And once I do get on a boat, I'd probably be hoping for it to sink during the crossing. I ask you, young man, do you really think it makes sense for me to go to the consulate once they reopen it at the new address?"

I said, "No, it doesn't make any sense."

He stared at me for a while; then he left.

VIII

I left, too. A few steps farther down the street, a streetcar passed me. It stopped fifteen feet ahead of me. There was a slight delay at the stop. They were helping someone get off.

"Heinz!" I yelled.

For it really was Heinz who was coming slowly up the Boulevard de la Madeleine after they had set him down on the sidewalk with his two crutches. He recognized me, but was too out of breath to call to me.

He'd shrunk even more since our time together in the camp. His head looked even heavier, his shoulders, even skinnier. Looking at him I wondered anew why life should be imprisoned in a body so fragile that can be maimed and tortured. Yes, I really mean imprisoned. His bright eyes seemed to mock his imprisonment; his wide mouth was distorted by the effort of walking.

In the camp I'd often tried to make him look at me with those eyes of his. Their keen, attentive gaze would fix on someone, look for something within, and find it, too; and each time they would get brighter, just like a flame when fresh fuel is added. Maybe because of this I would keep looking for new chances to draw his eyes to me. It was only when his alert gaze rested on me that I realized he detected something in me that I myself didn't know was still there. And yet it would be obvious that Heinz wasn't much concerned about me. He liked the sort of qualities in people that I lacked, that weren't important to me. Back then, at any rate, I was convinced that they weren't important. I'm referring to unconditional loyalty which, in those days, I considered senseless and boring, dependability, which seemed to me impossible to maintain, and unswerving faith, which seemed to me as childish and useless as dragging old banners across endless battlefields. And every time Heinz turned away from me as if to say: You may be a fellow human being, but . . . Pride would keep me from approaching him again until that other feeling became stronger again than my pride. Then I would again try to draw his eyes to me, sometimes by offering to help him, sometimes with silly things.

I remembered all this now as Heinz came the few steps toward me. In the last few weeks I'd almost forgotten Heinz, forgotten what bound me to him. Actually, in Paris, and also when I was on the road I had thought a lot about him, had kept searching for him instinctively among the godforsaken hordes milling in the streets and at the railroad stations. Then in Marseille I stopped thinking about him. It's odd, almost as if the most important things in life, while still very much a part of you, are forgotten. And instead we fixate on unimportant things that become temporary obsessions until they fade.

When Heinz briefly leaned his head against me—he couldn't

free his hands—and his eyes again focused on me, I suddenly understood what those clear eyes were looking for and almost instantly found again: it was me, myself, and nothing else, and I instantly knew, to my enormous relief, that I was still there, that I had not gotten lost, not in any war or in any concentration camp, not in fascism, not while moving about, not during any bombardment, not in any disorder, no matter how violent. I hadn't gotten lost, hadn't bled to death; I was here, and so was Heinz.

"Where are you coming from?" we asked each other. Heinz said, "I was coming to Marseille from north of here and got off the streetcar right in front of your eyes because I have to go to the Mexican Consulate."

I told him that the consulate was closed for a few days. We sat down in a small, dirty café. Back then they still sold cake on four weekdays. I stood up to get us some. Heinz laughed when I came back carrying a large package, "I'm not a girl, you know." I could tell that he hadn't eaten anything like this in a long time. He said, "When we were escaping, my friends carried me out ahead of the Germans. They took turns. We crossed the Loire. I felt bad on the way, believe me. I was a burden to them. But then at the Loire there was a fisherman who said he'd take us across, but only on account of me. So it evened things out. Unfortunately, one of us—you probably remember Hartmann—he had to stay behind because the boat was full. Hartmann told me to get into the boat, and he stayed behind."

"It's really strange," I said, "that you got out faster then I did. The Germans caught up with me and passed me."

"You were probably alone. They hid me in a village in the Dordogne so that I wouldn't end up in another camp. Now they got me a visa. Why does the consulate have to be closed right when I get here?"

He glanced at me, laughed, and said, "I thought of you sometimes on the way."

"You thought of me?"

"Yes, I thought of everyone—you, too. The way you were always so restless, always jumping from one thing to another. One day this idea, the next another. I was convinced I'd see you again somewhere. What are you doing here? Do you want to leave too?"

"Not at all!" I said. "I want to see how this turns out. I have to find out how it all will end."

"If only we can stay alive long enough to see the outcome of all this. As it happens, I've been severely disabled, I can't tell you how bitter I am about having to leave. My name is on the German 'Wanted' list. Otherwise, I'd settle somewhere if I still had both my legs. But this way, wherever I go, it's as if I were my own 'Wanted' poster."

"I already know the city pretty well," I said. "Is there anything I can help you with? But then you probably won't let me help you."

He smiled, looking directly at me, and his eyes again shone as brightly as when we first saw each other on the street, and I felt once more that I still had the stuff in me that made his eyes brighten. "I know you well enough, after all," he said, "to know whatever else you do, whatever mischief you're up to, whatever nonsense you think up, that despite that you would never under any circumstances leave me in the lurch."

Why didn't he tell me that before, I thought, before we were all ground down in this mill? I asked him whether he had any documents.

"I have a certificate of release from the camp."

"How did you manage to get a certificate of release? Didn't we all climb over the wall that night?"

"At the last second, when everything was already topsy-turvy, one of the people in our group was smart enough to pick up a packet of blank release forms. I filled one out for myself. With that form I got a residence permit for the village, and with the residence permit I got a safe conduct."

He still had a few of those forms in his pocket. He gave me one, explaining that you had to be careful not to write over the stamp. That you had to fill out the form in such a way that the stamp seemed to be on top of the writing.

I asked Heinz if we could meet again. "You might need me. I

know a lot of places to stay in the Old Port district; I know a few tricks. Besides, I'd like to talk to you. I have things on my mind that I can't quite figure out."

Heinz looked at me closely. Suddenly I realized that things weren't going well with me. It didn't matter much to me, but I could no longer deny that I was in a bad way. I had only one chance to be young, and things weren't going well. My youth was vanishing in concentration camps and on highways, in bleak hotel rooms with the most unloved of girls, and maybe on a peach farm where I would at best be tolerated. Aloud, I added, "My life is a mess."

Heinz said he'd meet me the following week, same day, same time, same place. I was looking forward to seeing him again with childish joy, counting the days. And yet, I didn't go to meet him. Something happened that kept me from going.

4

I

ON THE same day I bumped into Heinz, George Binnet dropped by unexpectedly late in the evening. He was the only person in Marseille who knew where I lived. Yet he'd never before come to my room. Our friendship hadn't quite reached that point. He said his son had suddenly become ill; the boy had asthma, but it had never been this serious. He was in urgent need of a doctor. Their old neighborhood physician was a drunken, dirty slob who'd been thrown out of the navy ten years before, and settled in the Corsican quarter. Claudine thought there would be good doctors among the German refugees. And so he'd come to ask if I could find one among the people I ran into every day.

I'd been fond of the boy from the first day I met him. It was for his sake that I spent hours at the most ridiculous committee offices asking for money. And instead of using it as intended, for my departure preparations, I bought him things he needed. Whenever I was talking with the Binnets in their apartment, I'd be looking out of the corner of my eyes toward the window where the boy sat studying. Instinctively, I'd choose words he could understand. Sometimes I took him on boat rides or into the mountains. At first he didn't say much. The occasional sudden turn of his head, his eyes lighting up, struck me as the playfulness of a young colt. It was welcome even if no more than a game. In this gone-to-pot world, I found reassurance in a quiet, still-innocent look or the gentle yet proud gesture with which Claudine offered me some rice, or the boy's surprised smile when I entered the apartment. I soon realized that nothing escaped him; that he knew more about us than we knew about him.

At the time I probably exaggerated the seriousness of his illness. It seemed to me like an attack on his life, like an attempt by some power—maybe it was simply crude, nasty reality—to get rid of him, to close those bright, uncomfortable eyes forever. I was even more anxious than George to find a doctor. I asked around at my hotel. They sent me to the Rue du Relais, a tiny alley off the Cours Belsunce. There, they said, at the Hotel Aumage in room 83, lived a once well-known physician, the former director of the Dortmund Hospital. Hearing the term "former" I expected to find an old man. I had forgotten that time stood still for these people once they left their homeland. Knocking on the door of room 83, I heard the frightened voice of a young woman trying to calm her companion. At that unusual hour both were probably afraid of a police raid. The door opened. But no one appeared. I saw only a blue silk cuff on a slender wrist. I felt a twinge of envy, the kind that sometimes hits me for no reason at all, maybe because this doctor I didn't know was so useful and competent that he was needed, or maybe because he wasn't an old man and his wife, whom I couldn't actually see, was gentle, perhaps, and beautiful.

I said, "We need a doctor," and the woman's voice repeated, with just a trace of joy, "They need a doctor."

The man came to the door at once; he had a real physician's face. Though his hair was already pretty gray, his face was young. There's something special about this sort of youthfulness. A thousand or two thousand years ago, doctors looked like this, too; they nodded the same way, they gave you the same attentive and thorough yet impartial look, a look that has focused innumerable times on individuals, or rather their physical ailments that even a layman can recognize. That night we scarcely looked at each other. He asked me briefly about the sick boy. He complained that I was being too vague. I was flustered because of my affection for the boy.

Silently we walked along the Cours Belsunce—it was still a rough, half-finished street back then. Cars full of refugees were parked on the north side, laundry hung out to dry. There was a light in one of the car windows. We heard laughter coming from inside. My companion said, "These people have already forgotten that their cars have wheels. They consider this corner of the Cours Belsunce their home now."

"Until a policeman chases them away."

". . . to the other side of the Belsunce. Where they'll stay until another police officer chases them back to this side. At least they don't have to cross an ocean like us."

"Are you also planning to cross the ocean, Doctor?"

"I have to."

"Why do you have to?"

"Because I want to heal sick people. I'm being assigned a unit in a hospital in Oaxaca. If the hospital were located on the Cours Belsunce I wouldn't have to cross the ocean."

"Where is Oaxaca?"

"In Mexico," he said, surprised at my ignorance.

And I said, even more surprised, "You want to go to Mexico, too?"

"I once cured the son of a high-ranking Mexican official in the old days."

"Is it hard to get there?"

"Fiendishly hard. There are no ships that go there directly. And getting a transit visa is very difficult. The best way to go is to take an American ship from Lisbon. But to get to Portugal you have to go through Spain first. Now they're saying that there might be another way to get there, that is, taking a French ship to Martinique, and from there boarding a ship to Cuba."

I thought, Here's a doctor with a heart and soul. He could help people. His reason for leaving was quite different from the one my death's-head friend from Prague had. He just wanted to wave his baton again.

The two tramps who were always hanging out at the construction site between the Maternity Clinic and the Arab café were lying there now. Their arms, which in the daytime stretched out to beg, were now folded under their heads. They were sleeping, unaffected by what was happening in their country—feeling as little shame as trees do, molding and decaying. Their beards were lousy, their skin was scurfy. They had as little thought of leaving their homeland as trees might.

We crossed Rue de la République; it was totally deserted. The doctor looked around carefully in the maze of dark streets of the Old Port so that he'd be able to find his way back without me. The night was cold and still.

I raised the doorknocker at the apartment on the Rue du Chevalier. When Claudine opened the door, the doctor looked closely at her, the woman whose child he was to treat. Then he walked quickly through the tiny kitchen to the boy's bed. He indicated to us that we should leave him alone with the boy. George had already left for the mill. Claudine laid her head on the kitchen table. A narrow strip of the softest pink, the palm of her hand, was visible along her chin. To me she'd always seemed like a flower or a seashell. But now, because of our shared concern, she had changed into an ordinary woman who went to her job during the day, and took care of her husband and child, working very hard. For George she had no magical significance. For him she was much less but also much more.

She asked me what I knew about the doctor, and out of jealousy, I exaggerated my praise. Just then he came into the kitchen. In candid French he reassured Claudine that the boy's illness was less serious than it looked. It was important not to upset the child in any way. This last remark seemed aimed at me, although he wasn't looking at me and certainly couldn't blame me for anything. He scribbled a prescription. Then, in spite of his objections, I accompanied him to the Rue de la République. He wasn't paying any attention to me, nor did he ask any questions about the Binnet family. It was as if he didn't think such questions worthwhile, preferring to learn from his own observations. I felt like a schoolboy who can't help liking the new boy even though annoyed because the new boy is ignoring him. I bought the prescribed medicine that same night with the money the Committee had given me for my departure preparations.

By the time I came back up to the Binnets the boy was calm and sleepy. The doctor had promised to bring him a figure of a human body that could be taken apart on his next visit. Even as he was falling asleep he kept talking about the doctor.

That man was here only ten minutes, I thought, and already he's opened a new world of promises and dreams for the boy.

II

I'm getting to the most important part now. I remember the date. It was November 28th. My second residence permit was about to expire. I brooded about what to do. Should I go back, this time with the camp release certificate Heinz had given me? Or go up to see the Mexicans? I went instead to the Mont Vertoux. Back then I went there four or five times a week.

I'd just been at the Binnets' place. The child was almost well again. We had become well acquainted with the doctor—I won't say formed a friendship as he wasn't the right person for that. We enjoyed being with him; he was different from us. The first thing he always told us was how his departure plans were going, and all the new things that kept happening to him. He told us that in his mind he could see the white walls of the new hospital day and night, and all the sick patients without a doctor. I liked his obsessiveness. I was amused by his inflated self-esteem. By now the doctor was so familiar with the place where he'd be working that he assumed we must be, too. He already had the visa stamp in his passport. The boy turned his face to the wall whenever the visa discussions began. At that time I was foolish enough to assume it was because he was bored.

As soon as he put his ear down to listen to the child's chest, the doctor became calm, forgetting his visas. His face, the tense face of a harried man possessed by some delusion, took on an expression of wisdom and goodness, as if his existence was now governed by something quite different from the instructions of consuls and officials.

Sitting there at the café, I was thinking about the circumstances of his departure and about my own stay here. The Mont Vertoux is at the corner of the Quai des Belges and the Canebière. The light that day was bright and clear and it lightened my mood and everything else that afternoon, even the most useless and unimportant detail of my unimportant and useless existence. Nothing foreshadowed what was to come.

There were two tables between me and the counter. At one of them sat a small woman with straggly hair; she was usually there this time of day, always setting her chair at an angle to the table and always telling everyone the same story, yet the shock in her eyes each time she told it was fresh and new. The story was about how she had lost her child during the evacuation of Paris. He had gotten tired of walking, and so she lifted the boy up into a truck full of soldiers. Then the German planes came and bombarded the road. So much dust! So much crying and screaming! And her child was gone. It wasn't until weeks later that they found the child at a farm; he would never be like other children. There was a tall, gangly Czech sitting at her table who told everyone that he wanted to go to Portugal. And then he'd add in a whisper, that it was only so that he could go from there to England to join in the fighting.

I listened for a while, immobilized by boredom. At the other table sat a group of locals. Although not originally from Marseille, they had settled here and were managing to make quite a good living off the fear and the mad longing for departure of the new arrivals. They laughed as they told the story of two young couples who had rented a boat for a great deal of money—the men had escaped together from a camp. But the sellers had cheated the young people; the little boat had a leak. They got as far as the Spanish coast. There they were sent back. They tried sailing up the mouth of the Rhône and were shot at by the coast guard and arrested when they landed. I'd heard this story a hundred times before. It was only the ending that was new to me. Just yesterday the men had been sentenced to two years in prison.

The section of the Mont Vertoux we were sitting in was right on the Canebière. And from where I sat I had a view of the Old Harbor. A small gunboat was anchored by the Quai des Belges across the street. Over the heads of the people filling the café with their smoke and chatter I could see its gray smokestacks among the slender masts of the fishing boats. The afternoon sun hung in the sky above the Fort. I wondered if the Mistral had started blowing again, for the women passing by on the street had pulled up their hoods, and the faces of the people coming through the revolving door were tense from the wind as well as their worries. No one paid any attention to the sun above the sea, the crenellations of St. Victor's church, or the nets spread out to dry along the whole length of the pier. They talked without pause about their transit visas, their expired passports, the three-mile zone, and the dollar exchange rate, about exit visas, and again and again about transit visas. I was disgusted. I felt like getting up and leaving.

Then my mood changed. Why? Who knows what causes these mood changes. Suddenly I no longer thought all the chitchat was disgusting; it seemed fascinating now. It was the age-old harbor gossip, as ancient as the Old Port itself and even older. Wonderful, ancient harbor twaddle that's existed as long as there's been a Mediterranean Sea, Phoenician chit-chat, Cretan and Greek gossip, and that of the Romans. There was never a shortage of gossips who were anxious about their berths aboard a ship and about their money, or who were fleeing from all the real and imagined horrors of the world. Mothers who had lost their children, children who had lost their mothers. The remnants of crushed armies, escaped slaves, human hordes who had been chased from all the countries of the earth, and having at last reached the sea, boarded ships in order to discover new lands from which they would again be driven; forever running from one death toward another.

Ships must always have been anchored here, at this very place, because this is where Europe ends and the sea begins. There's always been an inn at this spot because it was on the road that led to the juncture of land and sea. I felt ancient, thousands of years old. I had experienced all this before. But I also felt very young, and eager for all that was yet to come; I felt immortal. Yet this feeling soon faded. It was too strong a feeling for one so weak. I was overcome by despair, despair and homesickness. I mourned my twenty-seven wasted years that had vanished in foreign lands.

Someone at the next table was telling about a ship, the *Alesia*, headed for Brazil, which had been stopped by the British in Dakar. Since there were French officers on board, all the passengers ended up in an African detention camp. How cheerful the teller of this tale sounded! Probably because, just like him, these people couldn't get where they were going either. I'd heard this story countless times. Oh, deadly dull gossip! I longed for a simple song, for birds, for flowers; I longed for my mother's voice, the voice that had scolded me when I was a boy.

The sun disappeared behind Fort St. Nicolas. It was six o'clock. Casually I looked over the heads of the people toward the revolving door. It was turning again. A young woman entered. What should I tell you about her? I can only say, she entered. The man who committed suicide on the Rue de Vaugirard would have expressed it differently. Don't expect me to describe her. I can only say she entered. That afternoon I couldn't have told you whether she was blonde or brunette, a woman or a girl. She entered. She stopped and looked around. There was an expression on her face of tense expectancy, almost of fear. As if she hoped—and yet was afraid—to find someone here. Whatever she was thinking, it had nothing to do with visas. At first she went diagonally across the part of the room I could see, the part next to the Quai des Belges. I could still see the pointed top of her hood against the large, by now gray, window. I was afraid that she might not come back, that there was a door in that part of the room leading outside, and that she might simply walk through it. But she returned almost at once. The look of hope, of expectation on the young face had already turned to one of disappointment.

Up to now, if a woman I might have liked walked into a place but didn't come near me, I never would have begrudged the other man her attentions; I never felt I was losing something irreplaceable. But not this time. The woman walking by me at that moment was different. She had come into the café, but not to find me. And that made me feel awful. Only one thing could have been worse—if she hadn't come in at all. Again, she looked carefully around the section of the room where I was sitting. She scanned all the faces, all the tables, the way children search, both thoroughly and awkwardly. Whom was she so desperately seeking? Who could cause so much anxious expectation, such bitter disappointment? I would have liked to beat up this man who wasn't there.

Finally she discovered our three somewhat out-of-the way tables. Carefully she looked at the people sitting at the three tables. Foolish though it might have been, for a moment I had the feeling that I was the one she was searching for. She looked at me, too, but the look was blank. I was the last one she looked at. After that she left. I saw her pointed hood once more outside the window.

III

I went up to the Binnets. The doctor was sitting on the boy's bed. He had already given the inevitable daily report on how things stood with his transit visa. He had put his gray, close-cropped head on the bare, dark body of the boy, and as he listened, his face, distorted by his transit worries, changed. The expression of haste and fear of coming too late and being left behind changed over into one of infinite patience. His desire to leave Marseille as quickly as possible no matter what, no matter who'd have to stay behind, was transformed into kindness. It seemed as if he had nothing else to do, and didn't want to do anything else but to listen to the sounds that told him how his patient might be cured. The boy, too, had calmed down, for the soothing effect he'd had on the doctor now came back to him. At last the doctor raised his head, gave the child a gentle pat and pulled down his shirt; then he turned to the family. He treated George Binnet, since he happened to be the only one there, as the child's father. It even seemed to me that the doctor had changed not only George's relationship to the child but also to his beloved Claudine by considering them both as the parents. Because a sick child needs parents. He had imperceptibly changed all the relationships in the room in order to facilitate the child's healing. But once the illness no longer held sway, he wouldn't care about any of them.

He was just explaining to the parents what foods to give the boy. I was sitting on Claudine's coal box, listening, watching. Then all at once I became alert and pricked up my ears. What I'd just experienced was so fleeting that nothing of it lingered behind except a delicate, burning sensation, and a feeling of thirst as though I'd abruptly dried up. I was suddenly madly envious of the doctor. He had cured this boy who, once he was well, would presumably be of no further concern to him. And he had a certain power over people, not because of any tricks or cunning but because of his knowledge and patience. I was jealous of his knowledge and of his voice. He was different from me. He wasn't suffering. His mouth wasn't dry. I was jealous because there was some quality in the man that I myself would never possess, just as he himself could never, by himself, obtain the proper visas, letters of transit, or residence permits.

I interrupted him gruffly. I said that medicine didn't work. That, in fact, it didn't really exist. That no person had ever actually been cured by a physician, that people got well as a result of some coincidence or other. He gave me a penetrating look, as if he wanted to diagnose my fervor on this particular point. Then calmly he said that I was right. On his own, he could do nothing except to avoid doing anything that might interfere with the patient getting better. At most and with the utmost care, he might supply what the patient needed physically or spiritually. But even if all this worked, there was still something else, and maybe it was the most important thing. And he couldn't really explain what it was. It was something that depended neither on the sick person nor on the doctor himself. Rather it came from the ever-present fullness of all treasured life. We listened, fascinated—then the doctor suddenly looked at the clock, jumped up, and left, calling out to us that he had an appointment with the Siamese consul's secretary, and that the Siamese consul was a friend of the head of a forwarding agency that gave out visas for Portugal without American transit visas. George laughed; the boy turned his face to the wall.

IV

The next day was windless and overcast. The air felt as gray as the gunboat still lying at anchor in the Old Harbor. People never tired of staring at it as if it could tell them what Admiral Darlan was planning to do with it. The British were approaching the Tripoli border. Would the French voluntarily surrender the harbor at Bizerte, or would they refuse? Would the Germans then occupy the south of France too?—These were the questions of the day. If the latter were to happen, the British might bomb Marseille to smithereens. That, for the time being, would solve all transit visa worries. I went to the Café Mont Vertoux. The table where I'd sat the day before was free. I sat down, lit a cigarette, and waited. Waiting at the same place made no sense. But where else should I have waited?

The hour at which the young woman had come there yesterday was already long past. Yet I found it impossible to get up. Maybe I continued to sit there only because I was dead tired. My limbs felt leaden, paralyzed by the stupid waiting. The café was crowded. It was a Thursday, a day when alcohol was served. I'd drunk quite a lot.

Just then Nadine came to my table, dear old Nadine. Would you like me to describe Nadine? I can picture her standing before me at will. I didn't care about her then or now. She asked me what I'd been doing all this time.

"Been going to the consulates."

"You? Since when did you want to leave?"

"What else am I supposed to do, Nadine? Everyone is leaving. Am I supposed to kick the bucket in one of your filthy detention camps?"

"My brothers are in camps too," Nadine tried to reassure me. "One is in the occupied part; the other one is in Germany. Every family has a couple of their men behind barbed wire. You foreigners are all so strange. I never wait for things to just happen." She lightly stroked my hair.

I didn't know how to send her away without hurting her feelings.

I said, "You're so beautiful, Nadine, I'm sure things have been going well for you in the meantime."

She answered me with a sly smile, "I was lucky." Then she bent down so that our faces touched. "He's in the navy. His wife is a lot older than he is. Besides that, she's stuck in Marrakech. He's good-looking. It's just too bad that he's a lot shorter than me." She performed a move she'd learned at the Dames de Paris, flinging her coat back a bit so that one could see the light-colored silk lining and her beige dress.

I was astounded by this explicit demonstration of her good luck. I said, "Don't scare the man off! I'm sure he's waiting for you now."

She didn't think making him wait for her would do any harm, but finally I managed to get her to leave by making a date to meet eight days from then. I could just as well have arranged the appointment for eight years later.

I saw Nadine walk past the window as she went up the Canebière. Shortly after that they lowered the shutters. Blackout rules. For me it was oppressive not to be able to look out, to see the water and the shadows in the street. I felt trapped, locked in with all the demons populating the Mont Vertoux that evening. One clear thought flashed through my mind so worn out from waiting: If a squadron of planes were to bombard the city, I didn't want to die in this place with them. But in the end, that didn't matter either. How was I any different from them? Just because I didn't want to leave? Even that was only half true.

Suddenly my heart began to pound. Even before my eyes caught sight of her, it knew who had just entered. She was in a hurry, just as she had been the day before, as if fleeing from or searching for something. Her young face was so tense that it hurt me to look at it. I thought, as if she were my daughter: It's not good for her to be here, not in this place, not at this hour.

She searched through the entire café, going from table to table. She came back to my section, pale with despair. But then she immediately began the search all over again. She was alone and helpless in this herd of escaped demons. She came close to my table. Her gaze now rested on me. I thought: She's looking for me, who else? But already her eyes had moved elsewhere. She made her way out.

V

I returned to the Rue de la Providence. My room seemed bare and empty, as if I'd been burglarized while I was gone. My head was empty, too. I didn't even have a clear picture of her in my mind. Even that vestige was gone.

I was sitting at my bare table when there was a knock on the door. A stranger came in, a short man, wearing glasses. He asked whether I knew by any chance where his wife had disappeared to; he had found their room unexpectedly empty. From his questions I gathered that he was the man I'd seen from my hiding place on the roof, being led off in handcuffs. Slowly I began to explain that his wife, unfortunately, had been arrested.

He became furious. I was really afraid that, given his stout neck, he might choke. He told me they had taken him in chains back to his original département, but the official there had been in a good mood and had told the guards to let him go. He said he was still hoping to make the ship in time, but now that they'd dragged his wife off to Camp Bompard, he'd have to pay her bail, or, to call it what it really was, her ransom. He immediately disappeared into the city to find some friends to help him. How I envied him! The plump little woman belonged to him. She couldn't get away from him, although it was too bad that she was stuck in a camp. But she couldn't vanish from his life. He'd walk his legs off, do whatever he could to get her back.

As for me, I had nothing, no one I could hold on to. I went to bed because I was cold. I tried to visualize the young woman's face, her figure. I sought to find an image of her in the thin, bitter cigarette smoke that gradually filled the room. The hotel was deserted. The legionnaires had left in search of entertainment. It was one of those evenings when everything and everyone has withdrawn from you as if by some conspiracy.

VI

I was awakened by yowling dogs. When I banged on the wall, it got even worse. I jumped up and went to see if I could get them to stop their racket. I found the adjacent room occupied by two powerful Great Danes and a woman with insolent eyes and crooked shoulders. She was wearing an ugly, garish dress. I assumed she had something to do with one of the small, seedy theaters in the alleys down by the harbor that presented all sorts of trash. I explained to her in French that her animals were disturbing me. She answered me flippantly in German that it was too bad but I had to get used to it because the animals were her traveling companions. All she wanted was to go to Lisbon once she'd received her transit visa. I asked her if her attachment to the two mutts was really so strong that she'd drag them along all over the world.

She laughed and began to tell me her story. "I could slaughter them here and now. But I'm shackled to them because of a series of remarkable coincidences. I already had a ticket to sail on a ship of the Export Line. My American visa was approved. But when I went to the consulate to ask for an extension, they said that I needed a new, incontestable affidavit, a sponsor, and statements by two American citizens saying I was completely spotless morally. Where was I, a woman who'd always lived alone, going to find two American citizens who would put their hands in the fire for me, vouching that I'd never embezzled money, that I denounced the pact with Russia and didn't support the Communists, and never was and never would be one, that I would receive no strange men in my room, that I was leading, had led, and would lead a respectable life? I was pretty desperate. Then I happened to run into a couple from Boston, whom I had met one summer when we were staying at a place at the seashore. The husband had a position with Electromotor; that was something the consul respected. They didn't like it at all here in France and wanted to leave immediately on the Clipper, except that they loved their two dogs and dogs weren't allowed on the Clipper. We were despondent and complaining to each other about our respective dilemmas when we realized there was a way we could help each other. I promised the two Americans that I would take the dogs safely across the ocean on an ordinary ship, and, in return, they gave me an affidavit. Now you see why I wash, brush, and care for these two dogs. They're my guarantors—I'd drag them across the ocean with me even if they were lions."

Somewhat cheered by her tale, I went out into the cold morning. I chose a shabby little café because it was cheap and it was on the Canebière across from the Mont Vertoux. I stared out at the busy street. One minute the Mistral was driving the rain into the throngs of people, the next minute the sky suddenly turned light. The windows of the café rattled. I was thinking about the Office for Aliens; I was planning to try my luck there the following morning, perhaps show them the camp release certificate Heinz had given me.

Suddenly the young woman—for once I wasn't even thinking of her—appeared in the doorway of the café. With one look she took in the entire shabby little place. Besides me, there were only three construction workers who had come in to get out of the rain, and so she didn't even come inside. Under her hood her face seemed even smaller and paler than before.

I hurried out into the street. The young woman had already disappeared into the crowd. I walked up and down the Canebière, bumping into people, disrupting their departure gossip, their march to the consulates. Far away, at the end of the Canebière, I caught sight of the pointed hood. I ran after her but she disappeared on the Quai des Belges. I followed her onto the Quai, up the stairs, through the bare, endless streets to St. Victor's Church. There she stopped in the entrance of the church, near the candle sellers. Only then did I realize that this wasn't the woman I was looking for, but another woman, a woman I didn't know with ugly, mean, shriveled features. She was haggling over the price of the candles to be lit for the good of her soul.

There was another sudden rainsquall, and so I slipped into the nearest pew. I don't know how long I sat there, head in my hands. I'd come again to the brink, to the edge of it all. In spite of that I kept on with the old game, even at the edge. Also, I remembered that this was the morning I was supposed to have met Heinz. But the time of our appointment was long past and with it, so it seemed, the best of what lay in store for me. How cold it was in the church! A damp gloom reigned not only inside St. Victor's but also near the half-open door. The Mistral even blew in, causing the little altar candles to flicker. How empty the mighty nave, and yet new people were constantly coming in from outside; where did they disappear to? I heard faint singing, but couldn't tell where it was coming from, for the church remained empty. The churchgoers were all disappearing on the other side of a wall. I followed them down a stairway that was dug into the bedrock. The farther down we went the clearer the singing. Soon a flickering light from the crypt fell on the stairs. By now we must have been deep under the city, indeed, it seemed to me, under the sea.

It was here that they were performing the Mass. In the thin smoke wafting up, the timeworn capitals of the antique pillars were transformed into the grimaces of sacred animals. The ancient priest had a white beard and wore a sumptuously embroidered white stole. He was like one of those priests from long ago who are stricken when their unholy, sinful city is condemned to sink to the bottom of the sea because it scorned the warnings of Him who created this rock. The pale choirboys, eternally youthful, were singing as they carried their candles in procession about the pillars. Light from the flames danced on their faces. A soft drizzling sound turned into the shaky breaking of waves. It was the sea roaring above us. The singing ended abruptly. The priest, in a voice both weak and hard, typical of old men, began to reproach us for our cowardice and our hypocrisy and our fear of death.

"Today, too, we came here only because this place seemed safe to us. But why is this place safe? Why has it survived the ages, with-stood the military campaigns of two thousand years? Because He who carved His house into the many rocks around the Mediterranean Sea did not know fear.

"'Three times I was beaten with rods; once I was stoned; three times I was shipwrecked; a night and a day I have been in the deep; in journeys often, in perils of waters, in perils of robbers, in perils of my own countrymen, in perils of the Gentiles, in perils of the city, in perils in the wilderness, in perils in the sea, in perils among false brethren.'"

The veins stood out on the old man's forehead, his voice died away. The church seemed to be sinking down deeper and deeper, and the people listened, trembling both with shame and fear, to the old man's bitter silence. Then the choirboys' singing began again in its unbearable angelic purity, raising futile hopes in us as long as the melody floated in the air. It was answered by a dreadful sound issuing from the old man's deep chest that evoked gloom and remorse.

I was struggling to breathe. I didn't want to get stuck at the bottom of the sea; I wanted to die up above, together with others like me. I rushed back up the stairs. The air was cold and clear. The deluge had stopped; the Mistral had blown itself out. Stars were already glittering in the battlements of Fort St. Nicolas across from St. Victor's Church.

VII

The Binnet boy was allowed to leave the house for the first time the following day. Claudine asked me to take him out into the sun. I liked my assignment. We walked slowly up the Canebière on the sunny side of the street. The peaceful closeness between us was there again, almost effortless. I wished the Canebière would stretch on forever, that the afternoon sun might stand still, and the boy would always lean his head against my arm as he was doing then. He was dragging his feet a little lazily and spoke only when I asked him a question. He said he wanted to be a doctor one day. Despite the fact that I had his full trust and the peaceful gaze of his eyes on me, I immediately felt a pang of envy. By then he was so tired that I was almost pulling him along. I suggested we go to a café on the Cours d'Assas. Unfortunately they had no cocoa or fruit juice, only some watery greenish stuff. Yet there was a glint of happiness in his face, such as usually comes in response to the more precious things so rare in life. I loved him very much. I looked over his head and out through the window at the still-sunny square with its contorted trees. There was a crowd in front of one of the large houses. "What's going on?" I asked.

"Over there? Oh, nothing," the waiter said. "Those are just Spaniards. They're lined up outside the Mexican Consulate."

I left the boy with his greenish juice and crossed the square. I looked up at the tall doorway, at the coat of arms. It gleamed brightly; the layer of dust had been removed. I was amazed. Now I could even see the snake in the eagle's beak. The Spaniards looked at me, smiling. Only one said in annoyance, "Get in line, sir!"

So I got in line. Ahead of me and behind, I heard them saying the same words and phrases I'd heard months before outside the Mexican Consulate in Paris. Now they were repeating with even greater certainty that ships were going to sail from Marseille for Mexico. Again they repeated the ships' names: *Republica. Esperanza. Passionaria.* They were sure the ships would be leaving since they even specifically mentioned the names; they wouldn't be wiped off the shipping companies' blackboards. Moreover, the ports they were sailing to would never go up in flames. There were no impassable straits on their routes. I wanted to sail on one of these ships with such fellow passengers.

And lo and behold, I reached the gate. The doorman sprang toward me as though he'd been expecting me. I almost didn't recognize the lean, leathery man from the Boulevard de la Madeleine. He held himself proudly and was well dressed, which just reinforced our hopes for a departure. They ushered me into the office. It was no longer a simple room, but an awe-inspiring space with counters and a railing. And behind the railing, at a massive table, sat my little official with the most sparkling and alert eyes in the world. I wanted to turn on my heels and leave. But he jumped up and called to me, "There you are finally! We've had them search everywhere for you. You didn't enter your address properly. My government's confirmation has arrived."

I stood there transfixed, thinking, So Paul really did have some influence. He really does have a certain amount of power on this earth. Dumbfounded, I did the silliest thing, I made a slight bow.

The official gazed at me in amusement. I could read in his sardonic look just what he was thinking—You can be sure I didn't lift a finger in your affair. Other powers were involved. But we'll see who has the last laugh. He had me step behind the railing, and while I was waiting there, some ten or twenty departure-crazed people walked past. I also saw the white-haired Spaniard again, the one who had asked my advice about whether it would be worthwhile coming here again. And here he was. He had come, in spite of my advice and his own bitterness. Maybe he hoped that once on the other side of the ocean, he would regain his youth or find a sort of eternal life that would give him back his sons.

They brought out my dossier, leafed through it, rustling the papers. Suddenly the little official turned to me, his eyes flashed, I had the impression that up to then he had only wanted to lull me. "What kind of documents do you have, Mr. Seidler?" He was looking at me quite joyfully, almost laughing. "There are several compatriots of yours here who have had their visas for two months already but are still waiting for confirmation from the German authorities that they are no longer considered German citizens. Only then will the Prefecture issue them an exit visa, permitting them to leave the country."

We looked at each other. We could sense an adversarial relationship, but we both derived pleasure from this evenly matched duel. I replied, "Please don't worry. I have a refugee certificate from the Saarland, as well as from Alsace."

"But weren't you born in Silesia, Mr. Seidler?"

We looked each other in the eye, amused. I said, "In Europe very few people have the citizenship of the country they were born in. I happened to be in the Saarland at the time of the referendum."

"Permit me, but I continue to be seriously concerned about you. In view of all this, you're almost French, and you'll have considerable difficulties getting an exit visa."

I said, "I'm sure that, with your help, I can manage it. What do you suggest I do?"

He looked at me, smiling, as if I'd just asked him something funny. "First you should go with my government's confirmation of your visa to the American travel bureau. There you should ask for a receipt showing that your ship's passage has been paid."

"Paid?"

"Certainly, Mr. Seidler, paid. The same friends who were worried about your life and who pushed through my government's visa for you have paid in full for your ticket at the Export Line in Lisbon. Here in your dossier is proof of payment. Does that surprise you?"

I certainly was surprised. So all Weidel had to do was die, and, voilà, his voyage across the ocean was paid for, and his dossier filled with the best of documents that would prove more and more useful the longer his corpse moldered in the ground. It seemed as if dying was all it took for his friends to remember him and smooth his way down to the last detail.

"Then you must immediately go to the American Consulate with this proof of payment and the confirmation of your visa and apply for a transit visa."

"From the American Consulate?"

He looked at me sharply, "No matter what other talents you may have, I'm sure you can't walk on water. There's no ship that goes direct to Mexico. So you'll need a transit visa."

"But they keep talking about a direct ship to Mexico."

"Of course, they talk. But these are just phantom ships they're talking about. The Export Line is a safer bet. In any case, see if they'll give you a transit visa. Besides, you look a bit worldlier than other writers I've come across. Not that I'm belittling your abilities as a writer! Anyway, try your luck at the American Consulate. And then ask for a transit visa for Spain and Portugal." He had said the last merely incidentally, as if referring to a situation he was convinced would never come to pass, and that expending too much effort on it was futile.

I went back across the square that was by now cold and quiet.

With my splendid new visa confirmation, they'll certainly give me another extension of my residence permit at the Prefecture. After all, I've got to make the various preparations now for my departure—getting transit visas, etc. will take weeks. Now they'll believe me when I tell them that I'm serious about leaving and so they'll let me stay.

The boy was chewing on his straw when I got back to the café. The glass was empty. I'd been gone for about an hour. I felt guilty and was afraid to look him in the eye. But it wasn't until we were walking home that he said, "So now you're clearing out, too."

"What gave you that idea?"

He replied, "Well, you went to a consulate. You came suddenly and now you're going away suddenly."

I held him close, kissed him, and swore that I'd never leave him.

VIII

The doctor was already sitting there when we got to the apartment. He scolded me for making him wait for his patient. He then led the boy over to the bed and listened to his chest. I stood there feeling reprimanded and sad. The boy was all tired out and fell asleep almost immediately.

The doctor and I left together. We really had nothing to talk about but agreed it was bitter cold. I turned in the direction of the Quai des Belges and he followed me, I don't know why. More to himself than to me he said, "To think I could have left today!"

"You could have left today?" I said. "Why didn't you?" We were now facing into the icy wind, and he scarcely opened his lips when he replied, "I would have had to leave a woman behind. She doesn't have her documents yet. We're hoping to travel together at the first opportunity."

"And aren't you afraid of losing your position in the hospital over there if you wait here for this woman?" I asked. "Remember, you're a doctor, first and foremost."

For the first time he looked at me. "That precisely is my insoluble problem. I worry about it night and day."

Making a great effort because the wind was blowing right down my throat, I said, "But actually there's nothing more to worry about now. After all, you stayed."

"It's not that simple," he replied almost gasping since he had both the Mistral and me to contend with. "There are also some compelling external reasons that have delayed my departure. As always in such cases, one's inner considerations sometimes coincide with external circumstances. The money for my passage is in Lisbon. I had intended to leave from there. I was still waiting for my Spanish transit visa and then suddenly, from one hour to the next, there was word about a small ship leaving for the island of Martinique, a cargo ship carrying goods to Fort de France, along with a dozen officials, and there's room on it for thirty passengers. So now I have to raise the money for the passage, get the necessary papers, pay the security deposit, and quickly arrange to be one of the thirty passengers. And at the same time to manage this good-bye.—Do you understand?"

I said, "No."

We glanced at each other sideways, our necks tensed as if the wind might blow away our looks. I stopped at the corner because I wanted to get rid of him. He certainly wouldn't want to stand on this icy, windy street corner just to hear my opinion. But the matter must have been extremely important to him since, despite the cold, he asked, "What is it you don't understand?"

"That a person wouldn't know what matters most to him. It will come to light anyway."

"How?"

"My God, man, by his actions, how else? Unless nothing matters to him. Then he'll be like that piece of white paper over there that looks like a bird."

He looked with great concentration at the deserted Quai, only sparsely lighted by a darkened streetlamp. It was as if he'd never before seen a scrap of white paper blowing in a gust of wind. I added, "Or like me."

He turned abruptly to face me, looking at me with the same concentration. Then he said, "No." His teeth were clattering with cold.
"Nonsense. You only assume this pose, this attitude so that nothing
and no one will surprise you."

With that we parted. I had the same feeling I used to have when,
as a boy, the top student in our class finally thought I was worthy of
taking part in a special, privileged game, which, it soon turned out,
was nothing special at all. And now, to top it off, I'd also been infected once more with the dismal transit talk.

IX

By then I was quite numb from the cold and I entered the first café I
saw. It was called Café Roma. The warmth made me dizzy. Even as I
stood there, unsteady on my feet, looking for a table, I sensed with
some unease that someone was watching me. The dizziness left me; I
became aware of a group of men at one of the tables. Among them
was the little official from the Mexican Consulate. He was watching
me with laughing eyes as though amused to see me there. I realized
that all the men at the table were from the Mexican Consulate. Even
the doorman with the proud dark face was there. I told myself that
the little official had a right to drink his coffee wherever he wanted
to on this icy evening. Moreover, in his daily routine he must certainly meet as many transit applicants as a pastor meets churchgoers.
I didn't sit down but pretended to continue my search for a table. At
that point the Mexicans all got up to leave, and I sat down at the
table they had vacated, which was too large for me alone.

As usual, I sat facing the door. A healthy man who's been hurt
doesn't think night and day about his wound. But the awareness of
his injury remains with him, a fine undeniable pain, even while he's
working, talking, or walking. It hadn't left me for one second, no
matter whether I was out for a walk with the boy, drinking, spending time at the consulates, or talking with the doctor. I searched for

her wherever I happened to be, everywhere, no matter what else I was doing.

I hadn't yet touched my glass of wine when the door was pushed open and the young woman walked in. She took a few steps, stopped, and looked around breathlessly as if the bleak Café Roma were a place of execution, as if she'd been sent by a higher authority to stop a sentence from being carried out. But to me her coming, whatever her reason for coming, seemed to be a direct consequence of my waiting. And so because I felt she had come too late and because I didn't want to be too late, I left my glass on the table and went to stand by the door. After she passed me with her face turned away. I followed her. We crossed the Canebière. It wasn't as dark outside as it had seemed from inside the café. The wind had stopped. She walked into the Rue des Baigneurs. I was hoping to find out where she lived, where she belonged, under what conditions she survived here. But she just walked back and forth through the many narrow streets between the Cours Belsunce and the Boulevard d'Athènes. Perhaps at first she intended to go home and then suddenly changed her mind.

We crossed the Cours Belsunce and then the Rue de la République. She went into the maze of alleys behind the Old Harbor. We even passed the house where the Binnets lived. Its door with the bronze knocker seemed to me like one of those chunks of reality that enter into one's dreams. In the Corsican quarter we walked by the fountain in the market square. Perhaps she was searching for a particular street here, a house. I might have offered to help her. But instead I just walked behind her as if I feared that one word from me might be enough to make her disappear forever. One door was draped with silver-edged black sashes, the custom in this country when a dead person is lying in a house. In this way this wretched street became a proud portal for the almighty Visitor. It seemed like a dream in which I myself was the dead man, and at the same time it touched my heart. She walked up the stairs that led to the sea. Suddenly she turned around. Her face was right across from mine. She didn't recognize me. It was absurd. She walked right past me.

For a moment I looked down at the nighttime sea. It was almost completely blotted out by cranes and bridges. Patches of water were visible between the moles and piers, a bit lighter than the sky. A line ran from the outermost point of the Corniche with its lighthouse, all the way to the left mole of La Joliette. It was the horizon—a thin and unprepossessing line and only recognizable because it was lighter than the water. A line, inviolable and unreachable, but which eluded everything. Suddenly, from one moment to the next, I was overwhelmed by a desire to leave. I could leave if I wanted to. I could do it all. And my departure would also be different in that it would not be driven by fear. It would be an honest, old-fashioned departure befitting a human being traveling toward that distant, fine line. Suddenly I came to. When I turned to look for the woman, she was gone. The stairs were deserted, too. It was as if she had intentionally lured me up there.

X

I returned to the Rue de la Providence. I wasn't tired at all. What was I going to do? Read? That's what I used to do on free evenings like this. Never again! I felt that old boyhood reluctance to reading a book, that reaction against invented stories about a life that wasn't real. If something had to be invented, if this cobbled-together life we were living was too wretched, then I wanted to be the inventor of another life, but not on paper.

But here I was in this intolerably bare room of mine, and I had to find something to do. Write a letter? There wasn't anybody left on this earth I could have written to. Maybe my mother—but she might already be long dead. The borders between France and Germany had been closed for a long time. Go out again and sit in some café? Was I already so badly infected by those milling crowds that I had to be one of them?

Finally I did start writing a letter. I wrote to Marcel, Binnet's cousin. I asked him to talk to his uncle about me, to tell him that I'd come from the Saarland. After all, they should be able to find a spot for me on such a big farm. Even though I was living in Marseille and I had grown to like the city, was even attached to some things here . . . I stopped because at that moment there was a knock on the door.

It was the short legionnaire, the one who had put me to bed on my second night in Marseille. His chest was covered with medals, but he had taken off his burnoose. I had nothing to offer him besides a torn-open pack of Gaulois Bleu cigarettes. He asked me if he was interrupting me. In answer I tore up my half-written letter. He sat down on my bed. He was definitely a lot smarter than me—as soon as he'd seen the light under my door he'd given up foolishly fighting his loneliness. He confessed something I'd known for a long time: "I thought it would be paradise to have a room all to myself. And now all my buddies are gone; they've all left. And I miss them!"

"Where did they go?"

"Shipped back to Germany. I hardly think they'll be slaughtering a calf to celebrate the return of their prodigal sons. They'll put them to work in some especially unpleasant factory or assign them to the most dangerous posts at the front." He sat up very erect on the edge of my bed, a short, sturdy man surrounded by a spiral of smoke. He said, "The Germans came to Sidi-bel-Abbés; they set up commissions there. German style. They issued a proclamation, calling on all legionnaires of German birth to report to them, no matter why they had fled Germany. The Fatherland, et cetera, the magnanimity of the German people, all would be forgiven, and so forth and so on. So the German men in the Foreign Legion came forward, both ordinary soldiers and those in the middle ranks. The German commission, disregarding the promises made in their proclamation, checked them all thoroughly but took only a few. The rest they sent back. But those men had broken their French oath by having gone to the Germans. And now after the Germans rejected them, the French put them on trial. As punishment they were all sent to work in the mines in Africa."

I didn't like his story. It troubled me. I asked my guest how he had passed the commission alive.

"With me it's something else," he said. "I'm Jewish. For me the magnanimity of the German people was never even a consideration."

I asked him why he'd joined the Foreign Legion. That question seemed to stir up a whole swarm of unpleasant thoughts for him

He said, "I ended up in the Legion because of the war, and was committed to staying in it for the duration of the war. It's a long story and I don't want to bore you with it. I was released finally because of my injury and my medals. I'd rather have you tell me what happened to the beautiful young woman I envied you for, the first week I met you."

It took me a while to realize he meant Nadine. He said he'd almost gone blind looking for her as soon as he noticed that she was no longer my lover. He spoke of Nadine as I myself might have talked about the other one. His impassioned words hit me like an icy wave of terror. It was as if a gust of wind were blowing into the mists of my own enchantment.

5

I

I DIDN'T run into the young woman again in the next few days. Maybe she'd given up her futile search, or found the person she was looking for. Or perhaps she was already on the high seas, possibly on that boat to Martinique whose departure everyone had been speculating about that week. I had a feeling I'd find her again, somewhere, somehow. But even though I tried to force myself to stop expecting to see her, I always picked a seat facing the door.

The stream of the departure-obsessed swelled steadily hour by hour, day by day. No police raid, no decree by the Prefect of Bouches du Rhône, not even the threat of concentration camps, could keep the number of those hoping to leave from surpassing the number of people living here permanently. I considered all those who had already departed as refugees in transit. The refugees passing through this place had left behind their real lives, their lost countries. They were fleeing the barbed wire of Gurs and Vernet, Spanish battlefields, fascist prisons, and the scorched cities of the North. By now I knew many of their faces. No matter how alive they pretended to be, or how animated their talk about audacious escape plans, colorful outfits, visas for exotic lands, and transit visas, nothing fooled me about their plight. I was only amazed that the prefect and the other authorities and officials of the city continued to act as if the flood of departures could be dammed by mere human means. I was afraid that I might be caught up in the tide—I, who still felt alive, and absolutely determined to stay here. I feared I might be dragged into the stream by temptation or by an act of violence.

I went to the department that dealt with foreigners who were there on a temporary basis. There was a small group of us with all sorts of visa confirmations, safe conducts, and concentration camp release certificates. A fat official looked at us as if we'd come from another planet, not just from another country. He seemed to feel that the privilege of permanent residence here applied only to individuals from his own privileged country. They sent me to another department because a residence permit with so many extensions was either illegal or would have to be changed to a limited-residence permit.

I found myself waiting in line at the Rue Stanislas Lorein. You know the place, Didn't you stand there yourself in the rain and snow that terrible winter when there was a shortage of bread? Lines of people waiting for food, or actually, for the right to eat it in this city. There were Czech and Polish *prestataires* waiting there, soldiers who seemingly no longer had any role to play. They weren't even needed as cannon fodder since an agreement had been reached with the enemy. They were irrelevant here and so had laid down their weapons. Armies of ragged men who, as chance would have it, had barely survived, some just pretending to be alive. But they all had to be registered. Waiting in line, I met my little orchestra conductor again. He was shivering with cold—as if he'd crept out of a grave to be registered again with the living. I found the foreign legionnaire from the room next to mine. I found a gypsy carrying her children in a shawl on her back. And I found myself there, too, waiting with the rest of them.

Of course, you're also familiar with the cavernous Prefecture and the horde of frizzy-haired bureaucratic goblins that work there, digging out dossiers from the walls of shelves with their little paws and red-lacquered claws. And then, depending on whether you've hit a well-disposed goblin or a malicious one, you leave the cave either happy or gnashing your teeth. They gave me a magic paper, a new invitation to appear at a later date. They indicated that a general proof of departure wasn't enough, and that I would only receive a limited-residence permit if I brought along specific proof that I had booked passage on a ship, the date when my ship would leave, and a transit visa, giving me permission to pass through the United States.

II

I was stunned by all this and decided to go to the Mont Vertoux to catch my breath. The first thing I saw in the café, once I could see clearly, was the young woman. She was leaning against the wall behind the table where I liked to sit. I quickly pulled myself together and sat down. For minutes her hand rested on the back of my chair. Someone at the adjacent table leaned over to tell me that he'd found a boat that would take him to Oran this week along with a shipment of copper wire. He'd also arranged his route from there to Tangier at the English Consulate. The fellow had developed the technique of an actor's stage whisper that could be heard around the room. The revolving door turned, disgorging the woman from the hotel room next to mine with her two dogs, which bounded toward me barking joyfully. Tugging at their leashes, she greeted me with a laugh. Two people at the table across from mine started arguing about how Gibraltar seemed to be fogged in as soon as a ship was reported. And all this time the young woman's hand still lay on the back of my chair. I looked up at her. Her brown hair, cut after a fashion, was casually covered by her hood. Suddenly she made the only gesture possible: She held her hands over her ears. Then she left.

I was already on my way out the door when someone grabbed my sleeve; it was Paul. "Hey there, your Weidel might have thanked me," he said.

I wanted to shake him off, but he put his foot into the revolving door, and I actually fought that small, effeminate but tough foot in its ugly russet-colored shoe.

"Hey!" said Paul, "I really talked my tongue off for your Weidel. There were some major, even justified impediments. I had to use my influence. I spent a lot of my time, ploughed my way through lots of committees. But evidently even a simple gesture or a word of thanks is too much for Weidel."

"Forgive me, Paul." It took great willpower to calm the pounding of my heart. "But it's all my fault. I should have thanked you on his behalf a long time ago. But going like that to a committee, even making such a gesture—things that are a cinch for us—are impossible for him by his very nature."

"That's ridiculous!!" Paul said, "He didn't seem to have any difficulty making certain gestures in certain other directions."

I felt I had to make it up to him and invited him to have an aperitif with me. "You can't turn me down now," I said. "You're the one who's always treating. And to follow your suggestion . . ."

He relented and we sat down for a drink together. But I sensed that he was bored with me. He kept turning his head in all directions, obviously restless. In the end, he excused himself and moved to another table occupied by a group of men and women who greeted him warmly.

III

I followed the kind advice of the official at the Mexican Consulate. After all, people had long since stopped trying to give me advice. I went to the travel bureau.

The little agency was unprepossessing, lackluster, as if the administrative offices for the Last Judgment had been moved into a tobacco shop on some street corner. Yet it was big enough for anyone who'd made it this far. Dressed up or in rags, they stepped up to the counter and pleaded for a berth on a ship. Some had valid transit visas but hadn't yet paid for their passage; others had paid-up passages but expired transit visas. All their begging and whining was directed at a broad-chested, brown-skinned man with oily slicked-down hair. I'd met him once before in a café in the Corsican quarter. He had been there with his fellow countrymen when I came in for a glass of wine with my friend, Binnet. Now he was trying to suppress a yawn, which when it finally did come, coincided with the sobbing of a young woman whose passage could not be rebooked. She pounded on the counter with her little fists, but he barely looked at her. Then he crossed out her booked passage once and for all and began poking around in his ear with his pencil.

Again I ran into the little conductor. His eyes glinted feverishly as though a light had been turned on inside his skull. Quivering with joy, he informed me that he had the final summons to the American Consulate in his briefcase; his transit visa was at last ready to be picked up; his contract had just been renewed; his exit visa was assured; and his ship passage was properly booked.

A police officer leading a prisoner had come through the door; he stopped and unlocked the handcuffs on the man's wrist and pushed him inside. He was a short, stocky man. As he serenely massaged his wrist, I thought he looked familiar. When he greeted me I recognized him as the husband of my first neighbor in the hotel. He told me pretty calmly that his wife had already been transferred from Bompard to Gurs, the large concentration camp on the slopes of the Pyrenees. He had returned to his département where she intended to follow him. But she was prevented from doing this because of a new decree that applied only in his département, namely that all foreigners able to bear arms would be forcibly deported. The decree was eventually rescinded, but before that happened he had tried to escape, and hence his renewed arrest and the handcuffs. In the meantime, of course, all his papers, every last one, had expired. So he managed to persuade them to take him to Marseille so he could try to get a new booking. The Corsican, yawning and poking around in his ear, listened to the man's story; then with another yawn he said it was impossible. Through all of this, the police officer had been listening attentively. The handcuffs clinked again, and he pushed his man back out the door.

A well-dressed fellow entered next; I couldn't guess either his age or where he was from. He was handed a wad of money that he quickly and casually counted. Then he peeled off a few bills and threw them down on the counter, asking, no, demanding that his passage be rebooked for the following month because of visa delays. Our eyes met as he brushed by me on his way out. I had an inkling of a connection between us, but couldn't quite put my finger on it at that moment. I wanted to know who he was. Yet there was certainly no warmth in the cold look that he shot at me from an intentionally almost expressionless face.

It was my turn next. I showed my visa confirmation. Yawning, the Corsican noted that Weidel was the same as Seidler. A man with this name had definitely been expected for quite a while, his dossier was prepared, his passage paid. The Corsican said there was nothing to prevent him from booking passage on a ship for this man once he added a transit visa to his other visas. And once he got an American transit visa, transits for Spain and Portugal would be child's play. He looked at me briefly. The look felt like a drop of fluid, I even wiped my face. I stepped back and read the confirmation of my paid passage, which he had made out for me without argument. As I left I looked back at him—I was nonplussed to find his fat brown face had come alive, he was actually smiling at someone.

Naturally it wasn't one of us who'd been able to interrupt his constant yawning. The smile was directed at a shabby little man who had suddenly come to stand in the doorway. He was wearing a dirty coat. His ears were red from the cold. He spoke right over the pleading voices of the would-be travelers, who weren't paying any attention to him. The Corsican, though, gave the little man his full attention, even as he held the point of his pencil suspended over the file lying before him. "Listen, José," the little man said, "Bombello is coming along only as far as Oran. We're still waiting for that shipment of copper wire."

The Corsican said pleasantly, "If you leave unexpectedly, give my regards to our friends in Oran. Above all, regards to Rosario." He blew him a kiss. The little man laughed sadly, then scurried off like a mouse.

IV

Out of sheer boredom I decided to follow him. The wind was so
strong, it was raising whitecaps on the water of the Old Harbor. He
turned up his coat collar, but it wasn't enough to protect his ears.
Neither one of us was properly prepared for such a winter. But since
he came from the South, I was better able to withstand it. I followed
him along on the right side of the harbor. He stopped in front of a
tiny, miserable-looking café. The remnants of a painted sign, a pathetic squiggle, informed passersby that this house had served African customers in bygone times of summer and peace. The little man
darted through the beaded curtain covering the doorway. I waited
two minutes before following him in—again because I had nothing
better to do. The little man was already sitting with some others—
four or five fellow mice as well as a sad-faced mulatto and the old
barber from the shop next door, whose shaving brush had probably
turned to ice. They were all busy doing nothing. The proprietor had
come out from behind the counter and was sitting with two streetwalkers, both blue with cold. They all stared at me. The café was in
the grip of cold and ennui. The stone floor was too cold even for fleas
to be hopping around on it. And the damned strings of beads clack-
ing softly in the wind did little or nothing to keep the cold out. I'm
sure it was the bleakest place in Marseille, maybe along the entire
Mediterranean. The worst sin ever committed here was probably
having an aperitif on an alcohol-free, icy Wednesday.

A little glass was placed before me; they were all still doggedly
watching me. I decided I'd wait till someone spoke to me first. My
silence seemed to be driving them crazy; after about twenty minutes,
the little man held a whispered conference with his neighbors. Then
he hustled over to my table and asked whether I was waiting for
someone. I said, "Yes."

But he wasn't the sort of person who'd be satisfied with a one-
word answer. "Are you waiting for Bombello?"

I gave him a quick look. His mousy eyes became uneasy. "It's no use waiting, sir," he said. "Something happened to him. He can't come before tomorrow."

"Gentlemen," I said, "will you allow me to finish my drink with you?"

I joined them at their table. After a while, I cautiously asked about the boat to Oran.

It was a Portuguese freighter, they told me. They were still waiting for a load of copper wire. It had to be released by the German commission. From Oran the boat would sail to Lisbon, probably with a cargo of leather. They asked me whether I had the necessary documents.

"If I did," I said, "I wouldn't be waiting for Bombello, but could go direct to the Transports Maritimes."

The little man now started complaining. The affair was much too risky, their work permit was at stake, and they might lose their license. I wondered if they'd ever had a proper license. And so gradually we began to talk about how much a passage would cost. I wrung my hands.

All I'd wanted was to wile away some time in the middle of the day. I didn't have the slightest use for a passage from Oran to Lisbon. They were just on the verge of offering me a new and far more reasonable price when someone awkwardly parted the bead curtain with both hands. It was the young woman. She'd probably been running against the wind trying to catch up with someone. She held on to the nearest chair for support. I got up, took a step toward her. She looked at me. But if she recognized me, it was only as one of the many transit applicants everyone keeps running into in this city. Maybe my face had changed too much. As I looked at her, I felt more than bewilderment. I was afraid. It was as if something were clinging more and more tenaciously to my heels ... something no coincidence or fate could explain. She ran out again and all at once the foolish fear left me. I was only dismayed because she was gone. I hesitated only a moment before running after her, but the street was already deserted. Perhaps she'd hopped on a streetcar passing by on its way to the center of the city.

I went back to my seat at the table. They were all smiling a little; they'd warmed up a bit. As for me, I needed some warmth now, and would accept it wherever I found it. The barber asked whether I'd quarreled with her. The words coincided amazingly with my own feeling that I had known her for a long time, that a long life together lay behind us, and that we'd had a falling-out. The incident won the men in the café over to my side. People tend to see you in a more favorable light when you reveal something about yourself that they can understand. They advised me to try for an immediate reconciliation. You never know what might happen, they said; don't wait till it's too late. As I was leaving, they invited me to come again the next day; Bombello would be there in the evening around nine.

V

From there I went to another café—what else was I to do? This one was called Brûleurs des Loups. As I walked by the Café Kongo, I saw the Corsican sitting in the heated glass terrace. He recognized me and smiled. I thought it was probably because I was closer to his heart than his customary *prestataire* clients.

Sometimes you find real Frenchmen sitting in the Brûleurs des Loups. Instead of talking about visas, they talk about sensible things like the shady deals that go on. I even heard them mention a certain boat that was sailing for Oran. While the Mont Vertoux customers prattle on about all the details of booking a passage on a ship, these people were discussing the particulars of the cargo of copper wire.

The Old Port was blue. You know that bright afternoon light that shines its cold light into all the corners of the world, yet leaves them bleak and dreary. A fat woman with a fancy hairdo was sitting at the long communal table. She was devouring countless oysters, stuffing herself out of grief. She had been refused a visa, rejected once and for all, so she was eating up her travel funds. And there wasn't much else you could buy besides wine and oysters.

The afternoon was passing. The consulates were closing. The

transit seekers, tormented by fear, streamed into the Brûleurs des Loups and every other conceivable place. Their wild talk filled the air, a senseless mixture of intricate advice and sheer helplessness. The thin light on the various piers was already being reflected in the darker surface of the Old Harbor.

I was just putting some money on the table with the intention of going across to the Mont Vertoux, when the young woman stepped into the Brûleurs des Loups. She still had the sad, gloomy expression of a child being made fun of in a game. Carefully she searched all the tables with the same sorrowful, devoted care that childlike women in fairy tales take when they perform a useless task assigned to them for no reason all. For again, her search proved futile. She shrugged and left. I thought of the advice I'd been given that noon: Don't wait till it's too late!

I followed her out onto the Canebière. By now I knew that this determined rushing about would not lead her to her goal. The Mistral had stopped quite a while ago. And without its icy blasts the night was quite bearable, a Mediterranean night. She crossed the Canebière just before the Cours d'Assas. I could see that she was suddenly too tired to go another step. She sat down on the nearest bench.

The bench was right across from the Mexican Consulate. In the dark I recognized the large oval shield with the eagle perched on the cactus. To the young woman, I assumed, it was nothing more than a dully gleaming surface, and the door merely one of the thousands of doors in a city locked up for the night. Yet I had the persistent feeling that this emblem had come to play a role in my life. That it had found me and become attached to me a little like some other emblem might have become attached to a Crusader in bygone times. I didn't know exactly why or how, but from now on it would decorate my shield, my visa, and my transit permit—if I were ever to acquire one. And now there it was once more.

I sat down at the other end of the bench. The woman turned to face me. Her eyes, her face, her entire being pleaded to be left alone, to be left in peace, and I immediately got up.

VI

I walked to the Binnets' place. Claudine was busy picking the genuine coffee beans out of the ersatz coffee, which this time consisted of dried peas instead of barley. She'd used up the entire month's coffee ration so that she could brew a single cup of genuine coffee for her guest, the doctor. The doctor was despondent today.

He had allowed the Martinique ship to sail without him and booked passage on a ship sailing from Lisbon the coming month. But he had been refused a Spanish transit visa. Something he certainly had not foreseen. When he investigated, he discovered that the consulate had mixed him up with another doctor who had the same name and had headed the medical corps of the International Brigades during the Civil War. I asked him if he'd ever been in Spain.

"Me?" he said. "No, never. Although in those days there probably wasn't anyone who didn't ask himself at least once whether he was needed there. At the time I had the prospect of being taken on at the Saint Evrian hospital. That would have made use of my knowledge for the foreseeable future."

"And did the hospital take you on?"

"The situation dragged on like everything else in this country," he said wearily. "It dragged on endlessly. Then the war came."

"But your namesake must surely have come back from Spain long before that."

"I made inquiries about the man. He arrived in Marseille even before I did. And that's what turned out to be unlucky for me, for the fact is that he didn't apply for a transit permit. If he had, he would have been refused right away. Then the whole mix-up would never have happened, and they would have let me cross Spain. But the man didn't even apply for a transit permit. People who knew him told me he crossed the mountains with forged papers and almost reached Portugal. An adventurous fellow, this namesake of mine! So I was rejected for a transit visa because a doctor with the same name had been flagged at the Spanish Consulate."

While the doctor told his story, I was watching the boy. His eyes were fixed on the doctor's lips. I would have given anything to know what he was thinking, listening so intently to the man's tale of paper-jungle adventures and mistaken identity woes.

Claudine brought the coffee. It hit us like strong wine, for we hadn't had the real stuff in a long time. We were wide awake. Suddenly, I wanted to help the doctor. I told him I knew of a way to get to Lisbon via Oran. Did he have any money? The boy, who'd been watching us, seemed even more interested in my offer to help than the doctor. But then he abruptly turned his face to the wall and pulled the covers over his ears.

At that point the doctor got up—too soon, it seemed to me, after he'd been served such a precious cup of coffee. All he wanted now was "to hear any advice I had, in detail and alone." With his arm in mine he dragged me through the streets. I had to explain all the details, even though they weren't quite clear to me yet. I wondered whether he'd really make use of these tips I was passing along to him. He listened eagerly to all the possibilities, even the most absurd. At the corner of the Rue de la République he invited me to have supper with him. I accepted, even though I knew that he wasn't asking me because he liked me but only because I had a tip for him. The next day he'd probably tell them in the café that he'd had supper with a man who had given him a tip. In spite of that, I accepted. After all, I was alone and afraid of facing the rest of the long evening stretching before me in my cold room with a pack of Gaulois Bleu and the tormenting vision of that same face.

We entered the pizzeria. I took a seat facing the open fire. The doctor had them set the table for three. He looked at the clock and ordered a pizza for twelve francs. They brought the usual rosé. The first two glasses of rosé always go down like water. I like watching the open fire, you know, and the way the man hits the dough with his bent wrist. Yes, things like that are the only things in the world I really like. That is to say, I like things that have been and will always be there. You see, there's always been an open fire here, and for centuries they've beaten the dough like that. And if you were to reproach me because I'm forever changing and going to different places, then I'd reply, that it's only because I'm doing a thorough search for something that is going to last forever.

After the second glass the doctor said, "Please tell me again everything you know about the passage on the boat to Oran."

So, for the third time I told him about discovering the sad-looking little mousy man at the Corsican's and following him so that I could find out more about getting a passage, in much the same way the doctor was pursuing me to get information about getting a passage on a boat. The doctor was facing the door this time, not I. And suddenly the expression on his face changed. He said, "Please repeat it all for Marie."

I turned around. The young woman was coming over to our table. She didn't speak, merely nodded slightly to him in an old mutual understanding.

The doctor said, "This gentleman has been kind enough to give us some good advice."

She looked at me briefly. Sometimes it's easier to recognize a person from a certain distance rather than close up. I made no effort to reveal my identity to her. Meanwhile, the waiter brought over a pizza the size of a small wagon wheel. He cut each of us a triangular slice. The doctor said, "Marie, please eat something, you look so tired."

She said, "Again it was all in vain."

He took her hand. It's not that I was jealous. I just had the feeling that I was about to take something away from him that wasn't really his, something he couldn't possibly deal with. I grabbed his wrist and turned his hand a little so that the woman withdrew her fingers and I was able to see the face of his watch. Regaining my composure, I said I'd have to leave soon. He was disappointed and said he'd hoped that I had the evening free to have supper with them. Marie wasn't hungry, and he couldn't possibly eat the pizza all by himself. He would use his bread ration. But above all, I must tell Marie the whole story before I left. He poured me another glass of rosé. After I had downed this glass, too, I realized that if I got up and left now, the woman would certainly not follow me; she would continue to sit there with the doctor. So I poured myself another glassful and told the entire long, trivial story for the fourth time. The woman listened with complete disinterest as I told it. But the doctor couldn't get enough of the nonsense. That's right, I think it's all a lot of nonsense —exchanging one burning city for another burning city, switching from one lifeboat to another in the middle of the bottomless sea.

"But you'd have to go by yourself," I told him. "This sort of journey is nothing for a woman. It would be quite out of the question."

She broke in suddenly, "There's nothing out of the question for me. All I want is to get away from here. I don't care by what means. I'm not afraid of anything."

"It has nothing to do with being afraid. They can hide a man anywhere. They can drop him off in mid-journey. But these people would never risk taking a woman on board their boat."

We looked each other in the eye. I think at that moment she recognized me for the first time. I don't mean that she recognized me as someone she had run into often, but rather as someone who had crossed her path before, for good or for evil.

The doctor ordered another bottle of rosé to replace the one I had emptied almost single-handedly. And while I was drinking, I weighed her words: *I want to get away from here. I don't care by what means.* This confession coming from her lips, though I'd heard the same thing hundreds of times a day, seemed fresh and new in its foolishness and matter-of-factness; as if she was assuring me, here in front of the open fire and the sliced-up pizza, that death would some day destroy her features, too. I even took a moment to think of this most natural sort of destruction, the inevitable end of everything that's destructible. Her small pale face appeared close to mine, still untouched, in a rosé-tinged, glittering rosé world. The doctor grabbed for her hand once more. By reaching for the bottle, I managed to obstruct him just in time with my elbow.

The doctor said, "You wouldn't be able to leave by that date anyway. And when you are ready to leave, you may as well go via Spain."

I poured each of us another glass of wine. And even as I was emptying my glass, I realized that I had to push the man away from the table, out of the pizzeria, out of the city, and across the ocean, as quickly and as far as possible.

VII

I'll admit it—I didn't let the couple out of my sight after that. I'm not at all ashamed of it either. And rather than be annoyed, they truly seemed glad of my presence. I used the passage to Oran as an excuse. I talked things over with the doctor and the little mousy man and even with Bombello, whom I'd met by then. He was a lean, mustachioed, ordinary-looking Corsican; he didn't have much more than the one passage from Ajaccio to Marseille to his credit. I told the doctor that the cargo they were waiting for might still be stuck for weeks or it might suddenly be released, and if that happened the boat would be leaving from one hour to the next. And I asked him if he was irrevocably committed to the trip. With lowered eyes he said he had finally made up his mind: he was ready. He was counting on meeting Marie in Lisbon.

I passed most of my time waiting in Binnet's apartment under Claudine's suspicious eyes. She was puzzled by these longer visits of mine. The boy also waited in silence for the doctor whose visits became shorter as the boy's health improved.

The doctor would drag me along to the pizzeria to wait for Marie. On one occasion, while we waited for her, he told me, to my astonishment, that he had promised to bring me along because the presence of a stranger would remove some of the apprehension and anxiety that would inevitably accompany their good-byes. And, he said, he was glad to do anything that would make Marie a little more cheerful and calm her anxiety. We often had to wait a long time before she arrived. I could always tell when she entered a place from the expression on the doctor's face—it would suddenly and inexplicably change to an odd one of jealousy and apprehension. But even as the two of us were waiting there, I visualized Marie running through the city, going from one place to another, in this search of hers, which

I was no longer a witness to, since I now ended up at the same table with her in the evenings. Once I casually asked the doctor about this, and he said, just as casually, "Oh, good lord, it's the old visa scourge." His answer didn't sound quite sincere, and I was surprised because he was usually needlessly frank and honest in his confessions.

One ice-cold evening, he and I were waiting as usual. The pier outside the pizzeria had been swept clear by the wind. The few lights in the houses on the other side of the harbor blinked as if from a distant coastline. I wondered whether my companion was really as calm as he pretended to be. If the German commission were to release the cargo tomorrow, thus signaling his departure, he'd no longer be able to keep watch over Marie's life. Just then I saw from the contraction of his eyebrows, the narrowing of his eyes, that the small shadow in the cape with the pointed hood we had been waiting for had just appeared outside the window, and then the door opened.

She was breathless, but not just from the wind. Her lips were pale but not only from the cold. She didn't try to hide her fear, but leaned down to her friend, whispered a few words to him. For the first time since I'd met him, he seemed perplexed, dismayed. He got halfway up out of his chair and looked around. Infected by his dismay, I, too, looked around the place. But the room presented no threat of any kind, only calm. The owner's family sat at the next table, with the same wine, the same food as ours. The owner, who was also the chief cook, was stroking his favorite daughter's cheek, and giving orders to the second cook, his son-in-law, who, just as Marie entered, had grabbed the rolling pin to prepare some more dough. There were two other couples in the place holding hands and touching knees; they sat there motionless as if the most fleeting of all encounters had fused them together for all eternity. You could count on your fingers the shadows, not including ours, cast on the wall by the fire. It was burning only moderately as not too many customers were expected due to the weather and the lateness of the hour. The small pizzeria at that moment seemed like the last haven in the old world; offering us shelter and a last period of grace in which to decide what to do: whether to leave or stay. How many men had these walls shielded as they sat in front of the fire, agonizing over whether to leave, thinking about the most important thing that held them here. In here, before the glow of the fire, it was peaceful and quiet, no matter what disastrous tidings the newspaper hawkers would croak at us as soon as we stepped out onto the Canebière. No one would ever dare put out this fire as it warmed all these tormented people who'd managed to come as far as the Old Port. Even those who were pursuing them, no matter how much fear and terror they were spreading, were not immune to fear.

The doctor at last got hold of himself; he shook his head, saying, "See for yourself, Marie, there's nothing wrong here." He added, "There was nobody here before either." Suddenly he pointed to me, "Just him."

I felt slightly uneasy because I can't stand having someone point at me. I said, "I'd better go now."

At that Marie grabbed my hand, crying, "No, please stay! It's good that you're here."

I saw that her fear had grown less by my mere presence and that she thought I would protect her from any real or imagined danger.

VIII

I was ready now to fulfill whatever demands the officials and the consulates made; I was ready to provide them with the most ridiculous proofs of my intention to leave just so that they would let me stay.

Still grimacing from fighting the Mistral, people were crowding into the anteroom of the American Consulate. Here at least it was warm. In the last few days, bitterly cold temperatures had been adding to all the other woes of the departure obsessed. The doorman at the United States Consulate, looking as powerful as a boxer, stood behind a table loaded with files that was blocking the stairway leading to the upper floors. With one small movement of his massive chest he could have pushed the whole dry swarm of visa seekers driven here this morning by the icy wind out onto the Place St.

Ferréol. The powder lay on the women's faces, stiff from the cold, like chalk. They had spruced up not only their children and themselves, but also their men in the hope of finding favor in the doorman's eyes. From time to time he pushed the file-covered table aside with his brawny hip to free a space like the eye of a needle, through which a privileged transit visa applicant could go upstairs.

I almost didn't recognize the orchestra conductor without his sunglasses. The icy Mistral of the last few days had utterly devastated him, insofar as a Mistral can devastate a skeleton. But his hair was neatly combed and parted; he was trembling with joy. "You should have started sooner. I'll be leaving the consulate today with my transit permit." He held his elbows close to his body so that his little black tailcoat would not be damaged in the crush.

Suddenly a wave of anger spread through the waiting crowd. The woman from the hotel room next to mine had come in, wearing a colorful outfit and serenely leading the two Great Danes on tight leashes. The doorkeeper, knowing that she was acceptable to the consul, had immediately cleared the way between the table and the stairs with an impassive respectfulness as if the two Great Danes were visa guarantors bewitched by a spell. I made use of the small breach to follow the dog lady. I threw the doorkeeper my application form, Seidler, aka Weidel. The doorkeeper yelled at me, then he saw the dogs greeting me familiarly, whereupon he allowed me to go upstairs to the consulate secretarial office.

Here again there were waiting rooms. The dogs scared half a dozen little Jewish children. They squeezed against their parents and their grandmother, a yellowed, stiff-jointed woman, old enough to have been driven out of Vienna not by Hitler but by an edict of the Empress Maria Theresa. A young woman came out through one of the consulate doors to find out what all the commotion was about. She must have been floating on a little cloud as soft and pink as her face all through the war and the wholesale devastation of the world. Smiling and fluttering her wings, she led the entire family, still apprehensive and gloomy, toward the consul's desk.

Even caught up as I was in my transit permit mania and immersed in my own visa-obsession fog, I felt a pair of eyes on me. I wondered where I'd seen this man before. He'd already examined everyone else in the room and having nothing better to do for the moment, he was calmly staring at me. He was holding his hat in his hand. Then it came to me—I'd seen him yesterday at the travel bureau, but I couldn't tell then that he was almost completely bald. We didn't greet each other, merely smiled scornfully, because we both knew that, for better or for worse, we'd be seeing each other a hundred times more, that our lives were linked as fellow transit applicants, even against our wishes, our wills, even against fate. Then the little conductor appeared. There were red spots on his cheeks. His hands twitched. He was counting photographs, all the time assuring us, "I swear there were twelve of them in the hotel." The woman from the room next to mine used the time to brush her dogs.

I'm embarrassed to confess that my heart was pounding; I was scared. For a while I stopped paying any attention to the people entering the upstairs waiting room after me. They came in slowly, one by one, breathing shallowly. It doesn't matter what the consul looked like, I thought. One thing was certain, he had power over me. Even though this power was restricted to his own country. Still, if he refused to grant me an American transit visa now, I'd be branded as a failed transit applicant, indelibly marked for all the officials of the city, and for all the other consulates. I'd have to flee again, and lose my beloved even before I'd won her.

I calmed down when they called out the name Weidel. I was no longer afraid of being unmasked or of being rejected. I sensed the immeasurable, the uncrossable divide that separated the man whose name had been called out and the consul who, flesh and blood— lean flesh and thin blood—sat impassively behind his desk. I watched with interest, as if from outside myself, this ghost being conjured up—a ghost summoned to appear who had long ago fled to some shadowy, moldering, swastika-marked necropolis.

The consul arrogantly looked me up and down, the living man who stood between him and the ghost. He said, "Your name is Seidler? Yet you write your books under the name Weidel. Why?"

I said, "Writers often do that."

"What made you apply for a Mexican visa, Mr. Weidel-Seidler?"

I answered his stern question frankly, modestly. "I didn't apply for it, I just accepted the first visa that was offered to me. My situation required it."

He said, "How is it, sir, that you, as a writer, never tried to emigrate to the United States, like so many of your colleagues?"

I answered, "Where could I have applied? To whom? How? I was outside the world. The Germans had invaded! The end of days had come."

He tapped his pencil on the desk. "The Consulate of the United States was open for business on the Place de la Concorde."

"How could I have known that, sir? I no longer went to the Concorde. People like us didn't dare show themselves on the streets at that time."

He frowned. I realized that behind him the typewriters were clattering, taking down the entire interrogation. Just a bit of additional clatter in the general din, the big fear of silence.

"Mr. Seidler, how do you explain that you have been issued a Mexican visa?"

"Favorable circumstances I would assume," I replied, "and some good friends."

"Why do you say 'some'? You know you had certain friends in the former government of the former Spanish Republic and they are in some way connected with certain circles in the Mexican government today."

I thought of the poor dead man so hastily buried, of his pitiful legacy. Aloud I said, "Friends in the government? Absolutely not!"

He went on, "You performed certain services for the former Republic, worked for its information service."

I remembered the little bundle of papers at the bottom of the suitcase, the complicated story that bemused me one sad evening—how long ago had it been? I said, "I never wrote anything of the sort."

"Pardon me, but let me help you remember. There is, for example, a description of the shootings at Badajos written by you and translated into many languages."

"Of what, sir?"

"Of the mass shootings of Reds in the Badajos arena." He gave me a piercing look. Probably he thought my astonishment was due to his display of such complete knowledge. I really was quite astonished. Whatever might have motivated the dead man to write about that incident—someone else may actually have told him about it—he probably lent it some of the magic that now lay in the grave with him. His magic lamp, extinguished and broken, lay buried beside him now, a lamp that lit up for eternity anything on which he focused its beam, mostly on precarious adventures, but once also on this arena in Badajos. How stupid of the dead man to blow the lamp out himself. After all, as the old tale has it, the genie will obey the one who has the lamp. I would have given a lot to read what he wrote about that event.

I said, "I've never written anything like that either before or after."

The consul stood there and looked at me with a look that might have been called penetrating, if only it had been penetrating the right man.

He asked, "Do you have someone to vouch for you here?"

Where was I supposed to get someone who would swear to the consul that the dead man had never before or afterward written something like that, someone who would swear that my dead man would never write about any mass execution of Reds in any arena whatsoever?—The typewriters had gone silent along with the interrogation. And when the silence threatened even this room, I thought back to the beginning of this long story; I remembered Paul. I said to the consul, "Of course, my friend Paul Strobel, at the Aid Committee on the Rue Aix." The name was added to other names, the files to other files, the dossier to other dossiers, and I was given an appointment to appear January eighth.

After that exhausting interrogation I wanted nothing so much as to flee to the nearest café. I left the chambers of the consulate, walked down the stairs into the large entrance hall where I could barely make my way through the crush of people there. Dismay and shock were on all their faces. An ambulance had stopped outside the gate, and as I stepped outside, they were strapping a man on a stretcher and carrying him off. I recognized the little orchestra conductor. He was dead. People were saying, "He collapsed while he was standing in line. He was supposed to get his visa today. But the consul sent him back because he had one photo less than he was supposed to have. And so his visa date was postponed and his passage became invalid. This upset him terribly. And then when somebody helped him count his photos again, it turned out that he had miscounted because two of the photos were stuck together. So he got in line all over again, and that's when he collapsed."

IX

I watched the ambulance carry off my little conductor forever. My uneasiness passed; after all I was still young and strong. I went into the Café Saint Ferréol. It's only three minutes' walk from the American Consulate. I was now entitled to sit in the U.S.-transit applicants' café. I heard footsteps behind me. The bald transit applicant entered behind me. We sat down at adjacent tables, thereby indicating to anyone watching that although we were drinking by ourselves we might at some point want to exchange a few words. We each ordered a Cinzano. Suddenly he leaned over to me and clinked glasses with me, saying, "Let's drink to his memory! We may be the only ones even thinking of him."

"I first met the man on his arrival in Marseille," I said. "The poor guy. One visa or permit was always expiring just as he was granted the next one."

"That's what happens if you don't start with the last one. The first thing I did when I got here was to find someone who would transfer his passage on a ship to me. Only then did I start with the visa process."

I asked him whether there really were people who'd give up passage on a ship.

He said, "In my case it was a woman who lived not far from me. She was looking forward to the voyage, but then she suddenly got sick. So she gave up the race."

I said, "Oh, what sort of woman was she, what kind of illness did she have?"

For the first time, he really looked at me closely. I detected no kindness in his gray eyes, but there was something more important than kindness in them. He answered me, smiling, "Your curiosity is really astonishing. You ask a man you barely know about the unknown illness of a woman you don't know." He looked at me even more closely, and then he asked, "Is it perhaps because you're a writer? Asking all these questions only to have something to write about?"

I was taken aback. "Me?" I said. "No. That's not it at all. Certainly not!" I'd been rash with my answer. Now I couldn't take it back. Instead I added, "In any case, I made sure that I had a ship ticket."

He said, "In any case! A ticket in any case! In any case a visa! In any case a transit permit! And what if all these preventive measures go against you? What if taking all these preventive measures takes more out of you than the dangers themselves? If you get entangled in a web of precautionary measures just because of your foresight?"

"Oh, come on," I said, "you don't think I'd put too much stock in all this nonsense. It's a game just like any other. It's a gamble you take by living in this world."

He looked at me as if he didn't quite know whom he was dealing with. He turned away, making it clear to everyone that he was sitting at a separate table, even though it touched mine. His face was stern; his posture stiff. I tried in vain to figure him out. When he left the café, he forgot to say good-bye.

X

The Café Saint Ferréol was full of people; some had completed their business at the American Consulate and some were about to apply for exit visas and fortifying themselves before going to the Prefecture. I would have preferred going to the Quai des Belges where you can at least watch the harbor. And yet I sat there as if paralyzed, debating whether I should go up to the Binnets or whether I was making a pest of myself there.

Suddenly my heart began to pound even before my eyes caught sight of her. It was Marie. She came in and walked among the tables. Her sadness was contagious; it made me feel anxious. I got up as she came closer. Joylessly, she shook my hand. I said, "Come sit down here at my table. I'll order you a drink. You've got to listen to me now."

Apathetically, she sat down next to me. She asked in a tired voice, "What do you want from me?"

"Me? Nothing. I just want to know what you're looking for. You seem to be searching from morning to night, in all the streets, everywhere."

She looked at me amazed; then she said, "Why do you ask? Do you want to help me?"

"Does that seem so strange to you, an offer of help? What or whom are you looking for?"

"I'm looking for a man. One time they say he's sitting there in that café, another time they tell me he's sitting in this one. And then by the time I get there, he's already gone. But I have to find him. My life, my happiness depend on my finding him."

I suppressed a smile. Her life, her happiness. I said, "Finding a man in Marseille can't be difficult. Just a matter of hours, if it's really that important."

She said sadly, "I thought so too at first. But this man is bewitched."

"A strange man. Do you know him well?"

Her face turned even paler. "Oh yes, I know him very well. He's my husband."

I took her hand. She looked at me gravely, frowning. "If I don't find him, I can't leave. He has everything I need. He has a visa. And he's the only one who can get me a visa. He has to explain to them at the consulate that I'm his wife."

"So that you can leave with the other one, the doctor, if I understand it all correctly?"

She drew her hand back. I had spoken a bit too harshly and I regretted it immediately. She hung her head and said, "Something like that; yes, that's about it."

I took her hand again. She absentmindedly let it rest in mine. I thought that was progress. Almost to herself she said, "The bad thing is that I can't find him, and I'm keeping the other man from leaving. He's been waiting for me for a long time, all in vain so far, I mean, the other one, the doctor. He's already postponed his departure. But he can't wait much longer. It's only on my account that he's still here."

I said, "All right. You have to get the story clear first; take everything in turn. Who's been telling you that the man, your husband, is here? Who's actually seen him?"

She replied, "The staff at the consulate. He was there just a little while ago to pick up his visa. The official at the Mexican Consulate talked to him in person several times; there's no doubt about it, and the Corsican at the travel bureau too."

Why was her cool hand turning cold in my warm ones? She slid her chair closer to mine. And for a second I wished her image would vanish, would blow away in the Marseille Mistral. She would probably have let me put my arm around her at that moment, like a child moving closer to a grownup because she's afraid. But her childish, unfathomable fear was infecting me. Speaking softly, as if we were talking about forbidden things, I asked her, "When he came to Marseille, where was he coming from? Was it from the fighting? From a concentration camp?"

Just as softly she said, "No, from Paris. We were separated when the Germans came. He got stuck there. As soon as I arrived here, I sent him a letter. I met a woman I knew, the sister of a man we had known. His name was Paul Strobel. And this woman had a friend who was engaged to a French silk merchant. From time to time he went into the occupied territory on business. I begged him to deliver the letter to my husband in Paris. And he did. I know he did . . .

"What's the matter with you?" she suddenly cried. "What's wrong?"

I let go of her hand—no, that's not true. I actually flung her hand down on the table.

"Nothing's wrong with me!" I said. "What could be wrong with me? At most maybe having to wait for my Spanish transit visa. But that won't take much longer. Well, tell me more, don't stop now."

"There's nothing more to tell. That's all there is."

Without looking at her, I said, "The consuls see hundreds of faces every day. A name doesn't mean anything to them. Maybe he isn't here at all. Maybe he's still in Paris. Maybe . . ."

She raised her hand abruptly in an almost wild warning. Looking directly at me and in a changed, rough voice she said, "There is no maybe. People have seen him in many places. He was seen four times at the Mont Vertoux. The official at the Mexican Consulate saw him in the Café Roma, not just at the consulate. The Corsican saw him at the travel bureau and later in a café near the Quai du Port. It's just that I always get there too late."

"You probably put pressure on the Mexican Consulate, pestered the staff with your questions? Maybe asked them to investigate the man?"

"Oh, no. Not at all. I didn't do that. Because I realized on my very first visit there, when I saw that the address he'd left with the Mexican Consulate wasn't correct, that he'd probably come here with false papers, maybe even under a different name. And so there was no way that I could have them check on him, or ask sensitive questions, because that might spoil everything for him and consequently for me, too. Do you understand?"

I certainly *did* understand. The sadness that came over me at that point will never leave me. That was the dead man's legacy for me. I was the one to suffer.

I said, "You wanted to get a visa. But you couldn't get a visa without a husband. So you persuaded him to come here, in the hope of a new life together."

She looked at me with clear, wide-open eyes, the eyes of a child that shies away from lying, no matter what other mischief she's done.

I continued with my questioning, "And now you're in love with the doctor?"

After a moment's hesitation that I grasped at eagerly, she said, "He's a very kind person."

"Good God, Marie, I never asked you about his kindness."

For a while we said nothing. "Doesn't it seem odd to you that your husband, if he really came here, hasn't tried to look for you, hasn't moved heaven and earth to find you again?"

She clasped her hands. Softly she said, "It certainly does seem odd. More than odd. But even so, he's got to be here. There are people who've seen him. Maybe he knows that I'm here with another man. And doesn't want to see me again, doesn't care about me anymore."

I took her hand again. I tried to overcome the sadness I felt, a premonition of disaster. Once we were alone, I'd straighten it all out. But first, I had to quickly get the second man, the doctor, as far away from here as possible. And I knew better than anyone else the nature of the other man's demands on her. At least I thought so back then.

I said, "You're probably afraid of seeing him again?"

She seemed to withdraw. "Of course I'm afraid after all that's happened. Seeing each other again after such a long time is almost as difficult as saying good-bye."

"And so it would be best for you," I said, "if it could all be done on paper. In the file that's at the consulate. They would put your name on his visa. You would get a confirmation of the exit visa. I have some connections. Shall I see what can be done?"

"And what if I run into him aboard the ship—While I'm with the other man?"

"The other one has to sail by way of Oran. I'll help him arrange that."

"It will end up with my being all alone here."

"Alone? Oh, I see. Why are you afraid of being alone? Are you afraid of being sent to Bompard? Don't forget that I'll be here. I will take good care of you."

She said quite calmly, "I'm not afraid. Because if I have to stay behind by myself, I won't care whether I'll be free or imprisoned in the camp at Bompard or in some other camp. On the earth or beneath it."

As I listened to her, I pictured an utterly deserted continent devoid of human beings, the last ship having sailed, leaving her totally alone in a wilderness that would rapidly overgrow everything.

6

I

BACK THEN they were all consumed by one wish: to leave. And they were all afraid of one thing: being left behind.

They wanted to get away, to get away from this broken-down country, away from this continent! They were consumed by waiting. And to make the time fly, they resorted to gossip. As long as you were talking about departures, people would listen eagerly. They loved to talk about visas bought and sold or letters of transit and new transit countries. But more than anything else they liked to hear about ships that were seized or never reached their destinations, especially when they were ships that, for whatever reason, had left without them.

I was afraid of running into someone at the Mexican Consulate who might know me. But my heart jumped with joy when I saw Heinz among the people waiting there. I even forgot my guilty conscience. I embraced him the way Spaniards embrace each other, pressing all his shot-up, brittle bones close to me. The Spaniards waiting there gathered around us, watching our reunion and smiling with the indomitable hearts of passionate people not yet hardened by war, detention camps, or the horror of thousands of deaths.

"Oh, Heinz, I was afraid you'd gone and left me forever. I'm sorry I couldn't keep our appointment back then. Something came up, something that happens just once in a lifetime. I wouldn't have stood you up for anything less."

He looked at me as he used to do in the camp when I tried to get his attention by doing something silly. Rather coldly, he asked, "What in the world are you doing here?"

"I'm on an errand for someone. I've been looking everywhere for you the last few days—or has it been weeks. I was afraid you'd already left."

His face had grown even smaller since our first reunion. The thinner and more emaciated he got physically, the stronger and firmer his gaze, as is so often the case with people who are ill and deathly tired. Since my childhood, no one had ever looked at me so attentively. Then it occurred to me that he looked at everything and everyone with the same attentiveness, whether it was the leathery-skinned consulate doorman or the old Spaniard who had decided to get a visa even though his entire family had been killed, as if he thought of that faraway country as a realm of the blessed where one could find one's family again. Heinz gave the same attention to them as he did the round-eyed child whose father, as long as I've been here, has been incarcerated after he had already seen his ship through the pier gate, or to the *prestataire* whose beard was even longer now giving him an owlish appearance.

"You've got to leave this country, Heinz, before the trap snaps shut. Or in the end you'll be swallowed up by the Germans. Do you have a transit permit?"

"They got me a Portuguese transit. From there I go on—via Cuba."

"But how are you going to get to Portugal? You can't go through Spain!"

"I don't know yet," he said. "We'll see."

Suddenly I knew just what it was that gave him his strength. We've all been taught that God helps those who help themselves, but this man lived every moment of his existence, even the darkest, convinced that he was never alone, that wherever he was and no matter for how long, he would always find people who were like him. People who'd be there for him and that there was no poor devil, no pathetic coward, no corpse so dead that they couldn't be persuaded to listen when a human voice asked them for help.

"Please meet me at the Triads, Heinz. It's three minutes from here on the Cours d'Assas. Trust me, I can give you some good advice. And this time I promise to come. Didn't you yourself say that I'd never leave you in the lurch? Please wait there for me."

He said dryly, "You can look around the place and see if I'm sitting there."

Then it was my turn. The official looked at me with his gimlet eyes, "What?!" he said. "You want your wife included on the visa? Without special permission from my government? You think you can just take that for granted? I certainly cannot do that. Your wife doesn't use your name. Why didn't you enter her name at the proper time on the line that asks for: 'Persons accompanying visa applicant'? Your wife is certainly quite lovely; I had the pleasure of meeting her. But nothing can be taken for granted. Sometimes one has to be parted even from the loveliest of women. Indeed, the Pope has annulled some marriages. I'm not pleased about this new complication, my friend. You will have to wait."

"Do you know how long I'll have to wait for the new visa confirmation?"

"Remember how long the first one took, and make arrangements accordingly." He gazed at me with a new craftiness. And yet precisely because he was trying so hard to penetrate my motives, I felt a renewed confidence in my own cleverness.

I said, "Please, I beg you, even though it's late, enter my wife's name where it asks for 'Persons accompanying the visa applicant.'"

It wouldn't hurt anyone, I thought as I was crossing the Cours d'Assas. Nobody would care whether the two of us escaped from this place or whether we stayed. The delay would actually be good for me, a grace period in which I could straighten things out. I was already reckoning in consulate time, a kind of planetary time in which you equate earthly days with millions of years because worlds can burn in the time it takes a transit visa to expire. I also found myself starting to take my dreams seriously—hadn't they been casting shadows on the white pages of my file, my dossier? Whatever seriousness I had before—and it wasn't much—had almost vanished in the face of all the sleight-of-hand and the countless tricks you had to use in this world just to stay alive, to retain your freedom.

Heinz was sitting at the same table where I'd sat with the Binnet boy the day I first went to the newly opened Mexican Consulate. I joined him. From where I sat I could see the people waiting outside the consulate. They were struggling with two policemen who wanted to push them out of a narrow rectangle of wintry sunshine into the shade.

Heinz asked me what advice I was selling. Apparently, he'd already seen through everything. If he looked at me just a little bit longer, a little more carefully, he'd manage to decipher all of it.—What all my visits to the Mexican Consulate were about, why I wanted to see Marie's friend the doctor as far away from here as possible, and how much I hated having the doctor hanging around. And he'd also see why I wanted to help him, Heinz, more than any other person, more even than myself. Yet I knew only too well that to him I was only one of the many people to whom he had to turn if his journey were to succeed. Still I wanted to be helpful, and would always be proud of having been one of those who had helped in his rescue.

So, almost against my will, I started to tell him about the load of copper wire, about the passage on the boat going to Oran that I had intended for an acquaintance of mine, but would rather pass along to him, to Heinz. He said he'd certainly give this some thought. He asked me to meet him that evening at an inn fairly far from here in Beaumont. As long as we were sitting together I was under his spell. But as soon he left, I realized that I didn't matter to him, that he never considered me one of his own kind, never thought very much of me. That made me angry, and I began to wonder why I was suddenly so intent on helping him even though it thwarted my own plans.

II

That evening, at the little café in the Old Port they asked me if I had made up with my wife. I said I had. They asked whether she'd be coming to join me. I said no, not this evening. We had made up, our days of chasing each other were over, and she was calmly waiting for me at home.

Bombello was there again and asked me whether the ship's passage was for myself. He said that as a matter of principle he filled such requests only for people he had seen and looked over in person. In spite of this laudable cautiousness of his, he had of course no inkling of the passenger swap that was taking place right under his nose, since he'd never laid eyes on the doctor. To be honest, he always treated people fairly within the limits of his profession. He never lied to anyone about facts, and once a price was arrived at he had never invented reasons to raise it. He now looked at me, blinking hard. It was a tic that had stayed with him from a time when something had gone wrong. With a taxi I took him and the Portuguese up to Beaumont. I saw right away that both of them were satisfied with their new customer. And I was amazed and envious that even these two men felt good to have Heinz speak with them so seriously and courteously. How much we all appreciate being taken seriously! Still, it's just one of Heinz's tricks, I thought, a stunt. He probably puts me on the same level as these two, maybe just a notch, or half a notch above them.

Later, after another meeting had been arranged, Heinz and I put the two men into a taxi and sent them back to their own café. Heinz invited me to stay for a supper of rice and Fioli sausage. They also served us wine. The place was almost empty in the winter. Situated on a remote road near the edge of the hills, it seemed forsaken despite being quite close to the big city. I found myself drinking a lot, and suddenly felt angry and exasperated. I sensed that Heinz was bored with me. Why had I done all this for him when he didn't really care about me or even enjoy my company, and would never see me again? I kept drinking. Parts of my life seemed quite clear; other parts were obscured by a gentle reddish-black rosé fog.

"You're leaving again, Heinz. I always thought, if we ever lived in the same city, we'd have so much to talk about and that I'd have all sorts of things to ask you. Now the evening's almost over, and I don't even remember what those urgent questions were that I wanted to ask. Our time in the same city is coming to an end and I haven't asked you about anything."

"But you helped me."

"And that's precisely why you're leaving now. You're lucky, you're not like me; you have a goal, a purpose."

"You could certainly find a way to leave, too."

"That's not the sort of goal I'm talking about. Sure, I can arrange that sort of goal for myself, a destination and passage on a ship; I can get myself visas for God knows what countries. Transit visas, exit visas—I'm your man for that. But what good is all that when it doesn't matter to me where I go, that almost nothing matters to me?"

"Still, you helped me."

"When I sit here with you, I can see you have something positive and definite in you and ahead of you, something firm that will never be broken, even if you yourself should be physically broken. I can see it in your eyes, Heinz, and it seems to me that I have a part in that, too. You probably don't understand a word I'm saying . . . because you can't imagine what it's like to be so utterly empty."

We listened to the wind, which sounded much the same up here as it used to back home in the mountains. Heinz said, "I can well imagine it. There is nothing I haven't already lived through. I know what it is to feel empty. I used to be big and strong like you. The first time I got up on my crutches and tried to walk through a door—the sun was shining through that door at me, evil and glaring—I saw my shadow, my chopped off shadow, and I felt really empty. I'm probably the same age as you. I feel that I must still have a vast amount of time ahead of me, time enough to go back home and be there when everything changes. Deep down I ask myself: How can it all change without me, when I sacrificed everything—my bones, my blood, my youth—so that it could happen? But common sense tells me that I have only a few years left to live, maybe just a few months." He looked at me, not the way he usually did, but indirectly, pensively, with the look of a man who needs help. It made me like him even more.

III

I saw the doctor again at Binnet's apartment. When I told him that his passage to Oran wouldn't work out after all, he took the news pretty calmly. He said, "At the Transports Maritimes they assured me that there'd be another ship leaving for Martinique next month. I had them book me on it. That's a lot safer than sailing via Oran, and in any case the difference in the time of departure isn't that much."

So, I thought, here I've been running around on your behalf, and all the time you had your own backup plan.

He continued, "Marie told me that you wanted to help her. Maybe you'll be able to do better for her."

"I doubt that her visa will come through before you leave," I said. "And even if it does, just think of all the things that would still have to be arranged: posting a bond, the exit visa, the transit permit."

He suddenly gave me such a piercing look that I had no chance to change my expression. Calmly he said, "I'd like to explain something to you, once and for all. I drove Marie in my trusty, shabby, little car through the fighting and out of the war. What's left of my car is probably still lying in the same roadside ditch where I left it five hours this side of the Loire. We got here safely. We could have gone farther. We could have escaped to Africa; there were still ships sailing to Casablanca back then. One could still book a passage. Everybody could still escape. But Marie began to waver. Up to that point she had followed me, then suddenly she began to hang back. The ships all left, one after another. I couldn't get her to board one. Even though she'd followed me from Paris all through France to this city, I couldn't get her to board one of the ships. And back then you didn't need a visa yet, or a transit permit; you just jumped on a ship and sailed. Marie kept making excuses; and meanwhile the ships all left. I threatened to leave without her. I wanted to force her to make a decision. But she refused, continued to hesitate. And it's Marie's fault entirely that I can't wait any longer now. I'd like you to understand the situation."

"You don't owe me an explanation about your feelings."

"Not about mine, certainly. But I want to warn you that Marie will continue to hesitate. Even if she suddenly decided to stay, even then she would secretly be wavering. And she'll never be able to make the decision to stay. She'll never make any definite decision before she sees her husband again—and he may already be dead."

I said, "Who told you he's dead?"

"Me? Nobody! I said, *may* be dead."

I became quite upset. "Don't count on it! The man could come back. He may already be in town. Anything is possible in wartime."

Looking at me calmly, his long face expressionless, he said, "You're forgetting one small detail. Marie, after all, chose to come with me while her husband was still alive."

Yes, it was true. I had to admit it was true. And it couldn't have hurt the dead man more than it hurt me. War had spread across the land; death had also touched her, and she had been gripped by fear. Perhaps only for one day, but by then it was already too late. That one day had separated her for eternity from her husband.

But what did I care about her husband? I was rid of him; that was all. And even if he were to come back to life, I still would have wanted nothing more than to be rid of him. Compared to him, I thought, this fellow sitting in front of me is just a pale shadow. Why does she want to follow him? Why is she leaving me in the lurch?

In a changed tone of voice, as if he wanted to distract or to reassure me, the doctor said, "From what you've said, I can tell what you think about this transit existence, this visa dance, all this consulate hocus-pocus. I'm afraid, my friend, you're taking this all too lightly. In any case I take it more seriously. If there is a higher order governing this world—it doesn't necessarily have to be a divine order, just a higher order, a higher law—then it would surely exert some influence on this stupid system of dossiers. You'd be sure of your goal, whether you go by way of Cuba, Oran, or Martinique; it wouldn't make any difference. You'd be certain of the brevity and uniqueness of life, whether it's measured in lunar years, in solar years, or by transit deadlines."

"Given all these lofty ideas of yours, I wonder why you flounder around so much, and what you're afraid of."

"That's quite simple. I'm afraid of death. A mean, senseless death under the boots of the SA."

"And you see, I'm convinced that I'm one of those who'll survive it all."

"Oh yes, I realize you're completely lacking in imagination when it comes to your own death. If I'm not mistaken, my friend, you'd like to have two lives; and since you can't have them one after the other, then two lives side-by-side, running on parallel tracks. It can't be done."

I was appalled. "Wherever did you get that notion?"

He replied casually, "Good Lord, you show all the symptoms. Your exaggerated absorption in strangers' lives, your amazing desire to step in and help, which certainly deserves our gratitude. But I tell you, it can't be done. You cannot do it. Moreover, if there really is no higher order, if it's all a matter of fate, blind fate, then it really doesn't matter whether your fate is pronounced by some consul, by the oracle at Delphi, by the stars, or whether you read it in the countless coincidences of your life, mostly incorrectly, mostly with bias."

I was about to ask him to stop his chatter, when he stood up of his own accord, bowed to Claudine, and left. All during this conversation we'd been sitting in Claudine's kitchen at her tiny kitchen table covered by a blue-checkered oilcloth. She had followed our words closely, even though we were speaking German. It was as if our incomprehensible words were being communicated to her in some other way. She was knitting, and her long-fingered hands, dark on the outside and pink inside, moving with the needles, reminded me of slender leaves fluttering in a breeze.

I must have sat there silently for a long time after the doctor left. Claudine asked, "What's the matter with you? You've changed in the last few weeks. You're not the same man you were when you first came here. Do you still remember that time? I threw you out. I was so very tired, and I needed to cook dinner for the next day. Something's wrong . . . I can tell . . . don't deny it. What is it? Why do you keep following the doctor around, getting involved in his asinine departure plans? That man is not the right kind of friend for you. He's a stranger, a foreigner."

"I'm a stranger, too."

"But not to us. To us you're no stranger. This doctor may be a good man. He cured my son. But he's still a stranger to us."

"Aren't you yourself a stranger here, Claudine?"

"You're forgetting that I came to Marseille intending to stay. For you this city is just a place of departure; for me it was a place of arrival. It was my destination, just as those other cities over there, across the ocean, are for you people. And now I am here."

"Why did you leave home?"

"That's something you wouldn't understand. What do you know about a woman who boards a ship with her child in a shawl because there's no room for her at home? Because they're hiring all sorts of people for the farms, the factories, for things she doesn't know anything about. And then you people come along with your cold eyes! You who take so long to do something that for us is settled in an instant. And who arrange in the blink of an eye something that takes us a lifetime. Besides, you're only asking me questions now to keep me from asking you about yourself. Have you stopped seeing Nadine? Do you have another girlfriend? Is she causing you grief?"

"Let's not talk about me. Tell me, Claudine, don't you ever feel like going home again?"

"Maybe, once my son is a teacher, or a doctor. Not now, not by myself. A leaf blowing in the wind would have an easier time finding its old twig again. I want to stay with George and with my boy as long as I can."

She wasn't fooling herself about the fragility of these four walls of hers. And maybe for that very reason they might turn out to be that much more stable and long lasting. In any case, I felt more strongly than ever that this was a real home. It probably all began with George's desire to touch her stranger's hand. George, who'd been transplanted to this city in the south by the stupid evacuation of his factory. Why is it that men like George always seem to find themselves surrounded by four walls, whereas nothing ever has any effect on me—neither happy nor painful? In the end I'm always left behind, alone. Unhurt, it's true, but nevertheless alone.

IV

I went to the Brûleurs des Loups and sat down. The people around me were all terribly agitated because a car marked with swastikas had been seen racing down the Canebière around noon. It was probably carrying members of a commission negotiating with the Spanish, Italian, and Vichy representatives in one of the big hotels. The people in the café were acting as if the devil himself had come rattling down the avenue bent on corralling his lost flock inside a barbed-wire enclosure. I think they were almost ready to walk into the sea because no more ships were scheduled to leave for the time being.

Marie came in quietly. I saw her reflection in one of the mirrors that covered the café walls as if to multiply the chaotic confusion of distorted faces. I watched tensely as she searched, going from one table to another, looking at all the faces. I waited breathlessly for her to come over to my table, the only person who knew that her search was futile. Suddenly I felt I had to put an end to this search of hers, once and for all. I sensed beforehand the devastation that I would cause with those four words of the cursed truth.

Just then she saw me; her pale face flushed red and her gray eyes glowed with a warm, gentle light. She said, "I've been looking for you for days."

I promptly forgot my resolution. I took her hands. Her small face represented the only place on earth where there was still some peace for me. And yes, peace and quiet at once descended on my hounded heart; it was as though we were sitting together in a meadow in our homeland and not in this crazy harbor café whose walls mirrored the floundering and dread of the refugees sitting there.

"Where did you disappear to?" she asked. "Don't tell me you still haven't had an answer from your friends at the consulates."

My joy evaporated. So that's why she's been looking for me! I thought. The same reason that lay behind her search for the dead man. I said, "No. I won't get an answer that quickly."

She sighed. I couldn't read the expression on her face. It almost looked like relief. She said, "Let's just sit here together quietly for a while. Let's pretend there aren't any more departures, no ships, no good-byes."

I was a pushover for a game like that. We sat there together for perhaps an hour, silent and peaceful, as if later on we'd still have an endless amount of time to talk, as if nothing could ever separate us. At least that's how I felt. I wasn't even surprised at how submissively she let me hold her hand, as if it were the most natural thing in the world—or, that it was utterly irrelevant to her who was holding it. Suddenly she jumped up. It startled me. Her expression was that strange, vague, and somewhat scornful one she always had when she thought of the doctor. I could already sense the wild chase, the turmoil that would overwhelm me once she left.

Yet I remained pretty calm even after that. We're both still in the same city, I thought, still sleeping under the same bit of sky; anything is still possible.

V

As I was walking home on the Cours Belsunce, someone in the glassed-in terrace of the Café Rotonde called out my old name.

It gave me a start, as it does every time someone uses my real name. But this time I felt reassured because most of the people here run around using all sorts of names, even if sometimes it's just their old name translated into another language. At first the group of people waving to me looked like strangers. Then I saw that they were waving because Paul was waving. I hadn't seen him at first. His head peered out from behind the shoulder of a girl sitting on his lap. It may have been this improbable and amazing sight—Paul with a girl on his knees—that made me speechless. Paul had taken advantage of it's being an alcohol day, and his heavy brown eyes sparkled. He kept pushing his thin bespectacled nose into the girl's neck. She had long, lovely legs and a pretty little face, and she seemed quite content with his display of affection. With each peck of his beak she probably thought that Paul was a powerful man, persecuted, yes, but powerful. Paul waved to me with his free hand, the one not holding the pretty girl. I hesitated. But the others at the table kept waving to me just because Paul was waving. "My old fellow *prestataire*," Paul called out, "now he's Francesco Weidel's pistolero." The others had gotten tired of waving and were staring at me. I went over and sat down with them even though I felt like a stranger at their table.

In addition to Paul and the girl on his lap, there were five others. A short, stout man with a double chin and his equally short and plump wife who wore a feather in her hat. There was a young woman of such beauty I had to look twice to make sure she was real—soft neck, golden hair, and long eyelashes. I even had a strange sensation that she wasn't actually there, but a vapor in the air. She sat completely motionless. Then there was a pencil-thin but tough-looking girl with a large insolent mouth. She was most certainly there and not a vapor. She continued to look me up and down out of the corners of her eyes, her head leaning against the arm of her boyfriend. He was an exceptionally handsome, tall, and erect fellow with a thin-lipped arrogant smile who paid no attention to me. He was a total stranger to me, yet he seemed familiar, though I had no idea why he should.

Paul said, "You remember Achselroth, don't you?"

I looked at him more closely. And yes, it was Achselroth. But hadn't Paul told me that he'd already left on a ship for Cuba? I shook his hand. His elegant civilian clothes seemed as much a disguise on him as had his *prestataire* rags in the camp. I remembered what Paul had told me before about Achselroth's betrayal, how he had left them in the lurch at the crossroads, back then when they were escaping. Apparently Paul had forgotten it all. And hadn't I, too, put it all behind me with a handshake?

Achselroth said, "I hear you met Weidel. So he did eventually get here. Lucky thing I didn't throw my lot in with you. Because wherever I go I bump into people who're sore at me because I behaved in an un-Christian way toward them. And Weidel always knew better than anyone else how to hold a grudge. I met him recently at the Mont Vertoux..."

"You saw Weidel?" I cried.

He turned to the others, "Look, he's already afraid that his master has forgiven and forgotten." Then, turning to me, "Oh no, on the contrary, he was still sore. He was crouched behind his newspaper to make sure I wouldn't see him. You know, of course, that Weidel always hides behind a newspaper so that nobody will talk to him. He makes little pinholes in the paper so he can watch the goings-on from behind his paper. He likes watching what people are doing. The material things that go on, plot twists in the old style, the big, ugly tale."

The stout man with the double chin mumbled, "A great magician—using the same old trick."

I'd been staring too steadily at Achselroth. When he frowned, I quickly turned my eyes to the gentle, angelic, lovely face of the golden-haired girl. Paul whispered to me, "She was Achselroth's girlfriend until a little while ago. He told her he was fed up with playing his half of the most beautiful couple on the Côte d'Azur."

Achselroth went on, "Anyway, in this case the ugly tale goes like this: You remember when we were escaping from the camp, don't you, Paul? The crossroads where I went on without you? *J'éspère que cela ne te fair plus du mauvais sang*—I hope there's no bad blood between us on account of that?"

"Well, anyway now we're together here in the same place," Paul said. Apparently he thought that was all that mattered.

"I had a big head start on the Germans," Achselroth continued. "I arrived in Paris before Hitler. I unlocked my apartment in Passy, I took my money, valuables, and manuscripts, some pieces of art, and got in touch with this dear couple," he pointed at the feathered lady and the man with the double chin, who both nodded seriously, "and this lady," he said pointing at the golden-haired girl who remained immobile and unconcerned as if the slightest movement might smudge her ethereal beauty. "Then this fellow Weidel turns up. He'd probably been running all around Paris looking for friends. He was pale and trembling. He was completely unnerved by the approach of the Nazis. And since there was still some room in our car, I promised he could come with us, that I'd pick him up an hour later. But, as it turned out, this lady's baggage took up considerable room, for she needed her costumes and clothes professionally. She simply couldn't live without her suitcases, and back then I couldn't live without her, so we had to leave without Weidel."

"Weidel always had a lot of controversial material stuffed in his pockets," Paul said. "Our committee has been busy for weeks with him. You could form a separate committee just to consider his case. We could only halfheartedly vouch for him at the United States Consulate. He'd gotten involved back then in some affair."

"What affair?" the man with the double chin asked.

"Oh, four years ago," Paul said. "The Spanish Civil War. Some brigade major came to see him and told him these horror stories. And Weidel, poor fellow, was impressed by what the man told him. And since he goes in for absurd atrocity stories of blood and horror, the outcome was a novella à la Weidel about a mass shooting in an arena before an inquisition court. The Spanish press office distributed the novella. I warned him back then not to get involved with those people. But he said that the story fascinated him."

"Oh, so that's why he got the Mexican visa," Achselroth said. "In any case, I'm glad that I won't have to be seeing his offended face in the next few years."

"Don't count your blessings prematurely," Paul said. "He'll probably get an American transit visa through our sponsorship. Maybe you'll be sailing on the same ship."

I asked Achselroth, "Why haven't you left yet? Didn't you get here weeks before us?"

He turned abruptly toward me and looked at me as if he suspected I might be making fun of him. The others stared at me, and then they all burst out laughing.

Paul said, "You're probably the only man in Marseille who doesn't know that story. I can introduce you to a whole bunch of people who've already been to Cuba." The man with the double chin nodded sadly, causing a third chin to form.

The woman with the feather moved closer to me. "In Paris, Mr. Achselroth put us all into his car along with this lady and her suitcases, so that there was no room for Mr. Weidel. But Mr. Achselroth needed us, and so there was room for us. We're writing the music for his play. He drove like the devil himself to stay ahead of the Germans. And so he saved us along with the music for his play. Nobody got here faster than we did. And he bought the visas for us that first week already. We were the first to go, but, sad to say, he was cheated. The visas were forgeries, and when we got to Cuba they didn't let us land. We had to turn around and go back on the same ship."

I thought how remarkably unbecoming what we call bad luck was to Achselroth. He seemed to be created for good luck, to be gilded with luck. He grimaced and said, "We've learned how to live dangerously. The music for the play is going to be written in the Western Hemisphere. All in good time. Now we have reservations to sail from Lisbon, all right and proper. We have friends among the consuls. The transit visas for Spain and Portugal are in our pockets. We can leave this place any time." He pointed to the lovely young woman, who started slightly, but then at once went back to her dazzling immobility. "On the other hand, I profited from the enforced return—my imagination was liberated from certain notions. There's an old superstition about sharing a common fate and that it results in what they call loyalty. If the Cuban authorities had been more humane I would have gone on believing that this young lady was still mine simply because she and I had shared an exciting time in my life. But then I had the rare opportunity of being forced to return to my starting point. I revised my documents and my feelings as well. And the ghost of loyalty vanished."

I looked again at the young woman and wouldn't have been surprised if she really were a pure figment of Achselroth's imagination that had become superfluous and flown off over the Belsunce.

I felt slightly uncomfortable as if I, a very ordinary fellow, had suddenly got involved with a company of magicians. As I was about to leave, the man with the double chin stopped me. He took me aside. "I'm glad I met you. I think highly of Mr. Weidel. He is very talented. I've been worried about him for quite a while, and I'm glad to know he's not in danger anymore. Back then when we drove off without him, I reproached myself for not having volunteered to stay and let him go in my place. He deserved it. Naturally I was too weak. And then when we were so unlucky with our trip to Cuba and had to come back here, it seemed to me that it was punishment for my weakness, for my excessive haste."

"Please don't worry. Biblical punishments like that are no longer being doled out nowadays. If they were, most of us would have to be sent back." I looked at him and realized that the fat that buried his eyes and formed the folds under his chin concealed his true features.

He put some paper money into my hand and said, "Weidel was always poor. He can use this. Please try to help him. He never knew how to make money."

VI

The next morning I got up early. I'd promised Claudine to get in line for sardines outside a little shop on the Rue de Tournon before it opened. Yet even at that early hour there were already quite a few women outside the closed shop. They were wrapped in shawls and capes because it was windy and cold. Although you could already see a bit of sunlight on the highest roofs, the street between the tall houses lay in heavy, ages-old shadow.

The women were too tired and stiff to complain. They were bent on getting their sardines. Just as animals lurk at a hole in the ground expecting something edible to pop out, they were watching the shop door, all their attention focused on capturing a few cans of sardines. They were much too tired to wonder why they had to stand in line so early in the morning for something that had once been so plentiful in their country, or what had happened to all their country's abundant surpluses. Finally the door was unlocked. The line moved slowly forward into the shop, as behind us the line grew longer. It now stretched almost to the Belsunce. I thought of my mother back in Germany who, in the early dawn, had probably also joined some line outside some store in her city for a couple of bones or a few grams of lard. Lines like this were now waiting outside countless shop doors in all the cities of the continent. If you put them end to end they'd probably stretch from Paris to Moscow, from Marseille to Oslo.

Suddenly, on the other side of the street, I saw Marie in her hooded cape coming from the Boulevard d'Athènes. She was pale from the cold. I called to her. There was a glint of happiness on her face as she came toward me. I thought if she were to stay with me now things would turn out well. And she did come over, and she stood next to me, so that the women wouldn't be afraid she had cut into line ahead of them.

She asked me, "What are they selling here?"

"Canned sardines. I need them for the sick boy for whom I came to get your friend back then."

She stepped from one foot to the other. The women behind me started to grumble. I quickly turned around and assured them that only I was on line. But they jealously watched to make sure Marie would not get into the line ahead of them instead of going to the end.

I asked Marie why she was walking about here so early in the morning.

"Going to the travel bureau and the shipping companies."

I figured she was setting out early on her daily search, though she'd actually stopped right at the beginning of it, stopped next to me, postponing her rounds for my sake. I would gradually have to get her used to looking for me. The people behind us were getting restless, craning their necks to see.

Marie said, "I'm afraid I have to keep going."

"There are only six people ahead of us, Marie. It'll be my turn soon. Then I can go with you."

The women again became restless, while letting a pregnant woman go ahead of them. In back of me they were talking about a woman who had once gotten ahead in the line by stuffing a pillow under her jacket. But the woman today was without any doubt carrying a new life under her woolen dress. Her face was stiff from the cold, but even so her expression changed from one of fear at coming too late to one of hope, a hope for more than just a can of fish. A look of patience now replaced the despair in her dull face.

"Look, people are getting in line ahead of us," Marie said. "I have to leave now."

Why don't I go with her, I thought. Why don't I just tell Claudine that the store was closed? Why do I keep waiting here in the cold?

VII

I had invited Marie to join me in a small café on the Boulevard d'Athènes. She didn't keep me waiting long, but even those few moments were filled with mindless despair. So it was like a miracle to see her come in and head straight for me. She threw off her wet cape and sat down next to me. "How's everything? Did you get anything done?"

I said, "I got quite a few things accomplished. But you mustn't interfere, it will only confuse matters. They'll call you at the right time. At that point they'll want nothing more from you than your signature."

She moved back a bit, cupping her chin in her hand so as to get a better look at me. She said, "All along, I thought a stranger was helping me whenever I didn't know where to turn. Some man I didn't know. And suddenly the stranger turns up, and it's you."

She lightly touched my hand in thanks. But today she seemed, aside from our mutual undertaking, much more distant, less frank, less affectionate.

She went on, "How long do you think it will take? Days? Weeks? Will it all be arranged in time? My friend wants to leave, you know. To leave soon."

I said, "He'll have to wait a little longer. I'm afraid that the passage on the ship I told him about won't work out. He'll have to be patient a bit longer. The three of us will have to make do here a little longer."

A shadow touched her face. "The three of us? Who's the third person?"

I said, "Me, of course."

She looked out the window at the people who were coming from the upper train station down to the Boulevard d'Athènes, weighed down with luggage. Soon some of them with children, suitcases, and bags came into our café. Marie said, "A train just arrived. So many people are still coming here from all parts of the country. From camps, hospitals, from the war. Look at that girl there with the bandaged head."

We moved closer together to make room for the new arrivals, a gloomy-faced woman, her two half-grown sons, and a girl with her head bandaged, younger, but too big for the wicker baby carriage she was in.

Marie wrung her hands in what seemed to me despair. But her voice was calm, she said, "What if I'm summoned to the consulate and I find my husband's there! What if they summoned him, too, and he's standing there. What then?"

I said, "Don't worry. He won't be there. They don't need him. We don't need him."

She said, "They don't need him. We may not need him. But he could be there just by coincidence. After all, it was coincidence that brought us together, you and me. And I met *him* for the first time, too, by chance, and the other one, the doctor, also. That was pure coincidence."

I didn't know why this business with coincidence and chance was so important to her. I didn't like it. It also occurred to me that I'd once had similar thoughts, similar to what she was talking about, but that I'd stopped thinking them because I didn't like them. I said, "He won't be there, not by coincidence and not because the consul summoned him. You needn't be afraid of that." I took hold of her hands; they were still intertwined and only relaxed once I held them in mine. The only thing that bothered me now was the way the newly arrived woman was staring at us. Like all people whose lives have been turned upside down and disrupted, she looked at any sign of love with suspicion.

VIII

I was now meeting Marie every day. Sometimes we agreed when and where to meet and sometimes we met accidentally. Now and then she would admit that she'd been looking for me in the cafés. She no longer searched for the dead man. I would put my hand on the table because I knew that her hand would take mine. She would sit close to me. I felt as if my luck had changed for the better.

With her head against my shoulder she would watch the people being disgorged by the revolving door as if it were a mill that was grinding them, body and soul, dozens of times daily. I knew many of them; she knew others, and sometimes we told each other what we knew about their lives as transit-visa seekers. Marie said, "We're part of them too." I wanted to say that I wasn't, but at that time I sometimes still thought I might leave with her. To stay here with her? Or to leave with her? The thoughts alternated in my mind.

Marie said, "A day seems so long. And all these slow days suddenly add up to a lot of time. I don't think my husband is in Marseille anymore. There's no use my searching for him. We may be passing by each other without even being aware of it. Maybe he's staying somewhere outside the city, by the sea, in a village. Maybe he only comes to town now and then. I'll wait for him to find me."

I said, "You'll get your visa without him, too. I'm quite sure of that."

"And when I do? What then?"

"Then once you have your visa you'll get a transit visa, and once you have that you'll get an exit visa. That's the way it works."

She said nothing. Her hand in mine, her head against my shoulder. A moment before, her expression had been happy, now it was gloomy as she watched the faces of the people going past.

Suddenly I became suspicious—was she putting her hand in mine now and looking for me just so that I would get her the damned visa, so that she could leave with the other man, the doctor? Hadn't she tried to persuade Weidel to join her just so that she could leave with the doctor? I looked at her suspiciously out of the corner of my eyes. I saw the shadow her thick eyelashes cast on her pale cheeks. I realized I didn't care about any of that. I was alive, and she was sitting next to me. I asked her, "Where are you from?"

I was happy to see the sadness leave her face, as if she was remembering something pleasant. She smiled and said, "I'm from Limburg on the Lahn."

"Who were your parents?"

"Why do you say 'were'? I hope they're both still alive. I'm sure they're still living in the same house on the same street. It's the young people like us who are dying now. I think my parents haven't been apart for a single day since they were married. But as a child I felt uneasy and anxious in the midst of my family in those low-ceilinged rooms. And their chatter went on and on, gentle and thin like the little fountain outside the window. I wanted to be elsewhere, far away from there...Can you understand that? In the fall the grapevines on the walls of our yard were red; in the spring the lilacs and hawthorn bloomed."

I said, "And they're still there."

"And there was meadow cress growing by the brook..."

"Wouldn't you like to go back?"

"Go back? No one's ever suggested that to me. And it's not really bad advice...but..."

"Yes, but..." I repeated Claudine's words, "a leaf in the wind would have an easier time finding its old twig again."

She said almost to herself, "A person isn't a leaf. A person can go wherever she wants to. And she can also go back where she came from."

Her answer moved me. It was as if a child had given a wise reply to a stupid suggestion. "How did you meet Weidel anyway?"

Her face darkened. I regretted having asked her.

Then, smiling faintly, she said, "I was visiting relatives in Cologne. One day I was sitting on a bench on the Hansa Ring. And Weidel came along and sat down next to me, in the sun. We started to talk. No one had ever spoken to me the way he did. People like that never came to see us. I forgot all about his grumpy face. I ignored his being so short. I think I surprised him, too. He had always lived by himself. After that we met often. I was proud to be with a man like him, so intelligent, so mature. One day he told me that he had to leave. He couldn't stand Germany any more. This was in the early Hitler years. My father didn't like Hitler either, but still he wasn't ready to leave his homeland because of him. I asked Weidel where he was going. He said, 'Far away and for a long time.' I said, 'I'd like to see foreign lands too sometime.' He asked me whether I'd like to go with him, the way you ask a child, just for fun. I said, 'Yes.' Again, just for fun. He said, 'Good. We'll leave this evening.'

"That evening I was standing at the train station. I was so scared when I saw his face that I started to tremble. He stared at me and I stared back. You have to understand, he had almost always been alone. And he wasn't particularly good-looking either. He was almost ugly, unattractive. And I was so very young. You see, he probably wasn't the sort of man who's easy to love, who's used to having someone love him. But he stood there and thought about it a moment, and then he said, 'All right. You can come along.'

"How simply it all started. For me it was the easiest thing in the world. But how complicated it all got, how mixed up. Who knows why or how. We went south. We stopped at Lake Constance. He showed me everything. Taught me things. And then at last, one day I was tired of learning things. And he was used to being by himself. We moved around to all sorts of cities. We arrived in Paris. He often asked me to leave the apartment. We were poor. We had just one single room. And so I walked through the city, up one street and down another, just so that he could be alone."

Her expression changed abruptly. She turned pale. She was staring at the idle, aimless stream of people on the other side of the window. She cried, "There he is!" I grabbed her shoulder. With a wild tug she freed herself. I saw now whom she had seen: a short, gray, rather fat man with a sullen face who was just then entering the Mont Vertoux. He looked angrily at Marie. He gave me a churlish look, too. I grabbed Marie, more firmly this time and shook her, forcing her back on her chair.

"Stop this nonsense!" I said. "That man is a Frenchman. Just take a closer look! He's wearing the ribbon of the Legion of Honor."

The man stood still, and his expression suddenly changed. He smiled.

His smile told Marie more than the little red ribbon. She said, "Let's get away from here."

We left and walked through a maze of streets down to the Old Port. But this time we were together, the two of us, my arm around her shoulders. I asked, "Did that man really look like your husband?"

"A little—at first."

We kept walking as if we were under a curse that wouldn't let us rest. Marie was the one who'd been cursed, but I didn't leave her alone. We passed a house in a narrow alley lined by tall buildings. The door of the house was draped with black and silvery-bronze fabric because death had entered there that day. Now, at night, it looked like the portal of a dark, gloomy palace. We walked to the end of the alley; it led to the stairway that went up to the sea. We climbed the stairs; I never let go of Marie's hand. We could see the moon and stars in the sky. Her eyes were full of light. She looked out at the sea. Her face reflected a thought she would never reveal to me, maybe she had never expressed it at all. And for me there was a hateful correlation at that moment between that inaccessible thought and the equally hated and inaccessible sea.

She turned away. We went back down the steps in silence. After

walking around some more, we finally landed at the pizzeria. How
relieved I was to see the open fire! How it put the color back into her
face!

IX

We'd already had quite a bit of rosé by the time the doctor came in.
Marie hadn't told me that she'd made an appointment to meet him
at the pizzeria. I wanted to leave, but they both asked me to stay with
such urgency that I felt they were glad not to be alone together. The
doctor asked me as he always did, "How are things going with Marie's visa? Do you think it will work out?"

As every other time, I said, "It will work out," adding, "if you'll
only let me take care of it. Any meddling can ruin the soup."

"The *Paul Lemerle* is probably going to sail this month. I've just
been at the Transports Maritimes," the doctor said.

"Listen, love," Marie suddenly said in a light-hearted, clear voice
—(she'd probably had three glasses of rosé by then) "if you knew for
sure that I would never get a visa, would you leave on the *Paul Lemerle*?"

"Yes, my dear," he said. He hadn't yet touched his first glass of
wine. "This time if I knew that, I would leave."

"And leave me alone here?"

"Yes, Marie."

"Even though you said that I'm your happiness, your great love?"
Marie sounded a bit insistent now but quite cheerful.

"I always told you that there's something more important for me
than my happiness, than my great love."

I was angry now. I said, "Please drink your wine. Have a few
drinks to catch up with us so that you can talk sense!"

"No, on the contrary!" Marie said, still in the same cheerful,
stubbornly insistent voice. "Don't drink anything yet. First tell me
exactly how many ships you'd allow to sail without you for my
sake."

"At most the *Paul Lemerle*. But don't depend on that either. I'll be thinking it over very carefully."

Marie turned to me, "Did you hear that? If you really want to help me, you have to do it quickly."

"You see?" said the doctor. "Marie has decided to leave now; it's definite. Please help us, my friend. The Germans might occupy the Rhône estuary any day, and then the trap would snap shut."

"That's all nonsense," I said. "That has nothing to do with your departure. What matters is what you think is the decisive factor for your departure. We'll know after you've left what the real deciding factor was—whether it was fear, love, or loyalty to your profession. It will all be revealed in the decision you make. How else, after all? At least we're still alive and ready to leave, not just ghosts flitting about."

The doctor finally drank his glass of wine. Then as if Marie weren't even there, he said, "You probably think that love between a man and woman is very important, don't you?"

"Me? Not at all! I value less glittering, less glorious passions more highly. But unfortunately there's something deadly serious mixed in with this fleeting thing called love. And it's been bothering me for a long time that this most serious important thing in the world is so intertwined with something so ephemeral and trivial. What I mean is, an obligation not to abandon or betray each other. This is an integral part of that questionable, ephemeral, transitory affair. But *it* is not questionable or trivial, or transitory."

Suddenly we both turned to look at Marie. She was listening with bated breath. Her eyes were wide. Her face was red from the open fire. I grabbed her arm.

"As you learned in your first year at school," I said, "in your first Bible study class: The body does not last long; it passes away, but before it does it can be scorched. If the Nazi trap closes, if the city is bombed, then it can be mangled or torn to pieces, it can be burned— how do you doctors describe it? First-, second-, or third-degree burns."

At that moment the big pizza the doctor had ordered arrived with more rosé. We drank it quickly. The doctor said, "In certain French circles they're already expecting Gaullist uprisings this spring."

I said, "I don't understand any of that. I just think people who've experienced so much betrayal, who've been abandoned so often and spilled so much blood would have to recover first."

"I don't think that the young cook over there kneading the dough has any desire to die this spring."

I said, "You don't understand what I'm trying to say—that isn't what I meant at all. Why must you insult the cook, you of all people. You do nothing night and day except worry about the best way to get out of here. His chance hasn't come yet; his hour hasn't struck yet."

"Now that you've concluded your argument, you can let go of Marie's arm," the doctor said.

We finished drinking our wine. Marie said, "I have no bread coupons left for a second pizza." So we got up. It was only after we stepped out of the firelight that I noticed how pale she was.

X

I met Marie in a small café on Place Jean Jaurès. We avoided meeting in the large cafés on the Canebière. She sat down silently facing me. For a long time we said nothing. Finally she said, "I was at the Mexican Consulate."

I was shocked. "Why? Without asking me! Didn't I tell you not to try anything on your own?"

She looked at me in surprise. Then she said softly, "My visa hasn't arrived yet. The little official assured me it was just a matter of days, but the departure of the *Paul Lemerle* is also a matter of days. They're now saying at the Martinique Line that the ship will be leaving sooner than scheduled because of a special government order. The little Mexican official was very polite, actually he was more than just polite. You probably know him too since you go there so often. He's a strange little devil. At every other consulate they make you feel as if you're nothing, a nobody. The consuls all talk as if they were talking to a nobody with a phantom dossier. At the Mexican Consulate it's different. Have you noticed his eyes? You get the feeling that he knows everything in your file, the real truth. He looked at me and said he was sorry, very politely but with such impolite alert eyes. He said he was sorry that my husband hadn't immediately applied for a visa for me under his name when he applied for his."

I concealed my fear. I asked, "What did you say?"

"I told him that I wasn't here yet at the time. Then he said, still courteous and always with the same look as if he was amused by my stupid lies, that I was probably mistaken since I was already here when his correct name was entered. He said there were of course all sorts of mix-ups in the dossier, all sorts of name changes, but he was used to those tricks. He laughed, not just with his eyes—he laughed out loud, baring his teeth. I didn't say anything. I don't know what papers my husband presented there. I shouldn't screw up his stuff. The official turned serious then and said that it wasn't his business after all, but he regretted the delay. He had always thought it his duty to minimize people's unhappiness by any official measures at his disposal.—But never mind the official. In the end I don't care what he thinks, even if he's right. My husband didn't apply for a visa for me because they told him that I was going to leave with another man. You understand?"

"But you will get your visa. I promise you."

She didn't say anything. She looked out at the rain. Suddenly I felt that I had to tell her everything, the whole truth, no matter what the outcome, for her or for me. There was a terrible silence of many seconds during which I tried to find the right words to begin, tried so hard that beads of sweat formed on my forehead.

She smiled slightly and moved close to me, put her hand into mine, and leaned her head against my shoulder. I stopped hunting for the right words with which to tell her the truth. I began to think that it would be much better to win her over to my side, body and soul, before she heard the truth. I said, "Look at that woman sitting over there with the pile of oyster shells. I run into her almost every day. She was refused a visa. Now she's eating up all her travel funds."

We laughed and watched her. I knew many of the people passing by outside in the rain or coming into our little café, wet and cold, looking for a place to sit down. I told Marie their stories and realized she enjoyed listening. I went on telling her stories so that the smile wouldn't vanish from her face and to keep the dark expression of sadness from coming back. That's what I feared most.

During the week that followed the doctor often asked me whether her visa had arrived as the Transports Maritimes had finally set a definite departure date. But I didn't go back to the Mexican Consulate. For the second time I had decided to let him leave without Marie.

7

I

I SAW THE doctor again at the Binnet apartment on January 2nd. He hadn't come to examine the boy, who for the time being was well and already back at school. He'd come to bring him a present. The boy didn't unwrap it. He just stood there, leaning against the wall, eyes downcast, teeth clenched. The doctor tried to stroke the boy's head, but he pulled away, and shook the doctor's hand only reluctantly.

As he was leaving, the doctor invited me to meet him at the pizzeria the following evening to celebrate his departure. I realized then that he really was leaving; that I would be left alone with Marie. I felt anxious, the way you do when a dream seems too real and at the same time something intangible, imperceptible, tells you that whatever makes you feel happy or sad can never be reality.

In that calm voice, habitually hushed for the sickroom, and with a serenely sober look he said, "Please, I beg you, do everything you can and as soon as possible so that Marie can leave, perhaps via Lisbon."

I was utterly dismayed.

"Help her get a transit visa, the way you helped her get the other visas. And above all, put an end to her indecision." On the threshold he turned and said casually over his shoulder, "In the end, Marie will never make a definite decision to stay. She thinks that her husband has already left and is in the New World by now."

For a while I stood there in Claudine's kitchen, stunned. Then suddenly I felt unreasonably jealous of the doctor, even more so than the day I first brought him to the Binnets' apartment. It was stupid of me. What was it I envied him for? He was leaving after all. Was it his strength? His essential character? I even thought for a moment that he knew more than he was telling me or maybe he was just better at keeping things to himself. In my confusion, my foolishness, I even felt there was a secret understanding between him and the dead man, and that both were silently laughing at me. I was roused from these ridiculous thoughts by a slight noise coming from the bedroom. The boy had thrown himself on the bed and was crying, his body racked with sobs. When I bent down, he kicked at me. I tried to console him, but he shouted, "You can all go to hell!"

I stood there, helpless, watching him cry; I'd never before seen anyone weep like that. The boy felt betrayed and deserted. His grief was real. I picked up the present and unwrapped it. It was a book and I held it out to him. He jumped up, took the book from me, threw it on the floor, and stomped on it. I didn't know how to comfort him. George Binnet came into the room just then. He picked up the book, and sat down. He began to leaf through the book as if he were more interested in it than in the boy. The boy got up and stood behind George, staring at the book; his face was swollen from crying. Suddenly he tore it out of George's hands and threw himself together with the book onto the bed. Holding it pressed to his chest he quickly fell asleep.

"What happened?" George asked.

"The doctor was here; it was his last visit. He's leaving shortly."

George said nothing. He lit a cigarette. I envied him, too, for being so uninvolved, for being at home.

II

I was the first to get to the pizzeria and had already drunk half a bottle of rosé by the time the others arrived. Initially the good-bye went better than I expected. All three of us were probably a little apprehensive. Presumably this was the last time I'd be able to spend some quiet hours with the two of them. And, of course, I thought it was their last evening together. I saw things clearly now, as if the impending good-bye had opened my eyes. I even understood now why Marie had followed the doctor this far; how he had always remained constant, steadfast and calm, even as he drove his shabby little car across the country, just ahead of the Germans. I couldn't help but wonder why Marie had not yielded to his calm after so much moving about, so much turmoil. That evening I also realized to what extent he had seen to every aspect of his departure—he had obtained his visa and the necessary transit visas, and he had already steeled himself against any emotions that might in any way interfere with his departure. I looked at him now with increased respect. Yes, he was ready and able to leave.

Marie was carrying it off well too. She took a bite of pizza and drank a little wine. She didn't betray any emotion. I couldn't tell whether she was sorry he was leaving or if it was a relief. The doctor again urged me to work on Marie's departure and help her in any way possible. He seemed confident of being reunited with her. Apparently he considered my feelings about all this irrelevant.

We left early and crossed the Cours Belsunce. A fair had been set up, but dusk was late and the many colored lanterns weren't showing to best effect. The doctor asked me to come up to his room to help close an overstuffed suitcase. I hadn't been back to the Hotel Aumage since the Binnets sent me to find a doctor for the boy. At that time I'd paid hardly any attention to the building on the Rue du Relais. While its façade was narrow and dirty, the hotel itself was surprisingly large with an enormous number of rooms, all opening off narrow corridors that led to a steep staircase. On the ground floor to one side stood a small stove, its stovepipe winding up to the third floor. It gave off a bit of heat. There was a large basin of water on top of the stove and some smaller vessels in the twists of the stovepipe. Several of the hotel guests were sitting around the stove using it to dry their laundry. They looked up curiously when we came in—all of them transients, for who would choose a place like this to stay permanently? It was the sort of place you could put up with only if you knew you'd be leaving soon. It occurred to me that it wasn't a bad place for the doctor to have hidden Marie. The Rue du Relais was a short ugly street, the only one behind the Cours Belsunce that didn't cross through to the Boulevard d'Athènes, but ended at the next cross street.

We went upstairs. The doctor unlocked the door at which I'd seen Marie's hand that first evening. Her blue dress was hanging on the wall. There were several suitcases scattered around, some of them still open. I locked one, tied a rope around another. Then I rolled up the blankets and tied a rope around them. As usual when packing, there was always one more thing to do. The hours passed. I sensed that the doctor didn't want to be alone with Marie. He opened a bottle of rum intended for the voyage. We all drank straight from the bottle. Then we sat around on the suitcases, smoking. Marie was quiet, almost cheerful. Suddenly the doctor said it didn't make sense to go to sleep anymore, would I help him to carry some of the suitcases downstairs; he'd ordered a taxi for five.

I looked at Marie—the same way as in my childhood when I had been drawn irresistibly to a painting that I couldn't bear to look at. Now too, my heart contracted, even though there was nothing unbearable in Marie's aspect. She remained calm and cheerful. Except that to me her expression seemed a bit off-putting, with just a hint of mockery. I couldn't fathom why.

The doctor and I went down and up the stairs a few times. With each trip we left Marie alone in the room. And each time, as we carried off another load, it was like another good-bye, until the final farewell installment was paid. Maybe she was mocking him because he had dragged her with him across the entire country, only to cross the ocean now without her. At one point they shook hands.

An oldish woman who was on night duty in the room at the bottom of the stairwell came yawning up the stairs to let us know that the taxi had arrived. I went down to help the driver load the luggage. It gave the doctor three minutes to be alone with Marie. Once in the taxi, he calmly told the driver, "La Joliette, pier number five."

I lit a cigarette and took a couple of puffs standing in the doorway of the Aumage. The doors and windows of the house across the street were still shuttered for the night. Then I went back upstairs.

III

There she was, squatting in one corner of the room. I had won. It was as if she were my trophy—the spoils of war. I think at the time I even felt ashamed that I'd won her so easily—by a throw of the dice rather than a duel. Her head was down on her knees, her hands covered her face. But I could tell from the sideways glances she sent my way from between two fingers that she probably knew what lay ahead of her. Once again, what else but love?

Of course I'd let her do as she liked for the time being. Allow her to grieve for the doctor to her heart's content. Eventually she would have to pack up her things and move in with me under my own roof. It was rather bold of me to think of the Hotel de la Providence as "my own roof." I wouldn't be able to plant a garden for her, but I'd take such good care of our documents that no policeman could harm us. Maybe we could even leave Marseille at some point and move to Marcel's farm.

Those were my thoughts back then. But to be honest, I had no idea what Marie was thinking. I didn't talk to her, didn't ask her any questions, nor did I touch her hair which was the only thing I really wanted to do at the moment. I didn't want to leave her alone, but I didn't want to bother her with words of comfort either. I turned away from her and looked down at the street. At that hour there wasn't much to see on the Rue du Relais. From the window you couldn't even see the pavement. I could have been looking down into an abyss if I hadn't known that the room was on the fourth floor. I felt uneasy, anxious. When I leaned out a bit farther to get some fresh air, I was able to make out, at the lower right side over the rooftops silhouetted against a light gray sky, the slender iron masts of the Old Harbor. We'll be taking the ferry a lot, just so we can sit in the sun on the other side, maybe we'll go to the Jardin des Plantes.

Evenings we'll visit the Binnets. I'll wander through the Corsican quarter to see if I can get a chunk of her favorite sausage without a ration card. She'll line up early in the morning for a can of sardines. We'll pick the real coffee beans out of our coffee ration the way Claudine does, so that on Sundays we can have a cup of real coffee. Maybe George will find me a part-time job. She'll be sitting by the window when I come home. Sometimes we'll go for pizza and a glass of rosé. She'll fall asleep and wake up in my arms. All those things will happen, I thought back then. All these ordinary little things together would make a powerful whole: Our life together. I'd never before wished for anything like that, having always been a wanderer and never settling down anywhere. But now, in the midst of this earthquake, the yowling of the air-raid sirens, amidst the wailing of the fleeing hordes, I longed for an ordinary life like a hungry man does for bread and water. In any case, Marie would find peace with me. I would make sure that she would never again fall prey to some guy like me.

Meanwhile, a new day had dawned. The garbage collectors at the end of the street were clattering with the cans. The fire hydrants had been opened, and powerful jets of water sluiced along the pavement washing yesterday's dirt into the streets below. The sun was already shining on the roof across the way. A car drove up, bringing the first guest of the morning to the Hotel Aumage.

I immediately recognized two of the suitcases on the sidewalk, the one I myself had tied up and the one with the padlocks. Then the doctor got out, giving some instructions to the driver. He had arrived not just with the luggage that had been in his hotel room, but also a large trunk he had brought to the Transports Maritimes two days earlier. I said, "Your friend's back again."

She raised her head, and hearing his voice and the noise on the stairs, jumped up. I had never before seen her look so beautiful.

The doctor came into the room. He paid no attention to Marie, who was leaning against the wall, that silent expression of mockery on her face. He was livid with rage. "We were all inside on the pier," he said. "Half the passengers had already gone through the police check. Suddenly they announced that a Military Commission had commandeered all the first-class cabins for some officers who were going to Martinique. They unloaded our baggage. So here I am." He walked around moaning. "All the effort to get a cabin, all the expense! I thought that with a prepaid cabin I could be sure that no one could stand in my way. Now this French Military Commission requisitions all the first-class cabins and lets the people in steerage sail. Those people might even get to their destination. Maybe they've already arrived there, while I'm still sitting here in the Hotel Aumage. Those fools will get there but I'm left to die here." Marie's eyes were fixed on him even as he went on and on. I could still hear him cursing on the other side of the door as I went down the stairs. I was cursing too.

IV

It was still early in the morning when I left the Rue du Relais. The day seemed to stretch endlessly before me. How would I fill this day—as empty as my life—or the night that would follow it like the grave. First I decided to go up to see George. But he'd already left. Claudine was busy scaling a large fish the black man from Magash on the second floor had given her. The fish would come in handy because all her meat coupons were used up, she said calmly, completely unaware of my state of mind. I didn't accept her invitation to stay for dinner. As if there were better tables set for me elsewhere and I had countless friends!

I called out to the boy, hoping to rouse his interest, "He's come back." He was lying on his bed, just as I'd left him after the doctor's departure two days ago. What did I care if the excitement might be bad for him, after all, his doctor was back now. He could cure him. Then I turned back to Claudine who was wrapping the fish in a towel. I asked her whether she thought sometimes about what would happen to her since George probably wouldn't stay with her forever. She looked me up and down, holding her chin in her long-fingered hand. "I'm happy just to have something to eat for dinner," she said scornfully. I was already at the door when she called after me, "And I have my son!"

I went up into the hills toward Beaumont. It was a sunny morning. I had no trouble finding the little house where I'd met Heinz and his two companions. In the daytime it was a pleasant, low building with a henhouse ladder outside that led up to the second floor. The café was on the ground floor.

Heinz had forbidden me to try to find him up here. But when you really don't know what to do, you'll grope around looking for someone who has something you yourself don't have like a sick animal sniffing for a plant that will make it feel better. The café was deserted. I climbed up the ladder without running into anyone, and when I called out Heinz's name, the landlady appeared at one of the doors and said, "That tenant left a week ago."

I asked her, "Has he left here for good?"

She said, "Yes, for good," waiting with crossed arms for me to leave her house. I was stunned. In my present mood it came as a heavy blow that Heinz was gone forever. It hurt that he'd left without saying good-bye.

Maybe the landlady was lying. In any case, I had to clarify things for myself, and so I went back down to the café in the Old Port. I parted the scruffy bead curtain. It wasn't too cold that day. Bright flecks of light dotted the dusty floor, where one of the girls sitting there had extended a skinny bare foot. The cat was playing with the girl's slipper making the others laugh. Bombello, they told me, had left; the Portuguese hadn't yet come.

I walked back along the Canebière to the travel bureau. One of the two big dogs my neighbor was supposed to take with her across the ocean was lying in the sun outside the door. The woman was signing for the final ticket. The second dog was sniffing for the Corsican without being able to see him behind the counter. Although going to the bureau was completely unnecessary, I fortuitously ran into the bald man who had prophesied at the American Consulate that we'd keep meeting until one of us jumped the course.

There was a young woman waiting, guarded by a policeman. She was probably one of those being detained at Camp Bompard until she either got a berth on a ship or was told finally that there was none for her, and then she'd be put permanently into a camp in the interior. Her stockings were torn; the black roots of her dyed hair were showing. The corners of her documents stuck out of a little, greasy leather bag she carried; they'd probably all expired by now or become invalid for some other reason. Who could love a woman like that enough to bring her to safety across the ocean? She was too young to have a son who might have been able to take care of her, too old to have a father still alive, too ugly to have a lover, and too sloppy to have a brother who would want her in his house. I should have been helping her, I thought, not Marie. The fat musician from Achselroth's gang who had once gotten as far as Cuba came in. He barely greeted me, as if ashamed of what he'd told me the week before. The Corsican was poking around in his ear with a pencil since there was nothing for him to write down—all the available places had already been assigned. And so, continuing to fiddle around in his ear with the pencil and yawning, he listened to the whining and wheedling of these sad people who felt threatened with death, imprisonment, or who knows what. Some of them would gladly have given their right hand to the Corsican if he'd only promise them a place on a ship, or just promise to put them on a waiting list for a berth on a ship. But he promised nothing, just kept yawning.

I was prepared to wait my turn. After all, I had plenty of time, nothing but time; and I didn't feel threatened by anything, not even by love. But he saw me and waved me over. I realized he didn't consider me one of the multitude of transients, but one of his own kind. The others enviously made room for me; I asked him in a whisper about the Portuguese guy. Still poking around in his ear, he said, "He's at the Arabic café on the Cours Belsunce."

As I was walking out, the fat man who'd once gotten as far as Cuba grabbed my sleeve, but I shook him off. I was in a hurry. I had an appointment to keep now; I no longer had lots of time to waste. I went to look for the Portuguese. How bleak the Cours Belsunce

was! How tough the waiting time between adventures! How boring
a life without danger!

A dozen men, Arabs maybe, of whatever nation might have considered itself lucky to get rid of them, were lounging on shabby cush-
ions wrapped in greasy burnooses. Their ongoing game of dominos
sounded both brisk and sleepy. I didn't turn around to look for the
Portuguese, convinced that everyone was watching me. And indeed
the man I was looking for rose from a dim corner, and came toward
me. He asked whether I needed him again. Since our last encounter
he'd acquired a meek yet insolent gesture of putting two fingers to
his lips. We sat down and they brought us some rather nice tea that
tasted of anise. I told him that I was just trying to get some information about my friend.

His little mousy eyes flashed when I mentioned Heinz's name.
Oh yes, he said, they'd put him on the boat to Oran. That was already a while back. From there he changed to a ship bound for Lisbon; the entire journey was in the hands of the Portuguese.

"A pretty expensive detour," I said.

"Oh no," he said. "They didn't make any money on it; they did it
for the man's sake. You knew him, after all, he was your friend." He
gave me a brief look, from which I gathered how greatly he overesti-
mated me just because he thought I was Heinz's friend. I was dumbfounded by the look from his mousy eyes. If Heinz really had
managed to induce this fellow to perform an unselfish deed, then
Moses getting water from a rock was pure child's play.

He'd probably forgotten Heinz in the meantime, but my asking
about the one-legged German had rekindled his curiosity. It occurred to him that one of the men who had taken Heinz must be
back already. And since he had just as little to do as I, he was willing
to look for the fellow.

The sun had suddenly disappeared; a cold wind made us blink.
The Old Harbor seemed strangely empty. The little gunship was
gone. Where to, I wondered. The idlers hanging around outside the
cafés in spite of the stormy Mistral were speculating about it. The
wind took our breath away. Even with all his scams the Portuguese

evidently couldn't afford a coat to protect himself from the cold. In front of the expensive hotels, the mussel and oyster vendors were packing up their baskets, which meant it was almost three o'clock. So I'd already wasted quite a bit of time. We went up a steep street. Although I walked through this section of town a lot, I wasn't used to seeing it from this vantage point. In the cold afternoon light the bare masts of the fishing boats were outlined against the chalk-white walls of the houses on the other side of the harbor, all reflected in water that was blue in spite of the Mistral. From up here the city seemed strange, like one of those unattainable, submerged cities they used to tell about in stories. By now I was familiar with the quarter's various hidden lairs. I knew their secret—four walls, the same as back home, a man, a woman who went to work, and a sick boy lying in a bed.

Panting, the Portuguese and I climbed the stairs in search of someone who knew of a badly mutilated man who had been seen in one of the ports of the Mediterranean Sea. What a chain of hands had been required! So many miles long, to hand the living remains of his body from one car to another, from one stairway to the next, from one ship to another. What had the old man in the crypt of St. Victor's said? *I was beaten three times; three times I was stoned, three times I was shipwrecked, I spent days and nights in the deep sea, my life was endangered by rivers, at risk in cities, in the desert, and on the high seas.*

We stopped in front of a dilapidated house. The interior was paneled in costly wood that gave off a strange smell. As we walked up the stairs, this smell was replaced by that of a print shop. On the door of the topmost apartment was the name of a seamen's association.

There were piles of freshly printed newspapers. The Portuguese spoke to a man whose smoothly combed hair, clean-shaven chin, and firm, clean hands, gave him the appearance of a regular French sailor. His gray, calm eyes had crow's-feet at the corners that hinted at long sessions of intense lookout at sea. He was coolly watching everything and everyone, listening impassively to the whispered words of the Portuguese, even as he kept counting off newspapers from the stacks and handing them to a fresh-eyed boy who then placed them in a basket. Apparently he knew my Portuguese friend and had formed his opinion of him long ago. (Later, after someone was arrested, this whole affair blew up. It turned out that these papers, which looked like nothing more than an official government appeal to join the army or the navy, had been so cleverly laid out that, by folding the paper in a certain way, they produced a Gaullist slogan.) My friend gestured to me, indicating that I might actually be able to get some information about Heinz from this fellow. So I whispered to him that Heinz was my friend, that we had been in a concentration camp together, that I had helped him with his trip, and now I was worried about what might have happened to him. The boy who was putting away the papers put his head close to the edge of his basket so he could overhear our whispered conversation.

"No reason to worry," the man said. "Your friend has probably arrived already." He wasn't at all inclined to tell me more than that. There was a momentary flicker of amused mockery in his calm face, maybe at the recollection of some detail of their trip, some prank, hoodwinking the harbor authorities somewhere. Before we came to see him here, he'd probably forgotten all about Heinz. Now his gray eyes warmed at the memory; he probably saw him again on his crutches, his mouth distorted with the effort of walking, his bright eyes mocking his own frailty. This warm shadow in the gray eyes of a French sailor was the last visible sign that remained of Heinz in this part of the world.

Back downstairs, my Portuguese friend gave me a nudge. His expression said, You owe me a drink! Although it was an alcohol-free day, we found a bar where the proprietor quickly added a shot of schnapps to our coffee. Then the Portuguese and I realized we had nothing else to say to each other and would just be bored in each other's company. We politely separated. The Mistral had stopped as suddenly as it had started. The sun had come out again.

I went back to the inner city by myself, idling away one or two hours looking in shop windows. All day long I'd been brooding about my bad luck, or what I considered my bad luck: in Claudine's kitchen, on my search for Heinz, in the Arabic café, at the Seamen's

Association, at the bar with the Portuguese—I thought of a lot of other things, too, but then I always returned to my bad luck. How had I been able to live by myself before this? I remembered Nadine. I went to the side entrance of Dames de Paris to wait for her. I didn't care about her at all. And yet I was glad to see her face light up when she saw me waiting on the sidewalk. She looked very good in her beautiful coat and fur hood.

The hard day's work didn't seem to have affected her. She hid any sign of weariness. Powder like yellow butterfly dust covered her neck, her face, and her pretty ears that were just visible inside her hood. She said, "You've come along at just the right time."

I was grateful and glad to hear her say this, even if thoughts of my bad luck kept simmering inside my head. She continued, "Just think, my major left. He suddenly received his orders. He's off to Martinique—a military Commission."

"The pain of parting doesn't seem to have affected you very much," I said.

"To be honest, I was fed up with him. He was jolly and funny and amused me at first, but he soon got on my nerves. Plus he was too short and his head was too small. Yesterday we went to buy a helmet for the tropics, and when he tried it on, it slid down to his nose. He was a decent man. He took good care of me as you'll see in a minute. That's why I worried about his getting on my nerves. Now we're the best of friends, but at a distance. And on the way back he'll stop in Casablanca to see his wife. I had enough of him, still, he was a good man. In times like these you sometimes have to grit your teeth and pretend as if—Come, let's go up to my place so that I can show you how well he took care of me. And I'll cook you a meal like you haven't eaten in a long time."

She still lived in the same old hole not far from the Dames de Paris. It was easy to make her happy by showing my amazement at how the place had been completely refurbished. Absolutely everything was new, the quilt and pillows, the dishes and stove, and all the things on her dressing table under her mirror, and the mirror too and all those secret things made of glass and enamel. We opened a lot of cans and bottles. An entire city quarter would have had to stand in line for that. She started the lengthy process of cooking, interrupting herself only to show me a pair of shoes or some item of lingerie, or to hold me close. She inquired about my departure plans, whether there was anything I needed.

I said, "No, my love, I'm happy."

"Maybe you *do* need something; how's the situation with your visas?"

I said at the moment I didn't need anything, not even a visa. She replied that, if I ever needed one, she had a friend, a former classmate, who worked at police headquarters.

I asked whether the friend was as pretty as she was.

"No, she's fat and serious," she said.

Then we set the table and ate the food, engaged in some prolonged and pleasurable activities that tired me a little, and even though they didn't entirely alleviate my unhappiness, they lessened it a bit.

Much later, I was still wide-awake. I thought she was asleep, so I got up and lit a cigarette. The moon was shining in through the window, which was rattling as if the Mistral hadn't yet blown over. Quite unexpectedly, I heard her voice, calm and wide-awake, "Don't be sad, my dear! It isn't worthwhile! Believe me." So she had noticed how things stood with me and done what she could to comfort me.

V

For quite a while after that I didn't feel like seeing anyone else. I didn't go back to see Nadine either. I'd sit in a café in an out-of-the-way corner where no one would talk to me. If someone came in whom I knew, I'd quickly hold a newspaper up in front of my face. Once I even poked two little holes into the page so that I could see everything without being seen. When things got too dull I visited the Binnets. How dreary it can get in the time between two firestorms on this trembling earth! The heart, hopelessly accustomed to

the chase, keeps demanding more and more. But this time I regretted going to see the Binnets because the doctor was there. He was in
a good mood again.

"There you are finally," he said as I came into the room. "Marie is
worried, wondering where you disappeared to."

"Busy with a transit visa matter," I said, immediately regretting
my reply.

"So you've suddenly decided to leave, too?"

"I want to have all the necessary stuff, just in case."

Hearing this answer, the boy glanced at me briefly. It was the
only sign he had given that he was aware of my being there. He was
reading or pretending to read. Now and then the doctor spoke to
him, but the boy acted as if the doctor were no longer there. He
hadn't shown any emotion when the doctor returned; he just didn't
care anymore. The doctor had left, had deserted him, had hurt him
with his departure. He could come back a thousand times, but the
parting had been final. And now suddenly I, too, had become a
shadow for him; no use in clinging to me or talking to me.

The doctor told us that the passengers who'd been turned away
would have first call on berths on the next ship to leave. He was in a
pretty good mood. He was no longer brooding about the unsuccessful passage, but was already thinking of the next one for which he
had been signed up, and which he rested his hopes on. "Marie will
get her visa too," he assured us. "Please go and ask about it soon."

I said I was not in the mood to do that anymore. My mission at
the consulate was finished; everything had been properly applied
for. All that remained was to pick it up, and Marie could do that
herself.

He looked at me because I had spoken rather gruffly. He said politely, without any mockery, "We've inconvenienced you. This time
Marie has really decided to leave. Didn't I predict that she would?"

I said nothing in reply. I got up to leave. How could he be so certain in this confusion of coincidences?

I decided to stay in my room that evening. Climbing up the steep
stairs to my room I always waved to the landlady behind her little

window, and sometimes I even complimented her on her hairdo. I always managed to pay my rent with the money I received for "departure expenses," and was surprised when she stopped me that day. "A gentlemen asked for you, a French gentleman with a little mustache. He left his card."

I couldn't quite hide my shock. Once back in my room I studied the card: "Emile Descendre, Wholesale Silks." I had never heard the name before. Must be a mistake, I thought.

I hate mistakes and mix-ups, especially when they involve me. I tend to invest all human encounters with exaggerated importance, as if they were arranged by a higher authority, as if they were inevitable, unavoidable. And in the Inevitable there can be no mistakes, right? I was still smoking and brooding over this when there was a knock on the door. My guest, hat in hand, was well dressed; he glanced at the card lying on the table in front of me. Automatically I bowed as courteously as he had and, offering him the only chair, sat down on the bed. He'd already checked out my room within the boundaries of politeness.

"Please excuse me for bothering you, Mr. Weidel," he began. "But you can understand why I wanted to look you up."

"Excuse me," I said, "but all the terrible events that have befallen your country and all of us seem to have affected my eyesight as well as..."

"Please don't be alarmed," he said. "We know each other without ever having met. You've never seen me before, but if it weren't for me, you wouldn't be here."

To stall for time I said that this might be an exaggeration. His healthy, ruddy, self-satisfied face turned glum, so I quickly added, "Although you may have played some role in it."

"I'm glad to hear you admit that much, at least. My card, my name will have told you that I am Emile Descendre."

I asked, "How did you get my address?" At first I'd felt a stirring of fear, but it was quickly muted by sadness, which can also act as a charm against many things. Whatever was going to happen to me, I didn't care.

My visitor replied, "It's all quite simple. I'm a businessman. First I looked up Paul Strobel. His sister is a friend of my fiancée, as you no doubt know."

I still didn't have a clear notion what this was all about, merely a kind of dim glimmer of a recollection: Paul, his sister, a fiancée, a silk merchant. I said, "Please, go on."

He continued cheerfully, "Paul promised to give me your address several times. He thought he'd written it down, but then he couldn't find it—either among his own papers or on the lists of the Committee on which he serves. Paul is a very busy man. He suggested I go to the Mexican Consulate."

I listened eagerly. Bobbing his neatly combed head like a dapper bird on a stick, he complained, "I should also tell you that I turned first to Madame Weidel. I met with her several times. Of course I could understand her delicate situation; I took that into account. So it's even more important for me to straighten things out with you— and also, because Mrs. Weidel said she didn't know your address and I didn't want to bother her, I decided to find you on my own. As I said, I went to the Mexican Consulate. There seem to have been really a lot of slip-ups in connection with your address. There must have been a mix-up there, because the house number they had listed doesn't exist. The street on which you probably used to live didn't even have houses built anywhere near as high as the number they had listed for you. On the advice of the gentleman at the consulate, I went to the Mexican travel bureau. The head of that bureau had only the address of the Mexican Consulate listed for you. So, in spite of the fact that I'm a businessman and have to think of expenses, I decided to track you down. The head of the travel bureau referred me to a Portuguese man whom you'd been seen with. I promised this gentleman a small favor. Although he didn't know where you lived, he knew a certain young lady at the Dames de Paris."

I thought, Oh oh, the little Portuguese mouse has been scurrying after me out of sheer boredom.

"Please don't be angry. I don't want there to be any bad blood between us. The young woman didn't give me your address. I had to go for help to her colleagues. Those girls knew all about you. And so finally I found out the secret, and that only because one of the young women at the Dames de Paris lives nearby, in the Rue des Baigneurs. Forgive me, but I can't allow my business to suffer just because your family situation has shifted. I have to see that my expenses are paid."

I said, "Of course, Mr. Descendre."

"I am glad that you see my point. Back when Mrs. Weidel referred me to you I hoped for a partial reimbursement, while we were still in occupied Paris, but unfortunately I was not able to meet with you then and so I entrusted this matter to Paul, whom I knew through his sister."

"What expenses do you mean, Mr. Descendre?" I asked.

He replied angrily, "So Mrs. Weidel didn't tell you anything! Probably because she has other interests now. Excuse me, Mr. Weidel, I wouldn't mention these matters if I didn't think that you've found consolation by now. I met the lady in the company of someone else, but for me expenses are expenses. And back then Mrs. Weidel promised faithfully to reimburse me for part of my expenses if I would take her letter. At that time I was very reluctant to make a trip into occupied territory. It was expensive and dangerous to be on the road such a short time after the invasion; I had to reckon with difficulties on the return trip even if I had a pass from the Germans. The demarcation line might have been unexpectedly closed or moved. My own fiancée implored me to give up my travel plans, but that spring I delivered raw silk bales to the firm Loroy, for use by the army to make balloons and parachutes. At the time I couldn't find out whether the firm I'd made the delivery to had been evacuated along with my raw silk, or if the Germans had seized it. In the latter case I would get paid for damages only with a contract for additional deliveries. I had a lot at stake, but your wife tipped the scales with her request—she knows how to ask men for things. She said you would be eternally grateful to me, that it was a matter of life and death for her letter to get to you, and that the expense incurred was of no concern. Moreover, it was forbidden to take mail along. They frisked you! The lady really knew how to persuade a man. I believe in great passions. And so the impression I got of her on my return was that much more painful.

"All during that difficult trip I saw before me her lovely young face. It's true, even though it may sound strange, I thought, 'The woman will be happy when I tell her I accomplished my task.' After all, it wasn't my fault that I couldn't actually find you back then. An unlucky star hung over your apartment, sir. You've had bad luck with your addresses; I couldn't reach you in Paris either. No one in the quarter where you used to live knew of your whereabouts—your registration had not been terminated or changed. But Paul, as I am pleased to see, did take care of the delivery of the letter. The lady probably doesn't want to go to her new friend to ask for money. But I can't help it if love withers, I have to pay attention even to trifling matters. If I didn't operate on that principle I would never have come to be president of the Descendre Company."

"Very well, Mr. Descendre," I said. "How much do the expenses for the delivery of the letter amount to?"

He named a figure. I thought about it. I had only the money that the man going to Cuba had given me for Weidel two weeks before. I counted it out on the table. Now and then you achieve as much with honesty as with lies. I said, "Mr. Descendre, you're absolutely right. You have properly fulfilled your task. You didn't leave anybody in the lurch. Nor was it your fault that you couldn't find me in Paris back then. Your letter got to me in spite of that; you have to take care of your expenses. But as you can see, I'm quite poor. I shall pay you as much as I can; though the circumstances of my life have changed, the letter still means much to me. I'll try to pay the balance of your delivery expenses as soon as I can."

He listened politely to what I said, moving only his head back and forth. Then he signed a receipt. He indicated that he was at my disposal here, and that he might also be able to speak for me at the exit visa department of Police Headquarters. Then, weaving a few words about literature into his good-bye, he excused himself. We bowed to each other.

VI

I sat down in the glass-enclosed terrace of Café Rotonde across from the Belsunce. Without intending to I overheard the conversation at the next table. It seemed that during the night a man had shot himself in a hotel in Portbou on the other side of the Spanish border because the authorities were going to send him back to France in the morning. Two frail, elderly ladies—one of them with two little boys, maybe her grandsons, both of whom were listening attentively—were taking turns in animated voices filling in the details. They had a much clearer idea of what had happened than I, and they thought it all quite understandable and reasonable.

How could a man have such enormous hopes for his journey's destination that going back should have seemed so unbearable? This country in which we were still stuck and to which they wanted to force him to return must have seemed hellish and unlivable to him. You hear about people who prefer death to losing their freedom. And yet was that man really free now?—Ah, if only it were so! One shot, a single bullet to this small entryway above your eyebrows and you'd be home and welcome forever.

I saw Marie, walking slowly along the side of the Cours Belsunce. She was carrying a wrinkled little hat in her hand. She went into the Café Cuba that's adjacent to the Rotonde. Was her friend the doctor waiting for her there? Was she still going on with her search? Ever since the doctor had come back, I'd been desperate to avoid her. Yet now I couldn't control myself, and I waited, my face glued to the window. She soon came out again with a vacant, disappointed expression. She nearly passed right by me. I ducked behind my *Paris Soir*. But she must have glimpsed something of me, my hair, my coat, or, if there is such a thing, my overpowering single-minded hope that she would turn around just once.

She entered the Rotonde. I ran to the inner room, and with a sick and evil joy I watched as she performed her search. There was something in the way she was searching, in her features, that told me that the man she was looking for was not a shadow, but flesh and blood, and he could be found if he wasn't hiding from her out of sheer perversity. When she entered the inner room I left through the back door that led out onto the Rue des Baigneurs. Again I ran through the streets as if the devil were after me. By my disappearance, my inexplicable invisibility, I would assure her continued interest in me. Let her look for me, as she'd proved herself capable of doing, night and day, without rest. Since my game had already begun, I could obtain the departure documents, one by one. I could even conceal myself on board her ship the day it sailed. And then on the high seas or on an island or in the strange, oppressive light of the new country I could appear before her as if by magic. Then there would be nothing that could come between her and me but my skinny rival in love with the long serious face. The dead we left behind would long ago have been buried by their dead.

With such dreams I retired to my room on the Rue de la Providence. The odd, sweetish, barbershop smell of my earlier visitor, the silk merchant, still hung in the air.

8

I

MEANWHILE the day of my final appearance at the United States
Consulate was approaching. I had definitely decided to secure a
transit visa for myself. Back then it was all a game for me. Not so for
the others waiting in the lobby to be allowed to enter the upstairs
waiting room. Their faces were pale with fear and hope. You could
tell that those who, like me, had appointments for today, had
brushed and tidied their best clothes and warned their children to
behave as if they were going to their First Communion. They had
done everything possible to look their best, to prepare themselves to
face the implacable consul of the United States, in whose country
they wanted to settle down or through which they wanted to travel
to reach another country where they would settle in the event they
ever reached it. And they were all discussing hurriedly and for the
last time, in voices hoarse with nervous trepidation, such matters as
whether it would be better to hide one's pregnancy from the consul
of the United States or to admit it. After all, this child, depending
on the will of the consul who decided whether or not to award a
transit visa, might be born on the ocean, on an island in that ocean,
or in the new land—taking into account also that this unborn child,
in case the date given the consul for its birth was not feasible, might
never get to see the light of this dark world.—And whether it would
be better to conceal the seriousness of an illness or to describe it in
poignant detail because, in the long run, an illness might be reckoned

as a burden to the American State. On the other hand, a person who according to a doctor's testimony was sure to die soon would be no burden to anyone.—And whether you could really admit to being poor or if you should hint at some secret source of money, even if you'd arrived here with only the Committee's ticket after your hometown burned down and with it all your goods and quite a few neighbors.—And whether it would be better to tell them that the German Commission might threaten you with extradition if the letter of transit was delayed, or whether it would be better not even to mention that you were a person threatened with extradition by the Germans.

And yet although all this transit whispering made me feel quite miserable, it was amazing to think that even though thousands, no, hundreds of thousands, had died in the flames of the air raids and the furious attacks of the Blitzkrieg, there were many more who were born quite without being noticed by the consuls. They hadn't asked for letters of transit, hadn't applied for visas; they were not under the jurisdiction of this place. And what if some of these poor souls, still bleeding physically and spiritually, had fled to this house, what harm could it do to a giant nation if a few of these saved souls, worthy, half-worthy, or unworthy, were to join them in their country—how could it possibly harm such a big country?

The first three who'd been called in came down the stairs smiling with joy—a short, stout man with two tall, well-dressed women. Each was holding an American visa, recognizable from afar by the little red ribbons drawn through the stiff paper, for what reason I have no idea. In a way you could look at the little red ribbon as a medal ribbon representing the American transit visa holder's Legion of Honor medal.

Right after these three came the bald-headed fellow I'd been running into for the last few weeks in consulate waiting rooms. He also had been processed on the upper floor, but he came down the stairs empty-handed and looking glum. I wondered about that since, in the course of our fleeting acquaintance, he'd seemed like a man who knew his way around and could get what he thought he needed. As he pushed through those still waiting, he caught sight of me and invited me to join him later at the Café Saint Ferréol.

At that point the woman who had the room next to mine appeared on the stairs with both dogs. She looked happy. She waved to me and wrapped the leashes of the dogs around her wrist so that we could chat. I no longer thought of her merely as a peculiar, ugly, insolent woman with crooked shoulders, and two huge dogs. She'd become a familiar and yet at the same time a remote, mythical figure, a kind of Diana of the Consulates.

"It turns out," she said, "that these two animals need a certificate stating that they are dogs who actually belong to United States citizens. I'd really like to slaughter both of them at this point, because it's their fault that I can't leave yet. But as their owners would scarcely sign my certificate of good character if I chopped the animals up for goulash, I'll have to go on taking care of them, brushing them and bathing them. Oh well, without them I wouldn't have a visa at all." With these words, incomprehensible to any casual bystander, she loosened their leashes and walked out to the Place Saint Ferréol.

In the meantime, my turn had come. My appointment with the consul was for January 8th at 10:15 a.m. My heart was pounding in anticipation of this contest that I had to win. But not dully, fearfully; it was pounding with eager anticipation. The guard at the stairs allowed me to pass; I entered the second anteroom. It was crowded; I'd have to wait some more. I quickly realized that all these people waiting here, all these men, women, and children belonged to one family. I recognized some of them from a previous day's waiting, and also the old shriveled woman. Today the entire family had come and they were all terribly upset, even the youngest of the children, trembling with shock and indignation. Whispering among themselves, they tried to keep their voices low, but there was always one who yelled out or sighed or sobbed. Only the old woman sat in their midst, without moving, as if mummified, showing all the symptoms of her debility and approaching end.

A young man, standing apart, leaning against the doorframe, was fiddling with his beret and smiling. He knew what all the fuss was about, what was at stake, and he didn't care. He was enjoying the situation. Then out of the consul's office, like an angel dispatched from the throne of God, came the young creature with the small breasts and blond curls. She must have spent the entire war on a rosy cloud, protected from all its rigors. She went to stand in front of the door to the second anteroom and told the family in a soft but stern voice that they must come to a decision; it was the same tone of voice that an angel might have used to urge these souls to repent or depart from there. They all stretched out their hands, even the youngest children, sighed, and begged for an extension, a postponement. I asked the young man with the beret what was going on.

"They're the children, grandchildren, great-grandchildren and other relatives of that ancient woman," he explained. "Their papers are all in order. The consul is ready to sign them on the spot. He'll allow them all to enter the U.S. except for the old woman. The consulate's doctor has determined that she has at most two months to live. And they won't allow people like that on any American ship; and why should they? But the family is obsessed, the way such people can be. They want the old woman to go with them so that she can die with them, or they all want to stay here with her until she dies. Just think! If they all stay here, then the old woman will die anyway, but their visas will expire, the transit visas will expire, and you know that in France they intern people who have all their visas and transits and don't get out. Anyway, they all ought to be interned, or at least locked up in an insane asylum."

At that point the consul's golden-haired messenger appeared again. I noticed her soft skin, but her voice was severe. A short man stepped forward from the group. I'd never have picked him out as the head of the clan. He calmly announced their decision in a mixture of languages reflecting the many countries through which he'd come with his relatives. They had decided to stay with the old woman as long as she was alive. For if he, her eldest son, were to remain here and his wife left with their sons, what would they do in a foreign land without him? Or if his youngest sister were to remain behind, who had just recently been married and was expecting her first child, how could she give birth without the man who was his brother-in-law at her side? And if the brother-in-law were to stay in whose name the business was registered... But by then the consul's messenger was already calling out the next name. The family left, helping the old woman down the stairs, cautioning each other to be careful. They looked sad and upset, but showed no regret.

Next, the young man whose name had been called out a moment before emerged from the office, announcing cheerfully that he'd been refused a visa because he had a prior conviction for a check forgery. He literally skipped down the stairs. Then they called out my name.

For one moment I thought everything was lost; the police might already be there, ready to take me away, and I wondered how I could leave the building before they put their hands on me. Once outside on the street I'd be able to squirm free of them. Nadine's room wasn't far off.

But all was *not* lost; Paul had apparently made the effort and given his colleague the best of testimonials on my behalf. His pride had conquered any other feelings he may have had. I mean, his pride in having the power to give a good character reference, having the power to advise the consuls of this world. In a way the character reference was of course an obituary. He could neither please nor hurt this man Weidel, who must have been an arrogant and taciturn fellow while alive.

I was politely ushered into the room where they put the finishing touches on the affairs of those they finally permit to leave.

I was asked to take a seat at the desk of the young person who had been assigned to issue my transit visa. I was sorry that it wasn't the girl with the blond curls, but this guardian angel wasn't bad-looking either with black curls and soft brown skin that must have felt like velvet. She looked me directly in the eyes, earnestly and severely, as if this were a preliminary examination for the Last Judgment. I was amazed at her questions. She carefully typed out my answers, all the facts of my past, my goal in life. The web of questions was so dense, so cleverly thought out, so unavoidable, that no detail of my life could have escaped the consul, if only it had been *my* life. I'm sure they'd never had a questionnaire so blank and empty on which they tried to capture a life that had already escaped this world and where there was no danger of getting tripped up by contradictions. All the details were in order. What did it matter that the entire thing wasn't true? All the subtleties were there, giving a clear picture of the man who was to be given permission to leave. Only the man himself wasn't there.

She then took hold of my wrist and led me to the table with the apparatus that took the fingerprints of transit visa applicants. Patiently she instructed me to press down my left thumb, then all the fingers and the palms of both my hands—not too gently, not too hard. Except that these weren't the fingers of the man whom they were granting permission to leave. How clearly I sensed through the richly ink-stained flesh of my hands the other man's fleshless hands no longer capable of such pleasures! My guardian angel praised me generously for doing everything so carefully. I asked her whether I would get a little red ribbon too; she laughed at my joke. Finally, as a proper and approved transit applicant I was led to the consul's table. He stood there very erect. Something in his face and gestures indicated that even though he'd performed the act he was about to perform as often as a priest performs baptisms, it was equally meaningful each time. The typewriters clacked away for a while longer, then came the pens. When everything had been signed often enough, the consul made a slight bow. I tried to emulate it.

Once outside the door, I examined my transit visa, especially the little red ribbon drawn through the upper right-hand corner. It seemed to be purely decorative without any particular purpose. Now it was my turn to appear on the staircase with those below looking enviously up at me.

II

When I entered the Café Saint Ferréol, I saw my bald-headed fellow *transitaire* hiding in a remote corner. I thought at first he might have had second thoughts about having invited me. He certainly didn't look like a man who was expecting company. I sat down in another hidden corner. From my seat I could see the entire room. The café had two entrances. One seemed to be used by people going to the Prefecture; the other by those applying for visas at the American Consulate. Gradually the café filled up.

I picked up a newspaper and held it up in front of my face. Marie appeared. We had sat in this very place, she and I, after my first visit to the American Consulate. It was here that she told me about the husband she couldn't find. And I had shaken my head at her difficult situation. Now I realized how easy it was to make oneself unfindable. How clumsy she was in her search! How superficially she looked in all the likely places! How easy it was for me to deceive her, simply by switching my seat behind her back to another table between two curtains behind two potted palms. It seemed her happiness at her friend's return had already evaporated. It was me she needed now. It didn't matter to me that she needed me only to give her advice about some visa problem. I knew she'd invented the problem as a pretense to see me again, to start the game all over again. But she was looking for more than just visa advice with her searching eyes, her restless hands, her white face. I was glad to give up seeing her face light up at the sight of me jumping up and calling out her name in exchange for being allowed to witness this stubborn search of hers.

There was only one thing that bothered me, and it bothered me a lot. How long would she keep it up? I had no doubt she was searching intensely now, but how long would she keep it up? Another five minutes? Till lunchtime? For the rest of the week? For another year?

She couldn't possibly keep looking for the man whom she'd met purely by chance on a bench in Cologne, or for me whom she might have seen on the Cours d'Assas outside the Mexican Consulate. How was she going to fill the interim period, not knowing whether it would be hours or forever, always with the same game played so convincingly that it seemed serious. I might be able to endure seeing her walking on the arm of her friend the doctor, once, ten times. I might not feel good about it, but I could take it. What I couldn't bear was seeing this game being played out to the end, on good days and on bad, until death would part the two of them too.

Marie had left the café. She was already crossing Place Saint Ferréol. To go on with her search? Or to give it up once and for all?

My view was suddenly blocked by a man stepping up to my table. It was my bald-headed friend. He said, "I saw you come in, but you didn't look exactly hungry for company."

I asked him to sit down. At that moment, of course, it was only so I could get a more complete view of the square. It was empty. In spite of the newspaper kiosks and freezing trees, the place seemed filled by an immense emptiness and immeasurable time. The wind seemed to be sweeping along vast blasts of time along with the usual dust. Marie, I thought, was not only gone without a trace, but timelessly, for now and forever. I became aware that the man was speaking to me, "I see you have a transit visa."

I flinched. All this time I'd been holding on to the stiff paper with the silly red ribbon in the upper right-hand corner.

My friend went on, "I have one too, but it doesn't do me any good." He brought his glass over to my table and ordered cognac, one for himself and one for me. He looked at me more closely with his cold, light gray eyes and then followed the direction of my gaze. A bunch of people came out of the Prefecture and scattered over the square, where time suddenly stood still. There seemed to be no intermediate stage between the chase and complete standstill. Yet all at once I felt that with this man at my table I was no longer sitting alone here, whatever sort of man he might be. And it was a kind of consolation. I turned to him, "Why isn't your transit visa any help to you? You don't look like the kind of man who doesn't know how to make use of his documents." I took a sip of my drink and waited until he felt like talking.

"I was born in a region that belonged to Russia before the World War," he said. "It became Polish after the war. My father was a veterinarian. He was good at it. Even though he was Jewish he was appointed to a semi-official position at an experimental farm on an estate. I was born on the estate. Wait, you'll soon see how all this relates to my present transit visa. This large estate was combined with two smaller estates as well as a mill and the miller's house. The millstream flowed between the mill and the apartment we were assigned. To reach the nearest village you had to cross the stream and two little hills. They were small hills, but so steep that they seemed to touch the sky."

Because I thought he had stopped at these recollections of his homeland, I said, "It must have been beautiful."

"Beautiful? Well, it probably was beautiful. But that's not why I'm describing the landscape for you. Our estate, the two other farmsteads, and the miller's house didn't have enough people living on them to count as a village. So we were counted as part of the next village, Pjarnitze. I gave all this information to the consul. I was being very precise; I thought I was being as precise as he was. I wrote: 'Formerly part of the community of Pjarnitze.'

"But the consul was even more precise, the map he had was more exact. It turned out that my home village, which I've never gone back to, increased in population so that now, twenty years later, it's become a town in the country of Lithuania. So my Polish identity papers are of no use to me anymore. I need to be recognized by the Lithuanians. And on top of that, the Germans have been there for quite a while already. The entire territory is under German occupation. So now I also need a new certificate of citizenship, and for that I need a birth certificate from a town that no longer exists. All this takes time. If there's a delay in getting my change of citizenship then I have to cancel my booking on the ship."

I said, "Why rush to cancel it? In your case there's no rush. You're not in any danger. You aren't one of those people who think this continent is going to blow up because armed hordes are once more on the march and burning cities. There'll be other ships. You'll be able to catch a boat."

"I have no doubt of that. I've been working on the preparations for this trip for quite a long time. At some point my documents will all be ready. And then there'll also be a ship I can take. I'll find one.

Except that suddenly I can't remember anymore why I was so obsessed with leaving. Was it because I was afraid? But I'm a pretty strong character and in general not afraid of anything. So someone must have hammered this fear into me. But now the contagion has subsided, and the fear is gone. I'm sick and tired of all this nonsense; I was already fed up with it the last time we met. I've finally had enough of it."

"You know as well as I do that they'll never let you stay here in peace."

"If I have to leave France, then I want to take a different journey. First thing tomorrow morning I plan to go on a rather modest trip. I'm taking the electric train to Aix. The German Commission has its headquarters there. I'll register with them, tell them that I'd like to go back to my hometown. I want to go back to the place where I was born."

"Of your own free will? You know, don't you, what's waiting for you there."

"And here? What can I expect here? You know the fairy tale about the man who died, don't you? He was waiting in Eternity to find out what the Lord had decided to do with him. He waited and waited, for one year, ten years, a hundred years. He begged and pleaded for a decision. Finally he couldn't bear the waiting any longer. Then they said to him: 'What do you think you're waiting for? You've been in Hell for a long time already.' That's what it's been like for me here, a stupid waiting for nothing. What could be more hellish? War? The war's going to follow us across the ocean too. I've had enough of it. All I want is to go home."

III

I went to the Spanish Consulate. I took my place in the line of transit applicants. It was a long line that stretched for a block along the sidewalk up to the gate. In front of me and behind me they were telling stories about Spanish transit visas which eventually arrived but so close to the date of the ship's departure from Lisbon that it would have been impossible to get there in time to board the ship. Nevertheless, I waited patiently, the way you wait when you're waiting for the sake of waiting, and when what you're waiting for is unimportant. I must have been pretty deep in the Hell that my friend had been describing at the Café St. Ferréol, if it didn't even seem bad to me anymore compared to all that I'd already experienced and all that still lay ahead of me—it was bearable and cool, with storytellers all around me.

And so, after a couple of hours, I finally reached the outer gate of the Spanish Consulate; behind me the line snaked into the street. In the meantime a cold rain had started to fall on the people in line. After another couple of hours I reached the front hall of the consulate. I don't know what mysterious order reigned here, but I was brought before a gaunt, thin-lipped official with a long sallow face. He questioned me with grave courtesy as if there were no long line waiting behind me reaching to the next street corner, which he'd probably never seen anyway because he was always inside and the human queue always outside. Holding my documents, he pored through a ledger seemingly searching for the name Weidel. Why should this poor forgotten name that might at most be spoken by his mother, if she's still alive, appear in that book? But it was listed. A dour smile contorted the official's thin lips. Politely he told me that it was futile for me to apply for a transit permit; I would never be allowed to travel through Spain. I asked him why. He said that I must know the reason better than anyone else.

I replied, "I have never been in your country."

He said, "You can hurt a country without ever having stepped on its soil." He was very serious and proud of being able to refuse me a transit visa. He'd tasted a bit of power with his tongue—which I got to see since he lisped—and had liked the taste of it. But something in my face must have displeased him. Maybe it was my expression of joy that surprised him and spoiled the taste of power. So Weidel isn't just dust, I thought, not just ashes, not just a faint memory of some intricate story that I'd find hard to retell, like the stories I was told at bedtime as a child just before I fell asleep and was only half awake. Something is left of him that's alive enough and arouses enough fear for them to close their borders to him, thereby closing off access to other countries as well. The culprits were probably those same articles that the American consul showed me on my first visit to his consulate. I would have loved to read them. Maybe by now they're already ashes too, but not forgiven in Spain. Yet they've given their creator the right to live in another country. I imagined a ghostly march by night through a country that Weidel had never set foot in while he was alive. And wherever he passed, shadows moved in the fields, in the villages, and on the pavement of streets he'd never seen. Corpses stirred a little in their poorly prepared graves as he passed by because he had done at least this much for them: writing only a few lines, but obsessed with the need of doing something, of intervening, much as for me it had been just one punch in the face of some SA boor. So there was some similarity between us, at least in this one respect in our otherwise rather humdrum lives—this stubborn need to take action, to intervene. The Spanish consular official was staring at me with his somewhat protruding eyes. I thanked him cheerfully as if he actually had signed my transit visa.

IV

I sat down in the Mont Vertoux to think things over. I hadn't eaten anything, nor did I have enough money left to buy a meal. I had a glass of wine instead. So it seemed the route through Spain had been denied us three: the dead man, the doctor, and me. We were destined to take another little boat, probably that decrepit crate the Transports Maritimes dispatched to Martinique every month. The doctor had seen it lying at anchor once through the gates of the pier. What was it he'd told me before that first unsuccessful departure of his? That Marie had now decided to leave. He probably thought he'd won the game now, but hadn't Marie also decided to leave back then when he raced with her in his car across the Loire over a half-destroyed bridge? He hadn't taken me into account, he couldn't have since I didn't exist back then. Nonetheless, I'd caught up with them, arriving out of nowhere at the right spot.

The Mont Vertoux was beginning to fill up. Flecks of bright sunshine dappled my hands. I began, mentally, to put the earthly legacy of my dead man in order. There was our joint treasure in Portugal. The Corsican had to help us get at it. We needed money for travel, and for the security payment the French demanded to make sure that we didn't get stuck in—what did they call it?—the Eastern Hemisphere. A bright lofty word that suited the dead man better than it did me with my strong fingers and those broad fingernails that always annoyed me. I called to the waiter and asked him for an atlas. He brought me a greasy, tattered travel guide that contained a world map. I looked for Martinique, which I'd been too lazy to do up to now. And there it was! A little dot between the two hemispheres which weren't some prefecture's trick, nor a consular invention, but real, from eternity to eternity.

I felt someone touch my shoulder. By then I'd lost track of how much I'd drunk. I looked up to see my neighbor from the hotel, his chest gleaming with medals. I don't know why we were always running into each other when I'd had a lot to drink. The short, stocky legionnaire always seemed to appear before me in a fog of glittering medals. He asked if he could sit with me. I said I'd be happy to have his company.

"How's Nadine?" he asked.

"Nadine?"

"It's as if she's bewitched. I go looking for her everywhere. I walk up and down the streets at night, I check out all the cafés."

"All you have to do is stand at the employee exit of Dames de Paris at six in the evening."

"Me? Never! I'd never have the nerve to do that. It has to look as if I'm running into her accidentally at some odd moment. But is something wrong? You can tell me. I feel there's something bothering you."

I did then what I always do when someone asks me an awkward

question. I asked him one in turn: "You owe me your story," I said. "How did you get all those things dangling on your chest?"

He said, "By preventing a couple of dozen young fellows who were in circumstances similar to yours from going to the dogs."

I laughed and asked him whether this was a habit of his and whether that's what had made him sit down at my table.

"Probably," he said, quite serious. Then, of his own accord, he started to tell his story, because he needed to. "When the war started I was still living in a village in the Var. The locals were tolerant of outsiders and maybe I could have gone on living there without problems till today. But my father lived in the Garonne Département, and there they were interning all foreigners under sixty. They said they would release my father only if I, his son, joined the army. I thought it over and decided it was my duty to enlist. Back then, like most people, I believed in a real war against Hitler. They gave me a checkup and found that I was in good health. I'd known that all along, but my physical condition was so exceptional that I was one of those "select" men who fulfilled the requirements for the Foreign Legion. So they sent me off to the Foreign Legion training camp. I was surprised, but thought it was all part of the war. And meanwhile they released my father from the internment camp...What's the matter?"

Marie was just walking past outside. She wore a strange gray coat that I'd never seen on her before. I thought she'd already vanished into the crowd, when she entered the Mont Vertoux. She wasn't searching as usual, but sat down quietly in a corner of the café, staring straight ahead of her. She'd obviously come in for a quiet moment by herself. I was happy she was there, even if she wasn't looking for me, glad she was alive, still alive.

"Nothing's the matter with me—anymore," I said. "Please go on with your story."

"They sent us to Marseille. They sent us up there." He pointed to Fort St. Jean on the other side of the Old Harbor. "It's cold inside the fort, it stinks, and filthy water drips down the walls which are covered with the slogan 'March or Die'; that's the unofficial motto of the legion. Every morning they marched us down to the sea. There's a small cove behind the fort, and it's strewn with lots of boulders. We had to roll these boulders up a steep set of stairs that had been carved into the hillside. Once we reached the top, we had to throw the boulders back into the sea. This was our special training. It was supposed to accustom us to obedience. Am I boring you?"

I took hold of his hand to assure him that he was in no way boring me. And as he continued, I watched Marie's face, so still in the evening light. She could have been sitting by that window for a thousand years already, going back to the days of the Cretans and Phoenicians, a young woman looking in vain for her lover among the masses of people. The thousand years had passed like one day. Now the sun was setting.

"One day we sailed to Africa. They jammed us into the hold of a ship. That ship had been carrying legionnaires to Africa for I don't know how many decades, how many thousands of years. The accumulated filth of generations of legionnaires, never scrubbed out! We arrived at another training camp. It was even tougher. The harangues of our superior officers were full of mysterious references, of threats implying that the best was still to come. We were sent to Sidi-bel-Abbès. The noncoms were old legionnaires. All of them had run away at some time from their homelands because they'd killed somebody, set a house on fire, or been caught stealing."

I could sense that it was important for him to tell the whole story from the beginning. Meanwhile I thought about how I could get on the ship on which Marie would soon be sailing. I'd been waiting for the moment when she would stop searching; and now it had arrived. Today, in the seventeenth month after her flight from Paris, the fifteenth month since her arrival in Marseille. I could give the exact figures to the dead man. I could calculate it all. And she'd been searching for me, for me or for both of us. Yet the way she broke off her search was quite different from what I'd expected. It wasn't precipitous, no wild 'if you're going to do it then do it properly.' It was a calm decision to accept what chance had wrought. But chance itself seemed surprised to find her sitting there with lowered head and downcast eyes, in a state of resignation that chance had never come across before and which was only due to the fact that chance looked a devilish lot like something else.

I heard my companion's voice, and I wasn't sure whether he'd been talking all this time or not.

"The officers were French. Many of them had gotten into trouble while serving in Europe. We were the only ones who were there because of the war, because we wanted to defeat Hitler. But nobody believed us. And if they'd believed us, they would have hated us even more. They'd gone through the same stiff training that we were going through, and for that reason they wanted to make sure that this should go on forever into Eternity; they didn't want it to stop suddenly or get any better.

"Then came the day we marched into the desert. Before we left I got a letter from my father telling me that he was about to sail for Brazil and asking that I follow him there as soon as possible. I cursed my father, something I'll regret the rest of my life."

I was careful not to do anything that might interrupt his narrative, listening without moving to reassure him of my interest; yet my eyes never left Marie. I knew that, at this very moment and at this table, my friend was about to bring this past life of his to a close. For what has been told is finished. Only after he's told someone about his journey, will he have crossed that desert once and for all.

"We arrived at Fort St. Paul. It's in an oasis with palm trees and wells. There were cool, stone houses. French legionnaires were sitting around in the shade, playing cards and drinking. We were hoping for better days. But these French legionnaires despised us; they'd been told we were a gang of lowlifes who'd accept all sorts of humiliations just to earn a few sous. They led us out of town into the desert. We could see the lights of the town from there. They made us pour gravel into the sand for our camp so that the ground wouldn't be too soft, so that we wouldn't get too soft."

Marie was sitting motionless, silhouetted against the harbor. I felt our cursed belonging together so profoundly that it burned.

My neighbor continued, "They marched us farther out, way out into the desert, toward a small fort not far from the Italian border.

Everything was yellow—we, the earth, the sky. The officers rode while we went on foot, the noncoms too. The officers despised us because they were riding and we were walking; the noncoms hated us because they were walking and we were walking. I don't remember how long we marched through that desert. It seemed like forty years, like in the Bible.

"We were still a week's march away from our destination. They said we were going there to relieve the garrison. Then the Italian planes came. We were two regiments, alone between heaven and earth. The planes swooped down. They might just as well have been hurtling down on a single ship on the high seas. We dug ourselves into the sand, and every time the firing let up we'd move on. And again and again new swarms of these birds of death would swoop down from the sky. At that point the men despaired. They lay down in the sand, and they just stayed there, waiting for death. Our water was running out. Please forgive me. Perhaps you've experienced similar marches? I'm just telling you all this in answer to your question about how I got these things dangling on my chest.

"Up to that point I'd had no chance to prove my courage. Dragging boulders up a hillside, crossing the sea in a ship full of vomit that hadn't been washed for centuries, sleeping in a porridge of squashed bedbugs, jumping off a four-yard-high wall into a ditch filled with broken glass and rocks when your only alternatives are to die jumping or being stood against the wall for refusing to obey orders—that's no proof of courage, although it may be proof of endurance. But now, in the desert, I swear I wasn't even aware that I was being brave. I was just trying to talk my fellow legionnaires into showing a little courage. Especially the younger ones. I convinced them that this had nothing to do with the Foreign Legion, that there was a law that applied to all men, namely, that you had to behave decently until the moment of your death. And this notion or delusion got all mixed up with a promise of water and of our eventual arrival at our destination. And for a few minutes, they believed me. They pulled themselves together, got up out of the sand and trotted on for another hour. I told them I was there with them and had to endure everything along with them, as if it was in any way reassuring for them to know that I was enduring it too.

"Around that time the captain occasionally began to take me aside, to discuss how long it might still take, what one could expect, how the last of the water should be parceled out and when and where. And all the time there were those planes, again and again they would come, at shorter and shorter intervals. Diving down, and firing at us. Several of my boys died in those raids, boys to whom I'd just been swearing by all that was holy that we'd soon be at our destination. Now and then, I'd shoulder a pack for one of them. I swear to you, it never once occurred to me that any of this had anything to do with bravery.

"Much later I found out that we were the only outfit to arrive at its destination in any kind of decent shape. The captain claimed I'd had a lot to do with it. Later, at the fort, I was awarded the Ordre de la Nation. The guards had to stand at attention before me. They pinned the medal on me. The Captain kissed me in front of the company. The strange thing about this whole business is that I enjoyed it. What was even stranger is that everyone suddenly respected me. I swear, I didn't care that the respect was for me. But suddenly there was respect again. Respect for something. It didn't matter whether it was for me or what sort of medal I was awarded or which country's medal it was. The strangest thing about this story is that I began to like them all, and they liked me. I suddenly began to love them, body and soul, all these cruel, horrible, shifty men, all these vile, wicked bastards. With all my heart; I loved them and they loved me. I've never found saying good-bye so hard as when I left them."

I asked, "How did you happen to get discharged?"

He said, "I was wounded. I'm going to be demobilized now. Then I can pack up my jacket along with all my medals. In the meantime my father died in Brazil. Before his death he ordered a large quantity of gloves. I have two unmarried older sisters, but they can't manage the glove business without me. So, as soon as possible, I have to go over there to give them a hand."

As we left we passed by Marie's table, but she didn't see me. "That woman over there," I said, "is waiting for a man who won't ever come back."

"I came back," he said with a sad note in his voice, "but no one's waiting for me. Only two old sisters. I'm not lucky in love. And as for Nadine, you don't seriously think she'd fall for me, do you?"

V

Early the next morning my landlady sent someone to my room to tell me to come downstairs. At first I thought the silk merchant had come back to ask for another installment on his traveling expenses. But once I went downstairs, I immediately recognized the young man leaning against the landlady's window and winking at me as an officer of the secret police. I expected the worst. I noticed my landlady watching with barely concealed malicious joy.

The man's lips curled as he demanded to see my papers. His tone of voice was quite nasty. I placed the documents neatly on the sill of the landlady's window. He was astonished. "You have a visa? A letter of transit? You're planning to leave?" He exchanged a look with the landlady whose expression of malicious joy had changed to one of disappointment. I guessed from their mutual vexation that in their minds they'd already split the reward for my successful capture—for which my landlady had denounced me to him. All so that she could start her grocery store a bit sooner. The official went on, "You told this lady you definitely wanted to remain in this city, that you weren't intending to leave."

I said, "The things I told my landlady are not sworn statements. I can tell her whatever I feel like telling her."

In a grim fury he told me that the Bouches du Rhône Département was overpopulated, and the regulations required me to leave the country as soon as possible, and that I could retain my freedom only on condition that I at once book passage on a ship, any ship whatsoever. I should understand, he said, that French cities aren't there for me to live in, but for me to leave from.

In the meantime, my neighbor the legionnaire had come out of his room. He was standing on the stairs, listening to the officer's harangue. After the man left, he took me by the arm and dragged me down to the Belsunce, telling me I had to go with him to the Brazilian Consulate at once. He'd heard a rumor that a Brazilian ship was sailing today, and the rumor seemed to be quite credible; by tomorrow it would be a sure thing.

At his words I suddenly envisioned a ship, in a mist of rumors on some ghostly dock, being built in great haste by the spirits of those anxious to depart. I asked, "What's the name of the ship?"

"The *Antonia*," he said.

VI

I thought that Marie and I could board this new, just-materialized ship together. And so I went with the legionnaire to the Brazilian Consulate. There we found ourselves in a throng of transit visa applicants I'd never seen before, all crushed against the railing. On the other side of the railing was a green room rendered more spacious by a large map. There were two desks. The room was empty. At first no one came. Everyone was anxiously waiting for the consul to appear, or at least someone from the consular staff, an official, a typist, anyone who would listen to them. They'd been told at the offices of the shipping company that a ship was leaving shortly for Brazil. Probably many of them felt as little like going to Brazil as I did. But in any event, a ship was leaving, and once on board a ship you'd escaped and could hope for better things.

We pushed our way toward the railing. The consul's office remained empty, but from some remote room hidden from our view came the faint aroma of coffee, as if the consul had vanished in a cloud of coffee. This unaccustomed smell was exciting. We could imagine a sack of coffee, in fact, a cellar stocked with supplies for the invisible staff. After we'd been waiting for several hours, a slim, well-dressed, well-groomed man came into the room. He gazed at us in amazement, as if we were a desperate, feverish gang of people who'd forced their way into his living room, begging for some unintelligible thing. We all raised our voices to plead with him, but he withdrew in horror. So we continued to wait; several more hours passed. Finally he reappeared, pushed some papers around on one of the massive desks, then stepped to the railing, hesitantly, as if afraid we'd grab him and drag him over into our world.

My friend, in his dearly won desert calm, was the only one who'd been waiting silently. Now he suddenly banged on the railing. The slender young man looked up startled. His eyes were attracted to the glittering medals. Hesitantly he stepped toward them. My friend quickly handed him his visa application. I wanted to press mine into the young Brazilian's hands as well, but with a gesture of exhaustion to all the others waving their papers at him, he left the room holding only my friend's documents. I had the impression he'd be gone for years.

VII

I was walking past the pizzeria without looking inside, when someone came up behind me and took hold of my arm. It was the doctor, more exited than usual. Or maybe it only seemed that way because he was out of breath.

"So Marie was right after all," he said. "I could have sworn you'd be gone by now. I almost persuaded Marie that you had disappeared as suddenly as you had come, that it was useless to keep looking for you."

"No, I'm still here. People like you, with your calm and self-assured manner, are good at convincing others."

He bridled at that and said, "You didn't even go to see the Binnets, and they're really good friends of yours."

I thought, Yes, the Binnets are old, true friends. I had ignored them. But I'm sick. I've been infected with the departure sickness.

"Marie's been looking for you everywhere, for weeks already.

There's a real possibility that we'll be leaving on the next ship for Martinique, the *Montreal*."

"Does she have a visa?"

"She doesn't actually have it in hand yet, but it could arrive any moment."

"Do you have money for the passage?" I asked, and for the first time I saw a spark of amusement in his eyes. It made me want to hit him in the eyes.

"Money for the passage? I had that money in my wallet when we crossed the Loire already—enough traveling money to take both of us to our destination."

"And Marie's transit visa?"

"The consul will give that to her when she presents her visa. Except..."

"Another except!"

He laughed. "Nothing important. No, this time it's a modest except. Marie doesn't want to leave until she's seen you again. She considers you the most loyal friend she's ever had. Your sudden invisibility has only increased her esteem for you. I think it would be good if you'd join me for a glass of rosé while we wait for her together, here in the pizzeria."

"You're wrong," I said. "I can't go in there with you now, I can't ever again drink a glass of rosé with you, I can't wait for her with you."

He took a step back, frowned, "You can't? Why not? Marie is set on seeing you. I'm sure we'll be sailing this month. It's all arranged. Marie wants to see you just once more before the departure. You can surely give her that small reassurance."

"Why should I? I can't stand farewell ceremonies, those last and next-to-the-last good-byes. She's leaving with you; it's all set. She may feel a little troubled. But, well, we can't give her everything."

He looked at me carefully, as if to understand better what I'd just said. But I walked away, not even giving him the chance to reply. I felt his eyes on my back, following me.

My landlady was lying in wait for me when I returned to the hotel. She gave me a nasty look, a nasty smile. It seemed to me that her teeth had grown longer overnight, sharper and brighter. She pressed her large bosom to the sill, "Well?"

I asked in return, "Well, what?"

"Where's your ship passage? By the way, your room has been rented starting the fifteenth of the month. You're supposed to have left by then anyway." She'd probably only been pretending all these months to be a landlady. In reality she was working in disguise for some secret authority as an exorcist. I had strong doubts about her appearance except for those vulgar breasts in the window. Below that her body might end in God knows what, maybe a fishtail. I turned around on the spot.

VIII

I ran out of the hotel and went to the Rue de la République, to the Transports Maritimes. People were crowded around the counter. The next ship was scheduled to leave on the eighth. All berths had long ago been booked. So I booked a place on the ship after the next one. They emphasized that they could only make out my ticket after I showed them my exit visa.

I went outside and looked at the ship's model in the window of the Maritimes. They issued exit visas only to those who could prove they had money enough to pay for both the voyage and the security deposit. The Corsican would have to help me with my treasure in Portugal. I had to go at once to ask for his advice. Just then someone touched my hand. It was Marie.

"What are you doing here?" she asked. "Did you decide to leave after all? We're used to your magic tricks. I wouldn't be surprised at all if you crept out of one of the smokestacks on our boat once we were out at sea."

I looked down at her brown hair. She continued: "Then you'd always be there to give me advice and help. I'd never be alone."

I picked up her word. "Alone?"

She turned away as if I'd caught her in a slip of the tongue. "I mean, of course, alone with the doctor. Where have you been all this time? I looked for you everywhere. You can never find anybody in this damned city when you're looking for them. You only find them by coincidence, by chance. A lot has happened in the meantime and I need your advice again. Come with me."

"I have no time." I put my hands in my pockets. But she took hold of my thumb and pulled me across the street into the big, ugly café on the corner of the Rue de la République and the Old Harbor. The fat, gluttonous woman who evidently hadn't yet devoured all her travel money was sitting near one of the windows of the café. The Czech who'd wanted to enlist with the English ever since my arrival walked over to stand at the counter. His face was dark and determined. Through the glass door, walking by outside, I saw the fellow who'd been refused an American transit visa because of a prior conviction.

All these casual chance encounters, these senseless, repeated meetings depressed me with their stubborn unavoidability.

Marie was sitting with her head propped in one hand. With the other she was still holding on to my thumb. I had to admit that I wanted above all to be with her, to be with her anywhere. I stopped fighting it and asked her, "Is something wrong, Marie? Can I help you in any way?"

She put her head on my shoulder. There was a look in her eyes I'd never expected, a look I'd never seen there before. It was a look of infinite trust. I took her hand in both of mine. I had a feeling she was about to tell me something new, something surprising. But my premonition was wrong. She said, "You don't know it yet, but I actually have a visa now. The Mexicans really gave me a visa. All I need now is a letter of transit."

"For that you don't need my advice. Just go to the American consul, he'll give it to you."

"I've already been to see the American consul. He said he'd give me one and made an appointment for me to pick it up. Here's the appointment slip. I'm supposed to receive the transit visa on the twelfth of this month, but the ship is scheduled to sail on the eighth. Do you think my friend the doctor, who didn't wait for me to get my visa, would now be willing to wait until I get my transit visa?"

"Couldn't you think of anything to tell them at the consulate to make them change your appointment to an earlier date?" I asked. "Some special plea, some reason, even a lie? Wasn't seeing you enough to move the consul to help you?"

"Don't make fun of me. He wasn't at all moved by my looks. And I couldn't think of anything on the spur of the moment. The consul saw from my file that the visa had been granted to me as the companion of a writer named Weidel. He asked why, if I was in such a hurry, I hadn't come earlier. Weidel, he said, had been there himself just a little while ago. I said that I'd received my own visa now. I was glad I could say that much at least. I was scared to death. My husband had been there a little while ago! Just a little while ago!"

Hearing her say that made me blurt out, "He may have left in the meantime."

"On what ship? If he went to see the consul only a short while ago? He couldn't have sailed on a ghost ship. Or maybe he went via Spain? He was here recently. He was here, and I was here. Yet there've been moments during the last few weeks when I even thought that he was dead."

I cried out, "Marie, what are you saying? I told you as much once, and you just laughed and gave me an angry answer."

"Did I really laugh back then? I wonder how many years it's been since I actually laughed. I may be young, but look at me in the mirror over there!"

I turned to look. And started in amazement at the sight of us sitting at the same table, holding hands.

She went on: "I see that I still look young. How can it be that I'm still so young, so very young? How can it be that my hair's still brown? I feel a hundred years have gone by since we first heard that the Germans were outside Paris. You never asked me about that. Here, in Marseille, everybody asks, 'Where are you going?' They never ask, 'Where are you from?'

"When the war started, my lover—I mean the first one, the real one—he took me to a house in the country so that they wouldn't put me into a detention camp. You're wondering why he didn't keep me with him?—I told you before that he was sick, that he wasn't always nice to me, that he wanted to be by himself most of the time. So then another man, the one who's now my friend, came to the house where I was staying. He was a doctor and he came there to take care of a child. He was kind to everyone. He came often; I was alone; we liked each other. By that time the Germans were getting closer. I was afraid to stay there, so I went to Paris, and suddenly the Germans were just outside Paris. I looked for my friend, the first one, the real one, but he was no longer at his old address. The house where he used to live was boarded up. No one knew anything of his whereabouts. By then the windows had been removed from Notre Dame and everyone was leaving. I saw a woman wheeling a cart with a dead child out of Paris. I was alone, running through the streets, looking into cars. Then suddenly on the Boulevard de Sébastopol someone called to me from a car. It was the doctor. It was like a miracle. Like the hand of God. But it was no miracle, not the hand of God. It was sheer coincidence. Still, at the time it seemed like destiny itself and I behaved accordingly. I got into his car. He said, 'Calm down; I'll take you across the Loire.'

"That's how it started. I felt I had to get to the other side of the Loire, and because back then I had to get across the Loire, I now have to cross the ocean. I should have stayed where I was and continued looking for him. It was my own fault. Can you tell me why I had to cross the Loire, no matter what? Oh, what a trip that was! When the German planes came swooping down low over us, we got out and crawled under the car. At one place we picked up a woman whose foot had been shot up. We had to dump some of our luggage so we could get her into the car, but it was too late—she bled to death. We left the dead body by the side of the road and drove on. Finally we arrived at the Loire. The first bridge we came to had been blown up; cars and trucks were scattered on the riverbank and some still hung in the ruins of the bridge. People trapped inside them were screaming. We held each other close, he and I. And I promised to follow him to the ends of the earth. At that point I thought the end was near, the distance short, and the promise easy to keep, but we crossed the Loire and arrived here in Marseille. Suddenly coincidence did indeed turn into a stroke of fate. I was alone with the man who had found me instead of with the man I'd been looking for. That which had been a shadow was now flesh and blood; what should have been just for a little while now had permanence; and what was intended to be forever was—"

"Stop that nonsense!" I said. "You know it's all nonsense. A coincidence never becomes fate; a shadow never becomes flesh and blood; and something that has real permanence never turns into a shadow. Anyway, you're lying. You told me a completely different story before. You wrote a letter to your husband..."

She cried, "I? A letter? How do you know anything about that letter? Yes, I did write a letter, but that letter could not possibly have reached him, such a terrible letter. I wrote it while I was fleeing. I wrote it right after we left Paris, on the lap of that other man. Back then no mail was ever delivered. I wrote other letters too, right after we got here. And those letters did reach their destination. They must have been delivered; my husband must have come here. At the consulates they say he was there. I was sure that if and when he comes, once he's actually here, he'll have to look for me and find me, no matter whether I'm unfaithful, beautiful, or ugly. Then when he sees me, he'll call out to me, 'Marie, Marie,' even if I was suddenly old or disfigured or unrecognizably changed in some way. In my heart I know that it's not possible for him to be here without his having called out to me. The consuls say he's here, but in my heart I know he must be dead. If he were alive he'd come and get me. They're wrong, those consuls. They've issued a visa and a letter of transit to a dead man."

Her hand between my hands was now ice cold. I began to rub it, the way you rub a child's hands in the wintertime, but my hands were too cold to warm hers. I felt I had to tell her everything, then and there. I was searching for the right words.

Then she said, quite calmly, "Maybe he got here before us. Maybe he's already left. Yes, that's probably the answer; he's already left. After all when a consul says 'a short while ago' the words mean something quite different than when we say them. Time is different for consuls. A couple of months mean nothing to a consul. I didn't dare ask them what they meant. Maybe for the United States consul 'a short while ago' means several months ago."

I took a firm grip on her wrist and I said, "There's no way you can catch up to him. You lost him a long time ago. You haven't found him anywhere in this country, not even in this city. You have to believe me, he's too far away for you to ever find again. He's beyond your reach."

A new, almost unbearable light gleamed in her soft gray eyes. "I know where he went. I'll catch up to him this time. This time nothing will prevent me. If the consul won't make out a transit permit for me, I'll leave this country on foot, without a transit visa. I'll go to Perpignan, and there I'll get a guide to take me across the mountains like others have done before me. I'll pay a boat captain to let me have some corner on a boat sailing to Africa."

"You're not going to do any such thing," I cried. "They'll arrest you and put you into a camp so that you won't be able to leave at all. Do you have any idea what things are like out there? First they call out to you, they call out three times, then they shoot."

She laughed and said, "You just want to scare me. It would be better if you'd help me the way you did before. You didn't need a reason then, you just helped me."

Letting go of her wrist, I said, "And what if you're right, and the consuls have made a mistake? What if your husband is dead? What then?"

Her gray eyes lost their sparkle. "How could the consuls be wrong? They don't miss a thing in your passport, not a line in your file escapes them. They'd be more likely to keep a hundred good applicants from leaving just because a letter's missing somewhere, rather than take the chance that one bad guy leaves who shouldn't. I only got this ridiculous idea that he's dead because they're forcing me to stay here. Once I can look for him, I'll know that he exists. As long as I'm searching for him, I know that I'll be able to find him."

Suddenly her expression changed. "The doctor's walking by outside. I'm going to ask him to join us. You know, he's really a good man."

"You don't have to praise him to me. I know his good points."

She ran to the door and called to him. He came in and greeted us in his usual calm way. "Sit with us," Marie said. "We need to discuss my transit visa situation. My two dear friends."

He took her hand and looked at her. He said, "You're cold. Why are you so pale?" He rubbed her hands just as I had done a few minutes earlier. Marie looked straight at me with her all-too-clear eyes. She seemed to be saying, See, he's holding my hands; it doesn't mean anything. We just ran into each other. It was a coincidence.

I thought, Maybe he really is a good person. And probably just because he is a doctor he believes in healing. But I don't, I don't believe in healing. At least not by this doctor. I had no doubts about which hand she should be reaching for once the truth came out. In my mind I turned to the dead man: We'll take her away from him soon. Rest assured, he won't keep her long.

I said, "Give me that piece of paper with the date. I'll see if I can do anything with it." She rummaged around and found the little slip of paper.

When we got up, the doctor took me aside. He said, "You see now, don't you, that the right thing is for Marie to leave now. I didn't get mixed up in it. That would only have delayed things." He added softly, "She'll find some peace at last. I'll make sure she gets across safely." It wasn't till later that I realized the full meaning of his words.

I didn't follow them out. I stayed at my table and watched them as they walked down the Quai des Belges, not holding hands but in depressing harmony.

9

I

I SPENT the rest of the day running up and down the Canebière with Marie's document in my pocket searching for someone who could help me. I knew now that Marie would no longer put up with any delay, coincidence, or trick. I finally understood the message I'd received in Paris that was intended for Weidel: "Join me any way you can, so that we can leave this country together!"

Her new friend, the doctor, was wrong; actually, she had never hesitated. We were the ones who had hesitated, the doctor and I, quarreling about this woman who had been determined to leave all along. She only stayed as long as she wanted to, and now that she wanted to leave, it would all go enormously quickly, so quickly that I'd never be able to catch up if I didn't immediately arrange things for both of us. I even wondered if I should go back to see the American consul again. I wracked my brains for a way to strike a spark of understanding in that consular brain. Nothing useful came to mind except the realization that I'd never before come up against such an incorruptible official. In his own way, he was a just man. He carried out his difficult duties as a Roman official might once have done, in that same place, listening to the emissaries of foreign tribes with their dark and to him ridiculous demands from gods unknown to him. The summons, once it was registered and signed by him, was unalterable. God himself, if there was one, would sooner take back a judgment, would sooner give the lie to His own inscrutable wisdom. In any event, if He existed, it would all end with Him anyway.

Moreover, He didn't have to fear that He would lose the little bit of power by which He still held fast to this struggling world.

I spent the next morning as well reflecting on the goodness of God. It was the day alcohol could be served. At the Café Source I caught sight of Paul and his girlfriend, along with Achselroth, the man who'd left Paul in the lurch, the thin girl for whom he'd left the other girl, the other girl, and the man who was going to Cuba and his wife. They were all sitting around a table in the café having an aperitif. They were quite content to be among themselves. To them I was probably just a pesky unavoidable hanger-on from the old concentration camp days. They didn't seem at all happy to see me when I sat down at their table.

Achselroth said, "How's your friend, Weidel? The last time I saw him he seemed offended and depressed."

"Offended and depressed? Weidel?"

"Why do you look at me like that? You shouldn't be offended if I tell you he seemed offended when I spoke with him yesterday."

"You spoke with him yesterday?"

"On the telephone."

"On the telephone? Weidel?"

"Oh, good God, no. Excuse me. Hundreds of people call me every day. I'm a sort of vice consul. Everybody needs advice. It wasn't Weidel at all who called; it was Meidler. For the last fifteen years I've been confusing the two. Yet they fight like cats and dogs when they're together. I'll never forget Weidel's face in Paris when I congratulated him on Meidler's film premiere. Incidentally, I saw Weidel's wife this week at the Mont Vertoux. I'd never get her mixed up with anyone else! She looked a bit frazzled and upset, though still very lovely."

"I always wondered," Paul said, "at Weidel's luck in getting that woman."

Achselroth answered him slowly, his handsome face hardening somewhat, "He probably picked her up when she was still a very young girl. At an age when children still believe in Santa Claus. He probably convinced her of all sorts of things, such as that men and women love each other." Turning to me he said, "Please give the young woman my sincerest regards."

I was surprised and somewhat disturbed that this man had retained such a clear picture of the real Marie. The man's mind, his memory, probably worked in such a way that he recorded everything clearly, even the most subtle things so that he could later write it all down, the same way a short-sighted or half-blind person can use some gadget to record everything in precise detail, like those cameras used in astronomy; whereas a sighted person is confused by fogginess and spots that eventually dissolve anyway. Achselroth had probably mentally recorded the most improbable and secret events, and this time it just happened to be Marie's turn. I began to feel apprehensive, but I tried immediately to figure out some way to get this man to help. He'd never do anything if he didn't think it would be worth his while, just like my poor, shabby Portuguese friend. He, at least, had done something selfless once. Achselroth, on the other hand, would never do something like that, never. He would keep drawing new people into his infinite emptiness, enticing them in, and never, ever find one over whom his own abyss would close. Did he know himself? I wondered. I didn't think so. Nature which had equipped him with a handsome face and good mind had played him a dirty trick. In this respect he was like an amoeba, an algae. Even my little shabby Portuguese was far superior to him in this regard.

I said, "I'll give her your regards today. By the way, you could prove your devotion in another way. The young lady is in a bad way at present."

He said, very polite, "What's the matter?"

"She needs a transit visa. She already has her appointment at the American Consulate. But the date doesn't work. The appointment has to be sooner, because the ship is leaving earlier."

He said, perking up, "From Lisbon? On the twelfth? Is it the *Nyassa*? I'm booked on her too. I've decided to pull up stakes here."

"Yes, on the *Nyassa*," I lied. I probably looked at him too closely, for his face turned expressionless. I added, "That's of course if she gets the letter of transit in time."

"That can be arranged," he said. "We'll make the most charming traveling companions. And if there's a storm and they need a scapegoat, they can throw Weidel overboard."

"You'll get him mixed up with Meidler," Paul said.

"Don't worry, I won't mix them up. I'll throw the right one overboard." Achselroth went on, beaming, "I did try once to leave Weidel in the lurch, but it was futile. It didn't work. We both got here. And I'm sure Weidel's going to be swallowed by a whale this time too and get there at the same time the rest of us do."

"I think he'll actually get there before we do," I said. "But right now, his wife needs a transit visa. And since you're a friend of the consul's..."

"It's precisely because I am a friend of his that I can't bother him with such requests."

"But you're smart," I said. "People like you. If anyone knows the ropes, it's you. Isn't there someone who can get a consul to change a date?"

He leaned back in his chair. For a moment he said nothing. Then he said, "There is one man in Marseille who has some influence with the consul. He just happens to be in the city this month and will probably also be sailing on the *Nyassa*. He heads a commission that's investigating the effects the war is having on the civilian population. His commission is bringing over boatloads of food for French children. An excellent fellow. He's a friend of the consul's. And at the same time a sort of spiritual advisor to him. The consul will do what he asks, what he says carries moral weight with him."

"Moral weight?"

"Right," Achselroth said, utterly serious, "moral weight. If he's convinced that it makes sense, then he'll convince the consul to act. But he himself has to approve; he'll never do something that goes against his conscience."

"Well, let's hope that his conscience will allow him to change the date on Marie's transit visa to a few days earlier," I said. "And let's hope, too, that the consul will listen to this man of God. There are cases in the Bible—"

Achselroth broke in coldly, "We're dealing here with the American consul."

I was afraid he might take back his offer to help, and hastily said, "Forgive me! I don't know anything about such things. You know best."

He took a fountain pen out of his pocket. I was intrigued by it. You could see the ink through the yellowish glass. He wrote two notes and put them into separate envelopes, saying, "Please give both of these to the young lady today. Ask her to keep me informed. The best time to reach me is in the morning between eight and nine. I'm an early riser."

As soon as I was alone, I ripped open the envelope addressed to Marie. She mustn't know about this; I'd take care of it all. Achselroth's handwriting was straightforward. The contents of the note were straightforward, too: "I've heard of your troubles. I shall try to help you. Professor Whitaker will agree to see you after you give him my letter. Please keep me informed."

I tore up the note. The other envelope was addressed to Professor Whitaker at the Hotel Splendide. I went there at once.

II

A couple of policemen were idling near the revolving door of the Splendide, and on either side were some fellows conspicuously sucking on cigars. I must have looked all right to them as they let me go in. It was warm in the spacious lobby. Once inside, I realized how cold it had been outside these past months. I sat down in an armchair to wait while a bellboy took my letter upstairs.

In the camp by the sea it was the barbed wire that had united us. We were all filthy and crawling with lice. Heroes and thieves, physicians, writers, and rogues—we were all in the same boat along with the poorly paid spies who were the most bedraggled of all. The people here in this large, warm hall, made even larger by reflecting mirrors, were all united in being well-groomed and neatly pressed.

These were the gentlemen from Vichy, the members of the German Commission, Italian agents, the heads of the Red Cross Committee, the leaders of the large American I-don't-know-what committee, and in the corners of the mirrored hall, among the potted palms, stood the world's best-dressed, best-paid spies, suspiciously inconspicuous, sucking on the best cigars of their respective nations.

A bellboy came over to tell me that Mr. Whitaker could see me in an hour. Would I be kind enough to wait or, if I preferred, I could come back later.

I waited. At first I enjoyed watching, but pretty soon I got bored. The warmth began to bother me too; I would have liked to take off my jacket. I had become a kind of amphibious creature in the constant cold of the hotel rooms, cafés, and official waiting rooms I'd been frequenting. I watched the people going up and down the stairs or coming out of the elevator and crossing the lobby, walking briskly or stiffly, imperceptibly greeting or ignoring one another, dead serious or smiling, but all true to their roles—expressing so precisely who they thought or wanted others to think they were that it looked as if someone were sitting in the hotel attic pulling the strings.

Just to drive away my boredom, I began to speculate about the profession of a short, delicate white-haired American with a large head. He was complaining about something to the porter who listened to him patiently. Then the American went up the stairs, not taking the elevator, and I assumed it was to get a couple of committees to do something.

Behind me I heard indistinctly the sound of German being spoken. I moved to another chair to get a better view. In one of the dining halls behind a glass door at a table covered by a white tablecloth sat a group of Germans. Some wearing dark suits, some in uniform. In the haze of smoke, mirrors, and glass I saw flashes of swastikas. My blood runs cold at the mere sight of swastikas, and I always notice them immediately wherever they are, much like a man who's terrified by spiders is always aware of them. But here, in this warm room on the Boulevard d'Athènes, those symbols were especially frightening, even more so than back home in Germany in the prison interrogation rooms or during the war when I saw them on the soldiers' uniforms. I was wrong to make light of the terror people felt as the swastika cars roared by—a terror so great they were ready to walk into the sea. Those cars had stopped here, on the Boulevard d'Athènes. Here the Germans had gotten out to negotiate with the lesser masters of the world. And once the negotiations were done—at a price set by the masters—a few thousand additional people would die behind barbed wire, a couple of thousand more people would be lying in the streets of cities with shot-up bodies.

On the wall across from where I sat, a large clock with gilt hands showed me I had twenty more minutes to wait before I could go upstairs to see the man of God. I closed my eyes. If the consul listened to this man of God, the matter of Marie's transit visa would be decided. She would have to leave. I would have to get on the same ship. I would have to leave this world that was dear to me and join those shadowy swarms as if I really were one of them, only to catch up to Marie. How had she gotten me to do what I feared most? I was filled with shame and regret. As a child I used to forget my mother when I went fishing. All it took then was for a log driver to whistle, and I'd climb up onto his log raft, forgetting my fishing tackle. He would take me along on the river only a little way, and already I would have forgotten my hometown.

It's true, I realized. Everything just passes through me. And that's why I was still roving about unharmed in a world in which I didn't know my way well at all. Indeed, even the fit of anger that had decided my life back then in my own country was only temporary. I didn't stay angry; I wandered around afterward, my anger gone. What I really like is what endures, that which is different from me.

I felt sad and anxious standing outside this man's door, this man who could shake the conscience of consuls. I wondered what he looked like. But here, too, there was first a waiting room, a waiting period.

Then the last door opened. The little man sitting behind a desk was the same delicate, large-headed American who had a little while ago complained to the porter and had used the stairs instead of the elevator. Despite the large head his face was small. It was a bit wrinkled. He looked at me sharply, from head to toe. The letter of recommendation from Achselroth that I'd sent up was lying on his desk. He read it with enormous attention as if the few lines could give him some spontaneous knowledge and understanding of all the connections. Then he looked me in the face, so keenly that I felt a stab. He said, "This letter has nothing to do with you personally. Why are you here instead of the woman?"

I had the feeling that this man was almost smarter than the consul. I answered meekly, "Please forgive me, I have come on behalf of the woman. I am her only support."

He sighed and asked me for all the documents. He examined them as carefully as he had the letter. You could tell that he could look through thousands of such documents without exhausting his powers of concentration. I was amazed that the truth should be revealed to him in a bundle of papers. But after all, they weren't any less dry than the thornbush in which God had once appeared. I also put the transit visa with the little red ribbon and Marie's appointment slip on the desk. He said, "You would like to leave on the same ship as the woman?"

"Yes, I would like to."

He frowned and said, "This woman doesn't have the same name as yours. Why?"

His look was so severe, his interest so genuine, that I could only answer with the truth. "It isn't my fault. Circumstances dictated against it."

He asked, " And what do you intend to do in the future? What are your plans? Your next professional undertaking?"

His look was piercing. I said, "I will try to learn a trade."

He said, a little surprised and with just a trace of sympathy, "How come? Aren't you going to write another book?"

Then under that severe gaze of his that demanded the full truth, it just burst out of me. "I? No. Let me tell you why. As a little boy I often went on school trips. The trips were a lot of fun, but then the next day our teacher assigned us a composition on the subject, 'Our school trip.' And when we came back from summer vacations we always had to write a composition: 'How I spent my vacation.' And even after Christmas, there was a composition: 'Christmas.' And in the end it seemed to me that I experienced the school trips, Christmas, the vacations, only so that I could write a composition about them. And all those writers who were in the concentration camp with me, who escaped with me, it seems to me that we lived through these most terrible stretches in our lives just so we could write about them: the camps, the war, escape, and flight."

He made a note and said with a glimmer of kindness, "This is a grave confession for a man like yourself. What kind of trade would you like to take up?"

"I have a talent for precision mechanics."

Then he said, "You're still young. You can still make changes in your life. I wish you good luck."

I said, "Without this woman I doubt very much that I would have any luck. Oh, if only you could help us. Your word carries great weight."

He smiled and said, "In a few cases, with God's help. Please take back all the papers except for the lady's appointment notice. I'll see the consul this evening at the meeting of our committee. In the meantime, please don't worry."

III

I climbed up to Fort St. Jean to be by myself and to look at the sea. Where the road took a turn and where the wind was the strongest I saw Marie coming toward me. The wind was blowing her toward me. I took her arm and in my foolishness wasn't even surprised at how readily she came with me, as if that gust of wind at the turn in the road had united us. I invited her to the pizzeria, and we went back down to the Old Port.

"I just wanted to be by myself," she said, "and to look at the sea."

We sat close to the pizza oven fire. In the brightly flickering flames her face seemed restless and hot; I had an inkling how it might look if moved by sudden joy or desire. Whenever I found myself alone with her, I felt the moment was at hand when I had to tell her everything. The waiter brought us some rosé, and we drank. I immediately felt lighter, it was like a threat lifting. Marie tugged gently at my sleeve. She said, "The consul has changed the date for my appointment. If you have friends like that, friends who can help me with my papers, why don't you have them help you? I can't believe that we'll be separating. Yes, that's right, look at me. I think you're going to turn up on the ship or on some pier or gangplank. Just as you did today, at a turn in the road in this strange city."

I said, "What's the use?" I looked at her closely, but the flickering fire made it impossible to read her true expression.

She said, "I could sit by this fire for hours, just listening to them knead and beat the dough. I could gaze at the fire and grow old doing it."

"In that case, why not go on sitting here?" I said. "Then I wouldn't have to follow you, wouldn't have to turn up on some ship or in a foreign city. We could sit here together, as often and for as long as we liked."

She looked at me sadly. "You know that I have to leave. Sometimes it seems that you're not really listening to me or that you think what I say doesn't matter."

She was right, I thought. She did have to leave. Telling her the truth now would just get things even more tangled. First let the ship set sail, leaving behind this cursed country, the good and the bad memories, the patched-together lives, the graves and all the absurdity about guilt and remorse.

"Well, tomorrow I have my date with the American consul. I'm worried. I pray to God he'll give me the transit."

"A strange prayer, Marie. People used to pray to their gods to send them a favorable wind. Do you think you can sit with me here for just a moment without constantly thinking about your departure?"

"You should be thinking about it too," Marie said, "you, of all people."

Her words made me think of the old man who had said something similar to me on my first evening in Marseille. For a moment I saw his eyeless, his bottomless face in the pizza fire, accompanied by the clatter of the rolling pin. Marie begged the waiter for a little slice of pizza, even without a bread ration. But he remained firm. He would only give us wine.

IV

That evening the hallway outside my room was clogged by a pile of luggage. It was guarded by the two dogs, now wearing new collars. In a little while my neighbor came to my door carrying some leftover wine, a bag of ersatz coffee, a bar of chocolate, and two eggs—all of which she wanted me to inherit. I could already imagine the look in Claudine's eyes when I brought her all this stuff. My neighbor was ready to leave for Lisbon the following day. There were even places booked for the two dogs in a special dog compartment on the *Nyassa*.

The beasts yelped happily as they left.

The next morning the hallway was again blocked with luggage. Two old people who had arrived on the early train were moving in. Both were short and round, with gray tousled hair. Despite their advanced age, they behaved like children. They had been tossed about with all their bags and packages in an uncomprehending world, but it had not managed to separate their wrinkled hands. The old woman borrowed a corkscrew from me to open a bottle of denatured alcohol. She noticed I was alone and invited me to share the weak early morning coffee she was making on her alcohol burner. And when my other neighbor, the legionnaire, appeared in their doorway, not having found me in my room, he was invited too. The coffee was ersatz coffee made from dried peas; the sugar was saccharin. The alcohol was some smelly ersatz alcohol, but the little flame filled our empty hearts with a substitute for home and hearth. When we asked where they were going, the old people said they were going to Colombia. The old man had escaped from Germany some time ago after they had set fire to his union hall. Their oldest son was in the German army and had been declared missing. The youngest son had done something bad back in Germany for which he'd been banned from their house. So he emigrated. Now it was this prodigal son who was inviting them to his home in Colombia. The legionnaire and I helped the old people put away their luggage. The Colombian Consulate didn't open till noon. The two old people sat down side by side near the window. The old man looked out at the Rue de la Providence. His wife began darning his socks.

V

The legionnaire and I, both of us with lots of free time, decided to walk along the Canebière from one café to the next, eventually ending up at Café St. Ferréol. Just to please him, I sent a note to Nadine at the Dames de Paris, asking her to come down to join us. He was startled and turned pale when she came and actually sat down at our table. She stared at his medals and asked him to tell her about them. But he was so flustered, he couldn't say a word, couldn't pull himself together. Here was his big chance and he was losing it—here suddenly was the young woman who had seemed so unattainable, and she was sitting at his table, laughing.

From there we went to the Brazilian Consulate. The inner room was as empty as the last time I'd been there. The people waiting at the barrier sighed and complained into the emptiness. The young man came out again, but this time only as far as the middle of the room—he'd gotten wiser. He was going to avoid the possibility that any of the visa applications being waved at him in desperation might stick to him as they fluttered across the barrier. He was about to withdraw again when my friend became quite frantic; he pushed the door in the barrier open, and with one leap he was in the inner room. He grabbed the young man's arm. I had followed him, and suddenly all those waiting pushed into the interior room behind us, shouting at the young man, "We've got to leave on this ship! We can't wait any longer! We have to get on that ship!"

Unexpectedly, the young man started cursing vehemently in Portuguese, but my friend didn't let go of his arm. Soon officials we hadn't seen before rushed out of the innermost room of the consulate and pushed the waiting horde back, all except my friend who refused to let go. Suddenly typewriters began to clatter; visa applications were collected. My friend was handed a piece of paper, and told that he must go at once to the consulate doctor, who could only see him right that minute. The doctor would give him a statement saying that his eyes were all right, because one could enter the country only if one's eyes were sound. Then they pushed him back again to the other side of the barrier, and out of the consulate. I rushed back in to retrieve my hat. By now the tumult my friend had started had subsided; the desks were empty again; the officials had withdrawn to the back rooms; and those still waiting sighed and complained because all the applications that had been gathered were still lying in one pile on top of the barrier.

How badly things were going for my friend. He certainly deserved better! The day after this happened he was demobilized. He put his medals into a cardboard box, and put the box into his suitcase. Then he asked Nadine to have lunch with him. He came back a little while later, looking pretty sad. She had smiled coolly, had been politely amusing; but had carefully sidestepped agreeing to see him again. He said, "Right at the outset I wondered if Nadine could fall for me of all people. And anyway, maybe she thought it foolish to tie herself down since I'd be leaving soon. But I'd gladly take her with me."

The Brazilian ship was scheduled to leave at the end of the week. He had all his papers, an appointment for the last visa, and his ticket was paid for. I went back with him to the consulate a couple of hours before opening time. The stairway was already packed with people overflowing into the street. From time to time a Brazilian appeared at an upper window, looked down, opened his mouth and closed it again, as if he was too weak to make a sound.

"Aren't they going to open the doors?" one man said.

"They've got to," said another, "because the ship is leaving today."

"Nobody can force them to open up,"

"We'll force them to," yelled a third.

"But that won't get us a visa."

My friend, silent and frowning, was already standing in line. The window opened again. This time a pretty young woman in a green dress looked down in puzzlement and laughed. The transit applicants answered her laugh with an angry shout. As I was walking home, I visualized them all, waiting endlessly. I thought they might still be waiting even as the ship weighed anchor—an empty ship sailing to an empty country.

That evening at the hotel the legionnaire knocked on my door. He said, "They won't let me go to Brazil."

"Didn't your eyes pass the test?"

"I had everything; I even had the eye doctor's certificate. And eventually the consulate did open. I even reached the room of the consul, but they said they had just received a telegram, and now they were asking for proof of Aryan ancestry. And so, in accordance with the laws of this country, I have to go back to my département of origin. I'm leaving today; I intend to return to the village I left when my father was imprisoned. It was in exchange for his release that I joined the army in the first place, although since then he has died. I'll wait there for a new visa. Besides I'm fed up with this city, and I want some peace and quiet."

He was taking the overnight train. I went with him to the train station, which was located high up on a hill. From there I could look down on the nighttime city, only dimly illuminated because of the air raid precautions. For a thousand years it had been a last home for people like us, a last refuge on this continent. I looked down from the station to where the land slipped silently into the sea, the first gleam of the African world on its white southern walls. But the city's heart, no doubt about it, continued to beat to a European rhythm, and if it were to stop beating, then refugees scattered all over the world would also have to die, like a particular variety of trees, which

—no matter where one planted them—would all die at the same time because they had all been sown at the same time.

I got back to the Hotel de la Providence just before dawn. The room to the left of mine was already occupied again. I slept very little because these new arrivals were making a lot of noise with their luggage. They knocked at my door a little later to ask for some alcohol for their stove. They turned out to be a young couple. The woman had probably been very slender and delicate once. But now, except for her calm face, she was broad and ungainly because she was expecting a child. Her husband was a strong and forthright fellow, who had escaped from a camp through a clever ruse. But now, since he had been an officer in the Spanish Army and they figured he would be handed over to the Germans, they decided to separate. He would leave immediately. He asked me to help his wife. Her no-longer beautiful face was calm; there was no sign of despair, or fear of being left behind alone. Nor was there any outward sign of her steadfast courage, now that she had only me as her support, someone she'd found at the last minute and by chance when they came to ask for some alcohol.

VI

I was waiting for Marie at the Café Saint Ferréol. It was ten in the morning, but the café was already full of people waiting to go to the Prefecture across the square or to the American Consulate. I knew many of these people, but there were also some new faces among them. For they kept streaming into the country's only port over which the French flag still waved. The masses wanting to leave the continent each week could have manned a giant flotilla. Yet not even one sad little ship was sailing on a weekly basis anymore.

Then I saw the girl from the camp at Bompard whom I'd met once at the Corsican's being led past by a police officer. She no longer wore stockings, the little fur piece she'd put around her shoulders in honor of the day looked mangy and moth-eaten. The police officer had to support her because her walk was unsteady. Most likely her last hope had just been shattered. Tomorrow they would probably send her from Bompard to a concentration camp where she'd collapse completely. In ancient times, these things were better handled. You could have bought a girl like that—her new master might have been cruel, or he might have been kind. He would have used her to work in his house, to take care of the children, to feed the chickens. No matter how ugly or worn down she was, she could still have retained some hope.

I saw three *prestataires* pass by, without weapons, without epaulets. Then Marie was standing in the doorway. She had her transit visa—I recognized it by the little red ribbon.

She came toward me and said, "Look, he gave it to me!" She wanted to order aperitifs for us to celebrate, but unfortunately it was a no-alcohol day; they didn't even have lemonade or real tea. Of her own accord, she took my hand, as in the old days. She gently stroked her face with it. I asked if she was pleased. She kept one hand on mine and one on her transit visa.

"You performed your magic again," she said. "You can do magic the way my other friend can heal. Whatever one of you can't do, the other one can."

"Marie, I'm afraid my magic is finished now. My skills will be useless from now on. No one needs them anymore. Just a walk to the exit visa department of the Prefecture and everything will be done."

"Not everything's done yet. I've been to the Prefecture three times already, all in vain. They told me I'd have to come back tomorrow. That they have to check my records first. Because everything depends on whether my husband has already been issued an exit visa. If he has, they'll give me one too. I think they gave it to him after he got his transit visa. So, I'll find out tomorrow."

Her hand which had been warm on mine, turned cool. I was desperate. I had to go see Nadine immediately. That last time I saw Nadine she'd talked about a girlfriend who worked at the Prefecture. She had to talk to her girlfriend today, as soon as possible. This business with the Office for Aliens had to be arranged by tomorrow.

Then Marie said, "I keep wondering what it might be like over there. Will it be the way it is here? Will it be different?"

"Where over there, Marie? What do you mean?

She raised her hand from the transit visa and pointed into the air, away from herself. "Over there, over there."

"Where over there, Marie?"

"Over there. When it's all over, will there finally be peace as the doctor believes? Will we see each other again over there? And if and when we *do* meet again there—will we be so changed that it won't be like a reunion, but more like what you always wish for in vain on this earth, a new beginning? A new, for-the-first-time meeting with your lover? What do you think?"

"Dear Marie, I've learned quite a few tricks in this city. By now I know pretty much how things work here. And I'm familiar with worldly affairs, even though they're pretty confused these days. I have good connections here and I don't know how anything works over there—I don't know my way around over there."

"My husband must have gotten there already. He must have thought that I left before him. Just like I thought he'd left before me. How can he know when I'll follow? On which ship? Will he expect me? I really believe now that when we get there, he'll be standing there, waiting for me."

"Oh, I see. You mean over there. In the country that gave you the visa. I haven't given that much thought so far. I think everything will be different over there. The air will be different, there'll be different fruit, a different language. And in spite of that, everything will be the same. Those who are alive will continue to live as before. The dead will remain dead."

She said slowly, contemptuously, "So you don't really believe he'll be standing there, waiting for me, meeting every ship that comes in."

"Over there, Marie, I don't think … "

All at once I saw Achselroth coming through the door with his girlfriend. Paul and his girlfriend were with him, as well as the couple going to Cuba. I grabbed Marie's hand along with her transit visa and pulled her outside and into another café.

"There was someone I didn't want to meet," I explained. "I didn't want him to see you either. I can't stand him."

She laughed and said, "Who was it? What did he do?"

"He's a really unpleasant guy, the sort of person you can't depend on, who'll abandon you every time."

"Abandon you?" Marie asked still smiling. "Did he run out on you once? A friend of yours? Who then?" Her smile vanished; she stared at me. "What's the matter? Whom did he abandon? Where? Why?"

"Please stop asking all these questions," I said. "Can't you just go from one café to another for my sake without ten times asking me 'why'?"

She hung her head and was silent. I waited, almost frantic for her to start asking again, to press me for information, to torment me into finally telling her the whole truth.

VII

I went to Nadine's department at the Dames de Paris. She was startled to see me there. Her supervisor was standing only three steps away from us. Nadine gestured for me to wait. She was just helping a customer try on a hat.

I felt good about waiting in this place, which was so unlike any of the other places I usually frequented. The supervisor asked me if she could help me, but I insisted on waiting for Nadine; I said that she knew what I needed, that my wife was her regular client. Every time Nadine took a hat off a stand and put it on her own lovely head, the customer's expression was one of hesitant hope, and then when Nadine put the same hat on the customer's head, the hopeful expression turned to one of embarrassment and disappointment. And I must say, the hat did take on a grotesque appearance. After Nadine had demonstrated her triumph in a superficially polite way with a dozen hats, a sale was at last concluded. It was a rust-colored hat with a wide brim and pointed crown, which looked quite good with what the woman could see of herself in the mirror, but not with the rest of her body.

"I'd like to buy a hat too," I said to Nadine since the supervisor made no move to leave. Nadine at once began to model several. As soon as the supervisor had moved away, I said, "You have to give up your lunch break for me. You have to go to the Prefecture right away. I hope your girlfriend is still there, the one you mentioned before."

"Oh, yes, Rosalie. She's actually my cousin. What do you need from her? Have you decided to leave?"

I didn't answer.

"Or is it that woman who was giving you so much trouble?" There was a note of contempt in her voice. "Good then. Let's do everything we can to see that she'll leave!" She fiddled with the hat stands. She twirled a hat on her index finger, a round child's hat that I think was very similar to the old crushed and crumpled hat that Marie never wore but always carried around with her.

"Please give me Rosalie's home address. I have to talk with her right away." Just then the supervisor came back. I took the hat and paid for it. Nadine wrote Rosalie's address on the receipt.

I interrupted Rosalie while she was eating dinner. My mouth watered when I smelled the bouillabaisse. She was at the table with her mother, a drab, fat woman—a lifeless, snuffed-out version of Rosalie. Rosalie was pretty fat too. Her shiny black, bulging eyes looked huge because of blue-black eye makeup. She reminded me a lot of that dog with eyes like wagon wheels. Unfortunately she offered me only a glass of wine, no bouillabaisse. Rosalie ate quickly, with pleasure, attentively waited on by her mother. For dessert there were tiny cups of genuine coffee.

I brought up the matter at hand. I put all the documents on the table. She wiped her mouth, then flipped through the papers with her small, plump hands.

She said, "You may be Nadine's friend ten times over, but I can't risk my job for you."

"But you can see that my papers are all in order; I have my visa and my transit visa. I need an exit visa by tomorrow. I'd be glad to pay you for your efforts."

She said, "Please don't mistake me for Nadine. For me there is only one reward, and that is being helpful to someone who's in danger."

I stared at her. So her face was only a mask—this mask of a fat, eye-rolling young woman, effectively hid the true but invisible face. Her real one was probably tough, kind, and brave. I was ashamed because I'd tried to get around her, to bribe her.

She said, "Why by tomorrow?"

"Tomorrow is the last day they're selling berths on the ship. And I can book a passage only if I have my exit visa."

"You haven't paid a security deposit yet."

"For the time being it would be enough to have proof that an exit visa will be issued to me as soon as I pay the security deposit."

By now she'd obviously stopped puzzling about some shipping company's trick. She asked only, "Are you absolutely set on leaving with this particular ship?"

"I am."

She put her head on her plump little fists and mulled over my file. She looked like a fortune-teller brooding over her cards.

"You have a refugee certificate—you migrated from the Saar to a French village. So you need the permission of our government to leave France. According to the birthplace listed in these papers you are German, so you need permission from the German Commission. Just a minute, please, don't interrupt me.

"I'm familiar enough with all sorts of documents to know whether they're in order or not. Yours don't seem to be ... Just wait a moment. Don't get upset! They're all right as far as they go, but as a whole they don't add up. I can't say exactly why they don't. I'd have to study them some more, which I don't feel like doing right now. There's also one question you have to answer me—after all, you're asking me to take a risk on your behalf, so in return I can expect a little trust from you. Would you tell me the truth about one thing, just to satisfy my curiosity? What do the Germans have against you?"

I was surprised. It had been quite a while since anyone had wanted to hear that old story, so far outclassed and outranked by everyone else's stories. Only this woman who in her official position must have heard hundreds of such tales every day was still willing to listen to mine attentively, with a kind of deference.

"I once escaped from a camp," I said. "I swam across the Rhine."

She looked at me, showing her honest, stern face. "All right. I'll see what can be done."

I was ashamed. For the first time in my life someone was helping me because of the person I was, and still this help was going to the wrong man. I took her small plump hand. I said, "I have one more request. If anyone in your department asks about me, today or tomorrow, wanting to know whether I'm leaving, please don't give them any information. And please keep what happened here today a secret. You must understand that it's important for me to leave without being recognized."

VIII

For the first time I was gripped by a powerful fear of being left behind. Many people I'd been fond of had already left. My advantage over them had once seemed enormous to me, but this was deceptive. Suddenly they had overtaken me. I saw Marie's face as if she were floating away, getting smaller and paler, like a snowflake. What if I really had to choose between taking the last ship and irrevocably staying here? I imagined myself no longer surrounded by the houses of those who were living here permanently, full of things, with smoke coming from innumerable chimneys, all the workers in the factories and mills, the fishermen, barbers, and pizza bakers. Instead I saw myself alone on an island in the middle of the ocean, or on a little star out in space. And I was alone with that black, four-armed giant crab, the swastika.

I rushed to the American travel bureau as if it were a sacred temple that would provide refuge to a human being hounded by the furies, facing an infinite desolation within himself. As soon as he saw me the Corsican turned to me even though there were many other frantic people waiting behind the barrier. He said, "He's in the Arab café over at the Quai du Port."

"I don't need the Portuguese anymore," I cried. "I need you. I've decided to leave too."

He looked at me, disappointed and amused, and said, "Then you'll have to get in line."

I took a place at the end of the line and listened for hours to the pleas, the threats, to the bribery, to the knuckle cracking of clenched hands. But that day everything seemed to come from my own heart. Finally it was my turn. The Corsican reached for my file, yawning and poking in his ear with his pencil.

He said, "You have lots of time. In three or four months there'll be a berth available on the American Export Liner from Lisbon."

I cried, "I want to leave this week, on the boat to Martinique."

"With what? Don't forget, your travel money is in Lisbon. Even if they forwarded it to us here, the boat would be long gone by then. And you wouldn't have dollars anymore, but idiotic francs. Your money would be worth a lot less and wouldn't be enough anymore for Lisbon—why all this nonsense?"

I said, "You've got to lend me money on the basis of the money that will arrive after I'm gone. I need only a small part of that money, and what's left will belong to you." I felt as if I had to wipe the look he gave me from my face. I drummed with my fist on the railing. He shrugged, gave a short, silent laugh.

He said, "No. I did that once, and it turned out quite badly. I love money, but in that case the harbor commission refused to let the people board the boat; the entire family was dispersed; there was no travel money left; they were all sent to camps, to Gurs, to Rieucros, to Argèles. They're still writing me nasty letters from three different concentration camps, as if I were the one who'd given them the infernal advice. I'll never do this sort of thing again."

I was beside myself. I said, "Please listen to me. I have to sail on that ship! It might be the last one."

He switched his pencil to the other ear and laughed, "The last one? Maybe! But so what? Why do you of all people have to be on it? If you didn't go, you'd be one of a huge number of people staying behind, the masses in this part of Europe. I'm just an ordinary employee of an ordinary travel bureau. Your reservation would be no guarantee that you'd survive events." Seeing the fury in my face, he took a step back. "And then, this particular ship to Martinique! You're mad! That's no ship for you. An awful, substandard wreck of a boat. It'll never get you where you're going." He put away my file, and turned away, ignoring me.

I was so angry when I got home that I banged my head against the wall. I felt like robbing someone just to get the money for the ticket. I had never quite believed that Marie would leave. Now the time had come. Maybe I could show someone proof of my treasure in Portugal. Maybe someone would lend me the money. But it was getting dark, and all office doors were already closed.

10

I

I WENT to the Brûleurs des Loups. This was a tough day for me. Too bad it was also one of the days they didn't serve alcohol. I smoked cigarettes and brooded. One moment I felt an overwhelming fear that Marie's ship might be the very last one; the next, I was calm again, filled with a vaguely optimistic confidence. But confidence in whom? In what? I didn't know.

Suddenly someone touched my shoulder. It was the doctor. He looked at me thoughtfully for a moment before sitting down at my table without my having asked him to. "I've been looking for you everywhere," he said.

"For me? Why?"

"No special reason," he said, but something in his eyes told me there *was* something special. "Marie went to the Prefecture. She's started packing. Three times she sent me to the Transports Maritimes to make sure the ship was really leaving, that nothing would interfere with its departure, and to make certain that our passages were booked. As reluctant as she was before, she's now eager to leave. She got her exit visa, but I have a feeling that something happened to her at the Office for Aliens."

I hid my dismay and said, "What could have happened to her there? She got what she wanted, and got it quickly."

"That's just the point. Her husband's exit visa had already been issued. I'm sure Marie tried to get the official to tell her more about it. They probably didn't give her any clear answers—otherwise she would have told me. Maybe they gave her new hope, maybe an ambiguous smile, some vague allusion. Maybe it was all just her imagination, or some mistake, but whatever it was, it was enough to make her rush home to pursue her departure preparations. It was as if she expected him to be there waiting for her on the other side of the ocean at some prearranged time."

"So, your wish has been fulfilled," I said. "She's leaving. You may not be overjoyed about her reason, but you should be able to find some solace in the thought that it will be very hard to find a man in a foreign country who couldn't be found in Marseille."

He looked at me a bit too intensely. For a brief time he said nothing. Then he said, "You're wrong. You can't help it, being who you are. But whatever the reason that made Marie decide to leave now, I'm glad with all my heart that she is leaving. I'm firmly convinced that she'll find peace, yes, real peace and healing as soon as the ship leaves the dock at La Joliette. Once on the high seas, once she's finally left this country and the past behind her, she'll be healed one way or another. Regardless of the reason that drove her to leave, she'll stop searching then for this man who doesn't want to be found. She'll stop trying to track down a man who obviously doesn't want to be tracked down, whose only wish is to be left alone, never to be tracked down."

He was saying exactly what I was thinking. And it suddenly made me angry. Contrary to all expectations, he'd almost won the game—he had the money; he had the documents. And I, who was a lot more nimble and clever, wasn't ready to leave. I said, "You can't possibly know that for sure. The man might be quite happy if she could ferret him out."

He said, "Stop worrying about a man you've never seen! His silence seems quite tenacious, his decision final."

We left the café together. We walked across the deserted Belsunce in silence. We had to watch our step so as not to get tangled in the fishing nets stretched out to dry in the huge square. They were weighted down with rocks and belonged to men who had fished all their lives and would go on fishing. The doctor turned at the Rue du

Relais; I went on through the maze of alleys to the Rue de la Providence.

II

At dawn I was already standing on the Rue de la République. I wasn't alone, as others had arrived while the stars were still out to wait for the shutters to be pulled up at Transports Maritimes. The talk among these poor souls shivering in the predawn cold was all about the imminence of a new war, about the Lisbon harbor being closed, that Gibraltar would soon be closed, and this would be the last boat to leave.

When I got to the counter, my voice sounded false to my own ears—it had this note of entreaty in it. And sure enough, the man behind the counter said, "We don't accept such changes in bookings. Your reservation is valid till noon, after that all advance bookings expire."

I hadn't quite left the counter when, listening to the pleading of all these other men and women, I was overwhelmed by a sort of shame at my own obsessive departure mania, ashamed that I'd got caught up in it.

Just then someone grabbed my wrist and said to me, "So you want to leave after all?"

I looked up at the face of my bald friend. I said, "I have my visa, my transit visa, and a prospective exit visa. But now it turns out I don't have a ticket."

He said, "Yes, you *do* have a ticket. You just don't know you do."

I said, "No, unfortunately I'm quite certain I don't have one."

He said, quite firmly, "Yes you do have a ticket. Here it is. I'm about to return mine and I'm giving it to you."

I tried to conceal my bewilderment. He was more agitated than usual, as often happens to people who've made an important decision that they're telling someone about for the first time.

"I'll explain everything. Come celebrate the transfer of my ticket

to you. I'm leaving too, but I'm headed in another direction." He
pulled me back to the shipping company counter.

I pulled away from him, saying, "You've made a mistake. I don't
have the money to pay for this ticket. And I have no money to pay
the security deposit that you need to get an exit visa, and without
the exit visa, no ticket for a passage on a ship."

He again grabbed my wrist and said calmly, "If that's all that's
standing in your way! Listen, you have a letter in your pocket that
says your trip has been paid for in advance. Your money for the passage is on deposit in Lisbon. I don't need your money here in this
place. I'd much rather that the money is outside France."

My heart was pounding. He still had a firm grip on my wrist, and
as he calmly explained things to me, I began to understand that I'd
played the game to the finish and won.

He sat down and began his computations while I stood and
watched. At last he said, "After subtracting the cost of the ticket and
the money for the Prefecture, you still have quite a little pile of
money there in Lisbon. I'm calculating the exchange rate at 60. Is
that all right? The amount you owe me is insignificant because passage on that filthy boat is so cheap. All you have to do now is to sign
this paper, asking that the bank in Lisbon transfer a small amount of
money from your account to mine."

He handed me a big wad of paper bills. I put the money into my
pocket; I had never before had that much money at one time.

Then he said, "You have just enough time to go to the Prefecture.
I'll wait for you here. When you come back with your exit visa, we'll
have my ticket exchanged for one in your name."

During all this time, even as he was settling the account and signing the papers, he had not once let go of my left wrist. It had remained in his grip as if in a handcuff. Now he at last let go and
leaned back. I looked at his bald, cone-shaped head. His cold gray
eyes were fixed on mine. "What are you waiting for? I can get rid of
my ticket a thousand times over right now. Just look!" He indicated
the people on the Rue de la République, all headed for the Transports

Maritimes office. Some had their luggage with them. They'd probably already reserved their tickets, had exit visas in their pockets, and
thoughts of departure in their pale, excited faces. But many of those
pushing their way to the shipping company counter had nothing at
all. You could tell which ones they were by their voices, their nervously twitching hands and lips. One could well imagine that they
sensed destiny at their heels and death waiting for them on the corner of Quai des Belges and Rue de la République. That he had let
them slip through to the Transports Maritimes, but with the threat:
If you don't come out with a ticket, then . . . ! And they came up to
the counter wringing their hands, without hope, money, or documents, as if this ship were the last one in their lives, the last that
would ever cross the oceans.

I mumbled, "Aren't you leaving?"

He said, "I'm going home. I can go back. To a ghetto, it's true, but
I can go back. But for you there is no going back. They'd stand you
up against a wall and shoot you."

He was right. And I knew that all he had to do was wave his
ticket in the air, and a mass of desperate men and women would
come crawling to him on their knees.

"I'll go to the Prefecture," I said. I'd decided to do it, then and
there. He again took hold of my wrist and led me away. He whistled
for a taxi, settled me in it, and paid the driver.

You know the Marseille Prefecture, don't you?—All those men
and women waiting from early morning till late in the evening in
the dark corridors of the Office for Aliens. A police officer comes
to chase them away, but they keep pushing their way back again
toward the exit visa department, on the chance that it just might
miraculously open a couple of hours earlier than usual. Each of these
ready-to-leave souls has experienced as much as a whole generation
of humankind normally might. One will start telling another next
to him how he escaped sure death three times already, but the man
next to him has also avoided death at least three times himself. He
listens only superficially, then he elbows his way into a gap in the

line, where another man will tell him how he has escaped death. And while they're waiting there, the first bomb drops on the city they had wanted to go to in search of peace, visas expire, a cable arrives on the other side of the door saying that the borders of the country that seemed like the last hope of refuge are being closed. And if you can't wrangle yourself forward with trickery and pure meanness to be among the first ten who can then race over to the Transports Maritimes with their exit visas, you'll find the passenger list will already be closed. Nothing can help you then.

I was one of the first ten. I looked for Nadine's girlfriend Rosalie. And then I saw her, sitting at a desk, her head supported on her fists, poring through files. I made my way to the far end of the railing so that I could talk to her without being interrupted.

"I've prepared everything for you." She said. "Did you bring the money?" She counted the bills with her plump fingers. Without looking at me she said, "Since you want to leave without being recognized, I advise you to be very careful. I can't emphasize this strongly enough. Police officers will be sailing on that ship, a civil police commissioner will be on board and will be examining all the passengers' documents in his cabin. That's the nature of this boat. Two months ago there was a case where a Spaniard was sailing in disguise, with forged documents. His sister was on the same boat. She had spread a rumor that her brother was dead, that he had escaped from Spain and then from a detention camp but had been killed in the Blitz. She wore mourning. But somehow she couldn't hide her joy when she saw that her brother had managed to get on board the ship. There are always spies among the passengers, don't ever forget that! And there was a commissioner sailing on that ship, too. Someone told him about the man, and that was the end of that. When the boat got to Casablanca for a stopover, they took him off the ship and handed him over to Franco. Be very careful!"

My bald friend was waiting for me outside the door of the Transports Maritimes when my taxi drove up. He again grabbed my wrist and pulled me over to the counter. The young shipping company clerk's face showed shock and amazement when he looked at the ticket I handed him. My friend asked him, "Is anything wrong? After all it can't matter much to you who uses the ticket."

"Doesn't matter at all. The only thing is, this is the third time this ticket has changed hands. Ordinarily people will crawl on their hands and knees to get tickets, and yet this ticket keeps getting passed on."

Afterward we stopped off at the first greasy café we came to on the Rue de la République.

My friend said, "I went to see the German Commission in Aix. Three officers interrogated me. When I put in my request to go back to Germany one of them laughed and mumbled curses. The other one asked me what I was going to do back home—he hoped I wasn't expecting them to welcome me with open arms.

"I said, 'It has nothing to do with being welcomed back. It's a matter of Blood and Soil. You do understand that, don't you?' He was a little taken aback. Then he asked about my assets. I said, 'I have a daughter in Buenos Aires; I had a brief love affair with her mother. I signed my assets over to the girl. Please don't worry about whether I have any money; I'm not worried about it.'

"The third officer listened to everything and said nothing. So I put my hopes in him. The only people you can talk to nowadays are those who remain silent. And so my request was approved and signed." He sipped some wine and said, "For thirty years I've been wandering through the world, at a time when other people planted trees in their homeland. Now all these people are leaving, and I'm going back home."

III

I went over to La Joliette, to the harbor commissioner's office. The reception room was relatively uncrowded, considering the thousands of people who were headed here. It was the last of all the waiting rooms. If a person, having waited wearily for his turn there, was not sent back without hope, then there were no additional waiting rooms for him, only the open sea.

A Spanish family came in. I was amazed to see that the old Spaniard was with them. The man whose sons had died in the Civil War and whose wife died as they were crossing the Pyrenees. He looked more alive than the last time I'd seen him; it was as if he were hoping to meet his loved ones again in another world on the far side of the ocean.

The old couple from my hotel arrived with their baggage and packages. They didn't think it was anything special to be among the very few permitted to enter this place. Innocently holding hands, even though burdened with all their many packages, they had traveled this exhausting path from consulate to consulate on which most others had gotten bogged down. I turned away to avoid having to answer any of their questions.

The harbor commissioner opened his office door and slipped behind his massive desk. He was a small man, a little like a squirrel, who looked as though he hated the sea. He sniffed at my papers, asked, "Where's your refugee certificate?" I pulled out the certificate Yvonne had given me. He put it with my file and stamped it. I was ready to leave.

IV

From the harbor commission office I walked to the edge of the quay. The large buildings on the piers blocked the view. Although the water between the piles was shallow, it was the beginning of the endless sea. One could see a handsbreadth of the horizon between the pier and the mole covered with cranes. An old, bedraggled boatman stood motionless a couple of yards from me, staring out across the harbor. I wondered whether his eyes were sharper than mine and he could see something I could not. Soon I realized he couldn't see any more either than the line between the mole and the pier where the sky and the sea touched, the thin line that is more exciting to people like us than the wildest, most jagged peaks of the craggiest mountain chains.

I walked along the quay and suddenly felt a feverish desire to leave at once. I could leave now, this very moment. Once on board the ship I'd steal Marie away from the doctor. I'd obliterate the coincidence that had brought them together on the Boulevard de Sébastopol in a time of desperation when they were fleeing mindlessly without a destination. I'd finally leave everything behind and make a new start. I'd laugh at the grim rule that says life can be lived only once and on a single track. If I were to stay behind here, I'd always remain the same fellow I was today. Aging gradually, I'd still remain a somewhat courageous, somewhat weak, somewhat unreliable fellow, who might with a lot of effort become more courageous, less weak, and a little bit more reliable without others even noticing. This was the moment to leave—later it would be impossible.

A small, clean ship, eight thousand tons or thereabouts, was tied up next to the pier. I couldn't read the name, but thought it might be the *Montreal*. I called over to the boatman, and he slowly came toward me. I asked him if it was the *Montreal*. He said the ship was the *Marcel Millier*, that the *Montreal* was anchored about an hour away from here, at Pier 40. His reply sobered me. I had already imagined this would be the ship I'd take, that it was my destiny. But my ship was anchored far away.

V

I took a cab to the Rue du Relais. For the third and last time, I climbed the stairs that spiraled up to the room where the doctor had hidden Marie. I thought it would be best not to give her any hint now of my plan, not even the slightest indication, and just turn up on the ship as if by magic. But I wasn't quite sure if I'd be strong enough to go through the motions of saying good-bye now.

I knocked; the door opened and I saw her hand covered by the hem of a blue sleeve. Marie took a step backward. I couldn't figure out the expression on her face. It was serious and a bit stiff. She asked brusquely, "Why did you come here?"

The stove was out; the weather had warmed up a couple of days earlier, and winter was on the way out. Suitcases stood around the room as they had the morning the doctor was going to leave. Everything in the room had been packed.

"I'm here to bring you a going-away present," I replied casually although my heart was pounding. "It's a hat."

She laughed and kissed me for the first time, a quick, light kiss. Then, standing in front of the mirror over the washstand, she tried on the hat. She said, "It even fits. You have such crazy ideas. Why did we meet only this winter just before I have to leave? We should have met long ago."

I said, "You're absolutely right, Marie. We should have met back then—where was it?—in Cologne, I should have been the one to sit down on the bench next to you instead of that other man."

She turned away and pretended to busy herself with packing. She asked me to lock a suitcase. We sat down next to each other on top of the locked suitcase. She put her hand into mine. She said, "If only I weren't so uneasy, so worried! Why am I so anxious? I know I have to leave, I want to leave, and I will leave. But sometimes I feel so uneasy, as though I'd forgotten something, something important, irreplaceable. I almost feel like unpacking all the suitcases, taking everything out again. And while everything's pulling me away from here, I wonder what it is that's still holding me back."

I sensed this was my moment. I said, "Maybe it's me."

She said, "I can't believe I'll never see you again. I'm not ashamed to admit that it feels as if you were the first man I'd met, not the last one. As if you were there when I was a child back home in our country, and yours was one of those wild, brown boyish faces that don't yet make girls think of love, but make them wonder what love might be like. One of the boys with whom I played marbles in our shady courtyard. And yet I've known you for a shorter time than any of the others, and only superficially. I don't know where you come from and why you're here. A visa stamp or the decision of a consul shouldn't separate people forever. Only death should be final, not a mere good-bye, not a departure."

My heart was pounding with joy. I said, "But mostly it depends on us. What would the other one say if I were to appear suddenly on the ship?"

She said, "That's just it—the other one."

I went on, more emphatically, "He's got a goal, his profession. He told us himself that it was much more important to him than happiness."

She put her head against my shoulder and said, "Oh him! Let's not pretend to each other. You know who is separating us. We don't want to lie to each other, now at the last moment, you and I."

I put my face into her hair, I could feel how much more alive I, the living man, was than the dead Weidel. She leaned her head on my shoulder. For several minutes we sat there with eyes closed. I felt the suitcase rocking under us, as if we were sailing gently on. Those were the last minutes of complete peace for me. Suddenly I was ready to tell her the truth. I cried, "Marie!"

She abruptly drew her head away and gave me a sharp look. She had turned pale, even her lips were pale. Maybe it was the tone of my voice, or maybe the expression on my face that warned her that something incredible was about to happen, an outrageous attack on her life. She even raised both hands as if to ward off a blow.

I said, "Before you leave I owe it to you to tell you the truth. Your husband is dead, Marie. He took his own life on the Rue de Vaugirard when the Germans marched into Paris."

She dropped her hands to her lap. She smiled. She said, "That shows you how little your advice is worth. That shows you how little your information is worth. Only yesterday, I found out for certain that he's still alive. So much for your truth telling."

I stared at her and said, "You don't know anything. What do you know?"

"I know now that he's still alive. I went to the Office for Aliens at the Prefecture to pick up my exit visa, and there was a woman, an official, who was working on my documents, she helped me. She was odd-looking, small and fat, but her eyes were kind, the sort of kindness I've never encountered before in this country. And she helped everybody. She gave them advice and helped them solve their problems. No file was too complicated for her. You sensed immediately that this woman was ready to help anyone and everyone, that she wanted to make sure we could all get out in time so that no one would fall into the hands of the Germans or end up in some concentration camp and die there for no reason at all. You could tell that she wasn't one of those lazy people who think that there's nothing to be done and all efforts are futile. Rather she was concerned that everything she had any control over would be done right, that nothing harmful would happen to anyone. You see, she was one of those people because of whom an entire people will be saved."

In my despair I said, "You've described her perfectly—I can picture her."

"Then I took heart," Marie continued. "I'd never dared ask anything before. I was always afraid I'd do more harm than good by asking questions. But now that I had all my documents, it couldn't hurt anyone. So I asked her about my husband. She looked at me as if she'd been expecting the question; she said she wasn't allowed to answer me. I pressed her, I begged her, please, if she knew, at least to tell me whether my husband was still alive. She placed her hand on my head and said, 'Rest assured, my child. You may yet be reunited with him on the voyage.'"

Marie looked at me sideways, smiling her sly little smile. She stood up to face me and asked, "Do you still have any doubts? Do you still believe the rumors? How can you possibly know? What do you know? After all, did you see him dead with your own eyes?"

I had to admit that I didn't. "No," I said. Only afterward did I realize how light her breathing was, and the slight, imperceptible note of extreme fear in her sarcastic questions. After my answer she said, sounding relieved and cheerful, "Nothing is holding me here anymore. How easy it is for me to leave now."

At that point I gave up. I couldn't catch up with the dead man.

He'd hold on to what was his forever, even in death and into eternity. He was stronger than I was. All I could do was to go away. How could I have possibly countered her argument? How could I have convinced her? Why even try? For then, though now looking back it seems ridiculous, I was infected for a moment by her foolishness. After all, what did I know about the dead man? Nothing but the gossip of a malicious hotel proprietress. What if he really was still alive? What if Achselroth really had seen him? Not separated from us by eternity but only by a newspaper into which he had poked two holes so that he could watch us unobserved and secretly begin to invent plot complications in comparison to which ours were insignificant?

I met the doctor on the stairs. He asked me to join him and Marie for an aperitif, the last one, all three of us, at the Café Mont Vertoux. I think I mumbled something about no alcohol being served that day.

VI

I went to the Rue de la République. Transports Maritimes was already open. I stepped up to the counter and asked whether there was still time for me to return my ticket. The clerk gaped at me openmouthed. Even though I'd whispered my question, and even before he'd fully comprehended what I was saying, the rumor spread among the people waiting in the room that a ticket had been returned. In fact, the rumor must have spread lightning fast, even into the city. For suddenly they were storming the doors, my ribs were almost crushed against the edge of the counter. The weakest, frailest people turned wild and belligerent in a last, insane hope of getting this returned ticket for themselves. But the clerk just raised his hands, cursing, and the rumor died down; the crowd shrank back, and he hid my ticket in a small side drawer behind the counter. I realized that it was intended for someone who'd asked to be put down for the first available ticket, someone who had already paid for this reservation, someone who had paid the kind of money these people could never pay. This was a person who'd never stand in line for a ticket, but who would just place a hold on it, a person who had power. The official frowned as he locked the little drawer. He compressed his lips in a slight smile like a man who wasn't losing anything in this little deal.

VII

I couldn't sleep at all that night. On the other side of the wall I could hear the young husband's last affectionate words to the beloved wife he was leaving behind with a child he might never see. He was sailing the next day.

It was still dark when I heard on the stairs the excited voices of the old couple who were going to Colombia to join their long-lost son. I got dressed and went downstairs. The Source was just opening, and I was their first customer. I swallowed a cup of bitter coffee. Then I walked down the Cours Belsunce. The nets were stretched out to dry. A couple of women mending them looked quite lost in the huge square. I had never seen them doing this before. I'm sure that I haven't seen most of the really important things that happen in this city. To see the things that matter, you have to feel that you want to stay. Cities shroud themselves from those who're just passing through. I picked my way carefully among the nets. The first stores were just opening, and the first newspaper boys were yelling the headlines.

The newspaper boys, the fishermen's wives on the Belsunce, the shopkeepers opening their stores, the workers going to work the early shift—they were all part of the masses who would never leave no matter what happened. The thought of leaving this place was as unlikely to occur to them as to a tree or a clump of grass. And if the thought ever did occur to them, there'd be no tickets available for them. Wars, conflagrations, and the fury of the powerful had passed over them. No matter how enormous the throngs of refugees the armies drove before them, their numbers were negligible compared to the masses who stayed behind despite everything. And what would have happened to me in all the cities I passed through as I was fleeing if these people hadn't remained behind? They were father and mother to me, the orphan. They were brothers and sisters to me who had no brothers or sisters.

A young fellow was helping his girlfriend fasten back a heavy door. Then, with incredible quickness and efficiency, he helped her set up a little cast-iron stove on which she baked pizzas. And already people were lining up to buy her pizza. Three exhausted streetwalkers came out of the house next door where the red light was still on. They were followed by a bus driver and a couple of businessmen. Even though she wasn't pretty, I thought the pizza maker was one of the most beautiful of women. She was like the women in those old fairy tales who remain forever young. She had always baked her pizza on that ancient little stove on this hill by the sea, in days when other peoples now long forgotten came by here, and she'll go on baking pizza for others yet to come.

My desire to see Marie just once more was stronger than my will-power. I went to the Mont Vertoux to say good-bye. Marie was sitting at the same table where she'd sat when she came there the first time. She looked so happy that I had to smile. Someone watching us might have thought the white paper she was waving around had something to do with our future together. But actually it was her travel permit stamped with all the stamps required for her departure.

"I'm sailing in two hours," she said. A rush of joy swept through her hair and lifted her chest and her face. "Unfortunately you're not allowed to see me off from the pier, but we can say good-bye right here and now."

I hadn't sat down yet, and she now got up and put her hands on my shoulders. I felt nothing but a presentiment of the pain that would surely hit me shortly, maybe even fatally.

She said, "You've been so kind to me!" She kissed me quickly on both cheeks, as they do in this country. I took her head in my hands and kissed her.

Just then the doctor arrived at our table. He said, "Ah, you must be saying your good-byes?"

"Yes," Marie said. "We wanted to have a last drink together."

He said, "Too bad, but there's no time left for that. You have to go to the Transports Maritimes immediately. You have to sign the baggage insurance papers. Unless you'd prefer to stay here ... "

He seemed to be quite sure of everything now. Too much so, it seemed to me. We both looked at Marie. She was no longer beaming. She said, and there was a slight, almost imperceptible tone of mockery in her voice, "I've already promised once before to follow you to the ends of the earth."

"Then hurry over to the Transports Maritimes and sign the papers!"

She shook my hand and left, finally, forever. I thought what you think when you've been shot or struck, that at any moment I'd be feeling an unbearable pain. But there was no pain at all. I kept hearing the sound of her last words, "... to the ends of the earth."—I shut my eyes. I saw a green fence with slender, wilted vines. I couldn't look over the fence; I could only see, between the fence slats, autumn clouds scudding across the sky; I must have been quite small still and thinking then that this must be the end of the earth.

The doctor said, "I should thank you for everything—you helped us."

I said, "It was probably just a coincidence."

He didn't turn away immediately. He gave me a sharp look, seemed to be waiting, maybe he had seen something in my expression to make him think I would say more. But I said nothing, so that in the end he just bowed briefly and walked away.

At last I sat down all by myself at the table. I was amused by that polite, brief, formal bow of his that put such a sudden end to everything. It was a sad kind of amusement, for suddenly, I don't know why just at that point, I was hit by grief for Weidel, for the dead man I'd never known while he was alive. We were left behind, he and I. And there was no one here to mourn him in this country shaken by war and betrayal, no one to render him at least some of what we call the last rites, to honor him. No one except me, who had fought over the dead man's wife with the other man in the hotel in the Old Port.

The Mont Vertoux was crowded. I overheard conversations in many languages about ships that would never leave, ships that had arrived at their destinations, and others that had run aground, been sunk or seized. Stories of people who wanted to serve with the English or join up with de Gaulle, of those who were forced back into camps, maybe for many years of imprisonment, of mothers who had lost children in the war, of men who had driven off leaving their wives behind. The ancient, yet ever new harbor gossip—Phoenician and Greek, Cretan and Jewish, Etruscan and Roman.

For the first time back then, I thought about everything seriously. The past and the future, both equally unknowable, and also this ongoing situation that the consulates call "transitory" but that we know in everyday language as "the present." And the conclusion I came to—it was only a hunch at that point, if a hunch deserves being called a conclusion—was of my own inviolability.

VIII

I got up from my table. I was tired, and my knees felt like lead as I walked back to the Rue de La Providence. I stretched out on my bed and lit a cigarette. Then I started feeling restless and went back into town. People around me were talking incessantly about the *Montreal*, which was sailing today, probably the last ship to leave. But in the early afternoon, all the talk suddenly stopped. The *Montreal* had probably put out to sea. Now all the talk was about the next ship that in turn would be the last to leave.

I went back to the Mont Vertoux and, from force of habit, sat down facing the door. My heart continued to wait, as if it had not yet grasped the emptiness that lay ahead from now on. It was still waiting—Marie might come back. Not the one I had known at the end who was tied to a dead man and only to him, but the Marie I had met that first time when the Mistral blew her to me threatening my young life with a sudden, incomprehensible joy.

Someone touched my shoulder; it was Achselroth's friend, the fat musician, with whom he had once gotten as far as Cuba. He said, "He's deserted me too now."

"Who?"

"Achselroth! I was stupid enough to complete the score for his play. Now he doesn't need me anymore. But I'd never have dreamed that he'd do the same thing to me, just slip away. I was very close to him, you know. Even when we were children, there was something about him, I don't know, he had some kind of power over me." He sat down, put his head in his hands, brooding. He came to himself only when the waiter placed the drink he'd ordered at his elbow.

"You ask how it happened? He probably has a lot of money. He probably spread it around at all the shipping companies in Marseille; he bribed a whole lot of officials and office staff; he collected a complete series of visas and letters of transit. That's what you call foresight. And he gave me his firm promise to take me along! But now that I think of it, he also once said that one ought to be careful about traveling with the same companion on two trips, especially if a previous trip went as badly as ours had. Someone probably returned a ticket at the Martinique Line, and he got it. He's sailing on the *Montreal*."

I couldn't manage to act as surprised as I had every right to be. I just said the first thing that came to mind, "Why despair over it? You're rid of him. You said yourself that he had some power over you even as a child. Now you're rid of all that."

"But what's going to become of me now? The Germans might occupy the Rhône Estuary tomorrow. And I won't be able to leave till three months from now at the earliest. I might be dead by then, deported, taken to a concentration camp, a little pile of ashes in a bombed-out city."

I tried to console him. "That could happen to any one of us. You're not alone." Simple-minded though these reassurances were, he perked up, looked around the room.

I think that was the first time he really looked at the things around him back then. For the first time he realized that we weren't the only ones involved in this; for the first time he heard the ancient chorus of voices giving advice, filling our ears with gossip, scolding and cursing us, making fun of us, teaching us, and consoling us all the way to our graves. But mostly they were consoling and reassuring us. For the first time, too, he saw the water and the lights on the docks, which were weaker just then than the setting sun reflected in the windows. He saw for the first time all these things that would never desert him, never let him down. He took a deep breath, heaved a sigh of relief.

"Achselroth may have been in a special hurry because he found out that the young woman he'd recently seen and taken a liking to from afar, would be on board the *Montreal*. She's Weidel's wife. Weidel, you know, isn't sailing with her."

I composed myself before answering. "Another one who's not sailing! But how do you know all this?"

"People know," he said casually. "Even though he has a visa, he's not leaving. There's something special about a man like that, don't you think? To have a visa and not use it to get away. But you're not like him. Weidel always did unexpected things. Maybe he's not leaving because his wife deserted him. She was seen with another man recently. So he's not leaving because everyone let him down, his friends, his wife, time itself. Because you know he's not the sort of man who'll fight things like that. He doesn't think it's worth it. He fought for better causes."

I suppressed a smile. "What was it he fought for?"

"For every sentence, every word of his mother tongue, so that his short, sometimes slightly crazy stories would be so clear and elegant that everyone would enjoy them—child or adult. Can you imagine doing something like that for your people and your country? Even if he was at times separated from his people, defeated by this war, that's not his fault. He withdraws with his stories, which can wait like him, ten years, a hundred years—By the way, I saw him just now."

"Where?"

"He was sitting back there by the window that looks out on the Quai des Belges. I'm exaggerating of course when I say I saw him. I saw the newspaper behind which he was hiding." At one point he stood up halfway, leaning to one side. "He's not here anymore. Maybe now that his wife's gone, he'll come out into the open and allow people to see him."

To hide my uneasiness, I asked the first question that came to mind. "Has Paul left already? He must be a pretty resourceful fellow with influence in the right places."

He laughed. "Evidently he doesn't have enough influence to get his own file in order. He has the visas and transits; they probably issued them on the basis of his "Enforced Stay in Marseille" certificate. But unfortunately they won't give him the harbor office stamp because they don't give that to anyone who's ever been expelled from Marseille. And it's precisely that little piece of paper on which the expulsion order is printed that gets stamped by the Harbor Commission. Paul will never be able to leave legally—and yet he can't stay legally either."

IX

The following morning I went up to the Binnets. I hadn't been there for some time. In my confused state of mind I hadn't felt like visiting them. The boy sat facing the window, doing homework. When he heard my voice he turned around and stared at me wide-eyed. Suddenly he came over and threw himself on me. He was crying, unable to stop. I stroked his head. I was touched, didn't know what to make of his tears.

Claudine said, "He thought you'd left."

The boy finally freed himself and said a little sheepishly but smiling, "I thought you were all leaving."

"How can you think such a thing? Didn't I promise you I'd stay?" To reassure him I asked if he'd like to go for a walk with me. In a unique peacefulness, we walked along on the sunny side of the Canebière, finally reaching the Triads. From our table there I could look out and see the gate of the Mexican Consulate. As usual crowds of Spanish men and women were waiting under the watchful eyes of some police officers. I asked for pen and ink and wrote, "Mr. Weidel has asked me to return his visa, his letter of transit, his exit visa, and the money he borrowed for the trip. I am also enclosing his manuscript, with the request that you pass it along to his friends who, I'm sure, will take care of it. It isn't finished for the same reason that Mr. Weidel is not able to leave."

I packed all the documents together and asked the Binnet boy to go across the street and give everything to the consular official in person. He was to say that a man he didn't know had asked him to deliver it. I watched him as he walked across the square and got in line with the Spaniards. He came out of the building again about half an hour later. I was glad to see him walking back between the trees. Eagerly I called out to him, "What did he say?"

"First he laughed. Then he said, 'It was to be expected.'"

I felt slightly uneasy hearing him say this. It seemed as if the little official with the alert eyes had read my entire story in this book of life as soon as he looked at my file on my first visit to the consulate.

George Binnet came to the door when I brought his son back, saying, "I'm supposed to give you a message from my friend François."

I said, "I don't know any François."

"Of course you know him. He said you once came to his seamen's association with a short Portuguese man. He helped a German friend of yours, a one-legged man. He sends you regards and wants you to know that the man arrived safely. And that the man thanks you, and he says that he is very happy to be over there now. He says the people over there are people from other countries, new faces, young faces. He's glad for the chance to see it all. He says for you to wait for him here."

George stirred his shaving soap until it was foamy and went on, "It's right that you should stay. What would you do over there? You belong here with us. What happens to us, will happen to you."

I said, "He wanted me to know all that?"

"Oh no. This is what I'm telling you. We know you. We would all tell you the same thing: All of us feel that way."

X

Barely a day had passed since the ship had sailed, when I got a letter from Marcel saying that I could come to the farm now. They were actually looking forward to seeing me there, because the spring farm work had begun. I reassured the boy by telling him that my going to work there didn't mean we'd be separated; that I was close enough to Marseille so that he could easily come to visit me anytime.

I'm not crazy for farm work; I'm a born and bred city boy. But Marcel's relatives are as honest as their relatives in Paris. The work isn't bad. The village is on a spur of a range of hills, not far from the sea. I've been there now for a couple of weeks. But the silence weighs so heavily on me that it seems like years. I wrote a letter to Yvonne in which I asked her again for a safe conduct, because the law still requires you to get permission to change your place of residence.

I went to the mayor of the village with all my impeccable new documents. I told him I had fled from the Saar, had spent the winter in another département, and had now come to work at a farm near the sea. From what I told him, he assumed I was a distant relative of the Binnets. And so, for the time being, this family and this country are sheltering me. I help them with sowing and removing caterpillars. If the Nazis overrun this part of France too, then maybe they'll let me do forced labor together with the sons of the family, or deport us somewhere. Whatever happens to them will happen to me as well. In any case, there's no way the Nazis would ever recognize me as a countryman of theirs. I intend to share the good and the bad with my new friends here, be it sanctuary or persecution. As soon as there's a resistance movement Marcel and I intend to take up arms. Even if they were to shoot me, they'd never be able to eradicate me. I feel I know this country, its work, its people, its hills and mountains, its peaches and its grapes too well. If you bleed to death on familiar soil, something of you will continue to grow like the sprouts that come up after bushes and trees have been cut down.

I came back here to Marseille yesterday to bring Claudine some vegetables and fruit for the boy. I help to feed him with food from the country. Here in the city, you can't even find an onion anymore.

I stopped off at the Café Mont Vertoux first and listened for a while to all that old harbor gossip that no longer affected me. It all sounded very similar to what I used to hear. But then I overheard something about the *Montreal*—the *Montreal* had gone down! It seemed to me as if that boat had left ages ago, a fairy-tale ship sailing the seas forever, its voyage and shipwreck timeless. But the news of its sinking doesn't keep masses of refugees from pleading for reservations on the next ship.

I was soon fed up with all this talk, and so I came here to the pizzeria. I sat down with my back to the door because I no longer expect anything or anyone. Yet I jump every time the door opens and have to use all my willpower to keep from turning around to look. And each time I check the new, faint shadow cast on the white wall. After all, Marie might turn up, the way shipwrecked people unexpectedly come ashore following some miraculous rescue. Or like the shadow of a dead person who's been ripped from the Underworld by sacrifices and fervent prayers. The partial scrap of a shadow on the wall in front of me was trying to connect with flesh and blood again. I could take this scrap of a shadow back with me and hide it in my refuge in the isolated village. There it would be aware again of all the dangers that lie in wait for the living, for those who really are still alive.

But then a lamp may have been moved or the door closed and the shadow on the wall fades, and with it so does the illusion inside my head. I turn to look at the open fire. I never get tired of watching it. At best I could imagine waiting anxiously for Marie as I used to do at this same table. Imagine her still walking up and down the streets of the city, the squares and stairs, the hotels, cafés, and consulates looking for her beloved. Looking ceaselessly. Not only here in this city, but in all the cities of Europe that I know, even in the fabled cities of other continents that I don't know. It's more likely that I'd get tired of waiting than that she'd get tired of her search for a dead man who can't be found.

AFTERWORD*

Perils Among False Brethren

Three times I was beaten with rods; once I was stoned; three times I was shipwrecked; a night and a day I have been in the deep; in journeys often, in perils of waters, in perils of robbers, in perils of my own countrymen, in perils of the Gentiles, in perils of the city, in perils in the wilderness, in perils in the sea, in perils among false brethren.

> —2 Corinthians 11:25–26 (as quoted in *Transit*)

PERHAPS the definition of a transit visa as found in Anna Seghers's novel would have been more appropriate as an epigraph, namely: "A transit visa . . . gives you permission to travel through a country with the stipulation that you don't plan to stay."

I have my reasons for preferring the second epigraph. The definition of a transit visa appears to be a simple one. It becomes complicated when you realize how many countries you have to travel through, how many ports you have to touch in order to reach a country where you will be able to stay. Someone who is just a refugee fleeing to a place where his own language is spoken, who is not merely given permission to travel through, but actually granted a place to stay and permanence, is in a far better situation than the stranger, the emigrant, who doesn't know if he will be liked in Portugal or disliked in Spain, if he will be welcome in Brazil, or under

*First published in the newsweekly *Der Spiegel* (June 6, 1964) and then as the afterword for the German edition of *Transit* (Neuwied: Luchterhand Verlag, 1985).

suspicion in New Zealand, or if his name is on some blacklist in the United States.

The appalling game with the authorities might begin with a corruptible or a non-corruptible consulate official or travel bureau employee. And not just now and then, but at least every third one of these officials is "proud of being able to refuse me a transit visa. He'd tasted a bit of power with his tongue—which I got to see since he lisped—and had liked the taste of it."

This novel, completed in 1942, is in my opinion the most beautiful Seghers has written. Perhaps it appeared so belatedly, almost too late here [in West Germany], because in the meantime, more than twenty years after it was first published abroad, too many on both sides of the East-West border have tasted power and have liked the taste; and then they like to argue here about things not even worth discussing, such as whether books like this should even be published here. Too many try to alter destinies by finger-pointing. It is still possible, in an election, to use the word *emigrant* in such a way that it damages one's opponent (as if an emigrant weren't a refugee; for he really is one, indeed even of a higher degree).

At any rate, one book-burning is enough for me. It was a pathetic affair that I witnessed in a Cologne school yard—embarrassed teachers, embarrassed students, and a couple of fanatics who couldn't quite manage to get a real fire going (it's actually very hard to burn a book). A flag was raised, a song was sung; then in embarrassment the group broke up, going their separate ways. Since that year, since 1933, embarrassment seems to characterize the way Germans live as a society; and it is part and parcel of the great German embarrassment that Anna Seghers's books are only now beginning to appear again here in the West.

The fact that this novel turned out to be the finest Anna Seghers wrote surely has something to do with the terrible uniqueness of the historical-political conditions she chose as her model: the situation in Marseille in 1940. The *Frankreichfeldzug*, or "French Campaign" —the German term makes it sound almost like a Boy Scout outing—was completed in the most painful of those twelve years (when so many had a taste of victory and found it rather to their liking!). The campaign flushed a great horde of emigrants out of Paris, out of all parts of France, out of the camps, hotels, *pensions*, and farms. They were all drawn to the one possible destination, Marseille:

> Phoenician chit-chat, Cretan and Greek gossip, and that of the Romans. There was never a shortage of gossips who were anxious about their berths aboard a ship and about their money, or who were fleeing from all the real and imagined horrors of the world... human hordes who had been chased from all the countries of the earth, and having at last reached the sea, boarded ships in order to discover new lands from which they would again be driven; forever running from one death toward another.

All of them experiencing what every refugee finds bitter, and potential refugees even more so: "I thought about the many thousands of people who called this city their own and quietly lived their lives here just as I had once done in mine."

Seidler, the young German mechanic who tells the story, starts cheerfully, with an almost brash masculinity, hardly touching on the political situation, rather taking for granted that the German army brought in by the Nazis and bringing the Nazis with it should invade France. Seidler escapes from Paris after being left behind by his friend Paul, taking along the suitcase and manuscript of the writer Weidel, who has committed suicide in a hotel. Pretending to be Weidel, Seidler applies for the dead man's visa, more or less pushed into this role by the consular officials rather than by any plan of his own. And so the terrible game begins: "It's a game just like any other. It's a gamble you take by living in this world."

Playing the game, he pulls along behind him like a shadow Weidel's former wife, Marie, while also attracting her as a person. The story, composed like a musical score, turns into a game centered around Marie, who in the meantime has become the companion of another man, a doctor, but after various manipulations she devolves upon Seidler—"she probably knew what lay ahead of her. Once again, what else but love." However, the doctor returns, and the game begins anew. Everything seems to be moving toward a happy end, with Marie and Seidler to be reunited on the departing ship. But then Seidler reneges, gives up the visa he obtained with so much effort, the ticket for the ship, and the security money. It is Weidel, the dead man, scoffed at by all and betrayed, who wins.

The story revolves around three characters: Weidel, Seidler, and Marie. Employing realistic stylistic means, Anna Seghers succeeds, or to be exact, succeeded two decades ago, in combining these incredible, almost inexplicable, unreal aspects of the situation, the abstract and crazy longing for a transit visa and the subsequent rejection of it. Out of a real historic political situation, she creates a novel that is simultaneously saga, epic, and myth—in the approaching figure of Marie, in the receding of Marie's shadow, and in the constant presence of the dead Weidel.

The trenchant and very realistic irony with which the minor characters are presented ("I thought how remarkably unbecoming what we call bad luck was to Achselroth," and an old Jewish woman looks as if she had "been driven out of Vienna not by Hitler but by an edict of the Empress Maria Theresa") does not destroy the circle of this magic. None of the minor characters, not Marie's new partner the doctor, or Paul the betrayer, or the Jewish Foreign Legionnaire, or Seidler's lover Nadine, or the Binnets—none of them intrudes on the enchanted Weidel-Seidler-Marie triangle.

The absurdity of the transit situation becomes clearest in the case of the woman who has the hotel room next to Seidler's. She feeds, cares for, and spoils two dogs because the dogs are the guarantee for her visa. They belong to citizens of a promised land that she may set foot in only because of the dogs.

It is not for me to reproach Anna Seghers for living where she lives [East Germany]. I don't quite see why even the coldest of all cold warriors would not want this novel to be available here [in West Germany]. Certainly it is no coincidence that our state honors refugees who speak our language yet has never established a relationship with those potential refugees who not only speak our language but also write in it. I doubt that our post-1933 literature can point to many novels that have been written with such somnambulistic sureness and are almost flawless. The story told here, the subject considered here, speaks more clearly and effectively than countless protests and resolutions against the circumstances under which an individual, who doesn't want to emigrate but has to flee from the East to the West, must struggle to obtain—perhaps paying with his blood or even his life—something even the best-intentioned official cannot issue him: that same exit visa for which thousands longed and demeaned themselves in the Marseille of 1940.

For anyone who would like to make writers aware of the dangerous conditions under which they live and write, I would refer them to the last danger enumerated by Saint Paul and cited by Anna Seghers: *Perils among false brethren.*

—Heinrich Böll

TITLES IN SERIES

For a complete list of titles, visit www.nyrb.com or write to:
Catalog Requests, NYRB, 435 Hudson Street, New York, NY 10014

* *Also available as an electronic book.*

DAVID KIDD Peking Story*
ROBERT KIRK The Secret Commonwealth of Elves, Fauns, and Fairies
ARUN KOLATKAR Jejuri
DEZSŐ KOSZTOLÁNYI Skylark*
TÉTÉ-MICHEL KPOMASSIE An African in Greenland
GYULA KRÚDY The Adventures of Sindbad*
GYULA KRÚDY Sunflower*
SIGIZMUND KRZHIZHANOVSKY The Letter Killers Club*
SIGIZMUND KRZHIZHANOVSKY Memories of the Future
MARGARET LEECH Reveille in Washington: 1860–1865*
PATRICK LEIGH FERMOR Between the Woods and the Water*
PATRICK LEIGH FERMOR Mani: Travels in the Southern Peloponnese*
PATRICK LEIGH FERMOR Roumeli: Travels in Northern Greece*
PATRICK LEIGH FERMOR A Time of Gifts*
PATRICK LEIGH FERMOR A Time to Keep Silence*
PATRICK LEIGH FERMOR The Traveller's Tree*
D.B. WYNDHAM LEWIS AND CHARLES LEE (EDITORS) The Stuffed Owl
GEORG CHRISTOPH LICHTENBERG The Waste Books
JAKOV LIND Soul of Wood and Other Stories
H.P. LOVECRAFT AND OTHERS The Colour Out of Space
DWIGHT MACDONALD Masscult and Midcult: Essays Against the American Grain*
NORMAN MAILER Miami and the Siege of Chicago*
JANET MALCOLM In the Freud Archives
JEAN-PATRICK MANCHETTE Fatale*
OSIP MANDELSTAM The Selected Poems of Osip Mandelstam
OLIVIA MANNING Fortunes of War: The Balkan Trilogy*
OLIVIA MANNING School for Love*
JAMES VANCE MARSHALL Walkabout*
GUY DE MAUPASSANT Afloat
GUY DE MAUPASSANT Alien Hearts*
JAMES MCCOURT Mawrdew Czgowchwz*
WILLIAM MCPHERSON Testing the Current*
HENRI MICHAUX Miserable Miracle
JESSICA MITFORD Hons and Rebels
JESSICA MITFORD Poison Penmanship*
NANCY MITFORD Madame de Pompadour*
NANCY MITFORD The Sun King*
NANCY MITFORD Voltaire in Love*
HENRY DE MONTHERLANT Chaos and Night
BRIAN MOORE The Lonely Passion of Judith Hearne*
BRIAN MOORE The Mangan Inheritance*
ALBERTO MORAVIA Boredom*
ALBERTO MORAVIA Contempt*
JAN MORRIS Conundrum
JAN MORRIS Hav*
PENELOPE MORTIMER The Pumpkin Eater*
ÁLVARO MUTIS The Adventures and Misadventures of Maqroll
L.H. MYERS The Root and the Flower*
NESCIO Amsterdam Stories*
DARCY O'BRIEN A Way of Life, Like Any Other
YURI OLESHA Envy*
IONA AND PETER OPIE The Lore and Language of Schoolchildren
IRIS OWENS After Claude*

RUSSELL PAGE The Education of a Gardener

ALEXANDROS PAPADIAMANTIS The Murderess

BORIS PASTERNAK, MARINA TSVETAYEVA, AND RAINER MARIA RILKE Letters, Summer 1926

CESARE PAVESE The Moon and the Bonfires

CESARE PAVESE The Selected Works of Cesare Pavese

LUIGI PIRANDELLO The Late Mattia Pascal

ANDREY PLATONOV The Foundation Pit

ANDREY PLATONOV Happy Moscow

ANDREY PLATONOV Soul and Other Stories

J.F. POWERS Morte d'Urban*

J.F. POWERS The Stories of J.F. Powers*

J.F. POWERS Wheat That Springeth Green*

CHRISTOPHER PRIEST Inverted World*

BOLESŁAW PRUS The Doll*

RAYMOND QUENEAU We Always Treat Women Too Well

RAYMOND QUENEAU Witch Grass

RAYMOND RADIGUET Count d'Orgel's Ball

FRIEDRICH RECK Diary of a Man in Despair*

JULES RENARD Nature Stories*

JEAN RENOIR Renoir, My Father

GREGOR VON REZZORI An Ermine in Czernopol*

GREGOR VON REZZORI Memoirs of an Anti-Semite*

GREGOR VON REZZORI The Snows of Yesteryear: Portraits for an Autobiography*

TIM ROBINSON Stones of Aran: Labyrinth

TIM ROBINSON Stones of Aran: Pilgrimage

MILTON ROKEACH The Three Christs of Ypsilanti*

FR. ROLFE Hadrian the Seventh

GILLIAN ROSE Love's Work

WILLIAM ROUGHEAD Classic Crimes

CONSTANCE ROURKE American Humor: A Study of the National Character

TAYEB SALIH Season of Migration to the North

TAYEB SALIH The Wedding of Zein*

GERSHOM SCHOLEM Walter Benjamin: The Story of a Friendship*

DANIEL PAUL SCHREBER Memoirs of My Nervous Illness

JAMES SCHUYLER Alfred and Guinevere

JAMES SCHUYLER What's for Dinner?*

LEONARDO SCIASCIA The Day of the Owl

LEONARDO SCIASCIA Equal Danger

LEONARDO SCIASCIA The Moro Affair

LEONARDO SCIASCIA To Each His Own

LEONARDO SCIASCIA The Wine-Dark Sea

VICTOR SEGALEN René Leys

ANNA SEGHERS Transit*

PHILIPE-PAUL DE SÉGUR Defeat: Napoleon's Russian Campaign

GILBERT SELDES The Stammering Century*

VICTOR SERGE The Case of Comrade Tulayev*

VICTOR SERGE Conquered City*

VICTOR SERGE Memoirs of a Revolutionary

VICTOR SERGE Unforgiving Years

SHCHEDRIN The Golovlyov Family

ROBERT SHECKLEY The Store of the Worlds: The Stories of Robert Sheckley*

GEORGES SIMENON Act of Passion*

GEORGES SIMENON Dirty Snow*